She's Not There

She's Not There

TAMSIN GREY

THE BOROUGH PRESS

Tamsin Grey asserts the moral right to
be identified as the author of this work

A catalogue record for this book
is available from the British Library

HB ISBN: 978-0-00-824560-3
TPB ISBN: 978-0-00-824561-0

This novel is entirely a work of fiction.
The names, characters and incidents portrayed in it, while at times based
on historical figures, are the work of the author's imagination.

Excerpt from *James and the Giant Peach* by Roald Dahl
reprinted by permission of Penguin Books. © Roald Dahl 1961

Excerpts from *The Courtship of the Yonghy-Bonghy-Bò* by Edward Lear

Typeset in Bell MT Std by Palimpsest Book Production Ltd, Falkirk, Stirlingshire

Printed and bound by CPI Group (UK) Ltd, Croydon CR0 4YY

MIX
Paper from
responsible sources
FSC® C007454

This book is produced from independently certified FSC™ paper
to ensure responsible forest management.

For more information visit: www.harpercollins.co.uk/green

In memory of the artist
Michael Kidner RA
1917 – 2009

JULY 2018

1

The invitation from Dora Martin caused that shift in Jonah's belly, like a creature waking up in its dark pit. 'Do we have to go?' he murmured, knowing that they did. The trek into London to see the Martins had become a July tradition. He pushed away his cereal bowl, last year's event flooding his head: the welcoming hugs and exclamations; the long, tense argument about politics; and then the vigil in the back garden, with the scarecrow and the wind chimes and the rabbits.

When the day arrived – a baking hot Friday – it turned out everyone was going to Frank's for a swim after school. Jonah waited until after band practice to tell his friend he couldn't make it.

'That's mad.' Frowning, Frank nosed his guitar into its sleeve. It was cool and mellow in the practice room, the blinds drawn down against the sun. Because of his bad hand, Jonah used a harness to help him hold his trumpet. Frank watched him take it off. 'Lola's coming!'

His friend's sly smile made Jonah blush. He turned away and watched Mr Melvin cross the room, open the door and step into the rectangle of blazing light.

'Who even *are* the Martins?' asked Frank.

'We knew them when we lived in London. Dora and my mum were, like, best friends.' The blinds flapped in a sudden gust, and Jonah got a flash of the sheets on the Martins' washing line billowing, the crescendo of wind chimes, and Dora, sprawled in her deckchair, her feet in a bucket of water.

'Come on, guys.' The other band members had disappeared and Mr Melvin was waiting to lock the door. Jonah settled his trumpet into its case.

'Get out of it. Say you're ill.' Frank zipped up his guitar, frowning again.

'I just can't, really.' Jonah made a wry face, but now his friend wouldn't look at him. 'It's — a kind of anniversary. They cook roast chicken.'

'Roast chicken? That's *mad*. It's like 30 degrees centigrade.' Frank spun away, towards the door.

'It was our favourite. Well, more my brother's,' he explained, but to himself, because Frank was ducking under Mr Melvin's arm. 'Roast chicken and roast potatoes.' He got a sudden flash of Raff, aged six, wolfing down a leg.

2

It had been agreed that Jonah could go to the Martins straight from school, rather than traipsing all the way home to go with the others in the car. The thought of the journey cheered him up. He hadn't travelled into London alone before. On the train, he put his backpack and his trumpet case in the luggage rack, shrugged off his blazer and sprawled across two seats, luxuriating in his independence. They'd been playing the 'Summertime'/ 'Motherless Child' medley in band practice, and the interweaving tunes played on in his head as he gazed through the fast-moving glass at the slow-drifting clouds. *Cumulus humilis.* He had been obsessed with clouds that summer, had learnt all their names. He saw the white sheets rising again, Dora's huge sunglasses, her yellow dress, the straggly hair in her armpits.

Dora Martin. Quite a famous artist these days. She had written the invitation, in her elegant, spiky slant, on a post-card featuring one of her paintings: '*It's that time again, and I'm so hoping you'll join us.*' He noticed that the creature – a kind of trapped emotional density – was awake again, and he shifted himself sideways, resting his head on his bent arm. It would be nice to see Emerald, who'd been in his class and would have updates on Harold and all the other Haredale kids. *Sometimes I feel like I'm almost gone.* He closed his eyes, letting the sleepy, mournful tune weave with the rhythm of the train.

He dreamed he was high above London, among the cool, silent clouds, looking down at the glittering sprawl. *You were our home.* He felt a leap of hope and dropped closer, looking for a sign of welcome, but the cranes rose and tilted, like slingsmen, the river shone like a ribbon of foil and, to the west, an acrid plume of grief rose from a blackened finger. He dove down like Superman, circling his old familiars: the Cheese Grater, the Shard, the Knuckleduster. Down further, between the chimney pots, into the grime of the centuries, and then southwards, along arteries and veins. The high street now, *their* high street: Chicken Cottage, Hollywood Nails, We Buy Gold. Left up Wanless Road, low under the bridge, the car repair yard, that smell from the warehouse. Dropping to the ground, he was his nine-year-old self now: bare feet on the warm pavement, fingers dragging along the fence. Opposite, the four shops, asleep, their metal shutters pulled down. And on the corner, there it was, their house, so familiar, but long forgotten. There was someone looking out of the sitting-room window, someone waiting for him. *Mayo?*

The train entered an urban canyon, sound waves bouncing off concrete and glass. He sat up straight, wiping the drool from his chin, and leant his forehead against the window. The tall buildings had fallen away, and the clouds were towering. *Cumulonimbus.* He suddenly remembered the clouds poster, Blu-tacked to his and Raff's bedroom wall, and the dream flooded him: the cool vapour, the eerie silence, the dizzying drop down; and their old house, right there, the scruffiness of it, every tiny detail. He hadn't seen it since they'd left; they had never gone that way in the car: but now, he realised, he could go and have a look at it, on his way from the bus stop to the Martins' house. A very short detour, to travel back five years. The shift again; the creature, wordless and sightless, like a blind baby seal, as his brother Raff's voice came to him, clear as a bell, down the years. *We need a time machine.* The two of them, in that messy kitchen, trying to work out what to do. Hands on his belly, he noticed his own face in the glass, his two eyes merged together. Then the train slid onto the bridge, and the breath caught in his throat. The million-year-old river, brown and glittering, full of boats, and the towers like giant androids, gazing glassily towards the future.

3

The car repair yard was silent, its gates padlocked, but there was that same oniony whiff from the warehouse. Same weather, of course, and the creature was moving again. Funny how, when it was asleep – and it was mostly asleep these days – he could forget it was there; that it had ever existed. He stopped at the bend in Wanless Road, setting his trumpet case down and wiping his palms on his trousers. Their house was still hidden from view, but he could see, across the road, the four shops. *The Green Shop, the Betting Shop, the Knocking Shop, and London Kebabs.* London Kebabs and the Betting Shop had their blinds down, and the Green Shop was all boarded up, but the Knocking Shop, on the face of it a hairdresser's, looked open.

'*Why is it called the Knocking Shop, Mayo?*'

'*Because of all Leonie's visitors.*'

'*But they don't knock, they ring the buzzer, Mayo, so it should be the Buzzing Shop, shouldn't it?*'

She had laughed and kissed him, and he had beamed with pride. He had loved making her laugh. Standing there, looking at Leonie's shop, he realised that the memory had brought the same grin to his fourteen-year-old face. He used to talk to her in his head when he wasn't with her, he remembered; tell her jokes and see her laughing face. He picked up the case and walked on.

After five years, it was a huge amount to take in at once. First, there was a new building where the Broken House had been. Scaffolding still, and no windows, just the empty squares for them to go in. Running in front of it, a new fence, higher and more solid than the old one, with proper 'Keep Out' signs. A gap, and then the corner house, half on Wanless Road, half on Southway Street, the end of the Southway Street terrace; a strange, wedge-shaped house, which had once been a shop, and had been through many conversions. *Their* house.

Apart from it wasn't their house. He stared, his eyes blurring. The same shape, and same size, but it had been all tidied and prettied, with pale blue walls and window boxes full of lavender.

Stupid idiot . . . He wiped his eyes on his sleeve. The house had sold very quickly, while he was still in hospital. It had been someone else's house for five years. He walked round into Southway Street and looked at the shiny new front door, wanting to kneel and peer through the letter box. He turned away instead and looked up Wanless Road, towards the flats where his friend Harold had lived, and where he and Raff had had the run-in with the bigger boys. Then he looked back the way he had come. The passionflowers had survived, their gaudy, sulky faces tumbling over the new fence.

'*They look like Bad Granny.*' Raff's six-year-old voice. He stepped forward and examined one in detail. Passiflora, a South American vine, named after the passion of Jesus Christ. He touched the crown of thorns, very lightly.

'Jonah?' A real voice, strident, familiar and – straightaway in his head, Raff again: '*Let's run!*' He gathered himself and turned. Her head was sticking out of the doorway. He gave a little wave, and she trailed out onto the pavement like a dilapidated peacock.

'Hello, Leonie!'

'Jonah! I *knew* it was you! Pat, look who's here!' She leant back into her shop, then turned, beckoning. He crossed the road and stopped with a bit of distance between them, but she stepped forward and took hold of his elbows, her bulgy eyes staring at him with a child's frankness. Resisting the old urge to lift his good hand to cover the scarring, he tried to return her raking gaze. '*Hench*'. Raff's word for her, because of her scary, weightlifter's body, towering above them. Now, she only came up to his chin. Same brawniness, though; and same breasts, jostling to escape from their blue satin casing. He quickly looked back at her face. 'Hello, Leonie,' he repeated, aware of the awkwardness of his smile.

'Mended good.' The tang of her breath. Same hairstyle, with the beads on the braids, but fewer braids now and silvery threads in them. Same plastic, sequinned fingernails; she brushed one along the scarring. 'Adds character. And you grown nice and tall. How long is it? Must be four, five years.'

'It's five.'

Leonie nodded. 'Near enough to the day.' She looked past him, at their old house. 'What you doing here? This the first time you been back?'

'Yes. I mean, I've been a few times, to visit friends, but not *here* . . .' They'd never come this way, in the car; they'd always stayed on the main road and taken the turning by the park.

'Pat!' She called into the shop again, her ornate hand on the door. 'She don't hear me. You by yourself? Where's your folks?'

'I'm meeting them at our friends' house. I came on the train, and they're coming in the car.'

'Pat! Where that dumb-arse woman got to.' She shouldered the door wide open. 'You better come in.'

He looked at his watch, hearing Raff's voice echoing through time: *'No way! She is HENCH and her sweets are RANK!'*

'Just five minutes. Have a cold drink. If she don't get to see you, my life won't be worth living.' She ushered him over the threshold, and there was that same long, thin room with the mirrors, and the whir of the electric fans. Like his own ghost, he drifted behind her, past the three hairdressing chairs, and the one ancient hood-dryer; the desk, with the phone, and the box of tissues. The beaded doorway, the white, squishy sofa, the sweets in a bowl, and – an embarrassing stirring, Raff's elbow in his ribs – *the magazines.*

'Help yourself to a sweet.'

'*RANK!*'

'I'm OK, thanks.'

Leonie slammed the bowl back down, and kicked off her shoes. 'Pat!' She padded over to the beaded curtain, her big flat feet leaving damp marks on the polished tiles. 'Losing her hearing. I keep telling her, but she won't have it. You better take a seat.'

The fans whirred and whirred. The footprints evaporated, and the beaded strands shimmied to stillness. Above the doorway, the tiny monitor showed the litter-strewn backyard, where Leonie's visitors waited to be let in. He got a sudden flash of her getting undressed, her blue satin dress dropping in a pile around her feet, and he cringed and tried to clear the thought from his head. He sat down on the sofa, which was as squishy as ever, but he was tall enough now to keep his feet on the ground. *The magazines. Oh no.* Remembering Raff's shocked delight, he leant forward. The top one looked respectable enough – one of those TV guides – but the one underneath it . . . He stared for a moment, then put the TV guide back on top. Suddenly deeply uncomfortable, he looked towards the door. Too rude, though, to just leg it. He leant back, closing his eyes against the electric breeze.

'The younger one was the looker. This one was always a bit drawn.' Pat, trim little Pat, tufty-haired, fox-faced, with a jug and some plastic beakers. 'World on his shoulders.' She put the cordial and the beakers down, and perched next to him on the sofa. 'Looks like life treating him better now.' She grasped the lapel of his blazer and peered at the coat of arms on the breast pocket. 'See, proper stitching – none of that stick-on.'

'Private school.' Leonie sank into the chair by the desk, and clasped her hands over her belly. 'Folks doing OK, then.'

Jonah opened his mouth, then closed it again. Explaining about the scholarship would sound like boasting.

'Cordial?' Pat reached for the jug.

'I'm OK, thanks.'

Pat looked at Leonie. 'Must be thirsty, on a day like this?'

Leonie shrugged. 'Maybe he don't like cordial. Maybe too sweet for him.'

'What about his hand?'

Leonie shrugged again. 'Why you asking me?'

Jonah drew his bad hand out of his pocket, and presented it.

'Your right one, is it?' Pat took hold of it, and Leonie tipped forwards to look. 'You right-handed?'

'Yes, but it's fine. I can do most things.' He waggled his remaining finger and thumb.

'Hope you don't get teased for it.' Pat set his hand down on his lap. 'Do your school friends know how brave you were, trying to save your little brother?'

'He don't want to talk about that,' snapped Leonie, and Pat clapped her hand over her mouth, chastened.

'It's OK,' said Jonah. 'Anyway,' he nodded at the case, 'I play the trumpet.'

'The trumpet!' Pat reached for the case and pulled it onto her lap. She opened it, and the trumpet nestled, gleaming, in the dark blue fur. 'Play for us!'

Jonah hesitated. 'I'm not sure if . . .'

'Just one quick tune! Or you need a drink first? Will I get him plain water?' Pat looked at Leonie again.

'It's just that the Martins are expecting me.'

'The Martins. I remember them,' Leonie was nodding. 'With the little girl. Same age as you. Yellow tails, each side. So they still live round here? They never come this way. Or if they do, I never seen them.'

'Her mother was sick,' said Pat. 'Must have passed by now.'

'No, she's better,' said Jonah.

'Better? I heard it was curtains.' Leonie looked dubious.

'Dora's fine. She's . . . we're having roast chicken.'

'Bit hot for roast chicken,' said Pat. 'Better with a salad, on a day like this.'

'But nice you stayed friends with them,' said Leonie.

'What about the dad? Remember, Leonie – with the veg boxes. He still in that business?'

Jonah shook his head. 'He lives in the country now. In an eco-village.'

'Eco-village?' asked Pat.

'Living off the land,' explained Leonie. 'No electricity or nothing. Do their business in the woods.'

Pat shook her head. 'So he left his sick wife.'

'No, she was already better,' said Jonah. 'And anyway they're still married. Dora and Em go and stay with him quite a lot.'

'In the eco-village.' Leonie nodded thoughtfully, as if she was planning a trip there herself. 'And does he come back to London? Will he be there now? To see you?'

'I expect so.' He tried to remember if Dora's email had said. Then he stood up, which was an effort, given how far he'd sunk into the sofa, and put his backpack on.

'You got to go,' Leonie sighed, and heaved herself up too.

'Or roast chicken might get cold.' Pat held out the trumpet case.

'Yes.' He suddenly felt how male he was, next to these middle-aged women: how tall, and strong and young. He took the case, and turned towards the door, trying to formulate a suitable goodbye, but was suddenly enveloped by Leonie. Her metal smell, her breasts, her damp armpits . . . He had to plant his feet firmly in order not to stagger back. She seemed to be crying. Still gripping the handle of his trumpet case, he put his free arm around her waist.

'Leonie, she still feels so bad.' Pat's pointy face had gone soft and slack.

'Bad? Why?'

'Here all day, looking out the window, and never saw nothing was wrong.' She patted Leonie's shaking shoulder. 'Enough now, Miss. Young man needs to go and eat roast chicken. And your 6.30 will be here. Need to bubble down.'

'That 6.30 always late.' But Leonie released him, and reached for a tissue from the box on the desk. She wiped her eyes, looking old, and Jonah felt a terrible tenderness for her.

'Don't feel bad. You were very good to us. Very kind.' She was so alien, so not of his tribe – and yet so familiar. He patted her other shoulder.

'Just glad . . .' Her voice was shaky, still full of tears. 'Just glad you doing so well.'

'Better get going.' Pat gave him a little push, but Jonah hesitated.

'You know . . .' He looked out into the sunny street and then down at his watch. The two women gazed at him. 'Maybe I have got time to play something quick. If – if that's what you'd like.'

'Yes!' Embarrassed by her own delight, Pat clapped her hand over her mouth again.

JULY 2013

MONDAY

4

On Monday morning Jonah woke up trying to say something. He was making tiny croaking noises, trying to get the words out, and his sheet was all tangled up in his legs. The room was full of sunlight, because of the fallen-down curtain, and outside the birds were screeching like crazy.

He sat up, kicking the sheet away, and looked over at the clock: 04.37. The sun must have just that minute risen, or rather Earth had just tipped far enough towards it. He was naked. It had been so hot in the night he'd pulled off his vest and wriggled out of his pyjama bottoms. His dream was like a word on the tip of his tongue. The birds had calmed down, but a dog was barking, and now there was a man talking, down in the street, right under the wide open window.

Jonah lay back down and tried to remember what it was he wanted to say, but the strange, hissing voice outside kept telling someone to shut their mouth. No one else was saying anything, so the man was either talking to himself, or talking into his phone. His tongue found his loose tooth, and waggled it. *'This tooth is movious,'* Lucy, his mother, had said at bedtime, in her Zambian doctor voice, her finger pushing it gently. *'It will be coming out on Wednesday.'*

He rolled onto his side and looked down at the book she'd read from at bedtime, lying open on the floor, surrounded by clothes. It was a poetry book by a man called Edward Lear. She'd read them 'The Courtship of the Yonghy-Bonghy-Bò', a very sad story about a tiny little man with an enormous head. It was her favourite. He and Raff preferred 'The Duck and the Kangaroo'. As he gazed at the picture of the Lady Jingly Jones, surrounded by her hens, telling the Yonghy-Bonghy-Bò to go away, he remembered his feeling, as she read, that his mother was a stranger, lost in an unknown world. Such a weird feeling; difficult to explain.

He tugged at his tooth. He'd made a bet with her – £1 it would come out *before* Wednesday – which he was sure he would win. His eyes travelled up to his cloud poster. The clouds were grouped into families and species. His favourite was *Stratocumulus castellanus.* Next to the cloud poster were Raff's three athlete posters: Usain Bolt, Mo Farah and Oscar Pistorius. Raff was a really good runner. Which reminded him . . . *Which reminds me, Mayo.* No, not Mayo, he'd started calling her Lucy, to be more grown-up. *Which reminds me, Lucy.* What was it that he needed to tell her? He noticed that the top left corner of the Oscar Pistorius poster was curled over, detached from its lump of Blu-tack. Oh yes, Sports Day. That was it. Sports Day had been cancelled the week before, because of all the rain, but everyone had been so disappointed that Mr Mann had decided they could squeeze in a shortened version this Thursday. There had been a letter about it. Probably still in his school bag.

He sat up again, to see the clock. 04.40, a mirror number. He climbed down the ladder past Raff's sleeping head, pulled on his boxers and crept out of the room. It was only three and a half steps across the landing and into Lucy's bedroom. Her curtains were drawn tight, so it was dark and the warm air smelt of her grown-up body. There were clothes all over the floor. Jonah stood on a coat hanger and said 'Ouch', but quietly. He reached her bed and climbed onto it, fumbling for the sheet and pulling it over him. The smell of her was stronger, more secret, and he rolled across to snuggle up. But she wasn't there.

Jonah rolled to the far side of the bed and looked at the crowd of things on Lucy's bedside table. Her Tibetan bells alarm clock, a wine glass with a smudge of lipstick on it, the mugs he'd brought her tea in, the days she'd stayed in bed. The card with the X on it was leaning against one of the mugs, and he reached for it. People usually did a few Xs, little ones, under their signature. This single X filled the whole card. One long kiss, then. He pictured his father Roland's face, with hopeful lips. The card had come with the flowers, was it Thursday or Friday? They were a mixture of roses and lilies, the roses red and fat like cabbages, and the lilies all creamy and freckled with gold. He'd brought them up to her, and she'd taken the card and told him to put the flowers in a vase. Which he had done, but without any water, so they had died. Jonah put the card back down and wobbled his tooth, seeing Roland's face again – his anxious frown, his sticky-out ears. They hadn't been to visit him for ages. Maybe he would ask if he could phone him up. He would tell him about the tooth bet first. Then he'd check about the flowers.

He rolled over again, back to the near side of the bed, sat up and swung his feet down to the floor. By the skirting board was her big tub of coconut oil, without the lid. The oil was thick and white, like wax, and there were three indents where her fingers had dug into it. It would come out in white lumps, but then, as she rubbed it into her skin, it would melt into transparent liquid. He crouched down and put three of his own fingers in the holes. They were wet and oozy: the wax was melting because it was so warm. He wiped his fingers on the sheet and went to see if she was in the bathroom.

His pupils, large from the darkness, had to quickly shrink again, because light was flooding in through the open window, bouncing between the mirrors and the taps and the water in the bath. The bathwater was green and shimmery, with a few black squiggly hairs floating on the surface. Jonah put his hand in and the light on the ceiling broke into ripples. The water was lukewarm and very oily, and when he pulled out his hand one of the hairs was coiled around his fingers. He got some toilet paper and wiped it off, and then he put the paper down the toilet. There was wee in the toilet, very dark, smelly wee, and Jonah flushed it, before leaving the bathroom and going to stand at the top of the stairs. He looked down and his heart beat faster, because the front door was open.

Jonah padded downstairs and out into the street. Under his feet the pavement was still cool, but the light was blinding. Their house was on a corner. The front door was on Southway Street, but the sitting-room window and the boys' bedroom window were on the other side of the house. Jonah looked that way first, towards Wanless Road, which was still in shadow. On the far side of the road, the metal blinds were still down over the four shops, one of them spray-painted with the word 'Pussy'. A wheelie bin, its lid thrown open, balanced precariously on the kerb. Then he turned his head and shaded his eyes with his hand to look down sun-drenched Southway Street. The pretty houses looked like they still had their eyes closed. Only the light moved, glinting on the parked cars and the netted metal cages around the spindly white trees.

Jonah turned and walked around the corner into Wanless Road. It was wider than Southway Street, with no trees, and wheelie bins were parked at intervals along the pavements, like Daleks. The Broken House was next to theirs, but there was a gap in between. It was older than all the terraced houses, and had been much bigger and grander, all on its own in its garden. They could see right into it from Lucy's bedroom window, but from here it was hidden by high, joined-together boards, covered in places by a tumbling passionflower, and dotted with 'Keep Out' signs. In fact, it was easy to get in. One of the boards had come loose and you could push it open like a door and slip inside.

Jonah walked through the stillness like he was the only thing left alive, dragging his fingers along the splintery boards. The loose board had been left ajar, and he peered through. The nettles had grown as high as his chest. The Broken House looked back at him, like a sad old horse. It was a long time since he'd been in there. As he turned away, with a start, he noticed Violet.

The fox was standing, still as a statue, on the bonnet of a filthy white van. Their eyes met, and although he knew her well, he felt shy of her, almost scared. He said, 'Hello, Violet', trying to sound normal, but his voice croaked, and all of a sudden she leapt onto the pavement and flitted into

the Broken House's tangled garden. Animals can sense your
fear, he remembered his mother saying, they can smell it,
and it makes *them* frightened. He looked after the fox for a
moment, and then at the white marks her scrabbling paws
had left in the van's thick grey dirt. There was a V-shape,
and two long scribbles, like a signature. He turned to walk
back to their house – which was when he saw the Raggedy
Man.

The Raggedy Man was standing against the wall of the
squatters' house; like Violet, so still that Jonah hadn't noticed
him. His feet were turned in and his arms hung down like
coat sleeves. '*Remember, he was a boy like you once,*' Jonah
heard Lucy say, but he quickened his step, crossing his arms
over his naked chest. The Raggedy Man was tall and black
and gnarled like a tree, growing out of his filthy, raggedy
pink tracksuit. He never said anything, ever, not a single
word. Jonah found himself saying, *A boy like you once,* over
and over in his head, as his feet padded quickly along the
pavement. He turned into Southway Street and, from the
corner of his eye, he saw the Raggedy Man put his hand in
the pocket of his tracksuit bottoms and pull something out.
Then his arm snapped out straight, the hand splayed
open . . . offering something? Jonah hesitated on his doorstep. There was an object glinting in the Raggedy Man's
palm. A coin? He darted a look up at the grizzly face. The
huge, angry eyes stared back at him. He looked away quickly,
scurried inside and closed the door.

5

He had only been out for a few seconds, but it felt like he'd come back from another world. Standing in the familiar jumble of the hallway, he could smell their wet swimming things, still in the bag. They'd gone to the Lido the day before, Sunday, on their bikes, early, to avoid the queue. Lucy loved to swim, but had sat on the edge, her wild hair crammed under a big straw hat, gold locket at her throat, her body wrapped in her enormous red sarong. As he'd glided like a manta ray above the slime-smeared floor of the pool, he had looked up and seen her strong brown feet dangling in the water. *Why won't you come in?* he had asked her silently. Her toes had rings on them – gold, like the locket – and her toenails matched the sarong.

Her red umbrella was leaning against the wall. He and Raff had taken it to school the day it rained. Next to the umbrella was the stepladder, which she must have pulled out from the cupboard under the stairs, as a reminder to get the curtain in their room back on its rail. Under the ladder was the can of petrol that, weeks and weeks ago, they'd walked all the way to the service station on the main road to get. They'd taken it on the bus, all the way across south London, to where they'd had to abandon the car the evening before. They'd been too late, though – the car had been towed away, so they'd brought the petrol back home. Getting the car back cost lots of money, which they didn't have. They didn't really need a car anyway. Next to the petrol was a pile of shoes, among which, Jonah was relieved to see, were her clogs. She must be here after all. He turned and pushed open the sitting-room door.

She wasn't there. Jonah looked down at her yoga mat, lying like a green lake amidst a jumble of Lego, nunchucks and cheese on toast remains. Part of Raff's Ben 10 jigsaw encroached upon the mat, like a jetty. He looked up. Through the sitting-room window, he saw the open-lidded wheelie bin balancing on the kerb.

She'd been burning incense in the kitchen, but the smell of the bin was stronger than ever. They hadn't emptied it for days – maybe weeks. Lucy had been ill for quite a while, off and on. Washing-up was stacked high on every surface, and the dirty clothes they'd collected up to put in the machine lay in piles all over the floor. He kicked through the clothes and went through into the tiny conservatory (if you could call it that), just big enough for the table, the three ordinary chairs and Raff's old Tripp Trapp ladder chair. The dead flowers had shed some more petals, onto the drawings they'd done of them when they'd got back from the Lido. Lucy had said she didn't mind they were dead. '*I prefer them when they get like this. Much more interesting.*' Maybe she had just wanted to make him feel better about them, but she had carried on, her voice low and dreamy. '*The intricate husks of them, like skeletons, on their way to dust.*' Jonah traced the line she had drawn, a fragile curl of dried-out lily petal. Her book was on the table, too, the book she'd been reading for weeks, even though it was very thin. There was a picture of a mask on the cover, an African-looking mask, with feathers and round empty eyeholes. Ants were crawling over the book and the drawings, and up and down the glass jug she'd made the orange squash in. There was a layer of black on the remaining inch of orange liquid: a floating blanket of drowned ants. The dead ants made him think of their holiday in the house with the swimming pool, and Lucy rescuing insects from the pool all day, using a net on a long pole. It was in France, the house. The Martins had taken them, as a treat, after Angry Saturday, and Roland getting sent to prison.

There were two new things on the table: a green wine bottle, empty; and a yellow mango, fat and ripe. The bottle was green, and the label was white, very white, with a grey drawing of jagged hilltops poking out of a sea of cloud like shark fins. The cloud was stratus, which wasn't all that interesting to look at from below, but from above it was all misty and rolling. Jonah picked up the mango. Its skin squished under his fingers. 'A Chaunsa,' he whispered. The King of Mangoes. The Green Shop Man had introduced them to Chaunsas, which grow in Pakistan, but only in July. Last year, the Green Shop Man had given her three of them, as a present.

Near the edge of the table were three little heaps. When he looked closer, he saw that they were made of the shavings from the coloured drawing pencils, mixed with crumbs and his and Raff's fingernails. She'd cut their nails after they'd done the drawings, and it had been about time; they'd been long and ragged and dirty, like witches' fingernails. The heaps were like tiny pyramids. He touched one of them gently, imagining her sitting at the table after she'd put them to bed, all alone, with her too-thick lipstick on, slowly pushing the fingernails and the pencil shavings and the crumbs together with her fingers. Then maybe her phone had rung, and it had been Dora Martin. And then maybe Dora had come round with the bottle of wine.

It would be good if Dora had come. She hadn't come for ages, and they hadn't been to the Martins' house for a while either. *They're still our friends, though. Aren't they?* He noticed how much he talked to her in his head, instead of just having his own thoughts. Did other children do that, to their mothers, or maybe their fathers?

There were no glasses on the table. He looked over at the pile of things on the draining board, and then remembered the wine glass by Lucy's bed, with the smudge of lipstick. If there was only that one wine glass, then maybe she had decided to pop to the Green Shop and buy a whole bottle of wine to drink on her own. Taken the last glass of it up to bed with her. He looked at the label again. Such a beautiful, soft drawing, and the words Cloudy Bay, in such fine, thin letters, with lots of space in between. It didn't look like the kind of wine you could get in the Green Shop. Then he saw that a steady stream of ants was heading down into the jug, despite the blanket of corpses. He thought about trying to divert them from their death, but the only thing he could think of would be to empty the jug and wash it, and the sink was too full of plates and pots.

Jonah looked up at the calendar. Yoga Poses 2013. The pose for July was Ustrasana, or Camel, and there was a picture of a woman, on her knees, arching backwards. The

pages of previous calendars had always got filled with
Lucy's scrawls, but this one had stayed very bare and
clean. He stepped closer, gazing up at the four and a half
rows of squares, thinking how each square was a complete
turn of the planet on its axis. The first two weeks were
all empty. Then, in the middle of the third row, Wednesday
the 17th, she'd written two letters, S and D. *An acronym.*
For the rained-off Sports Day. There was a squiggly word
beginning with C on the 18th, and then, on the fourth
row, she had circled the 26th, and written three letters,
P, E and D, in blobby brown felt-tip. *PED.* Trying to
think what they might stand for, he reached up to take
the calendar off its nail, and laid it on the table. Using
the dark blue drawing pencil, he crossed out the cancelled
SD, and wrote a new one in Thursday, the 25th. He
thought for a moment. She hadn't put 'Haredale's Got
Talent' on the calendar, even though Raff had been talking
about nothing else for weeks. He wrote in HGT, right
under SD. A busy day. He paused, and then went over the
letters again, because the blue pencil didn't come out that
well on the shiny calendar paper.

Jonah put the pencil down, yawned and looked at the
kitchen clock. 5.25. Where had she gone, so early? He turned
and tried the back door. It wasn't locked. Roland used to
tell her off about not locking the back door. The backyard
had a concrete floor, with brick walls on all three sides, the
Broken House rising up behind the far wall. In the middle
of the concrete floor was the brown corduroy cushion she'd
been sitting on the day before. Yellow-flowering weeds were
sprouting from the cracks in the concrete and from between
the bricks. Lucy's plant pots were sprouting weeds too, as

well as the things she'd planted. Her dirt-covered trowel
was resting against the wall. Her bicycle, which was a heavy,
olden-days one, but painted gold, was gleaming against the
back wall. Both the tyres were flat and weeds were growing
through the spokes of the wheels. It was all looking very
beautiful. He saw the watering can, and wondered if Lucy
had watered the pots before she went.

A movement made him jump and look up. The fox had
appeared on top of the back wall. Again their eyes met, and
again he felt scared of her.

His heart banging, he cleared his throat. 'Violet, are you
following me this morning?'

He had tried to sound calm and amused, but his voice
sounded thin and silly against the silence. *'Fear is like a
magnet,'* he heard Lucy say. *'It can actually make bad things
happen.'* He wondered if the Raggedy Man was still standing
outside, waiting to give him the coin. He turned away from
the fox, trying to stop his heart from thudding, and stared
at the dip Lucy's bottom had left in the corduroy cushion.
He remembered the loops and the lines and the spatters,
blue-black ink on the sunlit white page.

Brighter today.

That's what she'd written, sitting on the corduroy cushion.
He'd squeezed onto her lap, feeling her bosoms squishing
against his back, and looked down at the shape of the words.
Then a breeze had lifted the pages, and they had fluttered
and batted against each other, all covered in her squiggly
writing. And she'd reached forward with her dry, brown
hand and flipped the book closed.

He checked the pots. They hadn't been watered but under the surface the soil was still quite moist from all the rain the week before. In the biggest pot, which had honey-suckle growing out of it, and also delphiniums, there was something red and shiny sunk into the soil. A particular red. Definitely an object he'd seen before. A toy? One of his and Raff's old cars? His fingers closed around it. Not a car. Not a toy, even. He pulled it out, and something caught in his throat, because it was a mobile phone, just like Lucy's, a snap-shut Nokia. It probably *was* Lucy's. But why would Lucy bury her phone in a flowerpot? His heart banging again, he wiped it on his pyjamas, but it left a dirty mark, so he shook it to get the rest of the dirt off it, and it came apart. The back of it and the battery plopped back into the soil. He retrieved them and carried the three parts of the phone back into the house. He laid them out on the table, and fetched a tea towel to wipe them properly clean, before clicking them back together.

It was her phone. It had to be. No one else had those Nokias any more. He pressed the 'On' button. There was a bleep, and the screen lit up. It was showing a very low battery, but it seemed to be working fine. After a few seconds there was another bleep, and a missed call popped upon the screen. DORA. So she *had* phoned, and maybe she *had* come round with the wine. The last time they'd been to the Martins' must be the afternoon they'd taken Dylan round to mate with Elsie. Weeks ago. The phone bleeped again, and died. He weighed it in his hand, wondering where the charger might be, and remembering that chilly afternoon in the Martins' garden, watching the rabbits.

The charger wasn't in any of the wall sockets in the

kitchen, and it wasn't in the socket in the hall. In the hall he looked at Lucy's clogs again. They were wooden clogs, very old, kind of chewed looking, but so comfortable, Lucy said. They were the only shoes she'd worn for weeks. He put his own feet into them, remembering seeing her red toenails through the water. His feet would be as big as hers soon. DORA. The word danced in his head. Maybe they would go round to the Martins' after school. It would be nice to see the rabbits. And Saviour. He saw Saviour's warm brown eyes, and heard his friendly, cockney voice. *Fancy giving me a hand with the cooking?*

He stepped out of the clogs and went upstairs. The charger wasn't in the socket on the landing. Back in Lucy's room, it was still quite dark and, instead of continuing his search, he found himself getting back into her bed, half expecting her to be there after all. She wasn't. *Where have you gone, silly Mayo?* No, silly *Lucy*. He closed his eyes, and saw Dora, lying by the pool at the French holiday house, while Lucy, in just her bikini bottoms, walked up and down with her net. '*Nice to get away from it all!*' Dora's cheerful voice, her sunglasses, her long, thin body covered against the sun. '*Nice to get away from it all!*' She'd kept saying it, all the way through the holiday, as if . . . As if what? He rolled onto his side, seeing Lucy's net full of wet insects, her bosoms and her concentrating face as she tipped them out onto the paving stones; and got that weird feeling again, the one he got when she was reading the Yonghy-Bonghy-Bò poem. That she was separate from him, different, a stranger; and it wasn't just her grown-upness, or her femaleness, or her Africanness, which came and went with her mood. He pictured the three tiny pyramids on the kitchen table; and then the single, glinting disc on the Raggedy Man's palm; the stepladder, the red umbrella, the scribble Violet's paws made in the filth on the white van: and then he must have fallen asleep, because the next thing that happened was the ringing of the Tibetan bells.

6

The bells were a lovely sound. Jonah listened with his eyes closed, imagining the monks in their monastery in the misty mountains. Then Raff came running in, like a tornado.

'There's some guy swearing his head off in the street! You got to hear him, fam!'

Jonah opened his eyes and watched his little brother scamper around the bed, holding up his pyjama bottoms, which had lost their elastic. He realised he was still clutching the red phone, and put it down next to the lipsticky wine glass.

'What's that? Where's Mayo? Why have you got her phone?' One of Raff's cornrows had started to come out. 'Anyway, come on, you got to hurry. You seriously got to hear this!'

Jonah switched off the bells and followed his brother into their bedroom, where he was already leaning too far out of the window. 'Be careful, Raff!' He squashed in beside him, putting an arm around his waist. His skin felt very warm and dry.

'Oh my days! It's the bloomin' Raggedy Man!' Raff leaned even further, and Jonah tightened his hold. 'But he never talks!' said Raff. 'Why is he saying those things?'

Jonah looked down, and saw that the Raggedy Man had moved from outside the squatters' house and was on the pavement directly below. 'I don't know.'

'He got *issues*, man! Who is he *talking* to? Oi! You talking to us?' Jonah tried to clap his hand over Raff's mouth, but Raff wriggled out of his hold. He pranced, making signs with his fingers. 'Don't call me snake tongue, you fuckin' rat, you crazy fuckin' vampire bat!' he hissed, his cute face all mean.

'Don't say fuck, Raff.'

'Why? *He* said it!' Raff yanked up his pyjama bottoms. 'And *you* just said it, you fuckin' giraffe neck!'

'Anyway. It's time to get dressed.' Their school uniforms would be downstairs, among the dirty washing on the kitchen floor. Out in the street, the Green Shop door opened, and the Raggedy Man fell silent. The Green Shop Man came out, holding the stick with the hook on the end that he used to push up his metal blinds. Raff aimed an imaginary catapult at him, pulling back the stone in the sling, then letting go, his fingers exploding into a star, his lips blowing a kind of raspberry. 'Phwoof! Right in the head!' His pyjama bottoms fell to his ankles. He reached down to pull them back up. 'Is it Haredale's Got Talent this week?'

'Yes. Thursday.'

'Yesss!' Raff went spinning off, doing his dance again. 'Is Mayo writing her diary in the garden, like yesterday?'

'No.'

'Oh my days! It's Sports Day on Thursday too!'

'Yes.' It would be a bit of a scramble, Mr Mann had said, but he didn't want to deprive the athletes of their moments of glory; and parents who were already planning to come to the talent show could come early and kill two birds with one stone.

'Is she still better, or is she back to being ill?' Raff had stopped dancing.

'Better.' *Brighter.* The squiggly words on the fluttering page.

'Where is she, anyway?' Raff was suddenly very still, his tortoiseshell eyes fixed on Jonah.

'I'm not sure. Probably gone to the park.'

The Green Shop Man pushed at his stick. The huge noise of the metal blinds going up filled the air.

7

The pint of milk on the doorstep had already gone warm. It had a note under it from the milkman – a bill probably. Jonah carried the milk and the note into the kitchen. The mango and the bottle of wine were still there, and the ants were still crawling up and down the jug to their deaths. Raff sat down, and Jonah got the Weetabix out of the cupboard. The only clean bowls he could find were a wooden salad bowl and a white mixing bowl. Raff looked at the bowls and snorted.

'Or we could do some washing up,' Jonah said.

Raff raised one eyebrow. 'No way is I doing washing up, Little Peck!'

'Raff, you are not allowed to call me that.'

'Who you tellin', Dirty Little Peck?' Raff jumped up from the chair and shoved his face close to Jonah's.

Jonah moved away, ignoring him, which is what Lucy told him was always the best policy, and got on with putting three Weetabix into each bowl.

'Come on then, Peck!' Raff was snarling, his lips rolling back, showing his tiny white teeth. He lifted his arms, aiming his catapult at him. 'Peck versus the Slingsman! Phwooff!'

'Shut up, Raff!' He put his hands over his ears, but he could still hear Raff saying it, and making his stupid raspberry sounds.

'Little Peck. Fuckin' Peck.'

'Don't *swear!*' In a rush of rage, Jonah pushed Raff to the floor.

Raff jumped straight up and threw himself at Jonah, and they staggered through the kitchen and out into the hall, where Jonah managed to shove his brother off him. Raff fell back against the stairs, grabbing the stepladder as he went, and it fell on top of him, and he started crying, really loudly.

Panicked, Jonah shoved the stepladder away and knelt beside him. 'I'm sorry, I'm sorry,' he said. 'Are you OK, Raff? Where does it hurt?'

Raff just screamed louder, like when he was a toddler. 'Mayo!' he was screaming, over and over, and Jonah put his hands over his ears again.

'STOP!'

Raff stopped. They looked at each other for a moment, and then Raff slid himself off the stairs and opened up his arms, and Jonah knelt down and hugged him. They rolled over and lay side by side, amongst the shoes.

'What's she doing in the park?' asked Raff.

'Yoga.'

'But her yoga mat's in the sitting room.'

'Yes, but your Ben 10 puzzle's on it. She probably didn't want to break it.' Out of the side of his eye Jonah could see the yellow word on the rusty red of the can they'd filled up at the service station. GASOLINE. The American word for petrol. Closer in, by his temple, the chewed-up heel of one of her clogs. *Why haven't you got your shoes on?* he asked her silently.

'Jonah,' Raff whispered.

'What?'

'Is Bad Granny going to come?'

Jonah got a flash of Bad Granny's looming, brightly coloured face, and felt a shiver run through his body. 'Don't be stupid,' he said. Raff had sounded like a really young child, which he was, of course. Jonah wriggled his arm under his shoulders.

'Alright, me old Peck,' said Raff, but in a little cockney chirrup, not that horrible gangster voice. Jonah giggled.

'How nice to meet you, Lord Pecker!' he said in his Your Majesty voice, and Raff rolled around, snorting. Jonah chuckled. It was usually Raff who made *him* laugh. Through their laughing came a sound, which Jonah hardly heard, but Raff suddenly sat up straight, looking wide-eyed at the door. 'Mayo?' he whispered.

Jonah sat up too. Raff was holding his body very stiff. There was a moment's silence.

'What was it?' Jonah whispered.

'Someone. Looking through the letter box.' Raff got to his feet, but Jonah grabbed his ankle.

'Don't open it!' he hissed.

'Why?'

'It might be the Raggedy Man.'

'The Raggedy Man?' Raff crouched back down. Jonah reached for his hand. They both stared at the letter box, listening hard. A car came up Wanless Road and turned the corner.

'Why do you think it was the Raggedy Man?' Raff whispered.

'I don't know. Just because he was outside our house.'

'And he wants to come in?'

'I don't know. Are you sure you saw someone?'

Raff nodded. He lifted his arms and aimed his sling at the letter box. 'Phwoof.' He made the sound very quietly. Then he stood up and stretched, and pulled up his pyjama bottoms. 'Bags the wood bowl,' he said, in a normal voice.

8

Having breakfast in the enormous bowls made them laugh again, the way they had to reach down to get their spoons to the Weetabix. Then Raff said, 'Who sent them?'

Jonah looked at the skeletal flowers. *On their way to dust.* 'Roland,' he said.

'What, from prison?'

'You can still send people things. He sent you those posters of the runners.'

'Did Daddy give me those?'

'Yes!'

'I thought it was Saviour.'

'It was Roland. Last year, when the Olympics were on. You should remember that, Raff! Imagine if Roland knew you'd got him mixed up with Saviour!'

'Fuck off, Jonah, because I didn't mix him up with Saviour. I just thought Saviour gave me the posters.'

'Anyway. He sent Lucy flowers before.'

'When?'

'On her birthday.'

'So why did he send some now?'

'Maybe because she was ill? How should I know, Raff?'
Sometimes Raff's questions went on and on.

'But how did he know she was ill?'

'Maybe he phoned her.' Jonah suddenly remembered
finding her red phone in the flowerpot, and tried to think
what he'd done with it.

'Why didn't he speak to us, then?'

'I don't know, Raff! I don't know anything about it! I
don't even know if it was him who sent the flowers!'

'No need to fuckin' *shout*, fam.'

'Don't *swear*! You *always* swear!' Jonah picked up the
mixing bowl and tried to put it in the sink, but the sink
was too full.

'You got anger management, bro.' Raff shook his head
for a bit, squashing ants with the back of his spoon. 'Maybe
he sent them because he's coming out on patrol.'

'Parole.' There was no room on the draining board either.

'Maybe he'll get out in time for Sports Day.' Raff examined the ants on the back of the spoon. 'Do you remember
when he came to Sports Day with Bad Granny?'

'Yes.' Jonah put the bowl back on the table. He was
surprised Raff could remember. He'd been tiny, not much
more than a toddler.

'But it was before she tried to steal us.'

'Stop killing the ants, Raff.'

'Will he bring her this time?'

'Raff, he won't come to Sports Day. He's not getting out
that soon. Lucy would have told us.'

'She might of forgotten.' Raff squashed some ants with
the back of his spoon. 'Anyway, why do you call her Lucy
now? What's wrong with Mayo?'

'Nothing.'

'Is it because it's Zambian?'

'No. I just like calling her Lucy.' She liked it too. She liked it that he was getting so grown up.

Raff squashed some more ants. 'What about Haredale's Got Talent? I bet he'll get out for that!'

'Raffy, that's the same day, remember! And stop killing the ants!'

'Dey *ants*, Peck.'

'Ants are amazing!' Jonah grabbed the spoon off him and sat back down. 'Did you know they have two stomachs?' He watched the ants reorganise themselves. 'One for themselves, and one to store food to take back to their queen.'

'Queen gonna be hungry, den.' Raff snatched the spoon back and rolled it over a whole cluster of them.

'Raff! That is such bad karma!'

'Saviour says that karma shit is rubbish. He says everything's just random.' But Raff laid the spoon down. 'You know Bad Granny?'

'Yes.' Jonah looked at the empty eyeholes of the mask on the cover of the book.

'Will we know her again? When Roland comes out on patrol? Will he take us to see her?'

Shattered glass, Sadie's crazy face, and the peacock, screaming. 'I don't know.' After she'd tried to take them from school, Dora and Lucy had talked about going to court to get – what was it called? – a thing to stop her from coming anywhere near them. He wasn't sure if they'd actually done it, though. He opened the book. It was Dora's, she'd written her name on the inside cover, *Dora Martin*, in black ink, the letters very pointed, and all leaning forwards.

Underneath it, she'd done lots of scribbling in pencil, words and some doodles, but no, actually it was Lucy who'd done the stuff in pencil, he could tell by the handwriting, and the doodles.

'Raff.' He closed the book.

'What.'

'What does Peck actually mean?'

'Peck means Peck!'

'Doh! Did you get it off Saviour?'

'I didn't get it off no one. It's from my head.' Raff put down the spoon and stood up, very straight, with his arms by his sides. 'This is what it is!' He made a bobbing movement with his head. It looked like a move from a street dance, but also exactly like a pecking pigeon. It made Jonah laugh again, and try it himself. They both walked around the table pecking for a while.

Raff stopped first. 'Maybe it was the Angry Saturday man who sent her the flowers.'

'It wouldn't be him.' Jonah noticed the clock. 'Raff, we need to hurry! We're going to be late for school!'

9

Jonah hesitated before opening the front door, and looked from side to side before stepping onto the pavement. The Raggedy Man was nowhere to be seen. There were clouds now, great billowing ones: cumulus, not cumulonimbus, so it wouldn't rain.

'Mind, Peck!' Raff shoved past him. He had a toothpaste beard, his shirt was filthy and he was wearing trainers, which wasn't allowed. Jonah passed him his school bag, and hoisted his own onto his shoulder. They scurried along Southway Street, but stopped dead on the corner, because there was a fox lying just off the kerb.

'Violet!' Raff cried, clapping his hand over his mouth, but Jonah shook his head.

'It's not her. It might be one of her cubs though.' The back of the fox's body had been squashed into a bloody mess by the wheels of a car, but its head and its front legs were untouched. Jonah wondered if it had died straightaway, or whether it had lain there for a while, trying and trying to make its back half work. He wriggled his shoulders to shake off the thought, and took Raff's hand. 'Come on,' he said.

The bell started ringing as they went through the gate.

Jonah went with Raff into the Infants, and watched him run off into his classroom, before walking through into the Juniors' playground. It had nearly emptied out. Among the stragglers were Emerald and Saviour, and Jonah ran over to say hello. Saviour was squatting down so that Emerald could hug him goodbye, which he didn't need to do any more, because he was quite short, and Emerald had got really tall. Something about the way they were hugging, and the expression on Saviour's face, made Jonah stop a foot or two away and wait to be noticed. They didn't look like father and daughter: Saviour browner than ever, so brown you might not realise he was a white person, whereas Emerald's skin had gone just slightly golden. And Emerald was all fresh and neat in her school dress, with her long yellow hair in bunches, whereas Saviour was scruffy, in his torn T-shirt, and his paint-spattered Crocs, with bits of leaves and twigs in his curly hair. Jonah noticed that it was more grey than black now, his hair, and that you could see his scalp through it, hard and brown as a nut. His eyebrows were dark still; dark and bushy, which could make him seem cross, or at least lost in his thoughts – until he looked at you, like he did now, over Emerald's shoulder, with his kind, interested eyes.

'Jonah, mate. Where's the whale?' If you didn't know him, you might expect a deep, growly voice, maybe with a foreign accent, and be surprised by the warm, cockney lightness. He winked, and Jonah grinned and winked back, and Saviour reached up and high-fived him, because Jonah had been trying to wink for weeks.

'Fourteen runs!' Jonah said.

Saviour frowned.

'England won by fourteen runs! Didn't you watch it?' He and Raff had been glued to it the whole of Sunday afternoon.

'Course they did.' Saviour was wobbling a bit, because Emerald's hug was getting tighter.

'I didn't like that Hawk-Eye business. I didn't think it was really fair,' said Jonah.

Saviour nodded and stood up, and Jonah noticed he was getting fat again. He'd lost quite a lot of weight from giving up alcohol, but he was putting it back on. Emerald slid down onto her knees, wrapping her arms around his legs, and Saviour staggered, and put his hands on her shoulders. He didn't seem interested in talking about the cricket, so Jonah said: 'Lucy hasn't been very well.'

Saviour nodded again, looking down at Emerald. Her parting was dead straight and the bunches were like long silky ears which flopped around as she burrowed her head into his stomach.

'She stayed in bed for three days. I made her cups of tea.'

'Good on you, mate,' murmured Saviour.

'But yesterday she got up. We went swimming. Apart from she didn't actually swim.' Saviour had taken hold of one of Emerald's bunches and was twirling the yellow hair around his dark fingers. 'And she didn't watch the cricket with us. She went for a lie-down instead. But she doesn't really like cricket.'

Saviour let go of Emerald's hair and looked at his watch.

Jonah suddenly remembered the wine bottle. 'Did Dora come over to our house last night?'

'Dora,' said Saviour, as if he hardly knew her, but Emerald stood up and turned around, her bunches flying.

'No, my mum *didn't* come over. Because she's *really* ill. She's so ill she might even die!'

Saviour put his hand onto her pale head, and Jonah saw that his fingers were dark purple, almost black, from picking blackcurrants, probably.

'Really, Emerald!' Jonah said it with a smile, and a little look at Saviour, because Emerald was such a drama queen.

'Jonah, it's actually true – isn't it, Dad?' Saviour stared down at her with a strange, stiff smile on his face, and Jonah felt himself blush.

'Mum *is* ill, but that doesn't mean she's going to die, Emmy,' said Saviour. 'Not for a good long while anyway.'

Emerald put on her grown-up face. She said, 'You need to face the facts, Dad!' And Saviour's smile got wider and stranger, as if he might be trying not to cry. 'She's going to hospital this morning.' Emerald stroked her bunches, her grey eyes flicking between Jonah's face and Saviour's. 'To get her results. And tonight we're going to have roast chicken and roast potatoes for dinner.'

'Oh,' said Jonah. He couldn't think of anything to say, so he said, 'Anyway. I'd better go.'

He moved off, but Emerald let go of her bunches, picked up her bag and grabbed his arm. 'OK, wait for me, then. Bye, Dad!'

They left Saviour standing there in the middle of the empty playground, like a kind of scarecrow clown, with his orange Crocs and his purple hands and his leafy hair sticking straight up in the air.

10

Miss Swann had already started the Year 4 register. She looked up over her reading glasses. 'Emmy, Jonah, you made it! Awesome!' She was smiling, and the classroom smelt of her rosewater.

As he slid into his seat, Harold grinned at him with his loony grin. 'Yo, fam,' he whispered. They fist-bumped, and then Jonah looked back at Miss Swann. She was wearing a stripy summer dress with shoulder straps, and when she leant forward you could see her strangely long thin bosoms hanging down. Not bosoms. That's what Lucy called them, but no one else did. Most people said 'boobs', but it didn't feel right, calling Miss Swann's that. Maybe 'mammary glands'. *Her long, thin mammary glands.* Lucy would think that was funny. He smiled, picturing her laughing. Hers were nicer: fat and round, with puffy brown nipples.

In Assembly they rehearsed 'Star Man', which they'd be singing at the end of the Talent Show on Thursday evening. After the singing Mr Mann did certificates, and Jonah got one for his Broken House project, which he'd been working on all term as part of the Local History theme. All the Local

History projects were on display in the hall, and at the end of Assembly Jonah hung back to gaze up at his.

The house next door to us was built in 1862, by a rich Timber Merchent called Mr Samuels. It was a detatched Villa, in a Full-blooded Gothic Style, enlivened by vigorus Foliated Carvings.

He'd copied that last bit out from the London Survey website. He and Lucy had crept into the house to take the photos, showing the ruin it was now. One of the photos was amazing, looking up from the inside of the house, through the broken roof, to the sky. He imagined showing the certific-ate to Lucy when he got home from school, and telling her he would share it with her, because of the brilliant photo she'd taken – and Lucy sticking the certificate on the fridge.

'OK, Jonah, that's enough drooling over your own genius!' Mr Mann's hand came down onto his back, and propelled him out into the sunshine.

The playground was a swirl of children, flying about and screeching. The clouds had all gone, leaving a mysterious blue emptiness. All the colours are there, he remembered. It's just that blue light waves are shorter and smaller, so they scatter more when they hit the molecules. The endless-ness of the emptiness made his stomach drop, as if he was falling. Then he saw Harold, over by the fence, looking through into the Infants' playground.

'Is your mum better?' asked Harold as Jonah drew up beside him.

'Yes.' In the Infants, Raff and Tameron and their three

chorus girls were rehearsing the Camber Sands rap for the Talent Show.

'Can I come to tea, then?'

'Maybe.' Jonah remembered the first time Harold had come to tea, when they were in Reception. Harold hadn't been himself, to begin with. He hadn't wanted to play anything, or eat or drink anything, but had just stood with his hands in his pockets, mute. Jonah had been at his wits' end, but then Lucy had asked Harold what his favourite animal was. '*A peregrine falcon.*' He'd whispered it so quietly they had only just heard.

'*A peregrine falcon!*' Lucy had gasped. '*How fast can it fly?*'

'*Two hundred and forty-two miles per hour,*' Harold had told her. '*Which is the same as three hundred and eighty-nine kilometres.*' After tea, on the way back to his flat, Harold had held Lucy's hand all the way.

'Your brother's a boss dancer.'

Jonah leaned his forehead against the wire fence and watched. A crowd had gathered around Raff and Tameron and were joining in at the chorus. 'Ooh, Smelly Shelly! Uh, Smelly Shelly!'

'Who is Smelly Shelly anyway?' asked Harold.

'It's a shell. They found it on the beach, when they went on the school trip.'

'A shell!'

'Yep.'

'Did they make up all those words themselves? I bet your mum helped them.'

'A bit.' Her face came into his head, and he wondered if she was back in the house yet. 'Saviour helped more. He thought of lots of the rhymes.'

'Emerald's dad?'

'Yep.' Jonah leaned more heavily onto the fence, feeling the wire digging into his forehead.

'I think they'll win. Do you?'

'I dunno.' Jonah pictured Raff's face, glowing with triumph; Lucy's face, in the audience, crying probably. Crying and clapping. He smiled.

'Why are you smiling? Do you want them to win?'

Jonah slid his eyes towards Harold, who was inspecting him, his eyes tiny because of his thick glasses, his cheek resting on the wire. 'Is there even going to *be* a winner?' he asked. 'I thought it was more – just a show.'

'Well, if there *is* a winner, it should be them.' Harold looked back at Raff, who had started breakdancing. He shook his head. 'You might be Gifted and Talented, fam, but your brother's boss at everything. He'll win all the Sports Day races.'

Jonah shrugged. He rocked back onto his feet, and felt the grooves the wire had left with his fingertips. 'You know the universe?' he said.

'Yes.'

'Do you think it really goes on forever?'

Harold shook his head. 'No, there's other universes. Millions of them.'

'And then what?'

'I dunno. Can I come round to tea tomorrow?'

'I'm not sure.'

'If your mum's better, why can't I?'

'I'll ask, OK.'

11

In the afternoon it was RE. The classroom had got really hot. Miss Swann's boobs swung in her dress as she set out the painting stuff. Her hair, which was grey, even though she was quite young, had gone all frizzy.

'So we're all going to do a painting of something we've learned about Hinduism.' There were drops of sweat glistening on her top lip. 'Put on your overalls, please. Isiah. What are you going to paint?'

'The burning bodies!' said Isiah, with relish, and everyone started talking. They'd been doing Hinduism all term: the Diwali festival, some of the gods, the idea of karma and reincarnation, the Om symbol. It was Pearl who had told them about the dead bodies, burning beside the River Ganges. She'd seen them on a trip to India with her family.

'The burning bodies. Cool. Anyone else? What about the Diwali festival?' Miss Swann was setting out the paints and the water pots. She sounded tired.

'Their melting faces!' shouted Isiah. 'And their skulls, cracking open!' All the laughing and shrieking made it feel even hotter.

'You can't even see their faces,' said Pearl. 'They're all wrapped up in cloth.'

'Like mummies!' shouted Will Rooney, and Jonah thought of Lucy. *Are you back yet?*

'How do they burn them?' Tyreese was asking. 'With petrol?' Tyreese was Raff's friend Tameron's elder brother. Jonah looked at his overall. He didn't want to put it on. It was too hot.

'No, with wood,' said Pearl. 'But some families can't afford enough wood to burn the whole of the body, and they throw the leftovers into the river. So they put all these snapping turtles in the river, to eat up the leftovers.'

The class erupted. Jonah stayed silent, deciding what to paint. Maybe a picture showing the karma idea: lots of boomerangs, turning round and coming back, whacking into the throwers. But no, it was more complicated than that. Beside him, Harold was already painting, but Will and Isiah were still screaming about the man-eating turtles. Trying to work out how to do the karma boomerangs, he watched Miss Swann wipe her top lip with the back of her hand. It was actually *too* complicated. He would paint Ganesha, the god with the elephant's head, instead. He slipped on his overall and picked up his paintbrush. Ganesha had an elephant's head because when his father came home from a long trip he didn't recognise him and cut his real head off thinking he was his wife's new boyfriend. He thought of Roland and smiled, because of course Roland would recognise *him*. He remembered the scene at the end of *The Railway Children*, the clearing of the steam on the station platform, Bobbie crying, '*Daddy!*' Such a happy ending. He closed his eyes, imagining Roland's silhouette in the steam: tall, with high, square shoulders, and a little head with sticky-out ears.

When they had finished, Miss Swann pegged the pictures up to dry on the washing line that ran along the wall behind her desk. Jonah's Ganesha had turned out quite good. He had one little wise smiley eye. Roxy, the girl who had only started at the school a few weeks ago, had done Ganesha too, but hers was just a pink blob with a trunk. There were lots of burning bodies, black shapes amid orange flames.

'I love the way you've done the fire, Daniella,' said Miss Swann. Daniella had done lots of curly waves, in red, orange and yellow. 'And, you know, the body, to a soul, is like a set of worn-out clothes. Burning the body is setting the soul free.'

Emerald had done an Om sign, and Jonah gazed at it, trying to remember what Om meant. Something interesting. Lucy would know, because they chanted it in yoga lessons. He looked at the clock. Ten minutes until home time. *Will you come and meet us?* She didn't usually, but maybe she would today.

'This is awesome!' Miss Swann was holding up Shahana's painting. Shahana was the only Hindu in the class. She'd done a burning body, but hovering in the air above it was a baby, or maybe an angel. 'Shahana, is this showing reincarnation?'

Shahana shrugged.

'Who can remember what reincarnation means?' Miss Swann pegged Shahana's picture up.

'It's when you get reborn,' said Pearl. 'Your soul escapes through your skull, and it stays in the sky for a while, and then goes into another body.'

'And if you're bad, you come back as an animal,' said Tyreese.

'That's it!' Isiah shrieked. 'I gonna be bad! Then come back as a leopard, and munch up my enemies!'

Everyone laughed and shot their hands up, wanting to say which animals they'd like to be reborn as. Emerald wanted to be a rabbit, and Tyreese wanted to be a python. Pearl wanted to be a unicorn. 'Peregrine falcon,' Harold whispered to Jonah. Jonah smiled. He was still trying to remember what Om meant, and put his hand up to ask.

'Do Hindus believe in ghosts?' asked Daniella.

'Ghosts. Yes, I think they do!' Miss Swann glanced at Shahana. 'You're a ghost before you get reborn. Just for a few days. Isn't that right, Shahana? And the cremation of the body, and all the other rituals, help the ghost to leave, and get on with its next life.'

'So is a ghost the same as a soul?' asked Clem. Jonah's shoulder was starting to ache, so he switched arms. Everyone was just shouting out, when it should be his turn.

'I don't think it's the same, no,' said Miss Swann. 'I think a ghost is a trapped soul. But anyway, guys . . .'

'I saw my auntie's ghost once,' said Shahana.

'Oh.' Miss Swann wiped her top lip again, and tucked her hair behind her ears.

'Do you know what she's come back as?' asked Pearl.

'She's still a ghost. She's trapped.'

'Why?'

'Because she was murdered.'

There were a few gasps. Miss Swann glanced at her watch, then at the clock.

'Did the ghost have a knife sticking in it, then?'

Shahana turned around in her seat. 'Daniella, he didn't even kill her with a knife, actually.'

'Could you see through her, or did she look normal?' asked Clem.

'She looked normal. She was in the kitchen, and when I came in she got up and walked out.'

'Did she touch you?' asked Clem. 'Was she freezing cold?'

'Shahana's got allergies!' shrieked Daniella. 'She got touched by a dead ghost!'

Everyone went mad. Miss Swann's top lip was glistening again, and her hair was free of her ears. 'Quiet! Time for one more question. Jonah?'

'Oh.' Jonah had had his hand up for so long it took a moment to remember. 'Miss Swann, what does Om mean?'

'That is *random!*' shouted Isiah. Everyone laughed, and Daniella leant across to poke him. Then the bell rang.

12

'Is she here, have you seen her?' Raff had come running out of his class.

'Shut up, shut up!' Jonah grabbed Raff's arm and pulled him across the Infants' playground.

'Shut up yourself, dumbhead!' Raff said, trying to kick his ankles.

'You don't have to talk so loud. Mrs Blakeston could have heard.'

'So what?'

They were out of school, standing by the crossing. Saviour and Emerald had already crossed and were walking up the hill, hand in hand.

'Let's go with them,' said Raff, tugging him. 'I want to see Dylan.'

'No, come on, let's go home and see if she's there.'

The dead fox was looking much deader now. Jonah wondered if its soul was already reborn, or whether it was a ghost, still, looking down at its smashed body. On Southway Street they passed Mabel and Greta, and their mother Alison, as they were going through their front gate.

'Hello boys,' said Alison. 'Everything OK?'

'Yes, thank you,' said Jonah. Alison didn't like Lucy, and she didn't think the boys should walk to and from school by themselves. Taking Raff's arm again, Jonah slowed them both right down, to make sure Alison and the girls were inside their own house before they got to their front door.

The door had been painted maroon, but a long time ago, and the maroon was all peeling off, showing the white paint beneath it. Jonah banged the knocker. Then he banged it again. Raff couldn't quite reach the knocker, but he shouted, 'Mayo!' a few times through the letter box, while Jonah kept knocking. Then they stopped. The sun beat down and Jonah felt sweat trickle from his armpits. The white patches in the maroon reminded him of the marks Violet's paws had made in the dirt on the van, and he stared at them for a moment, imagining they were some kind of code which, if he could crack it, would tell him what to do. He turned and looked over at the squatters' house. Their front door was open, and he could see all the way along the dark hallway, with its red and gold wallpaper, to the rectangle of light at the end.

'What shall we do?' said Raff.

Jonah gazed at the rectangle, which was the squatters' open back door. Were the two open doors, that blaze of light, another sign, a kind of call? He imagined walking down the hallway and out into the garden. The squatters would be sitting, or lying down, probably smoking, one of those big, fat sharing smokes, which had made Lucy ill. He felt Raff nudging him, and cleared his throat. 'Maybe we should ask Ilaria if we can wait with her,' he said.

'Nah, fam.' Raff shook his head and crossed his arms, his nose wrinkled. 'Remember those sausages.'

Jonah nodded. It was the only time they'd been in the

squatters' house – a long time ago, just after Angry Saturday. The three of them, Lucy clutching a bottle, had walked through the open door and down the hallway, with its crazy velvet wallpaper, and its smell of incense and mould. Ilaria had been in the kitchen, making the big, ghostly sausages she called nori wraps, which were vegan, she'd told them. She had given him and Raff one each, and they were slimy and floppy, with bits sticking out each end. Neither of them could bear to take a bite, and had carried them around, not knowing how to get rid of them. In the back garden there had been a bonfire, the squatters and their friends all squatting around it, holding their hands out to it, their faces lit orange in the growing darkness. Everyone was white, and drab and raggedy compared to Lucy, who was wearing her red jumpsuit and her red lipstick. The red jumpsuit had a gold zip up the front, and the zip had worked itself down, so that you could see where her bosoms touched each other. He'd reached up to try and push it back up again.

Then a man had offered Lucy a big smoke, and she'd taken a few puffs on it. The man had a single, very long dreadlock coming out of his chin, and Jonah and Raff hadn't liked him, but Lucy had started chatting to him, all giggly and bright. The dreadlock man had stayed quiet, and after a while Lucy had stopped talking and gone inside. He and Raff had found her in the sitting room, lying on the floor with her eyes closed, moaning. They had both been really worried about her, and had taken it in turns to stroke her forehead. Ilaria had come in with a glass of water, and Lucy had managed to sit up and sip some. After a while she'd been well enough to stand up, and Jonah and Raff had taken her home.

'Let's go back to school,' said Raff. 'She might have gone in through the other gate, and still be waiting for us.'

'OK.' Jonah followed him back the way they'd come.

The school gate was already closed, so you couldn't get in without pressing the buzzer, but they could see that both playgrounds were empty by looking through the railings.

'OK, let's go to the park, then,' said Jonah. He could see Christine, who was the school manager, and much stricter than any of the teachers, peering at them through the office window. 'Come on.' He tugged Raff's arm. 'We could practise, for Sports Day.'

'I want to go to the Martins',' said Raff.

'We can't. They're having a special dinner.'

'So? They won't mind us coming.'

'They might want to be on their own.'

Raff dropped his school bag on the ground and kicked it.

'And when Lucy gets back, she won't know where we are.' Jonah picked Raff's bag up and held it out to him, aware that Christine was still watching them. 'Come on, let's go home. If she's still not there, we can get in through the back.'

They crossed the crossing and walked down the hill again, Raff dragging his school bag along the ground.

'Raff!'

It was Tameron. He was squatting on the kerb over the fox, with Tyreese from Jonah's class, and their elder brother Theodore, who went to secondary school. Tyreese was poking at the fox with a stick and the others were watching.

'They shouldn't just leave it like that, man,' said Theodore.

'Look at its eye!' cried Tameron. 'You lookin' at me, Mr Foxy?'

'Should we burn it?' suggested Tyreese. He looked at

Jonah. 'You know, like the Hindus.' Theodore shrugged and pulled out a lighter.

'Come on, Raff,' said Jonah.

'Wait! I want to see it burning!' said Raff. Jonah stepped forward and peered over their heads. Theodore wasn't holding the lighter near enough, and anyway the flame was tiny. He looked at the fox's face. Its eye was open, and for a tiny moment it was like it was alive, alive and wanting his attention.

'Let me try, bro,' said Tyreese. Theodore passed him the lighter, and Tyreese managed to slightly singe the fox's fur before burning his thumb and dropping the lighter to the ground.

Theodore picked up the lighter and put it back in his pocket. 'Not gonna burn with just that little thing.'

'We need petrol!' said Tyreese.

'Petrol!' cried Raff. 'We got petrol!'

The brothers looked at him, interested, and he looked back at Jonah. Jonah shook his head.

'Why not!' said Raff.

'I don't think we should,' said Jonah. 'And anyway, we might not be able to get in.'

'Why not?' asked Tameron.

'Our mum might not be back.'

'I need to wash my hands, man!' Theodore got to his feet. 'Come on, let's go.'

'Can you get the petrol tomorrow?' Tyreese asked Jonah.

'Fox gone by tomorrow, Tyreese, roadsweeper take it away.' Theodore pushed his brother forward, and the three of them walked away down the hill.

13

They tried knocking on the front door again, but not for long.

'What, then?' said Raff.

'It's fine,' said Jonah. 'The back door is definitely open. We can go through the Broken House.'

Around the corner, he trailed his fingers along the splintery fence, as he had that morning, but Raff kept to the kerb because he was scared of the passionflowers. Just as they reached the loose board, they heard a shout from across the road. It was Leonie, leaning out of her doorway.

'Where's your ma?' she shouted.

'Let's *run*, fam!' whispered Raff.

'At the shops!' Jonah called back.

Leonie shook her head, tutting and muttering, and came out onto the pavement, tossing her hair and clip-clopping in her high-heeled mules. She stood with her feet apart and her hands on her hips.

Raff snorted. '*Hench!*' he whispered.

'You're not going in there, it's too dangerous, you hear me,' she shouted. The Kebab Shop Man came to lean in his own doorway, and she turned to him. 'Some child is going to get themselves killed in there!'

The Kebab Shop Man nodded, and lit a smoke.

'Come here!' Leonie shouted, beckoning them. Ignoring Raff's mutterings, Jonah took hold of his hand, looked right and left, and crossed them over. Leonie's bosoms were straining out of her pink lace dress. Her fingernails were pink too, pink and incredibly long, and her black braids tumbled out of the top of her head like a waterfall.

'I know you two boys got your heads screwed on,' she said. 'So I'm surprised at you, even thinking of going in that place. It's dirty in there, you hear me?' Like Miss Swan, she had beads of sweat in the groove between her upper lip and her nose. 'There's nasty things, poison, make you really sick.'

They both nodded.

'Or, failing that, the place will topple over, smash them little bodies of yours into a pulp.'

Jonah nodded again, squeezing Raff's hand. He looked over at the Kebab Shop Man, who shook his head, flicked his smoke away and disappeared back inside.

'OK, come,' said Leonie. 'You can sit with me and Pat until your ma pulls her head out the clouds and remembers her responsibilities.'

'No way,' whispered Raff, as she clopped back in. 'She is hench, and her sweets are *rank.*'

'You coming or what?' Leonie was holding open the door for them. Jonah took a firmer hold of Raff's hand.

It was lovely and cool inside, from the many electric fans. The lady from the betting shop was having her hair done. She was a tiny little woman, very old and very white, and she was so low in the hairdresser's chair she could only just see into the mirror. Pat was standing behind her, putting bright blue curlers in her thin white hair. In the mirror, the old woman's broken-egg eyes slid to meet Jonah's. She used to let Roland bring him and Raff into her shop on Saturdays, but she didn't seem to recognise him. He reckoned she must be over a hundred years old.

'Look who I found,' said Leonie.

'The young gentlemen! Such a nice afternoon, why ain't they playing football in the park?'

'That dumb-arse mother of theirs gone off to the shops, left them to fend for themselves in the street, can you believe it? No disrespect, boys,' said Leonie.

She led them to the back of the shop, her pink lace bottom swinging, and sat them on the squishy white sofa. In front of them, on the glass coffee table, stood a bowl of sweets and a pile of magazines.

'Someone needs to phone the council to come and mend that fence, before a child dies in there,' said Leonie, lowering herself into the swivel chair behind the desk.

'Go on, then,' said Pat.

Leonie sucked her teeth. 'And be hanging on the phone all afternoon and night. Got better things to do with my time. Help yourselves to sweets, boys.'

Jonah said, 'Thank you,' but he didn't like Leonie's sweets either. Out of the corner of his eye he saw a tall, pink shape appear outside the shop window, and he stiffened, because it was the Raggedy Man again. He was peering in, or maybe peering at his own reflection, his arms long and loose by his sides. It was a girl's tracksuit, Jonah realised. That was why it was pink, and why it was so short on his arms and legs.

'What's he want?' Pat moved forwards, waving her arms at him, and he stepped back from the glass.

'Leave him be, poor soul,' said Leonie.

'Leave him be! I don't want him staring in at me like a Peeping Peter!'

'Tom,' Leonie corrected her, gazing at the Raggedy Man, who was shuffling backwards and forwards now, like a car trying to park in a small space. 'Something got to him today.'

The Raggedy Man moved out of sight, and Leonie sat forward and looked at the computer screen, clattering her fingernails on the desk. Then her hand became still, and a deep silence fell. Jonah and Raff sat upright, watching Pat's hands wrapping strands of hair around the blue rollers. The old woman's messy eyes were now closed. Maybe she was dead. Jonah heard Lucy giggle in his head. But her ghost would be here, until they burnt her body. He glanced around him. *Was* a ghost the same as a soul? He tried to remember what Miss Swann had said. That a ghost was a soul that was stuck, waiting to go to Heaven, or be reborn? *'Leave him be, poor soul.'* But the Raggedy Man seemed more of a ghost than a soul, a sad, lost, waiting thing. Leonie pulled a tissue out of the box on the desk, and pressed it under her nose, leaning back in her chair. The loud electric buzz made the boys jump and the old lady's eyes fly open. Leonie put the tissue down and said, 'That's my 4 o'clock.'

'Bit early, ain't he?' said Pat. The old woman's eyes closed again.

Leonie swung round in her chair. Her legs splayed and her hands rested on her belly as she and the boys surveyed the man on the tiny screen above the doorway that led out to the back. He was a fat white man, in shorts and a vest and flipflops. As they watched him he looked edgily around Leonie's little backyard.

'Better get him over with. He won't take long,' said Leonie, and with a groan she got back to her feet. They watched as she disappeared through the doorway, and then as the back of her head appeared on the screen. The man moved towards her, and then they were both gone, and the yard was empty again.

Jonah sank deep into the squishy sofa. The noise of the fans was making him feel sleepy, and he closed his eyes. *Where have you gone, Lucy?* He got a flash of her face, but then Bad Granny came looming at him, and he opened his eyes and sat up. He felt Raff's elbow in his ribs, and looked down at the magazine open in his brother's lap. Pictures of naked men and women, sexing each other. Raff was giggling silently, full of shocked delight, but Jonah took the magazine off him and put it down on the coffee table. 'Let's go,' he mouthed.

Pat's hands were busy with the old woman's hair. They walked very softly past her, and to the front door. As Jonah pulled the handle, the old woman's eyes opened and slid to them again. Pat said, 'Off now, gentlemen, my regards to your ma.'

14

Raff was looking edgy, like the man in Leonie's backyard. 'They're just flowers,' said Jonah. There were hundreds of them, all over the Broken House fence, staring silently, with their purple spiky eyelashes and their downturned yellow mouths.

'I don't like them. They look like Bad Granny.'

Jonah snorted, but Raff's face was strained.

'It won't really fall on us, you know, Raff. It's been standing up this long, it's not going to suddenly collapse, just because we're in there.'

Raff nodded.

'You can wait for me round the front, if you don't want to come.'

Raff shook his head. 'Don't want to be on my own.'

'Well, OK, come, then.'

Jonah went first, picking his way carefully along the faint and narrow path that led through the rubbish-strewn vegetation. He looked up at the house, and its boarded-up windows were like blank, daydreaming eyes, and the doorless back doorway was mouthing a silent 'Oh'. It had been here, all alone, for a very long time now, he found himself thinking, and he tried to remember which fairy tale it was when the prince hacks through the forest to get to the sleeping castle.

Inside it was dark and cool, and it smelt of dust and bird poo. They could hear the pigeons, hundreds of them, bustling and burbling in the rafters. The back doorway led straight into the kitchen, which was reasonably solid, with a floor and a ceiling. There was a hulk of an oven, and two halves of a filthy ceramic sink lying on the floor beneath two taps. The light leaking through the entrance fell on the table in the middle of the room, and Jonah saw that there was an old camping stove on it, along with a metal teapot, a plastic lemon and a cluster of bottles and jars. By the table were two chairs, or frames of chairs, their seats missing, which made him think of the Yonghy-Bonghy-Bò poem. *Two old chairs, and half a candle. One old jug without a handle. These were all his worldly goods: in the middle of the woods.* He looked at the huge, square, robot face which had been spray-painted onto the far wall. There was a hatch right in the middle of the face, and he went and peered through it, into the mouldy smelling darkness which had been the dining room. When he turned, Raff was at the table, examining one of the jars.

'Honey,' he whispered. 'Does someone live here?'

These were all his worldly goods: in the middle of the woods. Jonah joined him at the table. 'Maybe,' he said. There was a smoke lighter, and half a candle, and a sticky-looking teaspoon. The bottles were empty, apart from one, which was about a third full of a dark liquid. He picked up another jar and opened it, and sniffed. A spice. He couldn't think of the name. He put the jar down.

'Come on,' he said.

The hallway was more hazardous, because most of the floorboards were gone. There was more graffiti, pictures and symbols, and some words, mainly names. To their left rose the staircase, still grand-looking, though one of the banisters had been broken by a fallen chunk of ceiling. Light fell through the hole left by the chunk, and they could hear the pigeons more clearly. To their right, the hallway led to the front door, which would have given onto the street, if it hadn't been boarded up, and the fence erected in front of it. The door was intact, with its stained-glass window, and there were pegs, still, running along the wall next to the door. There was even a coat hanging from one of them. Opposite the pegs was a side table, with a bowl in it, a china one, and Raff, his fear overcome by wonder, went and dipped his hand in. He pulled out a pair of gloves, but then dropped them quickly, with a quiet screech, brushing a spider off his arm. He ran back to Jonah, and they both looked into the sitting room.

It was huge, much bigger than the kitchen. Jonah knew there had originally been two rooms, but that the wall between them had been taken down. He wasn't sure, but he thought it would have been in the 1970s, when the house was a children's home. He pictured it as the children's playroom, with beanbags, and a ping pong table, and the Wendy house for the little ones. Now it was more like a cave than a room. The ceiling had fallen in, and the ceiling above it, so you could look up through the remaining beams and see the outlines of the upstairs rooms: the boarded windows, the doorways, the fireplaces, and even some patches of wallpaper. The floorboards were gone too, fallen down into the basement, along with lots of bricks and rubble from the upper floors.

Jonah jumped down onto the rubble, and a group of pigeons flapped hastily upwards. It wasn't too big a drop, but it was easy to hurt yourself, because what you landed on tended to move. It was dark too, apart from the pool of light under the hole in the roof. He turned to help Raff down, and they crunched forwards a little way, until they reached the shaft of light. Jonah looked up.

'It's like a swimming pool! We could dive into it!' That's what Lucy had said, the day they'd crept in together and taken the photographs. As he gazed up through the remaining beams into the lopsided rectangle of blue, a tiny silver aeroplane appeared. Watching it crawl its way across to the other side, he remembered a film they'd watched on TV one afternoon, a really old film, called *Jason and the Argonauts*. While Jason tried to find the Golden Fleece, the gods watched him from an airy white palace, in their swishing togas, through a blue rectangle of water.

There was a tiny plop, and Raff said, 'Yuk!' Jonah looked down. The gob of poo had spattered just in front of them. He looked up again, to the beam that formed one edge of the rectangle. It was covered with pigeons. He could see their tails sticking out, black against the blue.

Jonah peered forwards into the darkness and saw the bed. It was an olden-days bed, with four wooden posts. It must have plummeted down from the floor above when the ceiling fell in. Had there been someone asleep in it? What a surprise they must have got. Lucy had gone right up to it and taken pictures, but Jonah had kept back. It was just too spooky, with its mattress, blankets and pillows all tidy, as if it was still in use. *These were all his worldly goods: in the middle of the woods, these were all the worldly goods, of the*

Yonghy-Bonghy . . . Trying to silence the chanting voice in his head, Jonah looked away from the bed and over to where they were heading, the patch of light in the far wall. He whispered to Raff to follow right behind him, and stepped over a big piece of carpet, noticing the noughts and crosses pattern. The rubble rose and fell, sometimes steeply, and he had to keep peering down to check each step. He noticed two ping pong balls, pale, like giant pearls. To his right loomed the Wendy house. She'd taken a picture of that too. *'Such a dear little house, Joney, and it's like those Russian dolls, it's a baby Broken House inside the big one.'* Behind the Wendy house was a piece of concrete pipe. He'd crawled into it last time, but she'd been too big. Now his feet slid among a heap of books, mainly open, like fallen birds. Among the books were more ping pong balls, and a toy train, and a Monopoly board. Further along, a baby doll, one-armed, face down – yes, he remembered that doll, and the feeling of wanting to turn it over, to see its face. He was aware of the bed, over on his left, but he kept his eyes on the ground in front of him. Then they were there, below the hole in the wall that used to be a window. The board that had once covered it was propped against the wall underneath, providing a slope up to what had been the windowsill. It would have been quite easy for Lucy, or any adult, to take a couple of big steps up the board, but it was a scramble for the boys. Raff scraped both his hands on the rough brick ledge, and Jonah hurt his knee. Out in the narrow space between the Broken House and their back wall, they examined their injuries and dusted themselves down. Then they surveyed the wall, which was surprisingly high from this side.

'How does Mayo get over it?' said Raff.

Jonah looked at the kitchen chair that had been positioned against the wall to their left. The back of it was broken, but the legs and seat looked in good shape. 'Like that,' he said. 'Come on.'

They got on the chair together, and Jonah gave Raff a leg-up before hoisting himself up. They sat on the wall, their legs dangling against the warm brick, looking down at the familiar cracked concrete, the bright flowers, the gold bike, the corduroy cushion and the watering can. He got down first, lowering himself until he was hanging from the top of the wall by his fingers, letting go and remembering to bend his knees as he landed. Then he helped Raff down, and they let themselves in through the back door.

15

The house was really smelly now, much smellier than the Broken House, and there were lots of fat, black flies. Jonah propped the back door open and opened up the windows, so that fresh air would come in. Then he went to the bin and opened it. The stench hit him full in the face, and he quickly closed it again.

'I'm thirsty,' said Raff. Jonah picked a glass up off the draining board, rinsed it and filled it, water splashing on the dirty plates piled up in the sink. He passed it to Raff, and then opened the drawer that Lucy kept the incense sticks in. He took two sticks out of the open packet and the box of matches. Raff glugged the water down and put the glass back on the side. 'I'm hungry.'

Jonah opened the fridge. He saw a mustard jar, a lime pickle jar, a tomato ketchup bottle and a bunch of slimy spring onions. They really needed to go shopping. Jonah felt cross with her for a moment. Then he remembered his certificate, and pulled it out of his school bag. 'Look.'

'I saw you get it in Assembly, dumbhead.'

Jonah found a space for it on the fridge door, amongst the photographs and postcards and all the previous certificates.

WELL DONE, JONAH!
In recognition of your excellent work
on your local history project.

He stood back, and ran his eyes over the photos. They went back to when he was a baby, and even before. There was the one of Lucy in a bikini, which he didn't like, though at least she had her bikini top on. It had been taken long before he was born, and she was thinner, and her bosoms – no, boobs – looked even bigger, and she was thrusting them out, with her hands on her hips. Her lips were blowing a kiss to the photographer, who was presumably Roland, but it was difficult imagining her being like that with Roland.

'What special dinner are the Martins having, anyway?'

'Roast chicken.' Jonah stared at young Lucy's face, trying to imagine her being in love with Roland. They had met on a yoga holiday in Egypt. The photo might even be from that holiday, although Lucy had been ill for most of it. Roland had heard her in the night, in the bathroom, moaning, and he'd looked after her. He skimmed all the photos again, looking for Roland. There was one of him when he was maybe a teenager, with his arm around Rusty, his dog. Rusty was looking at the camera, and Roland was looking at Rusty, so it was his profile you could see, with his long knobbly nose and his quiff.

The only other photo with him in it was the one of their wedding day. The two of them, standing on some steps, Roland in a suit, and Lucy in a strange blue dress with a white collar. He was smiling, but she looked serious. She was slightly turned away from him, even though they were holding hands, and you could see her bump, in which a little tadpole Jonah had been swimming around. About a third of the photo had been torn off. Presumably because it showed Bad Granny.

The photo next to it was of Raffy, Baby Raffy, only just born, his stripy monkey toy in his tiny fist. Jonah had given him that monkey, in the hospital. Lucy had been sitting up in her big bed, and someone had lifted him onto her lap, and put the bundle that was Raff on *his* lap, and Raff's fierce little face had gazed up at him. Everyone had been amazed at the way he held the toy. *'What a strong baby! What a strong little baby!'* Jonah got a match out and lit both incense sticks.

'Maybe there's some sweets left.' Raff was looking at the Advent calendar, which was high up on the fridge door, fastened with four magnets at each corner. They'd made it together last year, with pieces of red and green felt. It had twenty-four pockets sewn onto it, and the word 'Christmas' across the top. When Christmas was over, Lucy had said she was so proud of the calendar she couldn't bear to take it down.

Jonah and Raff stepped forward together and dipped their fingers into the pockets. No sweets any more, they'd gobbled them all up, but Lucy's fountain pen was in pocket number 17.

'That's what she was writing with. In the garden,' said Raff, snatching it from him. Jonah nodded. It had been a present from Dora, along with the heavy, thick-paged book.

Brighter today.

'Where's her diary?' He turned, his eyes scanning the messy room.

'Here's her keys.' Raff used the pen to fish them out from between two piles of dirty plates. Jonah took the keys and looked at her elephant key ring. She was always forgetting her keys. The elephant reminded him of his painting of Ganesha, and the little wise eye. The sweet smell of the incense was filling the air. He put the keys down on the table and noticed the calendar, and the changes he'd made that morning. The first two weeks still so clean and bare, but now, with his dark blue additions, the third and fourth row were looking untidy. He squinted at the word beginning with C, and tried to think what PED might stand for. Then he flicked back to June. Vrischikasana, or Scorpion. A very difficult pose, a kind of handstand, but with your toes coming down to meet your head, like a scorpion's tail.

June had been busier. Lots of her loopy scrawls. He ran his finger along the rows of numbers, going backwards through time. *Dentist*. They hadn't bothered going in the end. He couldn't remember why. *Martins with D*. Oh yes, the day they took Dylan round, so he could mate with Elsie. They'd sat on a blanket in the garden, watching the rabbits ignoring each other. Saviour had brought out tea and cake. Rhubarb cake. It had been quite cold.

'I wish we had a time machine,' said Raff. He had taken the pen to bits and was examining the little tube inside.

Jonah kept looking at the calendar. Time, a whole month, one circling of the moon, turned into thirty squares on a page. 'What for?' he said.

'To take us to when she comes home. Then we wouldn't have to keep on waiting.'

'Or it could take us back to this morning. Before she went out.' Jonah flicked the calendar back to July. 'Then we could stop her from going.' He put his finger under the word beginning with C. It might be Clink. Or maybe . . .

'You can't actually do that.'

'Do what? Don't do that, Raff. The ink will come out and go everywhere.'

'Change things that have already happened.' Raff kept squeezing. There wasn't any ink in it anyway. 'Otherwise everything would explode. There's no point in going back. Only forward.'

'But if you go forward you lose some of your life.' Jonah thought for a moment. 'Well, not if you came back again.'

Raff nodded. 'You could go forward, see what's going to happen, like who gets a certificate in Assembly, and then come back and make a bet on it.'

'Well, you could bet on a horse race,' Jonah pointed out. 'You could put all your money on it, sell your car and your house, because you'd absolutely know which horse was going to win.'

'Daddy would like that!'

Jonah frowned, looking at the photograph of Roland and Rusty. Rusty had died, ages ago, before the Egyptian yoga holiday. He was buried in Bad Granny's garden. There was a gravestone, with his name. 'I don't think he would. He would think it was cheating. Which it is.' He looked back at the calendar. PED. On the last day of term. Perfect End Day? 'And anyway. Once you've gone forward, coming back again, you're actually going into the past. So putting the bet on in the past would make everything explode.'

'No, because you'd put the bet on in the new time, that came after you went into the future. The bit that nothing's happened in yet.'

PED. Jonah frowned at the letters, thinking about time travel. 'But when you're in the future, watching the horse race, then it's actually the present, isn't it? And the time leading up to the horse race must have actually happened, otherwise . . .' He closed his eyes, seeing the strange blankness of unwritten time. 'I think what must happen is that you split into two.' He opened his eyes. Raff was fiddling with the bits of pen again. 'So your old self just keeps going, and *not* putting on the bet, and then your *new* self . . .' He stopped again, trying to work it out. It was incredibly complicated.

'No such thing as time machines anyway, stupid Peck.' Raff dropped the pen pieces on the table and left the room.

16

Her clogs were still there, and the umbrella, and the petrol can, and the bag with the swimming things. The step-ladder was lying flat, taking up a lot of room. Jonah picked it up and rested it against the wall. Without saying anything, they wandered together from room to room, ending up in Lucy's bedroom, where the air was still thick with the smell of her body. Raff climbed into her bed and lay down.

'Why are they having roast chicken?'

'Because of Dora's cancer.'

'She's had that for ages.'

'She got better from it. But Em said now she's really ill and might die.' Jonah surveyed the room. A big tear in the paper lampshade showed the curly light bulb inside it. The wardrobe door hung open, clothes spilling out, and two of the drawers were sticking out of the high chest of drawers. Lucy's red silk dressing gown, with the dragon on its back, was hanging on one bedpost, and on the other was that smelly grey cardigan she'd borrowed the day they took Dylan to the Martins'. Her flowery top and denim shorts from yesterday were on the floor beside the bed, and her lacy pink pants were still inside the shorts. There was a dark stain on the cotton bit where her fanny went.

'Do you believe her?'

'I don't know.'

'Mayo said it wasn't actually that bad.' Raff kicked the duvet off the bed. His trainers had made dirty marks on the bottom sheet.

'When did she say that?'

'I dunno.' Raff sat up and swung his legs over so that he was sitting on the other side of the bed, facing Lucy's dressing table, which was just a small, ordinary table with a piece of mirror propped on it. Jonah went and sat beside him, and they both looked at themselves in the dusty, greasy mirror. Jonah looked more like Roland, who was white, with a long, thin nose, whereas Raff looked more like Lucy, with his browner skin and his afro hair, and his huge, golden eyes.

Raff leaned forward and reached for her lipstick, which was lying amongst some lipsticky tissues. It didn't have its lid on, and was all squashed and melted. Jonah noticed that two of Raff's cornrows were coming out now. Lucy had put them in weeks ago, nice and tight, so they would last, but nothing lasts forever. He watched Raff putting the lipstick on his mouth, remembering Lucy doing the same thing the night before. The cricket had finished, and he'd gone upstairs to find her. She'd had her back to him, and their eyes had met in the mirror. She'd scraped her hair into a tight knot on top of her head, which made her look weirdly beautiful. *That hairstyle really suits you, Mayo,* he had said. And then he'd said, *'Lucy, I mean.'* He'd smiled, but she hadn't smiled back; and her lipstick had been far too thick.

'What's up?' said Raff, with bright red lips.

'Nothing,' said Jonah, but the memory had brought a coldness into his belly. 'You look stupid with that lipstick.'

'I look cool, bébé!' Raff turned sideways to look over his shoulder into the mirror and blow a kiss at himself. Then he went over to her wardrobe and pulled out her sparkly fairy shoes. 'Roast chicken's my favourite. Why can't we go to the Martins'? We could leave her a note.'

Jonah had a flash of the Martins' house: of burrowing into that space behind the sofa and lying there, smelling what was cooking, and listening to Dora and Lucy talking. When they had first got to know them, when he and Emerald were in Reception, they used to go there nearly every day.

'Or we could just tell Dora to phone her,' said Raff.

The phone. Jonah turned to the bedside table. It was still there, next to the wine glass. 'Have you seen her charger?'

Raff had put his feet into the sparkly shoes and was clopping around the room. 'It's down there.' He pointed to the socket under the dressing table. Jonah crouched down, connecting the phone to the electric current. 'Why didn't she take her phone?'

'She must have forgotten it. Like she forgot her keys.'

'But where is she?'

The phone seemed to be charging. Jonah tried pressing the 'On' button.

'Jonah.' It was Raff's very young voice again.

'What?'

'Do you think Bad Granny will come and try and steal us again?'

'Stealing isn't the right word, really.'

'Why not?'

Jonah frowned. It was the word Lucy used, when she told the story, but he was sure there was a more grown-up way of talking about it. 'She didn't think Lucy should be allowed to look after us. But that's not the same as stealing.'

'Will she try again?'

'No. I don't think so.' The phone wouldn't turn on.

'Maybe we should tell the Martins Mayo's not here.'

'I don't think we should.'

'Because of the cancer?'

'Because they might decide to phone the police. And then the police will tell Bad Granny.'

'And she'll come and steal us.' Raff's voice had gone all husky. The phone suddenly bleeped. Then it bleeped a few times more, indicating missed calls and messages.

'Yesss!' Raff clopped over and pulled the phone out of Jonah's hand.

'Raff, what are you doing!'

'We've got a message from Mayo!' he said, pressing the buttons.

'They're not going to be *from* her, stupid! They're from people who phoned her! Give it to me! You'll delete them if you're not careful!'

Jonah grabbed it back off him. There was a missed call and a voice message and two new texts. He played the voice message first. 'It's Dora,' he whispered. Dora sounded cross and upset, tearful, even.

'What's she saying? Is she saying she's going to die?' Raff tried to get his ear right next to Jonah's, but Dora's voice had stopped.

'She said, what's going on, you ignore my texts and then phone me up at the crack of dawn.'

'Who, Mayo?'

'Yes. Shush.' He looked at the most recent text.

Awful in the hospital. Hubby lost it totally. You and me
need to sort things out. Come over with boys after
school?

'Let me look.'

'Wait.'

The earlier one, sent at 11.07, was in a different tone:

Worrying about you is the last thing I need right now.
PLEASE FUCKING REPLY

'Give it, Peck!' Raff snatched it.

'Raff, give it back. I want to look at the old texts.'

'"Come. Over. With. Boys. After. School",' Raff read out.
'Right, let's go.' He kicked the sparkly shoes off.

'And what shall we say about Lucy?'

'Say she didn't want to come. Anything. Come on, fam.'

'They'll think it's weird. They'll want to speak to her.'

Raff sat down next to him, sighing, but then jumped up
again. 'Hey! I know! Let's pretend to be Mayo, and write
that we're coming, but she's too busy!'

Jonah frowned. It was actually quite a good idea, although
pretending to be Lucy would be like lying.

'Come on, Joney! Then we can see Dylan!'

Dylan. Lovely, floppy Dylan. They hadn't seen him for
weeks. 'OK. What shall I write?'

'Say, boys coming over now, but I'm a bit busy.'

Jonah typed:

Sorry, I am OK but very busy so great if you could have
boys for tea shall I send them over now from Lucy

He showed it to Raff, who studied it. 'You don't write "great"
like that. It's g, r and the number 8.'

Jonah made the change, and pressed Send. Raff whooped
and started dancing.

'Put your trainers back on, then. And take the lipstick
off.'

'The Martins don't care about lipstick, fam!'

It was true. Saviour would laugh, and Dora would tell
Raff how glamorous he looked. Watching Raff prancing, he
imagined being with Saviour in the kitchen, helping him
with the meal; Saviour glancing sideways at him, saying,
'Penny for them.' He wouldn't answer, and Saviour's brown
eyes would get even kinder. 'That bad, eh?'

'Not that good,' Jonah whispered to himself. 'Lucy's gone,
and we haven't got any food. But the thing is, I can't tell
you.'

The phone bleeped. Raff came running to read the reply.
It was two words:

Fuck yourself.

'Oh Em Gee!' said Raff, his eyebrow shooting up. 'Is it really
Dora who wrote that? That is bad swearing, man!'

Jonah felt like crying. He lay down on the bed.

'Is it because she's going to die?' Raff sat next to him.

Jonah pushed his face into Lucy's pillow. Raff picked up
the phone and started pushing buttons. After a few minutes
he tapped Jonah's shoulder.

'Look.'

Jonah peered at the screen.

I am so soz. Please dont die xxx

'Have you sent it?'

'Yes.'

'Idiot.' Jonah put his face into the pillow again.

'Why?'

'People don't say stuff like that.'

'Yes they do!' The phone bleeped. 'Yesss!'

Jonah rolled over and watched him frowning at the screen.

'"Want to see the boys. Tomorrow, not now." Shit!' Raff
threw the phone onto the bed. Jonah reached for it.

Want to see the boys. Tomorrow not now. All too tired.
Em in bits.

'But they're having roast chicken! Let's just go!'

'We can't,' Jonah scrolled back to look at the old texts.
The most recent had been sent on Sunday morning.

Tonight X

Not from Dora. From a number, not a name.

'What are you doing now?'

'Nothing.'

'We need to do something, Peck!' Raff's fist bashed at his
shoulder.

Jonah stood up, putting the phone into his pocket. 'Calm
down, Raff. Let's go and have a look in the freezer.'

17

They found some ice cream in the freezer, and a pizza, which they cooked in the microwave, so it came out more like a Frisbee than a pizza. Jonah tried cutting into it and it splintered into bits. He chopped up the mango instead, which was difficult, and he cut his finger, and the blood mingled with the mango juice on the kitchen table. The mango was completely delicious, but they still felt hungry so they ate the ice cream, which was butterscotch. They ate it straight from the tub, and finished it, and then they felt sick and went and lay on the sofa in the sitting room. The cricket was finished so they watched the Tour de France, but Bradley Wiggins wasn't in it, and it was hard to work out what was going on.

'Where is she?'

'I don't know.'

Raff sighed. 'She must be dead.'

'Don't say that, Raff. Of course she's not dead.'

'Dead, or a bad man's got her. Otherwise she would of come back by now.'

Jonah felt in his pocket for her phone, and held it, feeling its solidness. 'The thing is, she might come back at any minute.'

Raff got up and went and opened the front door, and looked left and right. Then he slumped down onto the doorstep. Jonah went and sat next to him. Shadows had started to fall across the road, and it felt quiet and sleepy. The sky was still very blue, and Jonah thought about the gods in *Jason and the Argonauts* again, looking down, deciding what would happen next. Then Alison, Greta and Mabel appeared, from the direction of the park. Alison was carrying a big bag with a towel trailing out of it, so they'd probably been to the paddling pool. They were all quite pink, and Greta and Mabel were arguing. Alison was telling them not to, but then she noticed the boys and shaded her eyes to look at them. Jonah waved, but Greta hit Mabel, who burst out crying, and Alison was distracted from waving back. They went into their house and the road was quiet again, and Jonah felt a deep sadness steal up on him.

'Jonah.' Raff's voice was thoughtful, and he was sitting very still.

'What?'

'Why doesn't Alison like us?'

'Because she's not a very nice person.'

'Is it because of Angry Saturday?'

Jonah stared at Alison's dark green shiny door. 'I think she already didn't like us. Or didn't like Lucy.' He was remembering long ago, the itch of his spots and Raff crying all the time, and Lucy crying too, though she'd tried to hide it. 'Lucy invited them to tea once.'

'Really?' Raff sounded like he didn't believe it.

'We both had chicken pox and we couldn't go out anywhere, and it was really boring, and Daddy said Mabel and Greta had already had chicken pox and to invite them all over.' Roland was always telling her she should make more of an effort with people.

'I don't remember them coming to tea.'

'You were just a toddler. And anyway, they didn't.'

'Why not?'

Jonah stared at the green door. It had been lovely weather and Raff had been crying and crying, and Lucy had seen Alison coming out of the Green Shop with the girls in their buggy, and had put Raff down and run and opened the front door. He closed his eyes, remembering Alison looking down at him, commenting on his spots, and saying they'd got that one over with a few months ago.

'*So you can come in for a coffee!*' Lucy had cried, but they were off to the park to meet up with some friends. '*Pop in later, then! Come for tea! 5 p.m.!*' And Alison had replied, over her shoulder, that that would be lovely. Lucy had spent all day tidying up and had even managed to make a cake, in between walking Raff up and down.

'Because of Angry Saturday?'

'I already told you, Raff, it was before Angry Saturday.'

'So why didn't they, then?'

Jonah closed his eyes again. They hadn't come at 5 p.m., and they'd waited and waited, and then they'd gone to sit on the step to look out for them. And when they did finally appear, with lots of other mums with buggies, and Lucy had stood up, Raff on her hip, waving and smiling, Alison had waved back – but then she'd opened her own front door and all the mums and buggies had gone inside and the door had shut. And Lucy had sat back down, staring, with her sad, tired eyes, at Alison's dark green door; and Raff had started crying again.

'Is Alison racist?'

Jonah opened his eyes. Opposite, one of the squatters, the one with the bald head, came out and sat on the doorstep, just like them. The squatter was the opposite of the Yonghy-Bonghy-Bò, he realised, the Yonghy-Bonghy-Bò being tiny, with a huge head, and the squatter being big and tall, with a tiny head.

'Is she?' Raff nudged him.

'I don't know, Raff. Probably not.'

The squatter looked across and nodded at them, and got out his tobacco and rolling papers. It was finally starting to cool down.

'She's not coming,' Raff said.

Jonah watched the squatter light his smoke. The sadness was making his stomach hurt. He looked back at Alison's front door. *Alison doesn't like you, Lucy. No one likes you. Even Dora doesn't like you any more.* The squatter sucked. Jonah watched the smoke billowing out of his nostrils.

'Maybe we should phone Daddy,' said Raff.

'You can't just phone people in prison. It's more complicated than that.'

In the silence, they could just hear Alison's voice, shouting at Mabel and Greta. The squatter was leaning over his knees, squishing the smoke out on the pavement. Then he stood up and stretched his arms above his head.

Raff stood up too. 'Slingsmen,' he said.

18

Jonah was Slygon, and Raff was Baby Nail. Jonah kept winning, but Raff started getting fed up, so he let him win a few. He kept an eye on the clock, and when it got to 9 p.m. he said it was bedtime.

'That's not fair, I haven't won hardly any yet!' Raff threw his nunchuck down and went and lay on the sofa, face down.

Jonah stared down at Raff's back. Then he scrunched his eyes tight shut, to pray, or to make a wish, or to try and reach her, somehow. *Please come back.* He said it over and over in his head, but the only answer was the Slingsmen tune. His stomach lurched at the endless emptiness of everything, and he tried to get a sense of a god, watching him: Ganesha, with his kind little elephant eye, or the Christian god, his bearded face all cloudy. Or maybe a group of gods in their togas? Was what was happening a kind of test? If he did the right thing, would he get her back? And was *she* up there, with the gods, was she waiting for him to work it out, to pass the test, so that she could return; holding her breath, wanting to shout clues to him?

The Slingsmen tune tinkled on and on, with the occasional *phwoof* of a released missile. He opened his eyes, dropped his nunchuck, and pulled her phone out of his pocket. The smallness of it, the lightness, the scratched redness, the way it flipped open and closed: so familiar, it was like an actual part of her. He flipped it open and looked at the text from Sunday morning.

Tonight X

He glanced down at Raff, and walked out of the room.

In the kitchen he pressed the green call button and held the phone to his ear. As it rang, he batted away a fly, and looked out at the corduroy cushion in the yard. The phone rang and rang, and then it rang off. No voice telling him to leave a message; just silence.

He snapped the phone closed and laid it on the table. He went out into the yard and checked that the diary hadn't slid under the cushion. He walked back into the kitchen and looked for it on the windowsills and among the piled-up plates and bowls. Then he squeezed his eyes tightly shut again, trying to see her, to bring up her face. *I don't know what to do. Can't you send me a message? Or some kind of sign?*

Back in the sitting room, he wandered over to Roland's aquarium. The fish had died long ago, just after he'd gone to prison, and they'd emptied the water, and now the tank was full of random objects: chess pieces, a stripy scarf, a broken kite. No diary though. He looked down the back of the sofa, and then pushed his hands under Raff's body, feeling for the book. Raff pushed him away, swearing, and he rolled onto his back on the floor. There were flies, about ten of them, hanging out on the ceiling. The shape they made could be a messy J for Jonah. Or maybe an L for Lucy.

He stared at the insects, waiting for them to form a different shape, to start spelling out a word.

They didn't. Raff was crying now. Jonah got up and turned off the TV, and came back and perched next to him.

The sudden knock made them both jump into the air. They raced the few steps to the front door, Jonah arriving first and tugging it open.

'Where have you . . . !' he began, preparing to dive up into her arms, but he fell silent, because it wasn't her. It was Saviour.

19

The sun was setting now, and Saviour's face was glowing in the pink, spooky light. He was carrying a small wooden crate, and his fingers were still purple. Normally they were glad to see him, eager to let him in – but they both stood in the doorway, gazing out at him.

'Hello, Saviour,' said Raff, finally. Saviour nodded and cleared his throat, but instead of saying something, he offered Jonah the crate. His eyes were strangely pale: caramel instead of the usual brown.

'Thank you,' said Jonah, looking down. Plums, not blackcurrants; fat yellow ones, their skins breaking open, showing the squishy flesh. He turned and put the crate down, next to the petrol can.

'Are you going to let me in?' Saviour's voice was very croaky and his breath smelt like Lucy's nail varnish remover.

'Lucy's not here,' he said quickly. 'She's gone to yoga. She's only just left.'

Saviour looked down Southway Street, as if he might catch a glimpse of her going round the corner.

'Are you having roast chicken?' asked Raff.

Saviour shook his head. 'Not tonight.' The words were slurred, as well as croaky. He must have been drinking.

'Is Dora going to die?'

'Shut up, Raff,' said Jonah. Saviour's weird eyes fixed on him. His pupils were two tiny black dots, and it crossed Jonah's mind that an alien had taken over his body.

'You can come in if you want,' said Raff. Jonah nudged him, but Raff elbowed him back and jumped down from the doorstep. 'You can play Slingsmen with us, until she comes back!'

'Good plan.' Saviour took a breath and seemed to become himself again. He stepped forward, putting a hand on Raff's shoulder, but then stopped. His eyes had closed and his mouth hung open, his bulldog cheeks sagging low. It was like he had fallen asleep. He must be *really* drunk, which was strange, because he was meant to have given up alcohol forever. Then his phone started ringing, from the pocket on his shirt, and Jonah and Raff both jumped, but Saviour's eyes stayed shut. Jonah and Raff looked at each other as it kept on ringing.

'You should answer it,' said Raff, shrugging the hand off his shoulder and giving him a little push. Saviour's eyes opened, and he nodded and felt for his phone. Once he had it in his hand, he stared at the flashing screen.

'Answer it, then!' said Raff.

Saviour nodded again and held the phone to his ear.

'Dad?' Emerald's voice was small and tinny, but clear.

'Yes, love.'

Emerald's voice began to wail, and Saviour flinched, suddenly wide awake. He cleared his throat. 'OK, love. Don't worry. I'm on my way.' She kept wailing, but he cut her off.

Slipping the phone back into his pocket, his alien eyes came to rest on Jonah again.

'Saviour.' It was Alison. She had probably been watching them from her front window. Saviour's face stretched into a peculiar grin, but then he covered his mouth with his hand, as if he'd realised about his breath.

'Alison. How are you?' he said, through his fingers.

'Fine.' She said it emphatically, folding her arms tightly. She looked at the boys. 'How's your mum? Isn't it time you were in bed?'

Jonah nodded.

'Good. Saviour, I was wondering if I could have a word?'

'It's actually not the greatest time, Ali—' He pulled out his keys and looked over at his van, which was parked outside the Green Shop.

'It won't take a minute.' Alison took Saviour's arm. 'Goodnight, boys!'

Back in the sitting room, they watched Alison and Saviour reaching the van, Alison talking and talking as Saviour put the key in the driver door. He looked over at them, and Alison looked too, so they ducked down and lay on the floor.

'Can she tell that he's drunk, do you think?' Jonah whispered.

'Is that what's up with him!' Raff got to his knees, and risked another peek. 'She's too busy cussing Mayo,' he said, lying back down. They listened to Saviour's van drive away, and Alison's shoes clipping back to her house. Then there was just the tinkly Slingsmen tune again. Jonah gazed at Roland's aquarium, remembering the bright, flitting fish. *Four parrotfish, three angelfish and eight swordtails.* The fish food had run out, so they'd fed them cornflakes, and they'd all died.

Raff sat up. 'Who's going to read us a story?' His voice was very small.

'I'll read a story,' said Jonah. 'What story would you like, Raffy boy?'

20

It was very hot upstairs. They went into the bathroom and Jonah stood on the lid of the toilet and pushed the window wide open. The sky was all streaky, and the birds were singing – sweet little chirps in the dusk. A couple of flies had drowned in Lucy's bathwater, and neither of them wanted to put their hands in and pull out the plug. They brushed their teeth and took off their clothes, and Jonah bundled them all into the laundry basket, but then he took them out again, remembering that there were no clean ones. Raff got a book out of their bedroom, and they went into Lucy's room with it, because that's where she read to them sometimes, sitting up in her bed with a boy either side. Then they got in and pulled the sheet up over their naked bodies. Her smell was coming from the tiny particles of her left behind on the cotton, and in the air. Was that what a ghost was, millions of molecules, hanging together in an invisible swirl? He opened the book. It was one that they'd got out of the library ages ago, but never got round to reading, a proper chapter book, and the words looked very small and close together. Trying to get rid of the idea that Lucy was dead, he focused on the first sentence.

'"*Until he was four years old James Henry Trotter had a happy life*,"' he read. But sadness and worry gripped his stomach, and he let the book drop into his lap. Through the window, above the Broken House, he saw that the sky was finally darkening, and as he watched a single star came out.

'Why have you stopped?' Raff sat up and peered at Jonah's face. Jonah looked down at the book. Then he shut it and got up and went over to Lucy's chest of drawers.

Some of her underwear was spilling out of an open drawer, and he pushed it all back in and pushed the drawer shut. He climbed up, wedging his toes onto the wooden handles, and reached for the wire tray that lived on top of the chest. It was piled high, with letters and other bits of paper, and when he jumped back down with it, most of the papers slid out and fluttered to the floor.

'What are you looking for?'

'Her diary.' It wasn't there. He sat down and gathered up the fallen papers, which were mainly printed, and to do with money: lots from Jobcentre Plus, a couple from Smart Energy, a few from something called HSBC. As he gathered them up again, he noticed a postcard from the dentist saying they should come for a check-up, a letter about a clinic appointment, and one about their overdue library books, which made him shake his head. A white, handwritten envelope stood out from all the printed pages, and he stopped piling up the papers to look at it. Their address, of course, in handwriting he recognised; and there was a prison stamp on the back.

'What are you doing?' Raff sounded like he might start crying again. Jonah pulled the two sheets of letter paper out of the envelope.

Hello there, Lucy
Firstly, I want you to know that I don't blame you for refusing
to testify. I don't really blame you for anything.

Raff had come to stand next to him. Jonah looked at his
brother's feet, which were big and long-toed, like Lucy's, and
then at the date at the top of the page. The letter was from
2011, the year Roland had got sent to prison. Ages ago. He
stood up. 'I think we should go into our own room,' he said.

It was a tiny bit cooler in their room, and not as smelly.
They could hear Leonie murmuring to someone, in between
big drags on her smoke, and the other person grunting now
and then. Raff got into his bed and Jonah sat on the floor,
the carpet rough on his bare bottom. Raff said, 'Read the
Yonghy-Bonghy-Bò.'

Some of the words in the poem were hard, but he knew
it more or less off by heart. He tried to read it like Lucy
did, in the same soft, chanting voice.

> *On the Coast of Coromandel*
> *Where the early pumpkins blow,*
> *In the middle of the woods*
> *Lived the Yonghy-Bonghy-Bò.*

As he read, he remembered again the feeling from the
evening before, listening to Lucy's voice: his own mother,
unknown, unreachable.

> *Two old chairs, and half a candle, –*
> *One old jug without a handle, –*

These were all his worldly goods:
In the middle of the woods,
These were all the worldly goods,
Of the Yonghy-Bonghy-Bò.

Such a sad story. Such a strange, lonely man, who loves the Lady Jingly Jones, who is also lonely, with only her hens to talk to. But when he asks her to be his wife, and to share his worldly goods with her, she cries and cries, and twirls her fingers, and says no.

'Mr Jones — (his name is Handel, —
Handel Jones, Esquire, & Co.)
Dorking fowls delights to send,
Mr Yonghy-Bonghy-Bò!
Keep, oh! keep your chairs and candle,
And your jug without a handle, —
I can merely be your friend!
— Should my Jones more Dorkings send,
I will give you three, my friend!
Mr Yonghy-Bonghy-Bò!'

Raff sighed and rolled over. Jonah paused, staring at the picture: the Lady Jingly Jones, with her huge, feathered hat, weeping. Why had Handel Jones left her there on that heap of stones? And why did he send her hens? And would it *really* be so wrong of her to get together with Yonghy? Then he wondered if Handel might be in prison, like Roland, and Angry Saturday started flashing in his head. The sexing on the table, and then the peacock, with its terrible cry, and Bad Granny's hand, reaching for him, like a claw. Although

the way Raff was breathing meant he was already asleep,
Jonah started reading again.

> *'Down the slippery slopes of Myrtle,*
> *Where the early pumpkins blow,*
> *To the calm and silent sea*
> *Fled the Yonghy-Bonghy-Bò*
> *There beyond the Bay of Gurtle,*
> *Lay a large and lively Turtle, –*
> *You're the Cove,' he said, 'for me;*
> *On your back beyond the sea,*
> *Turtle, you shall carry me!'*
> *Said the Yonghy-Bonghy-Bò,*
> *Said the Yonghy-Bonghy-Bò.'*

There were another two verses, but it had got too dark to
read them. Jonah sat still, feeling himself to be very small.
Were the gods all talking about him, deciding whether to
help him? Or had they forgotten about him? Had something
more interesting come up? He closed the book and ran his
finger over the title on the front cover. The black letters
had been stamped into the red cardboardy stuff, so you
could feel them.

THE JUMBLIES & OTHER
NONSENSE VERSES

The book had been Lucy's mother's book, and it was on its
last legs. Lucy had Sellotaped its spine, to keep it going a
bit longer. There had been a raggedy paper jacket, but it
had fallen to bits. He opened it at the first page, where

Lucy's mother had written her name, very neatly. *Rose Marjorie Arden.* Arden, because she'd written it when she was a child, long before she'd married Lucy's father and become Rose Marjorie Mwembe. Underneath, in much bigger, messier writing, was Lucy's name: *Lucy Nsansa Mwembe.* She was still Lucy Mwembe, even though she was married to Roland. These days women who got married didn't always change their names to their husband's. Nsansa had a meaning; she'd told him, but he couldn't remember what it was.

He let the book slip from his lap, tipped to one side and curled into a little ball on the floor. They hadn't sung the song, he realised, the song she sang to them every bedtime; a kind of prayer, thanking God for the day, and asking him to look after them through the night. *Glory to thee, my God this night . . .* He sang the words in his head, picturing that old, Christian God, with his big white beard, all fatherly and silent, waiting to be noticed. Then he stopped, thinking instead about Rose. She had died a long time ago, when Lucy was a child. Lucy couldn't remember her that well, but she remembered the bedtime song, which was an English song; and that she'd called her Mayo, a Zambian word for Mummy. She had a tiny photograph of her face in the locket she wore on her throat, showing that she'd been white, with a very straight fringe of dark hair. Their other grandmother. Was she up there with the old, fatherly God, and the angels, with their white, seagull wings? Or had she been reborn? What would she have come back as? He tried to get a sense of her, of her smile, her motherliness, but all he could get was that tiny, faded face in the locket.

It was completely dark now. He curled tighter. They'd never met Lucy's father either, or her three half-brothers, who all still lived in Zambia. Lucy had run away from them, to England, when she was a teenager. Jonah pictured them, his black Zambian grandfather and uncles, sitting at a table, drinking beer and eating monkey nuts, under a purple-flowered tree; a jacaranda. *'Whatever happened to Lucy, by the way?'* said one of the uncles, and the grandfather broke open a papery monkey-nut pod, trying to remember.

Leonie was still murmuring away in the street below, and the Kebab Shop Man, because that's who it was with her, he was joining in more, in his strange high voice, but Jonah couldn't hear what either of them was actually saying. Every now and then there'd be a pause and the sound of a match striking, and a sharp inhalation. He drifted into a light sleep, and dreamed it was Lucy in the street, smoking and talking to the Raggedy Man. He went to the window and looked down at them, and a spotlight was shining a silver-white light down into the street, from the top of a very high crane. Was it a crane, or was it some kind of weapon? Lucy had her back to him, and Jonah called to her, but she didn't hear him. The Raggedy Man did, though, he looked right back at Jonah, and his eyes gleamed like silver coins.

When he woke up, it was much cooler, and the silvery light from his dream was in the room. Surprised to be on the floor, and awed by the light, he rolled onto his back. The light bathed his naked body and shimmered on the ceiling. Then he sprang up and went to the window. The street was empty, but above the gleaming roofs hung an enormous moon. It was actually sunlight, Jonah thought, just a shaft of it, from the other side of the world, bouncing off that ball of stone; but it was hard to believe, because the moon looked so alive, a mysterious sky being, and its light had a tenderness to it, like a caress. As he stared, he noticed the moon's little wise eye, like the eye in his Ganesha painting. And her voice came. She was singing to him, the bedtime song, in her softest, sweetest voice, and he turned and climbed up into his bed and closed his eyes, so that he could fall asleep before it stopped.

TUESDAY

21

Jonah woke up full of happiness. She was there, she'd returned, she'd crept in and kissed him. He'd been too sleepy to open his eyes, but he'd smiled and smiled. Now he stretched, and looked at the clock. It was 06.04. He slid from his bunk to the floor and hurried into her room.

The empty bed was like a punch. His belly churning, he checked the rest of the house, scurrying naked from room to room.

She wasn't there.

He went back to the bathroom, and sat himself on the toilet, wobbling his tooth with his tongue, his hands on his knees. Two flies were circling slowly above him, and there were now three dead ones floating on the oily surface of the bathwater. His stomach clenched and he moaned, and tried to relax. '*Soft tummy, slow breaths . . . Let it come,*' he heard her say.

There was hardly any toilet paper left, so he was careful to only use two squares. He washed his hands and returned to her bedroom, where he sat on the edge of the bed.

Brighter today.

He felt shivery, but instead of curling up under her duvet, he reached for her dressing gown. The red silk felt cold on his skin. The sleeves were too long, so he rolled them up and tied the belt in a knot, before searching the room for her diary.

He couldn't find it. He came to a standstill in front of the sparkly shoes, which Raff had left lying by the dressing table. He closed his eyes, concentrating, before going to the wardrobe and pulling out the rest of Lucy's shoes.

He sorted them into pairs and put them in a line across the floor, and then sat back on the bed and looked at them. The sparkly shoes, the scruffy winter boots, the black, very smart shoes with gold buckles, the yellow Converse boots, and the white, falling-apart trainers. Together with her clogs, which were still downstairs, that made six pairs. Jonah tried to remember if he'd ever seen her wear any other shoes. He couldn't.

He imagined Lucy's bare feet walking along the pavement. She liked being barefoot, and the skin on her soles was thick. As he thought about her feet his hand found its way into the dressing-gown pocket, and his fingers closed on what felt like a pen. He pulled it out. It was smooth and white and a bit longer and thicker than a normal pen. It looked modern, technological. He pulled the lid off. The tip was oblong, rather than pointed. He tried writing on his hand with it, but there wasn't any ink. Saviour would know what it was. Saviour liked gadgets. So did Roland, but being in prison, he wouldn't know about the newer ones. He put the lid back on and looked at the other end, at what looked like two tiny TV screens. The screens were white, with blue lines across them. He took the lid off again and tried pressing the tip to see if the screens would turn on, but they didn't. He looked more closely at the screens, daydreaming that aliens had made contact with Lucy and had given her this white stick. Now she was in their spaceship, high above him, but she could see him, through the screens. He couldn't see her, though, because of a malfunction. He imagined her waving, trying to get his attention, and he waggled the top of his finger at the screens.

'Are you their prisoner?' he mouthed. 'Or did you want to go?'

THERE'S A STAAR-MAAN!

The song flooded his head, with its story of the sad, strange being in the sky, lonely, but afraid of blowing people's minds. The leap from *Star* to -*man* was a whole octave, and then it dropped back to the seventh for *waiting*. Exactly the same as the leap from *Some* to -*where* and the drop back to *o* in 'Somewhere Over the Rainbow'. Was it Saviour or Roland who'd told him that? They both loved David Bowie, and they both loved gadgets, even though they hadn't liked each other much. The chorus ended, and he stared back at the white stick. He would take it to school, to show in 'Show and Tell'. Miss Swann would know what it was.

Down in the hallway he crouched over the crate of plums, thinking they could have some for breakfast. They were already covered in ants. Behind him, through the front door, he heard the milkman leaving a bottle on the doorstep. He waited a moment, and then collected the milk and took it into the kitchen.

He picked up a clean mug from the draining board, poured

himself some and drank. It was lovely and cold. Over
the rim of the mug was the backyard, and the marks on the
wall where his and Raff's shoes had scuffed against it on
their way down the day before. Above the wall loomed
the Broken House. A crow was looking out from the ragged
hole that used to be an upstairs window.

Then he noticed that the back door was ajar.

It was only open a crack. Jonah put down the mug,
remembering the feeling of her kissing him while he slept.
'Lucy?' he whispered. No, not in the dark, with her bare
feet, she couldn't have come all the way through the Broken
House and over the wall.

He pushed it closed. Maybe he and Raff had left it open.
Or maybe . . . The thought of the Raggedy Man made his
heart thump harder. He gazed around the kitchen, looking
for signs. Everything seemed the same as yesterday. Apart
from had there been a clean mug on the draining board?
He didn't know. His eyes came to rest on the picture of
Roland and Rusty on the fridge. When *was* he coming out
on patrol? Not patrol. That's what Raff had said. Lucy's
keys were still lying on the kitchen table. He picked them
up and slipped them into her dressing-gown pocket. Then
he found his Crocs in the pile in the hallway and went out
into Southway Street.

It was as still and as sun-drenched as the day before.
There was no Raggedy Man, but Violet was there, up on
the front wall of the house next door. The fox jumped down,
landing soundlessly on the pavement, only a couple of feet
from him.

He crouched down and whispered to her. 'Violet, have
you seen my mum? Have you seen Lucy, Violet?'

Violet stared at him with eyes like small brown marbles, and for a moment Jonah thought she might answer him, at least with a grunt or a yap. Then he remembered reading that foxes are silent, apart from when they are mating, or under attack. She walked past him, her paws soundless on the pavement, up to the corner of the street, from where she looked back for a second, before disappearing into Wanless Road.

Jonah closed the front door behind him, very quietly so as not to wake Raff. He followed Violet, round the corner of the house and past their sitting-room window. Ahead of him the fox rubbed herself along the fence of the Broken House. When she came to the loose board, she slipped through, just like the day before.

Jonah peered through the narrow gap into the tangled, litter-strewn undergrowth. Violet had stopped again, and was looking back at him. He crouched down and whispered to her again. 'But why would she come in here without any shoes on?'

He stood up and pushed at the loose board to make the gap wider, so that he could follow her.

'Hey, you! What you think you doing!'

The voice was male and very loud, booming in the early-morning stillness. Jonah jumped and looked around at the Green Shop Man, who was standing on the opposite kerb, holding his shelter-raising pole.

'How many times you need to be told! Get away from there!'

Jonah nodded and stepped away from the fence, and the Green Shop Man turned to the shutters. The noisy clatter of them kicked off the day, reverberating up and down the street. Jonah watched him pull out the green awning with the pole, and set up the fruit and vegetable stand. When he went inside the shop, Jonah crossed the road and followed him in.

The shop was dark, and smelt damp and spicy. The radio was on, but it hadn't been tuned properly. In between crackles it spat urgent handfuls of foreign words. The Green Shop Man was kneeling, piling spilt potatoes back into their crate. He glanced at Jonah briefly, a lock of black hair hanging over one eye. His face was perfect, like a film star's. '*Unfeasibly handsome.*' That's what Lucy and Dora called him.

'What you need?' he said, his eyes back on the potatoes. 'You need milk, or what is it?'

'We get our milk delivered.'

'So, then? Why you wearing that lady's thing? Move, now, mind out.' The Green Shop Man stood, holding the crate, and pushed past Jonah towards the door.

'Did anyone buy a mango on Sunday night?' Jonah asked in a rush.

'Mango on Sunday night?' The Green Shop Man had one hand on the door and the crate on his hip. 'Why you want to know that?'

'Someone bought us a mango and I want to know who it was. It was a Chaunsa, so I thought . . .' Jonah followed him back outside.

'So – you a little detective now!' He laughed, but not in a very nice way. 'Why you don't ask your mama who gave the mango?'

Jonah didn't answer. The Green Shop Man slammed the

crate onto the stand, and some potatoes bounced out of it again. 'Ten years old and already spying on his mama!'

'I'm nine years old.'

The Green Shop Man's hands scooped up the escaped potatoes. 'OK, Mr Nine-Years-Old, you go back home now, no more sneaky business. And get some proper clothes on, you look like a fool in that gown.'

The sound of drilling started up in the car repair yard, which alerted Jonah to the time. The alarm clock would be ringing by now, and Raff might have woken up. In a sudden panic he crossed the road, pulling Lucy's keys from the dressing-gown pocket. He couldn't get the key to turn, and called Raff's name as he wiggled it furiously. The lock finally gave way and the door swung open.

22

The sound of the Tibetan bells was floating down the stairs, and yes, Raff was awake, crouched down in the hallway with his back to the wall and his arms around his knees. He lifted his head, and Jonah gasped, because his skin had gone very dark and his cheeks were wet, his eyes, mouth and nostrils stretched wide open.

'Raffy, I'm here, I'm here!'

Jonah knelt down and tried to put his arms around him, but Raff's body was completely stiff. He was making tiny, scary sounds, as if he was suffocating.

Jonah grabbed his face with both his hands. 'Raffy, I'm sorry! Raffy, breathe!'

Raff gulped some breath, and then shoved him really hard. 'Fucking stupid . . . cunt!' He stood up and started kicking him.

Jonah crawled away from the kicks, into the kitchen and under the table. His heart thudding, he watched Raff kick all the chairs over, and then go upstairs, sobbing. Once he had gone, Jonah climbed out from under the table and stood up, wobbling his tooth, getting over the shock of Raff's state. 'He needs to be by himself for a bit. To cool off,' he

whispered to himself. The ants were still streaming into
the jug, and he felt a pang of guilt because he should have
tipped the cordial away and washed up the jug, to stop them
dying. Did ants have ghosts? *'To a soul, the body is just a set
of worn-out clothes.'* That's what Miss Swann had said. He
looked at the flowers, even more skeletal now, closer to dust,
thinking about Shahana's auntie. Could ghosts talk? Could
they send signs?

Are you dead, Mayo?

The only answer was the buzzing of the flies. He looked
down at the Camel woman on the calendar. She was in a
desert, a very yellow desert, looking up at a bright blue sky.
In a box beside her were the words: *'Good for digestion.
Relieves menstrual cramps. Opens the heart chakra.'* A fly had
landed on his cheek. He brushed it away and checked the
bread bin.

There was a small piece of bread, but it was rock-hard,
and he opened the rubbish bin to drop it in. The smell that
came out of the bin was as bad as ever, but what made him
feel sick was the way the rubbish was moving. He quickly
closed the lid, and then opened it again, to check it was
true. Yes, thousands of tiny, curly worms, wiggling amongst
the rotten food. How had they got in there, when the bin
lid had been closed? Then he remembered the lifecycle of
a fly – a diagram, in his insect book. Flies must have laid
their eggs on the food before it got tipped into the bin, and
now those eggs had hatched. He gazed at the tiny, disgusting
babies, trying to remember the name for them. Maggots,
that was it. He closed the lid again. It was Tuesday, so
the binmen would come the next day. They had to put the
rubbish out tonight; they couldn't forget again. But if

she wasn't back, how would he and Raff manage to lift the bag out of the bin, without the rubbish and the worms ending up all over the floor?

He pulled a chair over from the table and stood on it, to look in the food cupboard. There were a few tins and jars and he examined them one by one. He rejected the kidney beans, the mushroom soup and the anchovies, and climbed back off the chair with the jar of mincemeat. He couldn't twist the lid open, and he tried bashing it on the counter a few times, like he'd seen Lucy do. It worked: the loosened lid came off easily. The sweet, spicy smell was delicious. He found a teaspoon and sat himself at the table. 'Yummy,' he whispered, like she would. Lucy loved mince pies. They'd made piles of them one Christmas Eve, in Saviour's kitchen. Jonah levered out a lump of sticky black fruit and sniffed it, remembering the floury table and Saviour's big hands on the rolling pin. The first Christmas after making friends with them. He and Emerald had finished their first term in Reception, and Dora was painting Lucy's portrait. He saw Dora's face, all excited, with a blob of yellow paint on her nose.

He put the spoonful of mincemeat in his mouth. It was an odd taste, on a hot summer's morning. He closed his eyes. Dora and Lucy had just come down from Dora's studio, Dora in her paint-spattered overall and Lucy in her red velvet dress. The first batch of mince pies was in the oven, and air was full of the smell of them. Emerald and Raff were fighting about whose turn it was with the rolling pin, and Dora was going on about trying to get the *exact* tones of Lucy's skin, and what it was like to stare and stare at her friend's face. Saviour had wiped his floury hands and had poured sherry into tiny glasses, as Dora's warm, rough voice went on about cinnamon and lilac and chocolate; then Dora had taken Lucy's chin with her paint-caked fingers. '*Do you see, Saviour! Her mouth. The asymmetry? Which is what makes it so beautiful!*'

Mincemeat had got stuck in between his wobbly tooth and his gum. Cleaning it out with his tongue, he looked down at the table. He'd put the teaspoon down, and the ants were swarming eagerly towards it. He picked it up again, and watched them all turning confused circles. *Bad luck.* He dug the spoon back into the mincemeat. Dora and Emerald had gone off to get dressed up, and Lucy had joined in with the making of the mince pies; and Saviour had asked if they had mince pies in Zambia.

Jonah poured himself some more milk, just a little, because he needed to leave enough for Raff. He took a gulp, and felt the wet white moustache on his upper lip. As she'd cut the pastry circles and pressed them into the dips in the tin, she'd told them about Christmases in Zambia. Turkey, but with nshima, not potatoes. Jonah already knew about nshima, which was made from powdered corn. Saviour had been very interested, and asked how it was made, but Lucy wasn't sure because she had never done any cooking; not after her mother had died.

'*I didn't know your mother died.*' Saviour's voice, surprised and gentle. '*How? What of?*' Lucy had said a word beginning with S . . . like 'seaside', but not. Saviour had looked shocked, and said, '*Lucy, love,*' and laid his hand on her arm, but she'd shrugged it off. They'd made cakes together. English things, mince pies at Christmas. She and her mother had had a servant who did most of the cooking. And everything else, come to think of it.

'*I didn't even have to make my bed!*'

'*So what* did *you do?*' Saviour had asked.

'*I went to school. And we went to church a lot. I looked after my baby brothers. Half-brothers. My father married again, very quickly.*'

'My uncles,' Jonah whispered. The uncles he'd never met. The kitchen, Lucy's bright face, her fingers patting the pastry circles into the dips in the baking tray, all ebbed away. He was back in her silk dressing gown, which was slipping off his shoulders, and the ants were climbing the side of the mincemeat jar. He screwed the lid back on and imagined his uncles coming in through the back door. They were tall and thin, with very dark skin, and smart clothes, carrying briefcases. They stared down at him.

Do you know where she is?

They stayed silent.

Where is she? Is she dead?

They looked at each other, and then turned and walked out again. He looked down at the mincemeat spoon.

'*They dined upon mince, and slices of quince,*' said Lucy's voice. '*Which they ate with a runcible spoon.*'

'The Owl and the Pussycat'. From the red book upstairs. Rose's book. Jonah thought about the woman with the pale face with the straight, dark fringe in Lucy's locket, and imagined her reading the poems to little Lucy. After she'd died, had Lucy's father read them to her? Had Lucy read them to her little brothers? 'Did you, Mayo?' he whispered.

There was no answer, of course, and in the silence he saw her dead, very plainly: drowned, with her face just below the surface of the water, and flowers floating over it, and him, sitting on the bank of the stream, looking down at her.

A tear had rolled down his cheek. He brushed it away and stood up. Time to go and check on his own little brother.

23

Raff was curled up on Lucy's bed, still in his pyjama bottoms.

'We need to get ready for school now,' said Jonah. He tugged at the belt of the red dressing gown, but it wouldn't come undone.

'Where did you go?' Raff's voice was dull. Jonah saw that he was hugging one of the sparkly shoes to his chest.

'Just . . . to the Green Shop.' He went and perched next to him. 'Raffy, I'm so sorry. I shouldn't have gone out without telling you.' He put his hand on Raff's shoulder, but Raff shrugged it away. Jonah examined the knot and started trying to unpick it. 'We need to get dressed. We're going to be late.' He stood up again, knot undone, and let the dressing gown slide off him.

'Did you get some food from the Green Shop?'

'No. But there's some milk. I saved it for you. And some mincemeat.'

'Why are all her shoes out?' Raff rolled onto his side to look at them. 'Were you checking which ones she's wearing?'

Jonah nodded. He squatted, naked, by the shoes.

'She's not wearing any of them, is she?' Raff propped

himself onto his elbow. 'A bad man must have kidnapped her. No way would she go out barefooted.'

'She might have,' Jonah said. 'She likes being barefooted.'

'She wouldn't stay outside this long, without any shoes. She's in the bad man's house.' Raff sat up and swung his legs off the bed, suddenly urgent. 'She's a prisoner, fam! We need to phone the police!'

'But then Bad Granny will come.' Her passionflower face, looming out from her towering white turban; her jewelled, chicken-claw hands, and the peacock, with its hundreds of eyes.

'But how do you *know* that?' Raff's eyes searched his face.

Jonah cleared his throat. 'The police will phone her. Because she's our closest relative.' He was using his calm, grown-up voice, which usually got on Raff's nerves, but Raff kept quiet, listening hard. 'That's what they did on Angry Saturday. They took us all to the police station, and they phoned her up and she came and got us.' She'd been at a wedding, which was why she was so dressed up. Roland and Lucy had been taken away somewhere, and he and Raff were with a policewoman, in a tiny room with orange chairs. When she'd come in, looking so strange, Raff had burst into tears.

'That's it! It's the Angry Saturday man who took her!' Raff got to his feet, dropping the sparkly shoe to the floor.

'It's not the Angry Saturday man, Raff.'

'It flipping is, fam!'

Felix Curtis, reading his paper on the bench in the park playground; and the twins, Scarlett and Indigo, on the swings, their red hair brushing the ground, their long skinny legs all the way up in the sky.

'He must of come through the Broken House!' Raff's eyes were blazing. 'In the middle of the night, with his head smashed in, like a zombie!'

'Raff . . .'

'He must of come in through the back door, and come up the stairs and got her!'

'No one came and got her, Raffy. It won't be anything like that. She would have screamed, wouldn't she, and we would have heard her.'

'Not if he put a bandage round her mouth.' Raff was walking up and down, clutching his pyjama bottoms.

'Raff, listen.' Jonah stood up and grabbed him as he went past. 'Someone came, but they didn't put a bandage on her mouth. They brought her a mango.'

'A mango?' Raff frowned.

'The one we ate last night. And a bottle of wine.'

'And the flowers!' shouted Raff. 'I *told* you it was the Angry Saturday man who sent her the flowers. And then he came round, with a mango, and a wine, and he tried to sex her, but she wouldn't let him, and he tied her up, and dragged her out, and put her in his van . . .'

'Raffy, stop it!' Jonah sat on the bed with his hands over his ears, but Raff pulled them away.

'We've got to go round there, fam! You know where his house is! We've got to rescue her!' He tugged at Jonah's wrists, trying to pull him to his feet, but Jonah shook him off and pushed him away, hard, so he tumbled to the floor.

'They probably don't even live round here any more.' Jonah rubbed his wrists, thinking about the Curtises. 'Otherwise we'd see them in the park.'

'See who?'

'Scarlett and Indigo.' Sometimes it was their mum who had brought them. She had a ponytail, but he couldn't remember her name. She had come round to their house once and her eyes had been all red and puffy, and, in a quiet, icy voice, she had sworn at Lucy.

Raff had sprawled himself out on his back, thinking. Jonah watched his little belly rising and falling with his breath.

'So was Felix Curse Scarlett and Indigo's dad?'

'Curtis. Yes, he was.' Jonah hugged his knees.

'Were Scarlett and Indigo there then? On Angry Saturday?' Raff had rolled over and slipped his hands into the sparkly shoes. He walked them about, his knees following.

'No. It was their birthday, and their mum had taken them to Euro Disney.'

'Euro Disney! Sick!' Raff sat back on his heels, the shoes slipping onto his wrists like strange, enormous bracelets. Jonah hugged his knees harder. He hated remembering Angry Saturday.

'What about us? Were *we* there?'

Jonah nodded.

'Did we see them sexing?'

Jonah shook his head. 'Only Roland went into the house. He left us in the car.'

'Why did he leave us in the car? Did he know they were sexing?' Raff shook the shoes off his wrists.

'Probably. He knew she liked him.'

'Why did she like him?'

'I don't know.' Felix Curtis on the bench, with his coffee in a cardboard cup. 'He used to talk to her. While we played with Scarlett and Indigo.'

'What did he look like?'

'Just normal. But kind of – rich. With sunglasses. And a gold watch.' That big chunky watch, and then the hand, holding the cup, with very clean fingernails. Jonah put his forehead on his knees.

'Is *that* why she liked him? Because he was rich?'

'I don't think so.' Jonah pictured Felix Curtis's face very clearly, his sunglasses off, his greenish eyes, looking Lucy up and down. 'He was quite handsome. And funny.' She would sit next to him on the bench, and laugh and laugh. He pressed his forehead harder against his knees. Remembering her laughing like that was horrible.

'And how did Daddy even know she was in his house?'

'Because she'd left her bike outside.'

Her gold-painted bicycle, locked up on the railings, and little Raffy, in his child seat, leaning forward: *'Look, Daddy! Mayo bike!'* Roland had parked and gone to the front door, and after a while he'd looked through the letter box. And it had started raining, big fat drops on the windscreen, as Roland had walked around the side of the house.

'Were they in Felix Curse's bed?'

'*Curtis.* No. They were in the kitchen.' He and Raff had stayed in the car, waiting, until the ambulance came, and the police car; but he knew exactly what had happened, as if he'd actually seen it.

'What, *sexing* in the kitchen?'

'Yes.' It was a couple of days later that he'd heard the story, hidden behind the sofa in the Martins' conservatory. Lucy had told it in a shaky whisper, stopping and starting, and Dora had gasped and murmured and glugged wine into their glasses. Felix and Lucy had been drinking beer and eating cold ratatouille straight from the saucepan; and Felix

Curtis had taken off her clothes. When Roland had looked in from the rain, through the open French windows, Lucy had been lying on her back on the kitchen table, with her legs resting on Felix Curtis. He winced, remembering how he'd winced in his nest behind the sofa.

'And Daddy hit him!' Raff stood up and pulled his imaginary catapult. 'He slung him with his slingshot! Phwoof! Right in his head!'

'He hit him, Raff. He didn't have a catapult.'

'He punched him!' Raff punched the air, one fist then the other. 'Did Furtix hit him back?'

'No. Daddy hit him with a saucepan, and he just fell down, onto the floor.'

'Sick!' Raff took hold of an imaginary saucepan handle with both hands and whacked it against an imaginary head. 'You flipping Furtix! You fucking zombie!' He did some more whacks and swipes, his pyjamas slipping to his knees, and then to his ankles; and then he stopped. 'I wish the police hadn't caught him, though.' He pulled up his pyjamas and sat back down on the bed.

'They didn't have to catch him, Raffy. He didn't run away. Daddy's actually a good man. He didn't mean to hit Felix Curtis.'

'Why did he, then?'

'*Why* did *he, Lu?*' Dora had asked. '*I mean – I've never clicked with him, as you know. But I just can't imagine him* hitting *someone! Let alone with a saucepan.*' Jonah tightened his hold on his shins, remembering hearing Lucy's trembling answer, and not quite understanding, but feeling sick. Felix had seen Roland first. Lucy had only realised someone was there because of the strange, creepy smile on Felix's face.

She'd turned her head, to look where he was looking, and had seen him standing at the door, soaking wet. She'd tried to get up, but Felix had her legs. '*He just – kept going. It was like he* liked *it, that Roland was there.*' She had screamed at him to let her go, and he had, but the saucepan was already in Roland's hand. '*It all happened literally in a second. Like a car crash.*'

'I said, why *did* he, then?' Raff was shoving him.

'Because Felix . . .' Jonah rocked himself, trying to think what Dora had said. She had been really shocked, and had called Felix a 'rapist', but he wasn't completely sure what that meant. 'Because Felix kept going.' He mumbled the words into his knees.

'Going where?'

'Just . . . Roland got really angry, that's all. But then, straightaway, he was sorry. And he phoned the police and the ambulance.'

'Why did they put him in prison, if he was sorry?'

'Because he hurt Felix Curtis very badly. He damaged his brain.'

Raff was quiet again. Jonah could tell by the sound of his breathing how hard he was thinking.

'Jonah.'

'What.'

'If you had a time machine, would you go back and stop him from doing it?'

Jonah imagined himself in a tiny spacecraft, a globe, just big enough for his body, flying back over his memories. Slowly, over the last couple of days, hovering for a moment over the crowded Lido, spotting the splash of red that was Lucy, sitting on the side. Then quicker, the days rolling past, and the nights, he and Raff asleep in their bunk beds; birthdays and Christmas; the Olympics, that massive stadium. He hovered again, looking for himself: there, in between Raff and Emerald, Dora on the end. Onwards, to the holiday in France, another swimming pool; Lucy's net dragging through the water for the insects.

'Well, would you?' Raff nudged him.

Would he what? Oh yes, Angry Saturday. He closed his eyes and imagined himself getting out of the car, the rain on his skin, following Roland round the side, into the garden and through the French windows. '*Daddy, don't!*' Roland stopping, the heavy saucepan in mid-air, the eyes of all three grown-ups fixed on him.

'The thing is, Raff . . .' He opened his eyes. 'I don't know if everything would *explode*, but . . .' He paused, concentrating. Raff yawned. 'If I went back and stopped him, our whole lives would change, and the life we're in *now* wouldn't actually exist any more. And if *this* life didn't exist, then . . .'

'Forget it, fam. I don't actually care.' Raff stood up. 'I'm starving. We need to get some money and buy some food.' He stretched and looked around, and then picked the sparkly shoes up off the floor. 'We should sell these. I bet they're worth a lot of money.'

'But they're her favourite shoes!'

Raff shrugged. 'Serve her right, innit.' But he dropped the shoes back on the floor.

'I know!' said Jonah. 'My piggy bank!'

24

The piggy bank was on the windowsill in the conservatory, hiding in a jungle of candles, incense holders and postcards. It was squat and green, with yellow stripes, more like a very fat caterpillar than a pig, especially as it had lost its legs. Jonah picked it up. It jingled, and he smiled: there was definitely enough money in there for some bread, and maybe some butter.

'How come you've got a piggy bank, and not me?' asked Raff.

'Bad Granny made it for me. At her pottery class.'

'Wasn't that quite nice of her?'

Jonah nodded. 'She even gave me some money to put in it.'

'Why didn't she give me one?'

'It was for my birthday. And anyway you were too little.' He laid the pig on the table, on its back, and tried to prise out the rubber seal from its belly.

'How much money is in there, do you think?'

'Maybe quite a lot. I used to put my horse money in it.'

'Horse money?'

'From when we used to bet on the horses. With Roland. On Saturday mornings. Don't you remember?'

He wouldn't, he had been really little, but Roland always let them choose a horse each. He used to read out the horses' names from his newspaper, and how much they weighed, and how they'd got on in previous races, while he and Raff looked at the jockeys' silks, which were brightly patterned, like the fish in the aquarium. Then they all went to the betting shop and Roland lifted them onto the high stools. Children weren't really allowed, but the betting shop lady let them in anyway.

Jonah knocked the ants off the mincemeat spoon and used it as a lever on the rubber seal. Once it was off, he stuck his fingers inside the hole. There were a few coins, and a couple of them were quite big and thick. He turned the pig over and shook the money onto the table.

'That's loads!' Raff picked up a coin. 'Look! Two pounds!'

'Two euros.' Jonah picked up another coin. 'One euro.'

'So we can't buy anything with them?'

'No.' Jonah sat down and went through all of them, sorting them into piles. Four euros, eighty-five cents. Saviour had given them to him, he remembered, ages ago, on their way back from the holiday in France. *'Nice to get away from it all!'* He folded his arms on the table, and buried his head in them.

'Maybe the Green Shop Man would let us use them.' Raff sat down too, and shifted the piles of coins around. 'Maybe he'd let us buy some Coco Pops.'

'He won't,' said Jonah. Lucy must have taken all his English money. He sat up and suddenly swept the pig and the coins off the table. The pig broke into pieces, and the pieces and the coins scattered across the floor.

'Issues, Peck! Anger management!' One of the coins was still spinning. Raff reached with his toe to knock it flat. Jonah stared down at the Camel woman on the calendar. *You took my money, Lucy. You stole it. You just left me the stupid euros.*

'The Green Shop Man won't mind.' Raff slid off his chair and started collecting up the coins. 'Just this once.'

'Raff, he won't take euros, OK.' Slumped on the table, Jonah stared at the feathery mask on Dora's book. Below the mask was the book's title, *Heart of Darkness*. He traced the letters with his finger. Maybe it was that title that made the mask seem so scary. He flipped the book open to where the story began. The print was very small. The first paragraph seemed to be about a ship – about preparing for a journey. Her turned back to look at Lucy's scribbles on the inside cover, under Dora's spiky signature. First, she'd copied the signature a few times. *Dora Martin.* Then she'd written just *'Dora'*. And then a kind of poem.

Dora. Adora. Adorable Dora.
Who thinks I should read Proper Literature.
Who gave me a book about AFRICA
And put her name in it, to make sure I give it BACK to
  her.

Some drawings then – flowers and faces and fishes. Fishes, or maybe eyes.

But her real name is CORDELIA. How uncordial, Cordelia!
Giving me things, and then wanting them back.

'So how *are* we going to get breakfast, fam?' Raff was back on his chair, elbows on the table.

Jonah closed the book and pushed him the mincemeat jar,

and the bottle of milk. Her doodles had brought back that picture of her, under the water – dead – and he got up and walked into the sitting room. On the mantelpiece there was the postcard with the picture of a drowned girl, holding a bunch of flowers, lying in the flower-covered water. The card had been there for ages, as long as he could remember. He'd asked Lucy about the drowned girl, and Lucy had said she was from a Shakespeare play, but she couldn't remember which one. The girl had drowned herself because she was so sad that she'd gone mad. He picked up the card and looked at the other side. There was no address on it, or stamp, just a row of three hearts, drawn in black biro. One of the hearts had an arrow in it, and one of them had a zigzag splitting it into two, and one of them was whole, but the mounds at the top of it had nipples on them, so they looked like bosoms. Underneath the hearts there was an X. He tried to imagine Roland drawing the nipples on the heart, but couldn't. In small, printed words on the bottom right, it said:

OPHELIA 1851–52
SIR JOHN EVERETT MILLAIS

He put the card back on the mantelpiece. 'Raff!' he called. 'We need to go to school!'

25

'So you're coming over to ours today. You and Raff. That right?' Saviour had a frown on his face. He was wearing the same torn T-shirt and, from the smell of his breath, he hadn't brushed his teeth yet. Emerald stood next to him, pale and prim and proper, with plaits curled into circles, like Princess Leia.

'I think so.' Feeling himself blush, Jonah watched Raff run across the Infants' playground and go into his classroom. When he looked up, Saviour was staring at him. His eyes were back to normal, but underneath them were purple rings of tiredness. They gazed at each other for a few seconds, until the bell rang for registration. Then Saviour sighed and straightened Jonah's collar for him.

'Right then,' he said. He chucked Jonah under the chin, and kissed Emerald on the forehead. 'I'll see you both later.'

After he'd walked away, Emerald said, 'We didn't have roast chicken last night. My dad couldn't manage it. We're having it tonight instead.' She had grown even taller, he noticed.

'Oh.'

'But it's quite a small chicken, so there might not be enough for you and Raff.'

'Oh.' Jonah started walking towards the classroom.

Emerald followed him. 'It's actually not a *great* idea, you and Raff coming to our house.'

'Who said that?'

'Mum. She said Dad's got enough on his plate.'

'But she invited us.'

'I know. But this morning she said it might be a bit much. And also . . .'

'What.'

'She said your mum is really selfish sometimes.'

'OK, we won't come then.' Jonah pushed through the swing door, letting it swing back rather than holding it open for Emerald.

'Jonah!' She dodged through the door and followed him down the corridor. 'Jonah, you *can* come, as long as you play chess with me,' she said.

'Don't worry about it.'

'Daddy can cook sausages for you and Raff. It's just the roast chicken was meant to be a treat for me.'

'You always get treats, Emerald.'

'No, I don't. And my mum is really ill.'

Jonah turned to face her, so suddenly that Emerald nearly stumbled into him. Feeling his lips stretch into a snarl, he shoved his face close to hers. Emerald stared back, shaken.

'My mum is really ill,' he said, mimicking her know-it-all voice. 'And I am Emerald, the most important person in the whole wide world!'

He realised he was shaking. It was like his body had been

taken over by an angry troll. He wasn't shouting, but his voice sounded really vicious.

'What's the matter, Jonah?' she said uncertainly. 'Why are you crying? Don't cry!'

'I'm not crying, you stupid . . . cunt!'

Emerald's eyes opened wide, and Jonah turned away again, wiping his face, his heart racing. He couldn't believe he'd said 'cunt' and it made his legs feel weak. As he walked into the classroom he felt as if he might faint from the shock of the word, and gripped onto the back of Daniella's chair.

'Late again, you two?'

Emerald was already in her seat, but Jonah kept his grip on Daniella's chair, trying to steady himself and forget the terrible word he'd said. Raff had said it earlier, which was why it was there in his brain, ready to burst out of his mouth. He concentrated on Miss Swann. She was wearing the same kind of dress, but instead of stripy it was grey and silky. Her hair was better, but there were red blotches on her chest and throat.

'Jonah, are you alright?' she asked.

'Yes.' He let go of the chair and slipped into his seat next to Harold.

26

At playtime Jonah showed Harold the little white stick he'd found. Harold held it up, peering at the screens, then shook it hard, like a nurse shaking a thermometer. 'Where did you find it?' He looked at the screens again.

'In my mum's dressing gown.'

Harold pulled off the lid. 'Why didn't you ask your mum what it is?' He sniffed the tip. 'Did you ask her if I can come to tea?'

Jonah suddenly remembered the one time he had visited Harold's house, back when they were in Reception. A flat, not a house, very clean and tidy, but too full of furniture and ornaments. He'd taken a sip of his drink before Harold's mother had said grace, and she had told him off. Harold had been mortified. After the meal they had tried to play in Harold's tiny bedroom, but they couldn't get into the right mood. It had been a massive relief when Lucy had arrived to take him home.

'So can I?' asked Harold, still inspecting the stick.

'I didn't ask her.'

'Why not?'

'I couldn't. She's not there.'

Harold looked at him through his thick glasses. 'Where is she? When's she coming back?'

'I don't know.'

'Who's looking after you?'

'No one.'

Harold twiddled the white stick with his fingers and thumb, like he was a baton twirler in a parade. 'When did she go?'

'Yesterday morning. Or in the night. I woke up and she wasn't there.'

Harold stopped twirling. 'Do you think she's been kidnapped?'

'That's what Raff thinks. But I don't. Why would anyone kidnap her?'

'To sex her, maybe. Your mum is really buff.'

Jonah snatched the white stick back and turned away.

'Hey, fam! Wait!' Harold grabbed his wrist. 'We need to think this through!'

Holding himself stiff, Jonah allowed himself to be pulled back to face his friend.

'Maybe a robber came, and she saw him, so he *had* to kidnap her.' Harold's eyes, made tiny by the glass, were gleaming. 'So she wouldn't identify him. To the police. See what I mean?'

'Someone came, but it wasn't a robber,' Jonah said. 'They brought a mango. And a bottle of wine.'

Harold nodded, taking the white stick out of Jonah's hand. 'They'll have fingerprints,' he said. 'You'd better save them for the police!'

'We can't tell the police. And anyway we ate the mango.'

'That's OK. The wine bottle will have the best fingerprints. And DNA.'

'What's DNA?'

'It's like . . .' Harold scrunched up his face. 'Tiny bits of stuff, from the kidnapper's body. If the police get his DNA, they'll definitely be able to catch him.'

'I already said we can't tell the police, Harold!'

Harold tapped the white stick against his lips, frowning. 'Why can't you tell the police?'

'Because then Bad Granny will come and get us.'

Harold whistled, and shook his head. He knew about Bad Granny. He'd been there the second time she'd tried to steal them, the time she came to the school. Jonah looked across the playground. A football game had started; mainly Year 6 boys, but Tyreese was playing, and so was Isiah.

'But fam.'

'What?'

'Your nan. Is she, like, *evil*?'

Jonah nodded, but he suddenly saw Bad Granny's face, not her passionflower, film-star wedding face, but her real face, with its long nose and its sad, clever eyes.

'What did she do to you? When she stole you? Did she lock you up, or like . . .?' There was a shout, and some cheers. They both turned to look. Tyreese had just scored a goal.

'Raff broke her vase,' Jonah muttered. 'He was really little, and it was an accident, but she went totally mad.'

'Did she hit him?'

'She kind of – shoved him.' Out of the way of the glass, but with hard, angry hands. 'We tried to run away, but there was this bird in the garden, and it attacked us.' Remembering the terrible sound it had made, and the giant face, with all those shimmering eyes, made his belly hurt.

'A bird?'

'A peacock.'

'Sick! What was it doing in her garden?'

Jonah shrugged. 'It's hers. A film star gave it to her, as a present.'

'A film star! How come?'

'She works on films. She does the costumes. She knows lots of them.'

'Which one gave her the peacock?'

'I can't remember.'

'Was it George Clooney? I bet it was him. Or was it . . .'

'Harold, I can't remember who the film star was, OK!'

'OK.' Harold nodded, and they both watched the football game for a while.

'She did lock us up, actually,' Jonah said.

'What, because you tried to run away?'

'No. It wasn't until the next day. She knew my mum was coming to get us, so she locked us in the bedroom.' Roland's bedroom, with the picture of the horse on the wall. She'd pulled out a box of old toy cars and given them cups of milk and a plate of biscuits, and they hadn't known they were locked in until they'd heard Lucy's and Dora's voices downstairs.

'How did you get out?'

'She let us out, in the end.' It had been Dora who had persuaded her, who'd managed to calm things down.

'So it wasn't *that* bad.'

The bell was ringing and the footballers had stopped playing. Jonah shrugged and started walking towards the building. Telling it to Harold, it hadn't sounded that bad, but at the time, hearing Lucy shouting and crying, and realising they'd been locked in, it had been terrible.

'What was she like before all that stuff happened?' Harold fell into step beside him. 'Before your dad hit that man?'

'She was always horrible to my mum.'

'And your mum's really nice.' Harold nodded, waiting for details. Jonah tried to think. They had gone to Bad Granny's house quite a lot, before Angry Saturday. He remembered her reading him Roland's old picture books, and the time she'd taken him into the garden to show him Rusty's gravestone. There had been some massive arguments, and once Lucy had stormed out, and he had followed her, out of the front door, up Bad Granny's drive to the gate, where Roland had scooped him up. Lucy was already down the hill and running up the other side. *Run, run, as fast as you can, but you can't catch me, I'm the Gingerbread Man!* The Gingerbread Man was a story in one of the picture books that Bad Granny had read him.

'She hates my mum. If she knew she'd left us on our own, she'd love it, because it would be her chance to stop her from ever being allowed to look after us again.'

'And you'd live with her instead. And the peacock,' said Harold.

Jonah winced. That tiny beak, making that terrible noise. 'The peacock wasn't – it was mental, Harold. It wanted to kill us.'

'A killer peacock.' Harold looked thoughtful. They'd stopped walking, and he was trying to balance the white stick on the end of his finger. 'But if your mum doesn't come back, then at least . . .Well.' The stick fell. He dipped down to pick it up. 'Wouldn't it be better at your nan's than just you and Raff on your own? If she put the peacock in a cage, I mean?'

'But she wouldn't keep Raff.' His eyes blurring, Jonah snatched the white stick out of Harold's hand. 'She'd keep me, and she'd make Raff go to an orphanage.'

'Joking!' Harold looked properly shocked. 'Because of the vase? She wouldn't do that, fam.' He shook his head.

'That's what she was going to do. I heard her, on the phone, saying Raff was going into care.' The bell had stopped ringing and the playground was empty. Miss Swann was waiting for them by the swing doors, hands on her hips.

'Because of the *vase*, fam?'

Jonah shook his head. 'Because of his hair.'

'His *hair*?'

Miss Swann put her hands to her mouth to call to them. 'Jonah! Harold! Come *on*!'

27

Show and Tell was after lunch. Jonah felt nervous as he stood up, and hesitated before taking the white stick out of his pocket. Miss Swann was smiling encouragingly.

'What is it, Jonah? What have you got?'

'It's just something I found,' he said, holding it up.

'Awesome.' Miss Swann squinted at it, and came forward to get a better look. Her hair had gone frizzy again, and her grey dress was all creased and a bit damp.

'Where did you find it?' She took it from him. She looked taken aback, now, unsure of herself, and Jonah wanted to snatch the stick back off her.

'Just lying around,' he said. 'What is it?'

Miss Swann pulled the lid off the stick and peered at the tip. 'What do *you* think it might be?' she asked.

'I don't know. It looks like . . . something an alien might use.'

There were some giggles.

'There's no such thing as aliens, though, is there, Miss Swann?' said Daniella.

'Who wants to answer Daniella?' asked Miss Swann, and a forest of arms appeared.

'Can't you just tell us what it is?' blurted Jonah.

Miss Swann looked at him, surprised, and he knew he'd sounded rude. He dropped his eyes from her face to the red patches on her throat. 'I just want to know, that's all,' he murmured.

Miss Swann looked at the stick. He could tell she was thinking hard. 'I think it's a – a pregnancy test,' she said slowly.

'What's a pregnancy test?' asked Pearl.

'If a woman thinks she might be pregnant, then she can use this test to find out.'

'So it can tell if someone's going to have a baby?' asked Jonah.

'Yes,' said Miss Swann.

'How?'

'If a woman is pregnant, her hormones change. Does anyone know what hormones are?'

Some hands went up, and Miss Swann chose Solomon. Solomon hummed and hawed as he tried to explain, and Jonah felt another wave of impatience.

'Is she pregnant, then?' he asked. Solomon's mouth snapped shut and everyone's eyes swivelled to rest on Jonah.

'Is who pregnant?' asked Miss Swann.

'The person whose stick it is.'

Miss Swann cleared her throat. 'I think the test has been used,' she said. 'But I'm not sure if these blue lines indicate a positive or a negative result. We would need the instructions to be able to tell.'

'But if she was, and she didn't want to be, then the doctor sucks the baby out with a hoover thing,' said Daisy, and everyone started screaming.

'Enough!' shouted Miss Swann.

'It's true, though, Miss,' said Daisy. 'My friend's sister had it done.'

There were more shrieks, and Miss Swann shouted again. Once it was quieter, Jonah held out his hand. 'Can I have it back now?'

'Can't we all look?' said Daniella, leaning over her desk and reaching for it. It was usual, in Show and Tell, for an object to be passed around the class, so that everyone got the chance to see it up close.

'You know, I'm not sure . . .' said Miss Swann. Again she seemed to be thinking hard, unable to quite make up her mind. Then she said, 'If this is a used pregnancy test, and I believe it is, then this tip would have been dipped in urine . . .'

There was a roar of delighted disgust, and Daniella made a face and tucked her hands under her thighs. Miss Swann held her hands up for them to be quiet. 'Let's move on,' she said, suddenly brisk. 'Jonah, thank you for bringing in your very interesting object. Awesome! Who's next?'

'But can I have my stick, please?'

'Jonah wants his wee-wee stick!' shouted Isiah, and there was more laughter.

'Joney, I think the best place for it is the bin, probably,' said Miss Swann.

'It's actually mine so can you give it back, please.' Jonah pulled it out of Miss Swann's hand, and her eyebrows shot all the way up to her hair. The room was silent again. Jonah put the stick in his pocket and sat back down at his desk.

'Right,' said Miss Swann. 'Shahana, what have you brought in?'

28

Saviour was waiting in the playground. He'd already collected Raff, and they were holding hands, and Raff was saying something, and Saviour was looking down at him, listening. Raff's uniform was filthy, and his hair was crazy, sprouting out everywhere; but Saviour had shaved and combed his hair, and was wearing clean clothes, his long green Army shorts, and a white T-shirt, which made his skin look even darker. When he saw Jonah and Emerald coming, he smiled and let go of Raff's hand to hug them both. He smelt of chewing gum and his clean clothes.

'OK, you guys, let's go,' he said, releasing them. His belly stuck out into his T-shirt, but he was hench, so it didn't really matter; like the ugliness of his face didn't matter because of his interested eyes and his crooked smile. There was a photograph of him when he was a boy, hanging in the Martins' hallway, with the same smile and the same dark eyebrows, under a mass of curly hair.

Raff pranced down the road ahead of them, chanting his Camber Sands rap. Emerald walked with Saviour, holding his hand, tall and straight, her Princess Leia spirals still perfect. Jonah tried to get on the other side of Saviour and hold his other hand, but there wasn't really enough room on the pavement, so he walked behind, his hand around the white stick in his pocket. Emerald's pale yellow head came nearly to Saviour's shoulder. You might think, from the back, that she was his girlfriend, not his daughter. Except that she was so lanky. And no grown-up would have that hairstyle. Saviour's back was very broad. There was a patch of wetness on the white cotton of his T-shirt, between his shoulder blades. It was nice, being with a grown-up, even if it wasn't Lucy. He suddenly remembered coming home from school and seeing, on the kitchen table, that very first wooden crate. Mushrooms, silvery grey, with tiny little hats and long wispy stalks. He had held a clump up to his nose and they had smelt of dark forests. Lucy hadn't been sure how to cook them, and he hadn't been sure he wanted to eat any. She had tried boiling some of them up, just a few of them, with some spaghetti, and the water had gone black and the dark forest smell had gone all through the house. When Roland had got home from work, he'd asked what the terrible smell was.

'*Emerald's daddy gave them to us. He's a forager.*'

'*What's a forager?*'

'*Someone who goes into the countryside and gets food.*'

Jonah had fallen behind, so he quickened his step. Roland had been pleased that she'd made friends. She'd been lonely and thought no one liked her, and he'd told her not to think like that, and to try harder. And then the Martins had just – happened. Roland had been pleased to begin with, but then . . .

'Smelly Shelly! Uh huh, Smelly Shelly!' shouted Raff at

the top of his voice, jumping and hopping, half his hair loose from the cornrows. What would Roland do, if he knew Lucy had gone? What if he told Bad Granny? He wouldn't want them to be by themselves. Maybe they would be able to go and stay in the prison with him, in his cell. They would have to sleep on the floor. No, Roland would let them sleep in his bed, top and tail. *He* would sleep on the floor, the hard stone floor, with just a thin grey blanket.

'Gimme Smelly Shelly, please don't take it away!' They were in the park now, and Raff had climbed up the starflower tree, all the way to the top, and was leaning out between clumps of dark green leaves. In the spring, the tree blossomed into thousands of pink, curling stars. They only lasted about a fortnight, and Lucy loved them so much that they came after school every day so that she could look at them. It wasn't a tall tree, but Saviour called to Raff to be careful, and Raff disappeared, and then appeared again, lower down, swinging from a branch, his grin reaching to his ears. He could be that happy because he could forget about everything that wasn't happening right that second.

Jonah looked away. 'Are you going to have a baby, Mayo?' he whispered. 'Is that why Roland sent you the flowers?'

On the way through the park they stopped at the ice-cream van, and Saviour let them choose whatever they wanted. Raff chose an ice lolly in the shape of a space rocket. Emerald chose a strawberry Cornetto, and Jonah had a vanilla cone with a chocolate flake in it.

'Why aren't you having one?' asked Jonah.

'He's getting fat again,' Emerald explained. 'Mum says he needs to be the healthy one.'

'Is it because you've got too much on your plate?' Jonah asked.

Saviour smiled and ruffled Jonah's hair. 'Good one, mate,' he said, and bent down to take a lick of his ice cream. Jonah wished he hadn't. He might be looking better on the outside, but his insides can't have been very healthy, because his tongue was grey and cracked.

It was baking hot. They walked past the paddling pool, which was crammed with small children, and then along the path that led to the pond. Jonah walked close to the iron railings, bumping his fingers over them. On the other side of the railings, and down a grassy slope, was the hospital car park. The roofs of the cars shone like gold, and towering above them was the hospital where Raff had been born. Jonah thought of all the sick people lying in bed. Could they hear the children screaming in the paddling pool? Did they wish and wish they could be better, and be out in the park, eating an ice cream?

Saviour, Emerald and Raff had stopped in the shade of the trees around the pond, soaking up the coolness and watching the ducks. Emerald and Raff were licking their ices. Jonah realised he didn't really want his, now that Saviour had licked it. It was melting fast. He tipped it into a wasp-infested bin, and looked at the dead people's names. They were all around the pond, carved onto wooden benches. They'd used to come here a lot, him, Raff and Lucy, and talk about the dead people, and imagine their ghosts, sitting chatting on the benches.

'Getting on each other's nerves, probably!' Lucy had said. *'If I die, I don't want a bench down here, I want one up on the hill, so I can look at the view!'*

'*But won't you be in Heaven?*' Jonah had asked. '*Aren't all dead people in Heaven?*'

'*I think lots of them stay knocking around, for at least a few years. I definitely would, to keep my eye on you two.*'

The years showing how long they had lived were carved under the names, with some words, a bit from a poem or a plain sentence. Raff's favourite bench just said '*Snowy*'. Snowy must have been a dog, a little white terrier, like the dog in the Tintin books. Jonah's favourite was set back against the trunk of a gnarly old tree. The lowest branches of the tree came either side of the bench, as if they were about to hug it. The carved words said:

KUMARI
ETERNAL, RADIANT BEAUTY

There were no dates. Lucy said that Kumari was the name given to little girls who'd been possessed by a goddess, and that this was the saddest bench, because it was in memory of a child. '*She must be sick of hanging out with all these old people, around this dreary pond.*' Poor Kumari.

Jonah went and stood in front of Lucy's favourite bench. 'Olive Mary Sage,' he read.

'*She must have worn green, mustn't she,*' he heard Lucy's voice say. '*And her eyes were green. She was small and thin, and very clever.*'

Olive Mary Sage had lived from 1900 to 1995, nearly the whole of the twentieth century. Underneath the dates was carved:

SHE IS NOT FAR AWAY

Jonah imagined her sitting there, on her own bench, in the fancy, olden-days clothes she would have worn when she was young. A stripy green dress, he imagined, with a long skirt and long puffy sleeves, and green gloves and a little green hat, decorated with bunches of herbs and sprigs of olives. She looked up at him and nodded without smiling, in a polite, olden-days way.

'*She might have been a Suffragette,*' Lucy had said. '*She might have gone to prison, and gone on hunger strike, and nearly died. She was very brave. And sad, too, because she lost her sweetheart in the War. She never got over it. That's why she never married.*'

It wasn't definite that she wasn't married, but there was no mention of a husband or children on the bench. Her next-door neighbour, Hilda Jenkins, was a '*Beloved wife, mother and grandmother,*' and '*Sorely missed.*' Hilda hadn't lived as long as Olive, just from 1907 to 1984. She was too young to lose a sweetheart in the First World War, Lucy said, and then her husband would have been too old to fight in the Second. Jonah imagined Hilda as very grandmotherly – fat, with an apron on, and white hair in a bun. They had all decided that Hilda and Olive wouldn't like each other that much, and that their ghosts were probably really fed up of being neighbours.

'*But why doesn't Olive go up to Heaven and see her sweetheart?*' Jonah had asked.

'*Well, maybe they're both up in Heaven,*' Lucy had said. '*Olive will be with her sweetheart, kissing all the time, and swimming naked in green, bottomless lakes. Whereas Hilda, she'll be in her kitchen, making cakes with her grandchildren.*'

'*But her grandchildren aren't dead!*'

'*Oh, yes. Well, maybe she's found some dead children to make cakes with.*'

'*Kumari!*' Jonah had cried.

'Come on!' called Saviour.

29

They walked up the grassy hill, past the sunbathers and picnickers. It was still very hot, but a wind had started up and things were blowing around. Jonah watched a woman in shorts and a bikini top running after a plastic bag, and looked up at the clouds. Cumulonimbus. There was going to be a storm. At the top of the hill, the trees were all rustling loudly, and the shouts of the children in the paddling pool sounded very far away. From here, the view was amazing. Jonah turned and looked. Under the gigantic clouds, London sprawled and glittered like a vast pile of dragon's treasure. He imagined Lucy in a skyscraper, with a baby in her tummy, looking back at him, through a telescope. He lifted his hand to wave.

'Jonah!'

Saviour was holding open the park gate. Emerald and Raff were already through and standing on the pavement, waiting to cross. Jonah joined them. The houses opposite were like a row of eagles, perched above the park: tall, with hood-like roofs over glittering windows. He followed the others across the road, remembering the last time they'd come here, when they'd brought Dylan. They'd driven him

over, so it must have been before half-term, because it was
during half-term that they'd lost the car. Yes, it had been
the spring, the cherry trees had been in blossom. He remembered holding Dylan while Lucy locked the car, and looking
up at the clumps of pink.

Saviour led them through the front garden, which was
full of statues, all different kinds, from a grey, naked girl
with a missing nose and a missing arm to a brightly painted,
evil-looking gnome. There was also a toilet with a cactus
growing out of it. He and Raff had laughed their heads off
when they first saw that toilet. Saviour opened the front
door, and they all went into the house.

The hallway was spick and span, with everything slotted
into the wooden block of pigeonholes that stood against the
wall. A shaft of sunlight lay on the stripy-carpeted staircase,
falling from the window on the landing.

'Dora?' Saviour called. There was no answer, but something was banging somewhere in the wind.

They dropped their school bags, and kicked off their shoes
and socks, and Saviour shoved them all into various pigeonholes. The pigeonholes came from a post office, and there
were still postcodes written underneath them. Jonah breathed
in the dry, clean airiness. The floor, a stone jigsaw of brown,
cream and blue, was beautifully cold under his feet.

The floor in the long dining–sitting room was wooden
zigzags, like at Bad Granny's house – slightly waxy, and
you could smell the polish. Voices from the park drifted in
through the open front window. A hardback book lay open
on the stripy-cushioned window seat, and there were three
candlesticks on the long wooden table. Dora's lumpy, multi-
coloured oil painting of Lucy gazed down at them from the

wall opposite. Jonah gazed back. She was frowning, as if she didn't recognise them. Saviour had come in behind him, and he felt his hand on his shoulder, gently pushing him onward. Following Emerald and Raff, he ran his fingers along the top of the battered leather sofa, which was where the Martins watched television from. Above the TV were the antlers, decorated with fairy lights, twinkling, accidentally left on. The pinball machine was off, though, and the stool they used to stand on to play it had been pushed underneath, out of the way.

In the kitchen, Emerald and Raff put their ice-cream wrappers in the bin, and Saviour turned on the oven, before opening the fridge. Jonah caught a glimpse of the chicken, already covered in herbs and bits of bacon. 'Right then,' said Saviour. 'Who wants to help me pod the beans?'

Raff and Emerald both said, 'Me!' but Jonah walked on, down the steps and into the conservatory.

It was a grand, olden-days conservatory, nothing like the tiny glass lean-to at the end of their own kitchen. Dora's orchids, in pots along the windowsills, were all in bloom and the flowers – some blotchy, some speckled, some blank – looked like the faces of hundreds of tiny kittens. The mobiles were still hanging from the ceiling: paper birds and gauze butterflies, strings of seashells and a waterfall of long thin mirrors. The French windows were wide open, and the orchids were nodding, and the mobiles were spiralling, rustling and clinking in the breeze. Orchid heads were strewn across the stone-tiled floor, along with a few beans, which Saviour must have dropped coming in from the garden.

There was another statue, over near the door, gazing out

into the garden. Not a real statue, a mannequin, from a
shop, all smooth and white, apart from her lips and her
nipples, which had been painted with red nail varnish. Dora
had named her Ariadne the Sad. Jonah walked over to
Ariadne and gazed up at her lofty face; and then turned
to the rocking horse and patted its worn little head. The
first time they'd come here, Raff had been little enough to
sit on that rocking horse without his feet touching the
ground. It had been in the autumn, the very first term of
school, and there had been a fire in the wood stove and
yellow leaves plastered against the skylights. They had
bumped into them in the supermarket. They already knew
Saviour a bit – he'd talked to them in the playground, and
he'd given them the crate of mushrooms – but they hadn't
met Dora before. Emerald had been sitting up in the seat
of the trolley, like a baby, telling Saviour which biscuits she
wanted, and Raff had run up and said hello. He, Roland and
Lucy had followed, awkwardly, and it had been really embarrassing, because Raff had told Saviour that they didn't
actually like mushrooms. Then Dora had appeared, in her
long, pirate boots, swinging a leg of lamb.

He looked back at the sofas, which stood in an L-shape
around the stove. Dora's favourite sofa was brown leather,
like the TV sofa. It had a white furry rug on it and some
brown furry cushions. The sofa Lucy always lay on was
pink and squishy, and lower to the ground than Dora's. It
stood against the wall, but the back of it sloped up and
curled over at the top, which meant there was a small space
below, in between the sofa's base and the wall. The space
had been Jonah's little den. He would come down the steps
from the kitchen, and they'd be talking and talking, and

he'd drop down onto his hands and knees and crawl into that dusty cocoon.

Jonah sat down on the pink sofa, thinking about Lucy and Dora in the biscuits aisle. He put the palms of his hands together, like Dora had done when she saw Lucy, and Lucy had done the same thing back, and they'd both made little bows. It was like they both came from the same, faraway country, and they hadn't seen anyone else from that country for a very long time. But when Dora said, *'You must be the famous Lucy!'* Lucy's smile had been puzzled. And yes, seeing as it was before Angry Saturday, what had she been famous for? Dora had introduced herself, saying that her real name was Cordelia, but that she hated it.

'But it's so pretty!' Lucy had said.

'It's awful. When I was a teenager I tried changing it to Goneril.'

'Goneril?'

'Yes, because of King Lear. So I wasn't the goody two-shoes little sister.'

Jonah winced, remembering Lucy's knowledgeable nod. He'd known – he could always tell – when she was pretending something. He lay down on the sofa and pulled his knees up to his chest. Dora had found out everyone was calling her 'Gonorrhoea' behind her back, so she'd had to change it back again. Lucy had laughed a lot at that. They'd talked about Haredale, and Dora had said Emerald found school boring. *'She's not used to being treated like a kid, I guess. We've always let her join in with us.'* Lucy had asked why Emerald didn't have any brothers or sisters, which had seemed to him a bit nosy, but Dora hadn't minded at all. She'd said she would have loved some more, a Ruby and a Sapphire, but just as she'd been thinking about getting pregnant again, she got bloody cancer instead, and they'd nuked it, thank God, but they nuked everything else as well. And then she'd said that they *must* come to lunch, and help them eat the leg of what must have been a giant lamb.

Jonah looked around the empty conservatory, remembering Raff's shrieks of delight on the rocking horse, and Lucy and Dora laughing; Saviour trying to talk to Roland and handing out massive glasses of dark red wine, and the smell of the roasting lamb. Emerald had sung a song in French, and he and Raff had been amazed. Roland had said afterwards that she was *'an over-achiever'*, and also that he didn't know Lucy had read *King Lear*. Lucy had stomped off to their bedroom, and Jonah had gone after her and snuggled next to her on the bed. He'd asked her what gonorrhoea meant, and she had frowned, not understanding, but then she'd giggled, remembering, and told him. *'Little pitchers have big ears,'* she'd whispered, taking hold of both of his, and tugging them, very gently.

Jonah went and squatted at the end of the sofa, so that he could peer into the space behind it. The two brown furry cushions he used to lie on were still there. He was getting a bit too big now, to fit himself in. He stood up and looked down at the worn pink velvet of the sofa, imagining he saw the imprint of Lucy's body on them. Had she lain there the day they brought Dylan? Had he got behind the sofa and listened to Lucy and Dora chat? No, they'd gone straight out into the garden to introduce Dylan to Elsie, and show him the hutch, and they'd stayed out there, until they left. Lucy had been quiet, sitting huddled up in that grey cardigan, pulling blades of grass out of the ground. They hadn't stayed for a meal or anything. Dora had hugged Lucy as they were leaving, a really long hug, interrupted by Raff trying to push between them.

Jonah sniffed. The chicken must be in the oven. He turned and looked through into the kitchen. Raff was trying to pod the beans, instructed by Emerald. 'No, watch me,' she kept saying, 'you're doing it wrong.' He turned away, and put the palms of his hands together again. 'Actually it was just a yoga thing, wasn't it,' he whispered to Lucy. Like Om. Maybe he would ask Dora what Om meant. She would know. He looked out into the garden.

30

There were stone steps up to the patio, or the terrace, as Dora called it. The wind was whooshing, and the wind chimes in the apple trees were going crazy. There were lots of sheets drying on the washing line, and the wind kept whipping the sheets up into the air, giving him glimpses of Dora's white, octopus body, sprawled strangely on a cushion-stuffed deckchair. Sunglasses and a baseball cap covered her head and face, and a skimpy yellow dress covered her middle. Her arms were thrown back above her head, and her thighs had fallen wide apart. Her knees were bent and her shins and feet were in a green plastic bucket. The phrase 'kicked the bucket' came into Jonah's head, and his heart quickened as he wondered whether she was dead already. Then the wind dropped, and the wind chimes stopped, and everything became still and quiet, and the sun blazed down. He couldn't see any of Dora any more, just the bucket and the deckchair legs, and a book, splayed open on the pink paving stones.

Is she dead? He tiptoed up the steps and onto the patio, where he stood, not quite daring to go any further. He felt worried about Emerald coming out and crashing through the sheets to find her. If she was really dead, then how would Emerald survive? He remembered the egg-eyed old woman from the betting shop, having her hair done by Pat, and how he'd wondered if *she* was dead, and had heard Lucy giggling – not really, just in his head. Now he saw Lucy's face, very clearly, her eyes serious, questioning. *But what about if* I'm *dead, Joney? How will you two survive?*

Jonah closed his eyes. If they were both dead, Dora and Lucy, then they might be in Heaven together. He pictured them lying on their sofas, drinking their wine, both in white togas, like the gods in the film. *It's lovely here, isn't it?* Lucy, her voice lazy, arm trailing off the sofa, the stem of her glass threaded through two fingers. *But I should go down, really. I'm worried about the boys. Aren't you worried about Em?* Both rolling onto their tummies, looking over the edge of their sofas, down through the blue rectangle and into the garden.

There was a faint splosh. Jonah opened his eyes. Dora's wet feet appeared below the sheet. Not dead then. But one of the feet had a very dark bruise on it, and all the toenails were thick and yellow. Jonah felt terrified all of a sudden and turned, wanting to rush back into the house, but he was too late, because she plucked back the sheet and there she was, or some new, dying version of her, sitting forward in the deckchair, her glassy, insect eyes gazing out at him from under the brim of her hat.

'Jonah! Long time no see!' she said. It was definitely her voice, a New Zealand voice, light but earthy, with an interesting rasp to it. Jonah smiled shyly back.

'How you doing, mate!'

'Fine, thank you.' He was feeling awkward, like Roland – he got that awkwardness from Roland. He shouldn't be feeling like that, because the Martins were their best friends.

'That's good.' She stuck her sunglasses up on the brim of her baseball cap. Her face looked more or less the same. Dora was a bit younger than Lucy, but she looked older, because her skin was all crinkly, like scrunched-up tissue paper. Her tiny nose still had a diamond in it, and her eyes were still big and flat and grey, like televisions. She had another bruise on her arm, and she looked thin, thinner than ever. The yellow dress didn't suit her, it hung too loosely on her bony body, and the colour made her skin look even whiter. Jonah wondered why she didn't get tanned, like Saviour. He remembered her doing cartwheels the day she took them to the Olympics, and wondered if she could still do them, or whether her arms would just snap.

Dora pulled herself out of the deckchair and started unpegging one of the sheets, her feet leaving wet marks on the stone. 'How's your mum?' she asked, over her shoulder.

Jonah's fingers closed around the white stick in his pocket, wishing he could just tell her.

'I've got a wobbly tooth,' he said.

'Really? When's it going to come out, do you think?'

'Lucy said it would come out on Wednesday. I bet her it would be before, so it needs to come out today, for me to win.'

'Well, if it's loose enough, you could tug it out! Or would that be cheating?'

'I think so.' He watched Dora reach up, her white skin, the straggly armpit hairs. 'Dora?'

'Yes, love.'

He squeezed the stick, trying to decide. Then, in a rush, he asked: 'Can I put my feet in the bucket?'

'Of course.'

He stepped into the bucket. Feeling her watching him, he trod about, like it was a paddling pool, stirring the water.

'You are an amazing person, Jonah. Do you know that?' She had draped the sheet over her arm, and was unpegging another, with just one hand. 'I know it must be hard work, sometimes, being you. But you do such a good job. You deserve a medal really.'

Jonah carried on treading, feeling her watching him. You could only really take one step in that bucket, one step in any direction. He looked over at her book, and read the words on the cover. *Man's Search for Meaning* by Viktor E. Frankl.

'What does Om mean?' he asked.

'Om? I don't know. Nothing much. Ask your mum. She'll know.'

Jonah nodded. He stopped treading and looked back at the book cover, wondering what the E stood for, and remembered Dora's other book, with the picture of the mask on the cover, lying on the kitchen table at home. He should have brought it with him, to give back to her. He would have had to rub out all Lucy's scribbles, though.

'Oh, Jonah, I've just remembered!'

He looked up.

'What happened at your dad's parole hearing? Is he coming home?'

'I don't know.' His heart quickening, Jonah glanced back at the house. What had Raff said about Roland coming out on patrol?

'Oh.' Dora draped the second sheet over her arm. 'Well, if your mum hasn't said anything, then maybe . . .'

'What *is* a parole hearing?' Jonah started treading again.

'It's a – kind of meeting. The people on the parole board get together and listen to all the reasons why the prisoner should be allowed to go home.'

Jonah imagined the people, around a long table, with their hands cupped behind their ears, listening to Roland saying how sorry he was. 'And then they decide? At the hearing?'

'Or maybe after the meeting. I don't know exactly.'

'And if they decide he can go home, can he go straightaway?'

Dora stopped unpegging, thinking. 'I suppose so. They'd need to – let people know first. I don't know how long that all takes. Maybe there's a bit of a wait.'

'How many people do they have to tell?'

'Just – not that many.' Dora's face cleared. 'Actually, no, it's coming back to me. He's got a Parole Eligibility Date. That's why they had the hearing, to decide if he could go on that date.'

'What date is the – the Parole Edgibility Date?' Jonah stopped treading and watched the water settle.

'I'm . . . I thought it was really soon, but I'm not sure. And anyway – if your mum hasn't said anything . . .' She started pegging again. 'Lovey, I probably shouldn't have mentioned it. The parole board may have decided he needs to stay in prison a bit longer.'

'How much longer?'

'Not too long, hopefully.'

'Like, a few weeks?'

'I don't know, Joney. Yes, maybe.' She was sounding weary now, like she wished she hadn't started the conversation, but Jonah pushed on.

'And when he does come out . . .'

'Yes?'

'Will he come and live with us?'

'I'm not sure.' Dora had the sheets draped over her shoulder now, like a toga. 'To begin with, he'll stay at his mother's, probably. But he'll come and see you.' She reached up to unpeg another one. 'That'll be first on his list.'

'Dora?'

'Yes, lovey?'

'To buy food, for a few weeks . . .'

'What?'

'How much money would you need?'

'Money? Why, is Lucy flat broke again?' The tired dreariness that had come into her voice filled him with shame. 'Listen, don't worry about money. We can help out with money. I'll speak to her, OK.'

'OK.'

'Your mum will be fine,' she said. 'She just goes through her phases, doesn't she?'

He nodded, and looked through the water at his feet, side by side. 'You know when . . . ?'

'When what?'

He looked over at her. 'When Roland's mother wanted us to go and live with her.'

'Yes.' Dora turned to look at him over her shoulder.

'And Lucy was going to go to court. To get a thing to stop her coming near us.'

'A restraining order. She didn't bother in the end. I wrote her a letter instead. Which seemed to do the job.'

Jonah stared down at his feet. His toenails were too long. Lucy should have cut them when she cut his fingernails. 'Dora . . . ?'

'Yes, lovey?' She sighed.

'Could me and Raff come and stay with you?' It came out suddenly, without him knowing he was going to say it.

'Ouch!' A peg clattered to the ground, broken, and Dora put her finger to her mouth. The sheets over her shoulder slid off. She looked like she was going to cry.

'It's OK,' he said quickly, 'we'll be fine.' He stepped out of the bucket. He didn't know whether to go and hug her, or to leave her alone and join the others in the kitchen.

Dora took her finger out of her mouth. 'Jonah, has your mum talked to you about my illness?'

Jonah shook his head. He walked heel to toe in a circle, so the footprints would be joined up.

'The thing is that it's all quite hard on Em. It's hard on us all, but especially Em.'

Jonah nodded as he walked his circle.

'You know what Em's like. She's not sweet and kind like you, Jonah, she's an only child. And she's had me being ill a lot, and she just . . . well, she just finds sharing really difficult.'

Jonah nodded and nodded.

'Of course Lucy gets sad, and that's like an illness. But she cheers up again. Doesn't she?'

'It's fine,' said Jonah. He looked back at the book cover. Maybe E stood for Edward. Or that funny, olden-days name: Ebenezer. Not Emerald, anyway.

'I do think about you two boys a lot, you know, and I wish I could have you to stay, I really do. I just think Emerald would find it just a bit rough, right now. Do you see, Jonah, love?'

'Yes.'

'Come here.' She reached towards him, and he came close enough so that she could take hold of his hand. She tried to pull him into a hug, but he resisted. 'Oh, lovey.' Dora sighed, let go and picked up the sheets. 'I'll talk to her. When she comes to pick you up, I'll make her come in.'

'She's not picking us up,' said Jonah. 'She told us we could go home on our own.'

'She did, did she?' Dora sucked her finger again. 'She's avoiding me. 'It's because I'm ill again. She can't bloody handle it.' The sudden savageness in her voice made him wince.

'Mum!'

Emerald ran at Dora, nearly knocking her over, and Dora dropped the sheets and they hugged. Saviour and Raff followed. Saviour was carrying a tray with glasses on it, and a big jug of pink liquid and ice, which he put down on the curly white table.

'Hi Raffy!' said Dora. 'What's going on with your hair!' Raff put his hands up to his head. 'Get your mum to take it out, I would. You look so lovely with your big afro.' Dora pushed Emerald gently away and sank back down into the deckchair. Saviour passed her a glass of pink drink. 'How was school, guys?'

'Jonah called me a cunt.'

Jonah felt his face turn to fire. Saviour was looking at him, his eyebrows raised, but Dora was looking at Emerald, frowning.

'That doesn't sound very – likely,' she said.

'He did, though! Didn't you, Jonah!'

Dora's eyes travelled to him now. He readied himself to

try and explain, but his throat had tightened up and his mouth was very dry. He reached for the drink Saviour had poured him. The glass was a bit too full, and he raised it very slowly to his lips.

Dora looked away. 'Will you get the sheets, Hub,' she said softly. Saviour picked up the dropped sheets, and unpegged the other ones, bringing the rest of the garden into view. After the patio there was a stretch of lawn, with flower beds on either side, and then there was the vegetable patch, where the beans had come from, with trellises and netting and a scarecrow, which was actually an old tailor's dummy. It was wearing a pinstriped jacket and a straw hat with a green scarf tied around it. Beyond the vegetables were the apple trees, with their wind chimes, and under the apple trees was the rabbit hutch with its own wire-netted garden.

Dora turned her head, following Jonah's gaze. 'Oh!' she said. 'Do you want to look at the baby rabbits?'

Baby rabbits! Jonah and Raff looked at each other, their mouths open.

Dora said, 'Hey! Didn't Lucy tell you?'

She looked up at Saviour, who was folding the sheets loosely and dropping them into a wicker basket.

'When did they come?' asked Jonah.

'About a fortnight ago. Or is it longer? I texted her the minute . . .' Dora kept looking at Saviour as her voice faded off. Then she turned and looked at Emerald. 'Emmy, why didn't you tell these guys about the babies!?'

Emerald shrugged. 'I had other things on my mind, I guess.' She sipped her drink. A small moan came from Dora. Saviour put the last sheet in the basket and came and stood behind her. He pulled off the cap and sunglasses, and cupped her forehead with a big, purple-fingered hand. Dora's eyes closed. Emerald put her glass down. 'Come on then, guys.'

There were five baby rabbits, and they were very sweet. Emerald picked one up, but when Raff tried to grab another one, she said he shouldn't.

'They're used to me,' she said. 'But they'll be frightened of you. I tell you what, come here and you can stroke Lola if you like. As long as you're careful.' As if she was an adult, she took Raff's finger and stroked it over the rabbit's back.

'But I want to hold him,' said Raff, scooping the rabbit off her. 'See, he isn't scared. He likes me!' He held the rabbit up to his face and nuzzled him. 'Hey, Van Persie, you're my mate, aren't you my mate?' he said.

'Van Persie! What's that!'

'It's the name of a football player,' Jonah explained.

'You can't name a rabbit after a football player,' said Emerald. 'Anyway, it's my rabbit, and it's a girl rabbit and it's called Lola.' She tried to reclaim it, but Raff moved quickly away, holding it tightly to his chest.

'It's my rabbit, it's Van Persie.'

'It's not your rabbit!'

'Raff, give it back,' Jonah said. 'If Em wants that one, we need to choose out of the other ones.'

Raff wouldn't give it back. Emerald put her hands on her hips. 'Anyway, sorry guys, but none of them are yours.'

'Yes they are!' said Raff. 'Half of them are ours!'

'We're going to keep them all, I'm afraid,' said Emerald. 'They need to be with their mum.'

'What about Dylan? He's their dad! Where is he?'

'Dylan's in the hutch,' said Emerald. 'He never comes out,

he just sleeps these days. You can have Dylan back. The babies don't really need him.'

Jonah wanted to punch her. Instead he took a deep breath. 'Of course we can have Dylan back, because he's actually our rabbit, Emerald. We just lent him to you, so that Elsie would get pregnant.'

'And he's the babies' dad, so half of them are ours,' said Raff.

'There's five, so we can't have half of them,' said Jonah. 'But we could probably have two.' He was proud of himself for sounding so grown-up and reasonable, but Emerald called down the garden.

'Daddy! They can't have two of the rabbits, can they?!'

Saviour had sat himself at Dora's feet, and was kissing the inside of her wrist. 'Can't you just have a nice time playing with them, guys?' he called back.

Still holding the baby rabbit, Raff marched over to Dora and Saviour. Jonah followed, feeling very anxious.

'They're our rabbits too,' Raff said. 'You can't just keep them all!'

'Hey, Raff!' said Dora lightly. 'Let's wait till I've talked to Lucy, shall we?'

'Give it back!' Emerald had managed to pluck the rabbit out of Raff's arms, and he was in a proper rage. 'It's not fair! We should get Dylan, and three babies! And I want to take them home today!'

Dora moaned again. It was a tiny sound, but it made Saviour leap to his feet.

'Raff, we don't want a rabbit row,' he said. 'Let's keep our voices down, shall we?'

'Raff, lovey, come here,' said Dora, reaching out from the

deckchair, but Raff threw himself onto the lawn, sobbing. Jonah squatted down next to him and put his hand on his heaving shoulders. Emerald stood over them, stroking the rabbit.

'Raff, my mum is really ill, and she might even die, so if you behave like that we will have to send you home!' she said.

'Emerald!' shouted Saviour, as Raff started to scream. 'Will you stop being nasty to Raff! And will you STOP saying Mum is going to die!' He grabbed the baby rabbit off her and strode down the garden to drop it back with its mother; walked back and scooped the still-screaming Raff up into his arms.

'Right,' he said, 'who's going to help me make a black-currant tart?'

31

It was strange to be eating a roast dinner on such a hot, sunny day. They ate at the long table, underneath Dora's splodgy portrait of Lucy. The front window was wide open still, and they could hear faraway traffic, as well as shouts and laughter from the park.

Raff and Emerald got the legs, and Jonah and Saviour got the wings and some breast. Dora had a tiny bit of breast, but she didn't really eat anything. Jonah didn't eat that much either. Chewing was difficult, because of his loose tooth. Saviour was drinking wine, he noticed, red wine, but actually dark purple. Splodgy Lucy looked down at them, forever puzzled. Maybe she was puzzled because of all the colours Dora had used to paint her with, from navy blue to daffodil yellow.

Dora rubbed her bare arms with her hands, and then got up and closed the window. 'The weather's changing,' she said, to no one in particular. 'I think it's going to rain.' She sat back down. 'You couldn't get me a cardigan, one of you?'

Saviour knocked back his wine, and got up and went upstairs. Dora sat, wrapped in her own long arms, staring out of the window. Following her gaze, Jonah saw that she was right about the rain. One of the cumulus clouds had developed a hood – a pileus cloud – which meant a storm was definitely on its way. The cranes, rising up out of the London sprawl, looked like they were aiming at it. *Like slingsmen*. He, Raff and Emerald ate their blackcurrant tart in silence. He finished his first, and slipped away. He got Lucy's mobile phone out of his school bag, and took it into the toilet with him.

Please send boys home. Soz cant pick them up. Lx

He sent it, and then stood looking at the framed photo of Dora hanging over the toilet. It was from when she was very young, and at a party. She was wearing a tight silver dress and her hair was all spiky. She looked beautiful. He remembered lying behind the sofa listening to Dora telling Lucy about meeting Saviour. It was at a nightclub, and Dora was on drugs and feeling freaked out. *'I was dancing, and it was like I was going higher and higher,'* she'd said. *'You know, like a balloon. And then I saw him watching me, like an anchor.'*

Jonah imagined Saviour down at the bottom of the sea, sitting cross-legged and holding onto a piece of string. Underwater, he looked just like a sea creature, with his big mouth and his jowly cheeks, and his seaweedy hair. A big, silver bubble came out of his mouth and went wobbling upwards.

Jonah turned away from the picture. He thought about Roland, and how young and thin he was. He was the opposite of Saviour in practically every way. Tall, not short; smooth, not hairy; serious, not silly. Roland didn't know how to be silly. He was kind, though, and he would never be as grumpy as Saviour had been that morning. He tried to imagine Roland in a nightclub, but it was difficult. He didn't like drinking alcohol, and it was obvious from just looking him that he would be a rubbish dancer – too stiff and awkward. Saviour loved dancing. 'Boogying,' he called it. But Saviour liked alcohol too much.

The red phone pinged. Jonah looked at the screen.

No prob, will get hub to walk them over. We need to talk about rabbits xx

Jonah closed the toilet seat and sat down to think about the rabbits. Raff would be so happy if they could take some home. They could take Dylan home with them, at the very least.

He spent a long time on the next text, making sure it sounded like Lucy.

Rabbits! Please can we have some. Two will be enough, or even one. Put them in a box and the boys can carry them and Dylan too, also some food for them. Boys are fine to walk home by themselves xx

Waiting for a reply, Jonah stood up, put the phone down next to the basin, and looked in the mirror. He looked a lot like Roland. But browner. He thought about the moment of Roland's sperm reaching Lucy's egg: the beginning of his, Jonah's, existence. Or had he already existed, had he been a soul, up in the sky, looking down, waiting for his next life? He put his hand in his pocket and pulled out the white stick. Whose sperm had made Lucy's new baby? Felix

Curtis? Probably not. You probably can't even have a baby if your brain has been damaged. He got a sudden flash of the twins, Scarlett and Indigo, bouncing and bouncing on their trampoline. He'd forgotten he'd been in their garden. A barbeque, long before Angry Saturday. Lucy had spent ages getting ready, trying on different clothes, but in the end she'd worn her little red top and her denim shorts and her clogs. Roland had worn shorts too, but long, neat ones, and his special walking sandals, and his special walking hat. It was when he put on his daypack that Lucy had exploded. Why did he have to look like he was going on a 100-mile hike, when they were going to a barbeque around the corner? Roland had taken off the daypack and shown her the things he'd put inside: things like wet wipes and sunscreen, and a bottle of wine to give to the Curtises. Lucy had stormed out of the door. They had caught up with her halfway up the hill, and Roland had walked beside her, and he and Raff had walked behind, holding hands. Lucy's bottom had been all wiggly in her tight denim shorts, and Roland's daypack had jiggled on his back.

There still hadn't been a reply to his text. He went out into the hall and put the phone back in his school bag. He dug his hands in his pockets and looked around the Martins' hallway. There was the photo of boy-Saviour – cute, with a mop of curls. Jonah stared at the long-ago face. It was actually a sad face, even though it was smiling. He thought of Lucy as a little girl, motherless, reading her baby brothers the Yonghy-Bonghy-Bò. Then he suddenly realised that she might be back by now. She might have knocked and knocked, and then gone through the Broken House, and be really worried about them, and searching everywhere for her mobile phone. 'We're coming,' he whispered, turning away from the photograph, his heart beating faster with the need to get back.

The remains of the meal were still on the table, but everyone had got down. Splodgy, puzzled Lucy was there, of course, in the frame on the wall. Jonah noticed that Saviour's bottle of wine was empty. Through the window he saw that the sun was setting properly now, sinking down behind huge purple clouds, which were definitely nimbus. In the kitchen, he heard Dora's voice and stopped to listen.

'Maybe you should take some rabbits round,' Dora said. 'It's a bloody weird text, as *if* the boys could manage to carry two babies and Dylan across the park all by themselves, but maybe wanting them is a good sign.'

'They're still too little,' said Saviour.

'I don't think they are. They're eating food. I think they'll be fine.'

'I'm not taking any rabbits round,' said Saviour.

'What, not even Dylan!'

'Look. Let's forget about the fucking rabbits. They aren't the issue.'

'What is the issue?'

'The issue is the boys.'

There was a silence. Then Dora said, 'You know, Jonah asked if they could come and stay, earlier.'

'Well . . .'

'Well, what? Are you thinking we should have them?'

'Maybe. Just for a few days.'

There was another pause. Then Dora said, in a clipped, spitty voice: 'I think you've gone into some kind of denial.' Saviour murmured something, but she cut in, getting louder.

'I don't think you really get what it's going to be like, the next couple of weeks!'

'I do. I totally get what it's going to be like.'

'Then how could you even *think* of taking the boys in?!'

'I feel worried about them. They're not being looked after.'

'Saviour. It's going to take all we've got to look after ourselves.'

There was a moment's silence.

'She'll get better. She always does. And maybe getting some rabbits to look after will make her snap out of it!'

'Dora, *please!*'

The sudden blast of Saviour's voice made Jonah jump. His heart thudded.

'I'm sorry.' Dora's voice was very low.

'I've got enough on my plate without having to think about fucking rabbits.'

'OK,' she said. It sounded like she was crying. Saviour sighed and Jonah heard him moving across the room.

'I'm sorry,' he said. 'Baby, I'm so sorry. I didn't mean to . . .'

'I'm just worried about my – my fucking *useless* friend,' said Dora. 'One minute I'm worried about her, next minute I want to *kill* her . . .'

'It's OK, everything's going to be OK . . .' His voice went muffled as he hugged her. He said something else, and Dora moaned again, a loud, terrible moan, which sent Jonah flying upstairs to find Raff.

32

They left the house by themselves and set off across the park, but Saviour must have heard the front door close, because he came running after them. He didn't say anything, he just drew up beside them and walked along with them, looking straight ahead. The sky was full of cumulonimbus clouds, dark and brooding, but with weirdly bright pink bits in between, and below, the cranes had their tiny red lights on. Jonah walked fast, thinking of Lucy worried, and searching; and of her opening the door, crying out and hugging them both hard. Then he remembered the sight of her empty bed that morning, the blow to his hope, and his churning tummy. He slowed, and looked up at Saviour's quiet, faraway face.

'You know karma?' he asked.

'Yes.'

'Raff said you think it's rubbish, and everything is just random.'

'Did he?' Saviour looked towards Raff, who was a few feet ahead of them.

'So it doesn't make any difference, then, if you're good or bad? There's nothing you can do to – make things different?'

Saviour shrugged. He normally liked answering questions like this, but he obviously wasn't in the mood. As they walked on, Jonah's hand found the white stick again.

'Do you know what this is?'

He took it from his pocket and held it up. Saviour took it from him, and stopped and looked at it. They were under the trees by the pond, next to Kumari's bench, but it was getting properly dark so that Jonah couldn't see the writing on the bench, or the expression on Saviour's face. The trees sheltered them from the breeze, though, so he could hear his breathing, as well as the frogs croaking in the water. Raff had kept walking, out into the open, but now he turned and came back under the canopy of leaves.

'Where did you get this?' said Saviour. His voice had that thick sound, and Jonah remembered that he'd drunk a whole bottle of wine. He looked in the direction of the park gate, wanting to keep going, but also to get an answer from Saviour.

'I found it,' he said. 'Miss Swann says it's a pregnancy stick. Is it a pregnancy stick?'

'Where did you find it?'

'Just in the road. Do you know what the blue lines mean? Do they mean she's pregnant?'

'Do they mean who's pregnant?'

Jonah looked up at Saviour's shadowed face, trying to see his eyes.

Raff said, 'What is it? Can I have a look?'

Saviour looked down, showing Raff the stick. 'It's a test, to see if someone's going to have a baby,' he said. He turned to look at Jonah again. 'Jonah, where did you get this?'

'On the pavement.'

Something flitted over the pond, very fast, not a bird, a bat. Raff had the stick and was pulling the lid off.

'Miss Swann said that bit's got wee on it,' Jonah told him.

'Yukky!' said Raff, dropping the stick and the lid to the ground. Jonah squatted down and reached for them, but Saviour was quicker.

'Why did you show it to Miss Swann?' he asked.

'I wanted to know what it was. Can I have it back?' Jonah had started wishing he'd kept the white stick in his pocket.

'Jonah, what do you want with a pregnancy test you found in the street?' said Saviour impatiently. 'The best place for it is in the bin!'

'I want it back.'

Saviour stuck the stick in his own pocket and took Jonah's shoulders, squatting down so that their faces were level. Jonah could see his eyes now, and they were small and hard again.

'You didn't find it in the street, did you?' His breath was horrible. 'Whose is it? Why won't you tell me?' They stared at each other in the dark, Jonah feeling his anger rise, hot and icy at the same time.

'Tell me where you found this stick, and I will give it to you, Jonah,' Saviour whispered, gripping his shoulders tighter. Holding himself very straight and stiff, Jonah looked back at him.

'If you don't tell me, you don't get it,' Saviour said.

Jonah cleared his throat. 'I already told you.'

Saviour let go of him. 'OK, have it your way.' He stood up and threw the stick into the pond. There was a flurry of ducks, a splash and a quack or two. Jonah ran to the railings and tried to climb over them. He could see the whiteness of it, floating on the water, but Saviour grabbed his arm and held him back.

'You shouldn't of done that!' Raff shouted at Saviour. 'That was someone else's property! You should *not* of done that!'

'Jonah, for fuck's sake!' Saviour was struggling to keep hold of him. 'Why won't you tell me what's going on!'

Jonah managed to break free from Saviour's grip, and get over the railing, but when he looked down into the pond, all he could see was darkness. He squatted and paddled his hands in the water, but it was gone. He stood up, crying. It was proper, noisy crying, and he couldn't quite believe it was him.

'You shouldn't of done that, Saviour!' Raff shouted again.

'I'm sorry,' said Saviour. 'I'm so sorry, guys.' His voice was high and strange, a voice neither of them had heard before. He helped Jonah back over the railing, and Raff pushed past and threw his arms around his brother. Saviour sat down on the Kumari bench and slumped forward, his hands covering his face, his fingers digging into his forehead. Jonah and Raff both looked at him. 'I'm sorry, guys,' he said, still in that voice. 'I just don't know what the fuck to do.'

Jonah hesitated, impatient to get home, but not liking to leave Saviour in that state. The darkness was thickening around them, like a living thing. Were the ghosts there, watching them, wishing they could help? He wobbled his tooth with his tongue. It was hanging on a thin thread of flesh now. He could win the bet with her, he could pull it out with one tug and she would owe him a pound – but it would be cheating. He sat down next to Saviour and put his hand on Saviour's thigh. 'It's OK,' he said. 'Everything will be OK.'

Raff sat on Saviour's other side, and they both listened to Saviour sobbing. Then Jonah noticed the sound of a car engine. Through the trees he could see the truck's headlights, moving slowly down the hill towards the main gates.

'Everything's going to be OK,' he said again. 'Dora will be OK. The doctors will make her better.' He stood up and gave Saviour a kiss on the side of his head, and imagined Kumari the goddess girl taking his place on the bench, her gold sari shining in the dark. He could see her solemn face nodding, and her hand lifting into a thumbs-up. She would look after Saviour.

'Let's go,' he said to Raff. 'They're going to lock the park.'

They ran down the hill, past the humming hospital and the silent, empty paddling pool. As they got to the gate, big drops of rain started to fall.

'There's a man still in here,' Jonah told the park keeper. 'Up by the pond. He's crying.'

'Someone you know?' asked the park keeper, getting back into his truck.

'Yes. His wife has got cancer.'

The park keeper nodded. 'Alright then.'

33

They scurried through the quickening rain, holding hands. As they reached Southway Street there was a clap of thunder, and it poured. They arrived on the doorstep soaked. Raff knocked, then he opened the letter box and shouted, 'Mayo!'

Jonah felt for the keys in his school bag. As he did, he registered out of the corner of his eye that the Raggedy Man was there again, in exactly the same place, against the squatters' wall. He was standing very straight, with his arms by his sides, and Jonah knew he was watching them. He hurried with the keys, his heart thumping, hoping Raff wouldn't notice.

Inside, it was very dark. Jonah shut the door, and they stood, taking in her absence. He turned on the hall light and an insect started buzzing.

'It stinks in here,' said Raff.

The buzzing was coming from the crate of plums. Flies, or maybe wasps. He turned the light off again.

'Why did you do that?'

'So the insects go back to sleep.' It was actually called

torpor, the resting state of insects. Jonah started pulling his wet clothes off.

'I wish Dylan was here. Or Daddy. Or both of them. I don't like Saviour any more.'

'You'd better take your clothes off, Raffy. Maybe we should have a bath.'

Raff pulled his shirt over his head. 'At least we had some food,' he said. Jonah dropped his own shirt on the floor and reached through the dark for Raff. He hugged him hard. Raff hugged him back.

'I wish he hadn't cried.' Raff let his shorts drop and stepped out of them. 'I hated it when he cried.'

'He's got a lot on his plate,' said Jonah. 'That's why he's getting so fat,' he added. Raff burst out laughing, but then they both froze, because someone was knocking at the door.

They looked towards each other, hardly breathing, feeling the unknown presence on the other side of the battered wood. Jonah could just make out Raff's face, his shadowed eyes, his lips. 'Mayo?' he saw him mouth.

Jonah put his finger to his lips. He stepped closer to his brother. 'I think it's the Raggedy Man,' he whispered in his ear.

There was another knock.

'What does he want?' Raff whispered back.

'I don't know.' Jonah pointed up the stairs. They had tiptoed nearly all the way up when they heard the letter box flip open. Jonah froze, clutching Raff's arm, and they both gazed down at the door.

'Jonah!' Saviour called. The relief made Jonah weak, and he sat down on the top stair.

'Jonah! Raff! Are you in there?'

Raff sat next to him, and Jonah held his finger to his lips again.

'Boys! Boys, if you're in there, will you please open the door!'

Raff started giggling, and clapped his hands over his mouth. The feel of his brother's trembling body made Jonah giggle too, a bit too loudly.

'Jonah! Is that you? Are you OK?'

The fear in Saviour's voice made him pull himself together. 'Yes, Saviour!' he called softly, through the dark. 'We're actually just going to bed! Goodnight!'

'Jonah! Come and let me in!'

Jonah stayed quiet. He and Raff huddled together, listening to Saviour's ragged breathing.

'I know Lucy's not there, and I don't want to leave you by yourselves! Jonah?'

'He knows Mayo's gone.' Raff's whisper blasted warm air into his ear. Jonah shook his head.

'He doesn't. He's just guessing. Bluffing,' he whispered back.

The letter box finally dropped shut, and they heard him saying, 'Fuck!' a few times, which made them giggle again. Once they'd heard him walk off, they sat, listening hard. The insects in the plum box must have already slipped back into their torpor: the only sound was the soft drumming of the rain.

After a moment, Raff whispered, 'Are you sure we shouldn't tell him?'

'No. Dora doesn't want us to stay with them. They'll phone Bad Granny.' Jonah whispered too, not wanting to disturb the quietness of the house.

'Why will they?'

'I told you. She's our closest relative. She's the person that everyone will think *should* look after us.'

'Not the Martins. They know she's bad. It was Dora who stopped her trying to steal us.'

'I know. But it's different now, because Lucy isn't here.' He could see better now. He stood up, but Raff stayed where he was, his chin in his hands, his elbows on his knees.

'Raff,' he whispered.

'What?'

'What did Lucy say about Roland coming out?'

'She just said he was coming out soon.'

'Did she say anything about the parole hearing?'

'The troll earring?' Raff turned and peered up at him. 'What's that?'

'It's when they decide whether he can come out.'

'The troll?'

'No, Roland. On parole.' Maybe Dora was right, maybe they'd decided Roland should stay in prison for a bit longer. 'I'm freezing. Come on, let's have a bath.' Jonah crossed the landing and pushed the bathroom door open, but Raff stayed sitting on the top stair.

'You know on Angry Saturday.'

'Yes.' They'd left the bathroom window open and rain was coming in.

'Why did Bad Granny have a bandage on her head? Did Daddy hit her too?' He turned his head to look up at Jonah.

Jonah looked back at him, smiling. 'It wasn't a bandage, Raffy, it was a turban.'

'A turban? Is she religious? Has she got a dagger?' Raff's eyes gleamed.

Jonah smiled a bit more, imagining Lucy smiling with him. 'Bad Granny's not a Sikh, Raff.'

'Don't laugh. It's not funny.'

'Sorry.' The rain was dying down, so he didn't bother to close the bathroom window. Instead, he sat back on the stair next to Raff and put his arm around him. 'Bad Granny was all dressed up because she was at a wedding when the police phoned her.'

'She was getting married?'

'No! It was someone else's wedding.' A film star's, probably.

Raff leaned into him. 'Why *did* she try and steal us?'

Jonah sighed. 'She thinks Lucy's a bad person. She didn't think she should be looking after us.'

'Because she sexed Furtix?'

'She thought it even before Angry Saturday.'

'Why did she think it?'

'*It's actually racism, pure and simple.*' Jonah heard Lucy's voice and saw her angry face. Then Roland's voice, careful: '*I think it's a bit more complicated than that.*' He cleared his throat, working out how to explain.

'She thought she didn't really love Daddy, and she was just using him so she wouldn't get sent back to Zambia. If you're not from this country, but you want to stay here, you have to marry someone who is.'

They were both silent. Then Raff said: 'Bad Granny thought Mayo was bad. But it was *her* that was bad.' He sat up straight, shrugging Jonah's arm away. 'She tried to steal us, but she only wanted you, really. She wanted to put me in an orphanage. Because I broke the vase.'

'She was very angry about the vase.'

'Bad Granny got anger *management*, man!' The sudden loudness of Raff's voice made Jonah jump. Raff got to his feet. 'That's where Daddy gets it. That's why he bashed the man's head in.' He walked up and down the landing, swiping the air.

'Raff, Roland isn't – he's not actually like that.' Jonah brought his feet up and leaned his back against the landing wall. 'He was never angry. Sometimes he got a bit angry with Lucy, but hardly ever. And he was never angry with us.' He closed his eyes, trying again to think of the right words to explain. What was it Saviour had said that time, while they were making apple crumble? 'What he did to Felix Curtis – it was out of his character. He's not a bad person, he's a good person. A good person who did a bad thing.'

'Is it Mayo's fault, then?'

He opened his eyes. Raff was looking down at him. 'That's what Bad Granny thinks,' he said.

'That's what everyone thinks. That's why no one likes her. Apart from the Martins.'

Jonah closed his eyes again, remembering listening from that little space behind the sofa: Lucy crying, Dora all heated, telling her not to take any notice; she was right, it was that rapist Felix's fault, he actually deserved it, but it's always the woman who gets the blame.

'I broke her vase. But it was an accident.'

'Definitely. You were really little.' The vase had been on a low table by the sofa. It had shattered into tiny diamonds, lying all over the wooden zigzag floor.

'And she shouted, even though it was an accident.' Raff dropped to his knees.

'Yes. So can you actually remember it, Raffy?' How old had he been? Two? Three at the most.

'I can remember bits. Running outside. But that crazy peacock was there. Why was the peacock there?'

'It was Bad Granny's pet.'

'And she put us to bed in Daddy's old room. With the horse.'

'Yes.' The picture of a horse, a poster, over Roland's bed: a friend, its face so sad and understanding. Once Bad Granny had gone away, they'd got up and explored. 'We looked at Daddy's magazines.'

'What, like Leonie's magazines?' Raff looked at him, shocked.

'No, they were horse-racing magazines.' They'd looked at them for ages, those pictures of horses, all friends.

'And then what happened?'

Jonah frowned in the dark. 'I was worried you would do a wee in the bed. Because you still wore a nappy in the night. So I took you to the toilet. And that's when we heard her.'

'I remember listening to her on the stairs,' Raff whispered. 'She was talking really weirdly.'

Jonah nodded. On their way back from the toilet, they'd sat on the stairs and peered through the banister. She'd been sitting on the sofa, her turban off, her short, pink hair all tufty. Her voice had been all over the place, high and screechy, then low and growly. After a while he'd realised she was on her phone.

'What was she saying?'

Jonah stared down into the darkness, hearing Bad Granny's shaking voice. '*That fucking* fuck-up *of a woman. I* knew *she was a basket case, right from the start.*' Roland had brought her to visit Bad Granny, and Bad Granny had cooked a meal, but Lucy had hardly touched it. She wouldn't make conversation, or even look Bad Granny in the eye. And Roland had run around after her, like a dog, trying to work out how to make her happy. Like a Labrador. That's what Bad Granny had said. *'Like a bloody Labrador. When all he was to her was a ticket to stay in the country.'*

'She was saying she was going to keep you, and put me in an orphanage. Wasn't she?'

Jonah nodded.

'Because I'm browner than you.'

'He's much darker than Jonah. And that afro hair.' Her voice had calmed down by then, and she'd been cross-legged, leaning forward as she spoke, looking at some papers spread out on the coffee table. Jonah scrunched his eyes tightly closed. It was all scrambled up, what he'd heard at the time, and the story Lucy had told him and Raff. But Lucy hadn't been there. Her story was *his* story: what he'd told her the next day, when they'd got home. Had he remembered it right? Had she heard him right? Was the story she had told back to them the *exact* truth?

'If the orphanage van comes, I'll see it. I'll run away and hide.'

Jonah opened his eyes and put his arm around Raff's shoulders again. 'There's no such thing as an orphanage van, Raffy.'

'Yes there is. A man with a hat drives it. And he jumps out and catches children with his big net.'

Jonah smiled. The Child Catcher in *Chitty Chitty Bang Bang*. *'Lollipops! Ice cream!'* It was really scary, that bit. 'Raffy, that was just a film. There's no orphanage van.'

'Why was he only shouting *our* names?'

'Who?'

'Saviour. If he was . . . buffing.'

'Bluffing.'

'Bluffing. Why didn't he shout her name?'

'Because he was bluffing, of course.' He said it as if it was obvious, but it was difficult to get it clear in his head. He stood up. 'Come on. Let's have a bath.'

WEDNESDAY

34

The bells had been ringing for a long time in the Tibetan monastery, and he was on the point of discovering something; but then his tongue found his tooth, hanging by just a thread, and he realised it was now Wednesday. 'I think you're going to win the bet,' he whispered to her, half-dreaming, and she nodded and smiled. He circled the tooth with his tongue, seeing flashes of her face, and flashes from the dream. Was she back? No, the bells were ringing, she wasn't back, or she would have turned them off. But there had been some banging, he remembered, banging and drilling, like someone was mending something? Or had that been in the dream? Suddenly the tooth came away, very easily, and he opened his eyes and sat up, and spat it into his palm. So white, so tiny! Wednesday. She was right. She'd won.

The rain was still falling, and the air in the room was chilly on his shoulders. His tooth in his fist, he turned on his side and pulled the duvet over him. They'd dragged the duvets back onto their beds the night before. They hadn't had a bath, though, because it was still full of Lucy's oily water, with the hairs and even more dead flies. He gazed at the Oscar Pistorius poster, which had finally slid down the wall, so that Oscar was sitting, leaning against the skirting board, with his blade legs out in front of him. They'd seen him winning, getting his medal, at the Olympic Stadium – him, Emerald and Raff, and Dora on the end. His eyes were still sleepy, and he closed them, nestling into his own warmth.

It's still the Best Day of my Life, but it won't be for much longer. Do you know why?

Why, Joney? Her voice, so light and smiley.

Because when you come back, that *day is going to be the Best Day.*

Rainwater dripped, the bells rang and rang, and the ache of worry and of wanting her took hold. He sat up again and stared down at the tooth in his palm. He could show Raff. He looked at the clock – 07.49, time they were getting up anyway – and leant over the side of his bunk.

'Raff,' he whispered. There was no answer. The poem book was still lying open among the clothes on the floor, and he gazed at the picture of the Yonghy pleading with Lady Jingly Jones to marry him. 'Your proposal comes too late, Mr Yonghy-Bonghy-Bò,' he whispered. He leant further, to look at Raff. But Raff's bed was empty.

Still clutching his tooth, Jonah slithered down from the top bunk. There was a dent in Raff's pillow where his head had been. He ran into Lucy's empty room, and into the bathroom, and then down the stairs.

'Raff,' he whispered. The front door was open again.

Outside, it was grey and glistening, and his feet made tiny sploshes on the pavement as he walked around the corner into Wanless Road. Raff was there, staring at the passionflowers on the Broken House fence, beads of water in his hair and on his shoulders.

'Raffy.' Jonah felt a raindrop hit his neck and dribble down his spine. He sploshed to his brother's side. The flowers were even brighter in the wet grey light. A thousand Bad Granny masks, looking back at them.

'What are you looking at?'

'The council came.' Raff pointed, his other hand keeping his pyjama bottoms up.

'What?'

'Didn't you hear them?'

'Oh, yes.' The banging and drilling which he'd thought had been in his dream. Jonah stepped forward and touched the new silver screws. 'Did you see them?'

'No, they were driving away when I came out.'

The rain was gathering pace. Jonah pushed at the board. It didn't budge. 'Well, we can't get in this way any more. We'll have to remember the keys.'

Raff turned and walked around the corner, his pyjama bottoms dragging in the wet. Raindrops bounced off Jonah's shoulders. He opened his hand and stared at his tooth.

35

The alarm clock was still ringing when they got back inside the house, and the wasps were buzzing quietly in the plum crate. Raff was upstairs, sitting on the toilet, muttering to himself. Jonah leaned in the doorway. 'My tooth came out. Lucy won the bet.'

'Lay down in ma bed with ma Shelly by ma head . . .'

Jonah sat on the edge of the bath. 'Your hair is mad.' The night before he'd tried to unravel it all and comb it through, but Raff had wriggled and cursed and he'd given up.

'But I shoulda listened to what my mama said . . .'

'The milk hasn't come,' he said, watching Raff's dancing hands. 'I think it's because we haven't paid the bill.'

'Get me some arse paper, fam.'

'There isn't any.'

'Fetch me some, fam!' Raff aimed his imaginary catapult at him. 'I need to wipe my bum, don't I!'

Jonah went into Lucy's room and turned off the alarm. In the deep silence he surveyed the room. It was much cooler and the light was softer, but everything was exactly as it had been the day before. He gathered some lipsticky tissues from the dressing table to give to Raff, but then he went to the window and leant his forehead on the rain-spattered glass, looking out at the Broken House. It looked different under the dark clouds, not just desolate, but sulky – angry, even. There were pigeons all clustered in the upstairs window, like flies on the eye of an animal. He imagined reaching across with a giant arm and brushing them all away. The broken voice of the Broken House whispered in his head. *Please come*, it said; *why have you left me?*

He turned away, and his blurred gaze fell on Lucy's denim shorts, with her pink pants inside them. The clothes still held the shape of her. He knelt down and laid his fingers very lightly on the denim. Then he noticed the dark stain in the pants again. Was it blood? The stain was brownish and powdery, like dried blood would be. As he stood and turned his foot scrunched on paper, and he saw that he was standing on the old letter from Roland. He crouched over it, smoothing it out.

Hello there, Lucy
I want you to know that I don't blame you for refusing to testify. I don't really blame you for anything, apart from leaving your bicycle outside.

'Hurry up, fam!'

'Coming!' called Jonah.

If you had only taken it in with you, Raff wouldn't have seen it, and we'd have kept on going, home in time for the Queen Anne Stakes. But there it was, your golden bicycle, in broad daylight, when you said you were going shopping with Dora.

It was strange, reading Roland's words to Lucy. They were the words of his father to his mother, but it was like both people were strangers, like he was spying into their grown-up, private world. Forgetting about Raff, he started on the next paragraph.

> You'll have heard I got five years. Which means, apparently, that I'll be out in three, maybe sooner. My sentence should have been much longer, given the life-changing nature of the injury, and I should be very grateful to my lawyer. It all turned on 'mens rea', which, in case you're interested, is a legal term meaning 'guilty mind'. But I don't feel comfortable with my sentence. Why should it matter, whether or not I acted with intention, given the lives I ruined?

Although the writing was easy to read, lots of the words were difficult. He moved his finger underneath them, sometimes mouthing the sounds of the syllables.

> The way the lawyer put it, I was like a ball, struck or flung by a force outside me. The implication was, of course, that you were the player, the cause of it all. But I don't buy it, because if I'm a ball, then you're a ball, and the world is just a giant snooker table, and there's no point in anything, because we're all just snooker balls, bouncing off each other in an endless momentum.

The next paragraph wasn't as neat, and had crossings out.

> ~~Please be I know I can trust you to~~ Be sensible about things, won't you, Lucy. Watch your spending. Letting money flow is

all very well, but I haven't ever noticed it flowing back to you. I spoke to my mother this morning, and Lucy, she is very sorry for her attempts to take the boys from you. She was ~~feeling so angry with~~ in a terrible state when she did it, and she now knows it was a terrible thing to do. She accepts that she has ~~always been~~ never been fair on you, with her accusations and distrust, and she really wants to start building bridges. I know she has said some ~~stupid~~ vile things, over the years. But maybe you could try to understand the very protective feelings she has towards me. Lucy, please answer her calls. She wants to help financially, apart from anything else.

'Jonah!' Raff was really bellowing from the bathroom.

'Coming!' Jonah called again, but then he noticed the Martins' name, further down the page.

I'm sure the Martins are being very helpful, and I'm glad you've got them as a support. But don't get too entwined with them, Lucy. You'll say it's none of my business, but they treat you like their lame ducks, and I don't think it's healthy, for you or the boys. And please, Lucy, don't take any more money off them. If you did ever fall out with them, owing them money could make things really unpleasant.

'Fuckin' *Peck*! Bring me some toilet paper, man!'

'OK, Raffy!' Jonah put the letter down and took the lipsticky tissues to the bathroom. 'That's it, that's all there is. And don't call me Peck, alright.'

'Fuckin' Peck,' said Raff, looking dubiously at the tissues. Jonah sat back on the edge of the bath, thinking about money. How much had the Martins given them? They'd bought him and Raff the Wii player. They hadn't been able to believe their luck. And they'd paid for the holiday in France. He'd heard Dora talking about how much it had cost. But had they given Lucy actual cash? And what did Roland mean by 'lame ducks'?

Raff had flushed the toilet and was looking at himself in the mirror. 'Where my hat?' he asked, picking at the still-woven bits.

'What hat?'

'My trilby. I need it, for the show.'

'I don't know. Where did you put it?'

Raff shrugged. He hadn't worn it for ages. 'I'm hungry,' he said. 'We need some cash. We need to sell something.'

'At least we've got my tooth.' Jonah showed it to him. Raff turned and looked down at it, frowning. 'So we'll have some money tomorrow. Definitely one pound. Maybe more.'

'Peck! Don't tell me you believe in that tooth-fairy shit! Seriously!' Raff slapped his hand and the tooth fell to the floor.

Jonah's eyes filled, and he got up and went back into her bedroom.

36

'Who teefed ma toof, Mr Fairy!'

Raff came and sat on the edge of the bed. Jonah turned away from him.

'I brought you your tooth, fam.' Raff put his hand on his shoulder, and Jonah wriggled it off, but then Raff shuffled up close to him. 'You can put the tooth under the pillow if you want to, Joney boy,' he whispered. He stroked his face, the way Lucy did when he was sad.

Jonah rolled onto his back and stared at the ceiling. Lucy had always said that you had to believe in things, or nothing would be true. But did that mean that it was the believing in the thing that *made* it true?

'Raff, do you believe in God?'

'Nah.'

'Why not?'

'Because we come from chimps, innit?'

'God could still exist, though. Even if the Bible is wrong.' He closed his eyes. 'I felt him, once.' In Richmond Park, very hot, and they were lost and thirsty. Raff and Lucy had been ahead, Raff on Lucy's shoulders, and he'd followed them into the trees, all cool and green and mysterious, like they'd gone underwater. The feeling was of a current, running through his body, very strong in his hands.

'God's different from the tooth fairy, anyway,' Raff said. 'Why?'

'God's about the whole world. Tooth fairy's about toofs.' 'Teeth.'

Raff sighed. 'I know, fam. Just toofs sounds better.' He got up and went over to Lucy's chest of drawers. 'Anyway,' he said, dropping to his knees and pulling out the bottom drawer. 'Look.'

Jonah went and squatted by his brother. The drawer was amazingly neat, probably the only neat part of the house, and a sweet, forgotten smell rose out of it, like a loving ghost. On the left there was a pile of baby clothes, all carefully folded. On the right were cardboard boxes of various sizes, from shoebox to matchbox, some of them lidded, some open.

Raff picked up one of the smallest boxes and opened it. 'Look, fam,' he said.

Inside the box were some small white lumps, like pearls. Jonah gazed at them for a moment, his heart in his throat. He put a finger in the box and counted them. 'Eight,' he said. 'Six are mine and two are yours.' Raff opened his hand to let the seventh tooth drop into the box and closed the lid.

Jonah surveyed the drawer, a secret container of order. It was like the things inside were her precious jewels. He pulled out another box – red, battered, very old. It had a few pieces of folded-up paper in it. He opened one. The paper was thin and dry. It was a child's writing, but not his or Raff's. The ink was faded, and it was hard to read.

Today was quit fun we went to the zoo we sow crockodils and aslo
a snak in a tanck it was asleep and next to it was a tinny berd.
The berd wos so fritened.

There was a drawing of the bird, and the huge snake. The
bird was just two circles, with dots for eyes, little crosses
for its feet and a 'v' for a beak, but it did look frightened.

It is crool to put the berd in with the snak wot do yu think mayo
sinserly

  LUCY NSANSA MWEMBE PS I miss yu xxxxxx

'Who wrote that?' asked Raff, pulling it off him. 'Was it you?'
  'Be careful, Raff! No, it was Lucy. When she was a little
girl. It's a letter to her Mayo.'
  'What, but she never sent it?'
  'I suppose . . .' Jonah thought, drifting his fingers among
the folds of paper. 'Maybe when her Mayo died, she got
given it back.'
  'The writing is rubbish. She should of done finger spaces.'
  Jonah pulled out another piece of paper. A grown-up's
writing, but not joined up: the writing a grown-up does for
a child.

Dear Lucy
I hope you are being a good girl for Auntie. A little bird
told me you won your race in the Gala! Well done, and keep
it up. Maybe one day you will be a World Champion! I am
tired today, malaika, so just a short one today.
  Love Mayo xx

'Who's that one from?' asked Raff.

'From Lucy's Mayo.'

'I thought she was dead.'

'She is. It's from when she was alive.'

'"*Dear Lucy*",' Raff read, over his shoulder. 'Why is it in English?'

'She spoke English. She was white. Don't you remember the photograph? In Lucy's necklace?'

'Oh yeh. But why is she called Mayo, then?'

Jonah shrugged. 'She must have spoken Zambian too.' Not Zambian. There were lots of Zambian languages. The one Lucy's family spoke was Bemba.

Raff squinted at the faded letters. '"A little bird" . . . What kind of bird?'

'A little one.'

'Weird.' Raff tried to read some more. 'You can't even see it, fam! Did she write it with invisible ink? Was she a spy?'

'It's just old, Raff.' Jonah took both the letters and put them back in the red box. He looked at the baby clothes. On top of the pile was a pale blue sleep suit, dotted with yellow elephants. He picked it up and sniffed it. The forgotten, powdery smell, from when Raff was a baby and he was a toddler.

'I can remember you wearing this,' He shook it out and held it up. 'You used to crawl around, but your legs didn't stay in the legs, so you had these long empty legs trailing after you like tails.'

Raff took the sleep suit and sniffed it too.

'Do you remember it?' Jonah asked.

Raff shook his head.

Jonah reached across into an open shoebox, and pulled out two tiny white plastic bracelets. '"Raphael Bupe

Armitage",' he read out. 'Raff, this was your one. They put it on you so you wouldn't get mixed up with any of the other babies.'

Raff took it. He could only get two fingers into the bracelet. Jonah looked down at his own. 'Jonah Kabwe Armitage'. Kabwe meant 'little stone', but he couldn't remember what Bupe meant.

'What's this?' That little rattling sound. The stripy monkey! Tiny. Raff was dangling it from between his finger and thumb.

'That's what I gave you. When you were born.' In that big hospital room, Raff just a little bundle. 'I gave it to you, and you held it. You were a very strong baby, Raffy.' Strong and fierce.

Raff snorted and dropped the toy back in the shoebox. 'That's just what Mayo told you. You can't even remember.'

'Yes I can!' Could he? Or was it that Lucy had told him the story of Raff being born so many times that he had pictures of it in his head as strong as memories? He dipped his head to catch more of the smell that was coming from the drawer. 'What about ghosts, Raff? Do you believe in them?'

'Like the ones by the pond?'

'Yes, dead people. Their spirits. Waiting to go to Heaven.'

Raff shrugged. 'Maybe. Sometimes.'

'Have you ever seen one?'

'Have you?'

'Maybe.' Jonah thought about seeing his three uncles. 'I'm not sure.'

'That's it.' Raff sighed. 'How do you know if it's God, or spirits, or fairies, or if your head's just making them up?'

'Lucy says you can make things true if you believe
them.'

'Yeh, but she's full of shit.'

'Don't say shit, Raff! And anyway, she's not.'

'What's this?' Raff had picked up the letter from Roland.

'It's from Daddy. Just after he went to prison.'

'Oh.' He passed it to Jonah, and started leafing through
the pile of printed papers.

Jonah turned to the last page.

Time is going very slowly, which is changing the way I think.
Maybe it's just that I think more about the past. For example,
right now, I am remembering the first time I saw you, in
Dahab, up in the yoga room, with the sunset streaming in.
You arrived late, I was already lying on my mat, and I stopped
breathing, because you were floating in the doorway, all lit
up, and your face was like a Chinese lantern. You took the
space next to me, and I watched your feet, and your toes had
gold rings on them, and red nail paint. When you crouched
down to unroll your mat, you smelt of seaweed and coconut. I
lay very still, waiting for you to look back at me, waiting for
our eyes to touch. But when you looked, there was nothing. I
was nobody.

I had looked at pretty girls before, and realised that they
would never be interested in me. But it had never hurt quite
so much. I got over it, though. When you got ill a couple of
days later, you were just someone who needed looking after, and
I knew how to do that. And you were so ill that you let me,
even though it felt strange to you, because no one had ever
looked after you, before that.

So now I have written you a love letter. I have told you that *your face is like a Chinese lantern. I'm glad. I've always wanted to tell you that.*

I love you.

Ro

PS Can I ask you to do one thing, Lu? Even if you can't forgive her. Let Sadie see the boys? Just now and then?

'"Ro". Who's that?' Raff was peering over his shoulder.

'Daddy. Roland.'

'I didn't know he was called Ro.'

'*What do you think of this, Ro!*' Lucy, in her new red jump-suit. '*I got it from the Oxfam shop. It's genuine 70s!*' Her voice chirpy, a bit cockney; but she had mainly called him 'Roland', with her formal, Zambian voice.

'He wrote "I love you" and crossed it out,' said Raff. 'Who's Sadee?'

'Sadie. It's Bad Granny.'

'"Let – Sa – dee – see – the – boys." So he *wanted* Mayo to take us to see Bad Granny? Didn't he know she'd just try and steal us?'

'Raffy . . .' Jonah sighed. It was too complicated to explain.

'Does Daddy want me to go to an orphanage too?'

Jonah looked up from the letter. 'No,' he said firmly. 'Daddy really loves you.'

'Even though I'm browner than you?'

'Why should he care if you're browner than me?'

Raff shrugged and said nothing.

'He loves us both the same, Raff,' said Jonah softly.

'Even though I might not be his son?'

'Raffy! You *are* his son! We are both his boys! We're brothers!'

'Anyway.' Raff had had enough of thinking about it. He stood up, tugging at his hair again. 'What about food? I's *hungry*, man!'

'Get dressed then. We're going to get some breakfast.'

37

Alison's dark green door had a gold letter box, and a gold knocker, and a gold number 9. Jonah tried to smooth his shirt. Their clothes were all crumpled and damp and funny-smelling, but they'd put them on anyway. He looked at Raff, and tried to smooth his hair down onto his scalp. It didn't work. He reached up and banged the knocker.

They waited, listening to Alison calling to Mabel and Greta, and her steps coming towards them. As the door opened, there was a smell of shampoo and fresh coffee.

'OK, boys?' said Alison, frowning down at them. Her damp hair was making wet patches on her white shirt, and one side of it wasn't tucked in. Jonah looked down the hall and into the kitchen, where Greta and Mabel were sitting, looking back at him. They had their schoolbooks in front of them, which reminded him that Wednesday was the day you had to give in your homework.

'What can I do for you?' Alison said, looking at her watch.

'Actually . . .' The impatience in her eyes made Jonah pause. He looked past her again. Mabel and Greta were listening hard. He took a breath. 'We were just wondering if you had any spare cereal you could give us.'

Alison stared at him, and then looked back over her shoulder. 'OK girls, hurry up please, we're leaving in five.' She stepped out onto the doorstep and looked over at their house. 'Hasn't your mum been shopping?'

'She's not very well.'

'So she sends you over here.' Alison made a strange whimpering noise. 'The thing is, we've finished breakfast and the girls are doing their homework.'

'I didn't mean for us to come in,' Jonah said quickly. 'Just, if you had a bit of . . .'

'And actually it's my first day at a new job, Jonah. I've got to be there by half past nine and I've got to do my hair.'

'It's fine,' said Jonah. 'Come on, Raff.'

'Oh, don't just . . . !' Alison grabbed Jonah's arm. 'Have you *really* not got any breakfast?'

'It's fine.'

'I'm going to have to talk to the school about this.'

'Please don't. I'm sorry. We won't do it again.' Raff had kept on walking and was already nearly back at their house.

'Jonah, I don't want to get you into trouble, and I know it's not your fault, but your mum can't send you knocking at people's doors begging for food.' Alison was actually squeezing his arm quite hard, and anger burst out of him.

'Let go! I'm not begging, I meant, can we borrow it, and don't blame her because she doesn't even know!'

Alison dropped his arm and stepped back, shocked. Jonah turned and ran after Raff.

'Look right and left before you cross!' she called after him.

38

'That was one dumb idea, fam.' Raff was back in Lucy's bedroom, kneeling among her clothes.

'Well, you think of one, if you're so clever.'

'I already have. Pockets.' He was rooting around in her denim shorts. 'These are what she wore to the swimming pool, and she had to pay us in, didn't she.'

'We have to go to school, Raff.'

'I ain't going to school with no breakfast, fam.' Raff held the shorts upside down and shook them. The bloodstained pants fell to the floor. 'Yuk.'

'Hold on.' A whizzing had started in Jonah's brain. He looked around at all the clothes on the floor.

'What?' Raff looked up at him.

Jonah gazed down at the row of her shoes. He'd only been thinking about her feet. Barefoot was one thing, but to leave the house completely naked . . .

'You look weird,' said Raff. 'What's up?'

His heart thudding hard in his chest, Jonah went to the bed and dug under Lucy's pillows. Her nightie was there, the old yellow one that she had been wearing on Sunday morning, sitting on the corduroy cushion.

She wasn't even wearing her nightie.

'How much is this?' Raff had pulled out a few coins from the pocket of the grey cardigan. They were all brown. Jonah shook his head, and went to look in the wardrobe. Some dresses, her red jumpsuit, something swathed in plastic, because it had been dry-cleaned.

'Isn't it enough for Coco Pops?' Raff came to stand next to him and watched him leafing through the clothes. 'There won't be none in those,' he said. 'They haven't got pockets. What we need is to find her purse.'

Her purse. Yes, her purse. Jonah stared blindly into Raff's face. Her purse was bound to be here somewhere, because no one who went out barefoot and naked would take their purse.

'Swimming bag!' said Raff and shot out of the room.

The wasps buzzed ominously in the plum crate as they pulled the smelly towels and swimming costumes out of the bag. Her purse was at the bottom of the bag. Raff held it up, triumphant, then opened it and turned it upside down. A few plastic cards clattered to the floor, and some receipts. Amongst them, bluish and very grimy, was a five-pound note.

'Is it enough?' Raff whispered.

'It's enough for some Coco Pops, definitely . . .'

'Yessss!' Raff shot his fist into the air.

'. . . and maybe some toilet paper . . .'

'Yesss!'

'But the thing is, Raff,' he said, spreading the note out on his knee. 'We have to make it last.'

'Until when? Until she comes back, you mean?'

The wasps buzzed. Jonah stared at his swimming trunks,

remembering gliding like a manta ray, looking up at her feet with the toe-rings, and then the red shape of her, above the ceiling of water.

'Wait a minute.' He rummaged through the towels, and then turned back to the bag. 'Is her sarong in here?'

'Her sarong?'

'She wore it at the swimming pool.' Her red silk sarong, big as a bed-sheet – another present from Dora. It went round her body twice, tied in a big knot on her chest, and hung nearly down to the ground. 'Where is it?'

'I dunno.'

Jonah stood up. He ran back up to the bedroom and kicked through all the clothes. He knew he hadn't seen it, but just to be sure he checked in his and Raff's room, and in the bathroom. He came back downstairs and looked in the sitting room and the kitchen, and then stepped out into the yard.

The rain had stopped completely, and there was that steaminess in the air again, like on Saturday, when Lucy was still upstairs in bed. The corduroy cushion was soaked, and there was some water sitting in the dip Lucy's bottom had made. Violet was there, sniffing around the flowerpots. She looked up at him.

'It's not here,' he told the fox. 'So she's wearing it. She isn't naked.'

Violet jumped briefly onto Lucy's gold bicycle, and from there up to the top of the wall. Jonah watched her slink along it and then disappear down into the gully between the wall and the Broken House. Then a face appeared above the wall.

It was a head and nothing else, like Humpty Dumpty, but not like Humpty Dumpty at all, because it was the grizzly, charred-looking face of the Raggedy Man. Jonah froze, like an animal. The face disappeared. Still frozen, Jonah stared at the space where it had been. It appeared again, this time with hands, shoulders and a chest. The Raggedy Man was levering himself up onto the wall.

Jonah fled back into the house, closing the door and trying to lock it with trembling fingers. 'Quick, Raff, he's coming!' He gave up trying to turn the key and ran to Raff, who was sitting on the stairs, still examining the five-pound note.

'Who's coming?'

'The Raggedy Man! He's coming over the wall!'

'The back wall?' Raff stood up and strode into the kitchen.

'Raffy!' Jonah hissed after him.

'Oh Em Gee! Raggedy Man, what's your *game!*'

Jonah followed. The Raggedy Man was now complete, looming pinkly against the grimy bricks of the Broken House. They watched him walk along the wall, his broken trainers flapping, his head high. At the end of the wall he paused, and then dropped down into Wanless Road.

'Oh Em Gee!' Raff said again.

'He must live in there,' said Jonah. 'He must have been asleep in that bed when the council came and shut him in.'

'Coco Pops,' said Raff.

39

The radio was on loud in the Green Shop, and behind the counter the Green Shop Man was shouting into his mobile phone as he shoved a shopper's things into a plastic bag. Raff headed for the aisle with the Coco Pops. Jonah picked up a basket. Thinking of the smell in the kitchen, he stopped at the incense rack and pulled out a packet of Nag Champa. It was £1.99 so he put it back. He put toilet paper and a tin of beans in the basket, doing sums in his head. Raff now had the Coco Pops tucked under his arm and was looking at the sweets rack.

'We can't buy sweets, we haven't got enough money', Jonah told him. 'I don't know if we can even have the Coco Pops.'

'It's my money.' Raff picked out some bubble gum.

'No, it's not!'

'I found it. Baked beans are yuk.' Raff took the can out of the basket and tried to lodge it on a tray of chocolate bars.

'OK, but we need to buy proper things to eat.' He prised the Coco Pops from under his brother's arm.

'Who cares, fam!' Raff yanked the box away from him,

and Jonah tried to yank it back, but Raff wrapped his arms around it, squashing the cardboard.

'Raff, I just want to see how much they are!'

Raff's arms tightened, crumpling the box even more.

'Raff, I'm really hungry, so just stop messing about!' Jonah put the basket down and tried to wrestle the box from him. Raff kicked him hard on the shin. They scuffled, and the torn box fell to the floor, and Jonah stood on it, and the bag inside give way. Then there were Coco Pops crunching under his feet. He looked down at the mess, trying to keep Raff at arm's length.

'Hey! You kids!'

The Green Shop Man turned the radio off. In the silence, they looked at each other. There was a squeak as the little gate at the end of the counter opened, and they both dropped to their knees and started sweeping the Coco Pops into the gap under the shelving. 'If he makes us pay for it, I'm going to kill you, Raff,' whispered Jonah.

There was a shuffling noise, and two shoes appeared, right next to him. The shoes were made of that shiny black leather, but they were all cracked and battered, with frayed bits sticking up, so they looked like giant cockroaches. Out of the shoes came two wrinkly nylon legs, so thin Jonah could have touched his thumbs to his index fingers around them. He looked up. Bright, beady eyes under wonky, drawn-on eyebrows, a black furry coat and a red woolly hat. She was shaking her head and pursing her lips, but her huge cockroach feet were busy pushing more of the spilt Coco Pops under the shelf. Then she reached for the box and popped it inside her coat, just as the Green Shop Man came into the aisle. He still had his phone pressed to his ear.

'What you doing, idiot kids? Is my shop a playground now?'

He picked their basket up off the floor and handed it to the old woman. Shaking her head still, she took it and started shuffling away.

'Actually it's . . .' Jonah tried to reach for the basket, but the Green Shop Man slapped his hand away.

'Idiot!' he shouted, his anger suddenly rising to dangerous levels. 'Why you troubling an old lady, what you want from her!'

The old woman looked back at him, her mouth working, her crazy eyebrows moving up and down.

'It's actually . . .' Jonah looked up into the Green Shop Man's furious face. He wanted to explain, but Raff was heading for the door, and the Green Shop Man was shouting again. 'Your mama needs to know about this! You used to be good boys, but now look at you!'

Jonah turned and ran after Raff.

40

Raff was running up Wanless Road, the way they didn't usually go, away from the bridge and the car repair yard, towards the flats where Harold lived. Jonah ran after him, looking over his shoulder to see if the Green Shop Man was chasing them. There was no sign of him. He slowed down and shouted to Raff, but Raff was still sprinting, getting further and further away. *Run, run, as fast as you can* . . . The Gingerbread Man was cocky, but it was such a *scary* story, and the fox had got him in the end, thrown him up into the air and wolfed him down. Jonah increased his speed, trying to call Raff's name, but he was already breathless. He caught up with him just as he reached the flats.

'Where are you going?' he gasped.

Raff turned off the road and ran down a litter-strewn footpath between two buildings. Jonah followed him, right, then left, past Harold's flat and into a tunnel. They were soon deep in a maze of walkways, heading into the unknown heart of the estate. There was no one around, just cars and rubbish. *Run, run, as fast as you can* . . . Washing hung like flags from all the balconies, and spray-canned words and signs shouted out from doors and walls. Then there was music coming from somewhere, a rapping, screechy voice over a bone-shaking electric bass, and a smell of burning. Jonah's thudding feet were hurting. How was Raff managing to run so fast? There was no need anyway: the Green Shop Man was definitely not chasing them. He slowed, enough to be able to glance into a window as he passed it, and saw a very old man watching TV in just his baggy white underpants. When he looked back, he couldn't see Raff any more. There was no point in calling out his name, the music was too loud. He slowed to a walk, breathing heavily. The thought came to him that Lucy was here somewhere, in one of the flats, in her red sarong, with her boyfriend, their baby a tiny tadpole inside her tummy.

The music stopped. It was a relief to his ears, but there was something spooky about the sudden silence. It was as if something was about to happen. He turned into another narrow walkway, wishing he hadn't lost sight of Raff. The walkway took him out into a square and he lifted his hand to shade his eyes. The square was mainly a parking area, but there was a circle of grass in the middle, with a small playground on it. Raff had come to a stop there, and was in the athletes' recovery position, bent over, with his hands on his thighs. The square seemed deserted, but there could be people watching them from indoors. Was *she* watching them? Jonah looked up at the balconies, which stuck out on all four sides. They were like empty boxes in an open-air theatre, with just him and Raff on the stage.

Come out onto the balcony, Mayo. Was the boyfriend keeping her prisoner? *Shout out. We'll come and rescue you.* Somewhere, a dog started barking, and the sense of her being there, so close, melted away. His feet were sweating into his school socks and shoes, and he was thirsty, he realised, really, really thirsty. He looked over at the playground, which might have a water fountain in it. The green-painted metal fence around it had orange and white tape wrapped around it, and there was a sign saying, 'Unsafe. Do Not Enter'. He suddenly realised they weren't alone. Two hooded teenagers had ignored the sign and were sitting, motionless, on the swings.

Run, run, as fast as you can . . . Jonah licked his dry lips. The sky felt very close, like a grey quilted ceiling, and the light from it was making his head hurt. The boys on the swings must be boiling in their hoodies. Raff cleared his throat and spat a huge gob onto the ground, and the teenagers turned their hooded heads.

'Raffy,' Jonah whispered. Raff spat again and straightened up. The teenagers watched him as he walked to the padlocked gate and climbed over.

'Raffy.' Jonah called his name now, his voice quivering, as he moved towards the gate. 'Come back out! We've got to go to school!'

'Raffy! We've got to go to school!' mimicked the fatter teenager, his voice high and silly. The other one cackled and took a swig from his Red Bull can.

There's no such thing as baddies. Jonah looked up at the balconies. If he wished hard enough, could he make her appear? He looked back at Raff, who had jumped onto the climbing frame and was climbing to the top. Once there, he fished something out of his pocket. The bubble gum. *Thief!* Jonah looked over his shoulder. Would the Green Shop Man have noticed the missing packet? Would he have phoned the police?

The teenagers stood up. The one with the can was very

thin, with baggy jeans. The fatter one was wearing tracksuit bottoms. They walked over to the climbing frame, the fatter one's flipflops slapping the playground's rubber flooring. Jonah hoisted himself over the gate and went to stand next to the Thin One.

'Come down, Raffy!' he croaked.

'*Raffy*, you better do what you're told,' said Flipflop. He was white, with orange freckles, and he smelt of sweat and crisps. The Thin One was white too, with grey skin and dull, hooded eyes. When he noticed Jonah looking up at him, he drew his lips back, showing long yellow teeth. *Fear is a magnet. It can actually make bad things happen . . .* But Roland had said that was rubbish. He said bad things happened anyway, and that she shouldn't teach them to be daredevils. Jonah looked up at the balconies. There was no one else, anywhere. Just the four of them.

'Can I have a swig from your can, mate?' asked Raff from above, cocky as the Gingerbread Man. Both teenagers looked up. Raff, chewing, raised one eyebrow and showed a dimple. There was a moment's silence, and then the Thin One held up his can. Raff made his way down and sat on a bar. He took the can, legs swinging.

'Like the hair,' said the Thin One.

Raff grinned and drank, then offered the can back.

'Finish it,' said the Thin One.

'Ta, mate,' said Raff. He took the gum out of his mouth before knocking the drink back. He was gaining more and more confidence, but there was something in the Thin One's face and voice that made Jonah cold inside. He watched him fish a packet of smokes from the back pocket of his jeans and light up, his cheeks disappearing as his thin lips sucked and sucked, like a skeleton.

'Can I have a smoke too?' Raff had put the gum back in his mouth, and his cheeky eyebrow had darted up again.

'Raffy!' hissed Jonah. Raff grinned and dropped the scrunched can on the ground.

'He your brother?' the Thin One asked Raff. 'He needs to relax a bit, don't he.'

Raff's grin widened. Why was he such a fool? He was reckless, like Lucy. Jonah looked down at the packet he was now being offered and shook his head.

'Come on, mate. Help you relax,' the Thin One said. He looked over at Flipflop. 'This kid needs to relax, Jase. Shall we help him?'

Raff shuffled along the bar and tried to pull a smoke out of the packet for himself, but with an angry snarl the Thin One snatched it away. Raff's smile evaporated.

'Did I say you could have one? Did I? You half-caste runt!' The Thin One grabbed a bunch of Raff's hair and forced him to jump to the ground.

Fear is a magnet . . . But Jonah's belly had filled with ice. 'Let go of him,' he managed to whisper.

'You need to watch your manners!' said the Thin One. 'We saw you spitting. Do you think it's OK, to spit like that?'

'No.' Raff's eyes were huge and terrified. The Thin One made a tunnel with his lips and blew. The sight of the spit on Raff's cheekbone was like the force of a snooker cue, smashing Jonah's fear into an explosion of fury.

'You let go of him!' he shouted, hurling himself at the Thin One's denim legs. Flipflop dragged him off, smothering him with his wet clamminess, pinning his arms down by his sides. The Thin One still had Raff's hair, and Raff was whimpering, his eyes rolling to the side, trying to find Jonah's. Jonah tried to move but couldn't. 'Please don't hurt my brother,' he croaked.

'Have a cigarette and shut the fuck up,' said the Thin One, offering Jonah the packet again, but this time right into his face. 'Go on.' He shook one out, and rested it against his closed lips. 'Fucking take it, or I break this mongrel's nose.' He pulled Raff's hair harder, lifting him onto his toes, and Raff cried out again.

Jonah's knees were shaking badly, and his lips very dry and cracked, but he managed to take the smoke. Sticking out of his mouth, it felt very long, and it trembled like his body.

'Give the kid a light, Jase,' the Thin One said, slipping the packet back in his pocket. Flipflop let go of Jonah's arms and took hold of the back of his shirt instead. There was a tiny metal sound, and then a flame being held to the tip of the smoke.

'Suck!' said Flipflop. 'You got to suck!'

Jonah sucked. Smoke filled his mouth and heat hit the back of his throat. He coughed, and the smoke fell out of his mouth and onto the bouncy rubber. Flipflop reached down for it with one arm, pulling at Jonah's shirt with the other, so that his collar cut into his throat. Jonah gasped and grabbed at his collar, panic surging through him, but then Flipflop screamed and let go of his shirt. He knelt, nursing his hand. Raff, fierce and strong, had managed to stamp on his fingers.

'I said you need to learn some manners, you little piece of shit!' roared the Thin One, jerking Raff's head, but Jonah kicked, and it was an incredible kick, like the Karate Kid had taken over his body. The top of his foot thwacked denim and the squidgy package inside it, and a sound started – an amazing, high-pitched sound – which seemed to be coming from the Thin One's mouth.

'Run, Jonah, run!' screamed Raff. Flipflop had lumbered to his feet and was shouting and trying to grab them, but the Thin One was bent double, both hands on his crotch, still making that horrible noise. Jonah took Raff's hand and they both sprinted to the gate, Flipflop flipflopping after them. If they could just get over before he managed to actually take hold of either of them, before the Thin One recovered . . . Raff went first, tipping over on his tummy and slithering down onto his hands and knees. Jonah managed to vault it and pulled Raff up to his feet. Then they ran, back across the car park and into the concrete maze, faster than they had ever run, or ever would: faster than Oscar, faster than Usain, faster even than a peregrine falcon.

41

They had come out of the estate onto an unfamiliar road, and had kept on running for a while, with no idea of where they were going. As the roads got leafier and the houses got bigger, they slowed down. Both panting too hard to talk, they walked side by side.

Suddenly recognising where they were, Jonah pointed to the turning ahead. 'Bellevue Road,' he croaked.

Bellevue Road was olden-days-looking, with cobbles and Narnia lamp posts, and baskets of flowers hanging off poles. There were a few people sitting at tables outside cafés, and Jonah scanned their faces to check if there was anyone who might recognise them and ask them why they weren't at school. Still panting, Raff took his arm and pulled him into Harvey's.

They'd been to Harvey's a few times, with Saviour, who thought it was the best fish and chip shop in London. There was always a long queue, but it was worth it, Saviour said. At that time of day, though, it was empty, apart from the girl at the counter, who was reading a magazine. Raff went straight over to the drinks fridge and opened the door.

'Wait,' said Jonah. His mouth was so dry he could hardly

speak, but he knew that drinks in Harvey's would be much
more than in the Green Shop. Raff pulled two Coke cans
out of the fridge. They were freezing, you could tell from
the steam that came off them.

Jonah stared at them. 'Just one. We can share.'

Raff shrugged and put one back, and carried the other
one to the counter. Jonah pulled the five-pound note out of
his pocket.

'One pound fifty,' said the girl.

Jonah gasped, but Raff plucked the note out of his hand.
Once they'd got the change, they went outside and stood
in the shade of the awning. Raff tugged the tab off, releasing
air and liquid, in a creamy, glistening foam. Jonah watched
Raff's throat as he glugged.

'That's enough.' He reached for it, but Raff held up his
hand and kept glugging. When he finally passed Jonah the
can it was practically empty.

'Raff!' Tears sprang to Jonah's eyes, and he shoved his
brother hard.

'I left you a bit!' Raff steadied himself. 'You can always
buy another one.'

'You took the Thin One's drink, and nearly got us killed!
And you stole that bubble gum! I fucking hate you, Raff,
because you are not a snooker ball, you have a choice, you
are a bad person who does bad things, and I never, ever
want to see you again!'

Raff's face slammed shut. He shrugged and walked away,
hands in his pockets, across the road, past the flower shop
and around the corner, while Jonah gulped the last of the
Coke, scrunched the can and, still crazy with anger, threw
it hard into the road.

It looked weird, a piece of litter on Bellevue Road, and he looked around, expecting someone to tell him off. No one had seen. Shouting had made the crack in his bottom lip open up, and blood was now trickling down his chin. He sat down on the pavement, with his arms around his knees and his back to the shiny green bricks.

OK, Lucy, you need to come now. He pictured her, coming towards him over the cobbles, arms opening to scoop him up – but it was just his brain, imagining her. 'Dear God,' he whispered. He put his hands together and closed his eyes, trying to see God's face, but for some reason it was the Raggedy Man's he saw. *Please, God.* He opened his eyes and closed them again, trying to get rid of the Raggedy Man. *Please, make her come back. Please God. Make her come now.* But prayers only worked if you believed that they would. He closed his eyes tighter, trying and trying to believe, trying to get rid of the Raggedy Man and see Ganesha's twinkling eye. When he opened them, there was just the emptiness of the cobbles, and the Narnia lamp posts and the grey sky.

Wishing Raff hadn't gone, Jonah gazed at the woman choosing flowers out of the buckets in front of the flower shop. He licked his bloody lips, watching her pick out two lilies and tap her fingers on her chin, before going for some dark red roses.

'*The intricate husks of them, on their way to dusk.*'

Her murmuring voice, the pencil moving on the paper, her strange, sad eyes, gazing at her skeleton flowers. Why hadn't he asked her who'd sent them? What would she have said, if he had? The woman handed her flowers to the flower-shop man, who took them inside the shop. The woman took her purse out of her bag and pulled out two notes. Expensive. His hand closed around the four coins left in his pocket. *Was it your new boyfriend, Lucy? He must be rich, to be able to afford those flowers.* Angry Saturday started flashing again: the big house, the front door with the stained-glass poppy pattern, the screaming, the sound of the ambulance, its blue light. Trying to get rid of it, he stared hard at the flower-shop man, who had come back out with the flowers, now wrapped in dark green paper and tied with straw. The woman handed him the money.

Jonah pulled the four coins out of his pocket. Three pounds and fifty pence. It was alright for Raff, he wasn't the eldest, he didn't need to sort things out. *Letting money flow is all very well, but I haven't ever noticed it flowing back to you.* They'd been really poor since Roland went to prison. Before that, just a bit poor. Raff wouldn't remember, but Roland used to tell Lucy off for buying things all the time. What kind of things had she bought? He tried to remember. Clothes. Make-up. Wine. And *she* would say, back to Roland, '*Well, what about your betting?*' And Roland would point out that he never bet more than a fiver, and also that he quite often won.

Jonah gazed at the coins. His tongue found the hole in his mouth, and he heard her Zambian doctor's voice. '*This tooth is movious . . .*' She hadn't really minded about the betting; she just said it when he had a go at her about buying things. Sometimes she had even joined in, looking over their shoulders while they studied the form on Saturday mornings, and choosing her own horse from the list in the newspaper. She didn't even pretend to care about how much they weighed, or what kind of ground they preferred; she went by the sound of their names. On Grand National Day she had chosen a horse that was 100 to 1, and it had won, and she'd got £300. Roland had been amazed. *'Maybe there's something in your system.'* She'd smiled, counting her money, her eyes all sparkly. *'I keep telling you. You just have to* believe, *Roland!'* The horse was called something like Mon Momy, he remembered. The jockey's silk was a beautiful bright green, with a stripe of yellow and a splash of purple. Like a parrotfish. Like Roland's parrotfish, who had died.

Four parrotfish, three angelfish and eight swordtails. He and Raff used to sit and watch Roland's fish for hours. Dylan used to watch them too. If only they'd have bought some more fish food, instead of feeding them cornflakes. The next day they were all floating on the surface, swollen up. On their next visit to Roland, while they were waiting with the other visitors in the glass room, Lucy had told him not to say about the cornflakes.

'Let's just tell him the fish sadly died, and leave it at that.'

'But isn't that lying?'

'Not really.'

Roland had been so upset, and so puzzled about why they'd died, that he'd told him – blurting it out, across the prison visiting-room table. From the look that Roland gave Lucy, it was clear that not telling him *had* been lying. *'Thank you for telling me, Jonah,'* he'd said, and he'd reached over and cupped his face in his big knobbly hand. But when they got home, Lucy had said that a lie isn't a real lie if you told it to prevent harm or suffering, and that Roland might have been better off not knowing about the cornflakes.

Are you a good person, Lucy? Jonah jingled the coins in his hand and pictured her counting her notes, smiling and smiling. '*I keep telling you. You just have to* believe, *Roland!*' He stared down at the four coins. If he believed . . . if he believed what she believed . . . 'You know what, Raffy,' he whispered, 'I think I've got a plan.'

42

He set off in the direction of Southway Street, hoping that Raff had gone home. He walked quickly, excited at the thought of his plan, but as he put the coins back into his pocket, he felt the metal clump of door keys and realised that Raff wouldn't be able to get into the house, not even the back way, now that the Broken House fence had been mended. He transferred the coins into his other pocket, so that he wasn't weighed down on one side, and as he did so his dream suddenly came back to him, the one in the Tibetan monastery. A flash of red and a hand opening, showing him something – but then it had gone again. He tried to bring it back, but all he could get was a taste, a trace; then he saw, out of the corner of his eye, a teenager, a skinny white teenager, crossing the road towards him.

It was like his heart had exploded in his chest. He stopped, shaking, knowing he should run, but the force of the shock meant he had no control over his legs. Of course they weren't going to get away with it: after that kick, the Thin One was always going to track them down. Raff had probably already been caught and was being kept prisoner by Flipflop.

It wasn't until the older boy had stepped onto the kerb and passed him without looking at him that he realised it wasn't the Thin One at all – he didn't look anything like him.

He set off again, his heart still thudding, his legs wobbly. He had to find Raffy. He shouldn't have let him go off on his own. What if the real Thin One had already found him? What if he and his Flipflop friend were torturing him some-where? An ice-cream van passed him, and the sudden blast of its bright jingly tune made him jump. *'Lollipops, children! Come and get your lollipops!'* What if the orphanage van had come and scooped up Raffy, when he was all alone? What if he was never going to see him again?

Jonah slowed down, trying to breathe himself calm. There was no such thing as an orphanage van. There was no such thing as the Child Catcher. And the Thin One would have forgotten all about them by now. Raff would be sitting on the doorstep, waiting for him. He kept walking, the dread still with him. The parked cars all looked at him with their wide-apart glass eyes, their mouths full of letters and numbers. Should he look at the letters and numbers more carefully, try and work out what the cars were trying to tell him? Were those gods in their togas looking down and shaking their heads?

On Southway Street, a couple of the squatters were outside their house: Ilaria, in her usual grubby white clothes, and the one with the bald head and the weird earrings who'd been smoking on the doorstep on Monday evening. He was making a smoke now, one of those big ones which had made Lucy ill, licking the little white papers and sticking them together. The sky was whitening as the sun tried to bore its way through. There was no sign of Raff.

In the house, to let the bad air out, he left the front door open and batted his way through the flies to open the back door too. He went to check upstairs, just in case Raff had managed to get in somehow, but he hadn't. He sank down onto their bedroom floor and lay there for a moment, his face buried in his arms. *I've lost him, Mayo. I've lost Raffy. I shouldn't have . . .* He shouldn't have shouted at him about finishing the drink. And then he shouldn't have let him go off like that. He had anger management, like Roland. And either it was his fault and he would get punished by the karma boomerang, or he was just a snooker ball, in which case what was the point of trying to be good, trying to help other people, or do anything at all?

He propped himself onto his elbows and looked at the poor Yonghy's tortured face, and at the crazy Lady Jingly, weeping and twirling her fingers. 'I'm a-weary of my life.' He whispered Yonghy's words, tracing the line of Lady Jingly's long, slim body in its olden-days blue dress. 'If you'll come and be my wife. Quite serene would be my life.' Why *couldn't* she forget her stupid husband and live happily ever after with the Yonghy, and his chairs, and his candle, and his broken jug?

He went back down to the front door, and sat himself on the doorstep. A plane was going across the white sky, and the flies buzzed in the hall behind him. 'I actually feel really ill,' he said out loud, but Lucy wasn't there to hear him. Through blurred eyes, he noticed that there were more people about than usual. Ilaria and the bald squatter, sharing the big smoke, and the London Kebab Man, smoking too, leaning in his doorway; but also a group of people outside the Green Shop, all holding beer cans. Jonah checked the beer drinkers carefully. Not teenagers – they were all old, old and raggedy. One of them was the pirate man with the headscarf and the bright red face, who used to sing pop songs under the bridge, along to his two-stringed guitar. Once Lucy had let him and Raff drop some coins in his hat and, up close, the smell of him had been terrible.

But where was Raff? Jonah looked down Southway Street. Maybe, scared of bumping into the Thin One, and wanting lunch, he'd taken himself to school. Comforted, he looked back at the beer drinkers. The singing pirate and two women, one black and one white. He recognised them too, he'd seen them asking for money outside the train station. The white one was very small, with two sticky-out plaits. She looked like a little girl from a distance, but she was really old and wrinkly. The black one was younger. She had a shaved head and a gold tooth, and massive bosoms, jumbling around in her baggy black jumper. Not bosoms, boobs. They were being really loud, the pirate man shouting, the women cackling. Why wasn't the Green Shop Man chasing them away?

'Are you sick, too?'

It was Ilaria, calling to him from her doorstep, where she was sitting in the Lotus position, with each foot on the opposite thigh. She must be very flexible. Like Lucy. She had rings on her toes, like Lucy did, but hers were silver, not gold. The bald squatter must have gone inside. Trying to think what to say, he looked past her, into the gloom, noticing the crazy red and gold wallpaper. Their back door was open, like it had been on Monday.

'So you've seen Raff?' he called back.

'Yes. He couldn't get in.' She had the big smoke still, and she lifted it to her mouth and sucked. 'I don't think the teachers should be allowed to just release you like that.' She shook her head, holding the smoke in. 'You're too young. Especially Raffy. They should have phoned your mum.' Her words were quick and gaspy, and then the smoke came rushing out of her nostrils in two clouds, like she was a dragon. 'So she's back now, your mum?'

Jonah hesitated, and then shook his head. 'I've got a key.' He pulled it out of his pocket and showed it to her, but she'd turned to gaze over at the beer drinkers, who had all burst into screeching laughter.

Jonah stood up. 'Do you know where Raff went?' he called. She turned back, frowning, the smoke between her lips again. Then she coughed and banged her chest. 'Do you . . .' – he tried again, because she didn't seem to have heard him, but she interrupted him.

'That friend of yours was looking for you.'

The Thin One. Jonah felt that freezing of his insides. 'Which . . .?' He licked his lips.

'Is it Christian?' Ilaria took in some more smoke. 'Short guy. Heavy. Very tanned.'

'Oh, Saviour.'

'Saviour!' She smiled. 'He was knocking and shouting for a while. But earlier.'

Jonah nodded. He would have noticed that they hadn't arrived at school, and come round once Emerald was safely in the classroom. Knocking and shouting. He remembered Raff's question from the night before. 'Was he shouting for us?' he asked.

Ilaria smoked, nodding. 'Yes, for you. Who else?'

'I mean, was he . . .' He stopped. It was too complicated. 'Do you know where Raff went?'

'Back to school.' Ilaria nodded down Southway Street. 'I offered for him to come in here and have some beetroot juice, but he didn't want to.'

'Beetroot juice?' said Jonah, weakly.

'Yes. I just made it. Would you like some? Good for vata.' She unfolded her legs and stood up, throwing her smoke into the gutter.

'No, thank you.' Jonah felt himself smiling, at both the thought of Raff's face when he was offered beetroot juice, and of him now safely queuing for lunch in the school hall.

'Your brother didn't want any either.' She folded her arms. 'I can see he would feel shy, to come into our house. But we are quite friendly! Do you remember when you came to our party? Maybe you were too little.'

'I remember,' said Jonah. 'Anyway.' He looked down Southway Street, jingling the coins in his pocket. His plan. He would tell Raff. They'd go straightaway after school.

'Why not come inside, and wait for your mum?' Ilaria was on the kerb now, holding her hand out, inviting him to cross the greasy tarmac. 'We put the hammock up. Would you like to lie in the hammock?'

Jonah shook his head. 'Not right now, thanks.' The thought of lunch was making his stomach gurgle, and he was itching to see Raff, but he paused, not knowing how to leave Ilaria, who had folded her arms again and seemed hurt.

'Ilaria.'

'Yes.'

'Do you know what Om means?'

'Om?' She shrugged, her hands in her armpits. 'It's the sound of the universe.' She nodded up at the sky.

He looked too. The stratus was definitely thinning. The

sun would break through soon. He set off down Southway Street, jingling his coins; and then turned and waved, and she waved back, before disappearing into her red and gold corridor.

43

Jonah pressed the buzzer by the gate, and Christine bustled out of the school office and down the steps to let him in. 'What time do you call this?' She was wearing her usual blouse and jacket, and looked far too hot in them.

'I've been ill,' he said. 'We both have.'

'So where's your note?' She was steering him into the building, her hands on his shoulders. Feeling his shrug, she dug her fingers hard into the spaces around his bones, and he winced, and she let go. 'If I don't get a note by tomorrow, it goes down as unauthorised absence, Jonah. And the same goes for your brother.' She pushed back her sleeve to look at her watch. 'If you want anything to eat, you'd better be quick. They've nearly finished serving.'

Raff wasn't in the lunch hall, presumably because he'd already finished and was out in the playground. Jonah made a start on his meat pie, but it was cold and the pieces of meat were bouncy, like rubber. He pushed the plate away and went up for pudding, but there was none left, only fruit, so he put an orange in his pocket. He'd stopped feeling hungry anyway. All he wanted was to see Raff.

Outside, he peered through the fence into the Infants'

playground. Raff didn't seem to be there. Neither did Tameron, though, so maybe they'd been given permission to practise their rap in a classroom. He turned and wandered among the running, shouting children in the Juniors' playground, until he spotted Harold, sitting with his back against the toilet block wall.

'Have you found her?' Harold looked up at him, his glasses blazing in the sun.

'Her?' Raff was so much on his mind that it took Jonah a second to understand. 'Oh. No.' Jonah dropped down next to him and pulled out his orange. The peel was very thick and tough. He dug his fingernails into it, noticing how dirty they were, and realising his headache was still there.

'So where you been?' Harold was looking at him, his tiny, curious eyes now visible.

He shrugged and gave up on the orange, and they both gazed across the playground. Emerald and Pearl were standing by the fence, deep in conversation.

'Pearl's getting boobies,' said Harold. Boobies. Jonah looked at the two tiny bumps on Pearl's chest. 'You know periods,' he said.

'The blood thing.' Harold frowned.

Jonah stretched his legs out in front of him and leaned back, feeling the warm brick through his shirt. 'When the blood comes out, it's the egg coming out, right?'

'Yeh, bro. Disgusting.'

'But if the egg turns into a baby, then the period doesn't happen, does it?'

'This is to do with the white stick, right?' said Harold. Jonah nodded.

'Well, what?'

'Nothing. Just, maybe the stick said she wasn't pregnant.'

'Where is it? Let me look.' Harold held out his hand.

'I haven't got it.' Would it have sunk down to the bottom of the pond, or still be floating on the surface?

'Why not?'

Jonah remembered Saviour's snarling face. He shrugged again.

'What, you lost it! What is *wrong* with you!'

Jonah felt his jaws clench. The playground noise was too loud for his head and he closed his eyes.

'Have you still got the wine bottle? That's the best clue, because of the DNA . . .'

'Shut up, Harold.'

'What?' He felt Harold's body stiffen beside him.

'Nothing. Just . . .' He kept his eyes closed, feeling the warm brick again and the warmth on his face. 'You know how you go to church, and say prayers and stuff.'

'Yeh.'

'Well, does God ever say anything to you?'

'No.' Harold sounded very definite.

'But he hears you. And he . . .'

'To be honest, I don't even believe in him.'

'Oh.' Jonah paused. 'Why not?'

'Think about it, fam. The Bible says God created light in one day, right? By making the sun. And the sun is how many light years away, exactly?'

'I don't know.' Jonah could see where this was going.

'Say if it was only one light year away. So God had to wait a whole year before he could make the rest of it. Don't make sense.' Harold stretched and cracked his knuckles.

'It was a big bang that started everything off. Before that there was just nothing'.

Jonah was silent, remembering the underwatery feeling in Richmond Park.

Below the shouts and screams came the sound of grown-up, female footsteps. A shadow fell over his face, and the smell of rosewater. Miss Swann. He opened his eyes and looked at her legs, which were very white, with tiny black dots: sliced-off hairs, about to grow back out.

'*There* you are. Christine said you'd turned up. Where have you *been*, Jonah?'

He looked up. She was wearing another summer dress, a stretchy, clingy one, with a blue and white pattern. Her throat was blotchy still, and her forehead was all crunched up in the sun.

'I wasn't very well.' Jonah got to his feet, brushing gravel off his shorts. 'Neither was Raff,' he added.

'Is that so?' Miss Swann looked at her watch. 'Why don't we go inside,' she said. 'I want to have a quick talk with you before the bell rings.'

44

In the empty classroom, Miss Swann pulled a chair over to her desk for Jonah. The stretchy dress showed her hip bones and the droop of her belly. Lucy had a dress like that, a red one. Lucy's suited her better. Miss Swann sat down. He could smell her sweat, as well as the rosewater.

'You've been very pensive lately, Jonah. Do you know what pensive means?'

Jonah shook his head.

'It means quiet and thoughtful.'

He nodded.

'And troubled, maybe even sad.' She tucked her hair behind her ears, and he caught a glimpse of her armpits, which were bare, like Lucy's, not hairy, like Dora's.

'Are you sad, Jonah?'

Jonah shook his head. He was remembering Dora and Lucy talking about Miss Swann, after a Parents' Evening. On the sofas, him listening in that little cushioned space.

'*She's not bad looking. Bit washed out.*'

'*Yes, she could take better care of herself. Her hair is awful!*'

'I don't want to pry – do you know what "pry" means,

Jonah? It means being nosy. I hope you don't think I'm being nosy.'

He quickly looked into her face, not wanting her to think he thought she was nosy, and her eyes were full of kindness and worry. He stared at the blue and white pattern on her dress instead, his eyes blurring. *Should I tell her?* He strained to see Lucy's face, to hear the answer. He couldn't.

'I don't think you're nosy.' He cleared his throat.

Miss Swann leaned slightly forward, and he suddenly felt as if he *would* tell her. He would let himself cry properly, and she would put her arms around him and pull him onto her lap, and he would choke the words out.

'So what's up?' Her voice was low and soft.

He opened his mouth, but as he did, Lucy's laughing voice cut in. *'Her hair is awful!'*

'I'm OK,' he said.

'How's your mum?'

Tears suddenly forced themselves out of his eyes. Miss Swann opened the drawer of her desk and pulled out her box of tissues. He took one, and she watched him wiping his cheeks.

'Do you trust me, Jonah?'

Jonah nodded.

'If you trust me, why can't you tell me what's wrong?'

He looked back at the pattern on her dress. They were birds, the small curved shapes, or maybe flying fish. But was there actually such thing as a flying fish? After a while he said, 'Miss Swann?'

'Yes, Jonah.' She leaned forward, her hands clasped in the dip of her lap.

'You know the sun?'

She nodded, frowning.

'How far away is it? I mean, how many light years?'

She leaned back and looked out of the window, silent, lips pressed together, and he thought she wasn't going to answer. But then she said, 'It's more like light minutes, in fact. I don't know exactly. But not very long at all.'

Jonah smiled a little, thinking about telling Harold.

'Emerald's dad was asking about you. You know he's worried about you too.'

'What did he say?'

'He said . . .' She paused, and he knew she'd decided not to tell him the main thing that Saviour had said. 'He asked if I'd seen you. And he asked about your brother too. What's up with Raffy, then?'

'Tummy ache.'

'Is that what you had?'

Jonah nodded, wondering about Saviour. What had he said to Miss Swann? *Did* he actually know Lucy was gone?

'But yours got better?'

'What?'

'Your tummy.'

'Yes.'

'But Raff's still poorly.'

'No, his got better too.'

'Oh,' said Miss Swann. 'So he came in with you? Christine didn't tell me.'

Jonah gave another tiny nod. In the silence that followed he heard the ticking of the wall clock.

'Have you ever heard the expression, a problem shared is a problem halved?' Miss Swann asked, very softly.

Jonah gazed into her eyes, which were blue, with darker blue outer circles.

'If I told you a secret, would you keep it and not tell anyone?' He put his hand to his mouth, because the words had blurted out of him all by themselves.

Miss Swann looked out of the window again. 'Is it a secret from a long time ago?' She was thinking hard, probably about Angry Saturday. He stayed silent, and she turned back to him. 'Or is it something that's happened recently?' She leaned forward, and he could see the pores in her nose and the clogs of black in her eyelashes.

'But will you tell anyone?' he whispered.

Miss Swann drew back, the lines on her forehead deep. She pushed her hands between her thighs and rocked a little, backwards and forwards, thinking. 'Jonah, I cannot promise to keep your secret,' she said quietly. 'I wish I could. I want to. But I know that if you were to tell me that you or any other child was in any kind of danger, then I would have to take action to protect you. And that action might well involve telling other grown-ups.' She paused, and in the silence he saw the peacock's hundreds of eyes and that sharp, hissing beak. 'Does that make sense, Jonah?'

The peacock, screaming and running at them. The memory was so strong that Jonah closed his eyes and put his hands over his ears. The peacock's screams, Raff's screams, his own screams; taking Raff's hand and pulling him; running and running, looking for somewhere to hide.

'Jonah, please. Jonah, look at me!' Miss Swann's hands were on his shoulders and her voice had gone all frightened. He straightened up, shrugging her hands away. He didn't want to look at her any more. He wanted to get away now, go out into the playground, or anywhere, and forget the whole conversation.

'Are you in danger, Jonah?' She had her hands on his face now, cupping his cheeks, which felt weird. 'If you are in danger, then you must tell me.'

He shook his head. Her hands dropped away. 'Is someone you know in danger?'

Are you in danger, Mayo?

'What *is* it, Jonah?'

'It's nothing. Just my tummy's still a bit sore.' He needed to go and check on Raff. He couldn't wait until school was finished. He had to see him right now. He was still clutching the tissue. He put it down. 'Can I go now?'

'Not yet.' She tucked her awful hair behind her ears again and scratched at the rash on her throat, making it redder. She started speaking, in a fast, quivery voice. 'Jonah, you are an extremely capable, intelligent child, but you are carrying too much on your shoulders.'

The bell started ringing. He needed to go right now if he was going to catch Raff before he went into his classroom.

'Jonah, I need to know you are safe.' There was a proper break in her voice, like she was going to cry.

'I need the toilet,' he said. Her hands were cupping his face again. 'Miss Swann, please can I go to the toilet?'

She dropped her hands and sat back. 'Off you go, then.'

45

He hadn't managed to get to the Infants' block in time. The door had already been shut and as he'd pushed at it Christine had seen him and escorted him back to the Juniors. 'You've had all of lunchtime to see your brother,' she'd said. 'The bell's gone, and you need to be in class.'

Now he was slumped in his seat next to Harold and Miss Swann was reading to them. 'David was the youngest of eight boys. He liked to play musical instruments, and write poems.' He had only been half-listening, or maybe not listening at all, he realised, because he had no idea why she was reading this particular story. He looked at the words she'd written on the whiteboard.

COURAGE = DOING THE RIGHT THING EVEN IF IT IS DIFFICULT

'David wasn't old enough to go and fight the Philistines. He had to stay in the fields and look after the sheep.'

Her voice sounded so tired that it made him tired. He closed his eyes, and saw Raff in a toga, carrying a staff, walking along with all his sheep. The toga was too big for him, and so was the staff.

'But then David's father heard about a Philistine giant called Goliath, who was goading the Israelites to find one man brave enough to fight him.'

Goliath, like the Thin One, but much, much taller, towered above Raff, his full-body armour glittering.

'David's father sent him to join his brothers. He took food, and also his catapult. David was a very good slingsman . . .'

Slingsman. Like the Wii game. He saw the Thin One towering above London like a Transformer, his head among the weird, spaceship clouds. He and Raff were crane operators. They looked over at each other from their tiny cabins, grinning, and making thumbs-up signs, and then turned to their controls, gliding themselves into position, aiming their missiles at the Thin One's brow. The clouds. What were they called, those clouds? Something beginning with L. Then it came to him. 'Lenticular!' He said it aloud, waking himself up, and everyone turned and stared at him.

'Lenticular, Jonah?' asked Miss Swann.

A whistle sounded in the playground, and then running feet and shouting. Jonah looked: Mrs Blakeston's class, practising for Sports Day. Tameron was winning easily, because Raff wasn't in the race. Because Raff . . . Jonah scanned every child. Because Raff wasn't there.

'What are you doing now?' asked Miss Swann.

'I need to go. I need the toilet.' He had got to his feet and was heading for the door, but she was in his way. He tried to duck around her, but she caught him by the wrist. 'I need to go *now*!' he shouted, twisting away from her, but her fingers tightened.

'Jonah got diarrhoea,' said Daniella. 'Must have been sucking on his wee-wee stick.' No one laughed. They were all just staring at him.

'It's only five minutes until home time,' said Miss Swann. 'Can't you wait five minutes?'

Five minutes. Jonah looked at the clock. *Where are you, Raffy?* Five minutes was too long to wait. He shook his head. 'I need to go. You have to let me.'

'OK, but I want you to come back. With your mum. I want to talk to her.' Jonah nodded again. 'She's picking you up today?'

'Yes.'

'OK, well, I'll come out and find you in the playground.' She let go of his wrist and he shot towards the door. 'Tell your mum, Jonah!' she shouted after him. 'I need to see her! It's important!'

46

Where are you, Raffy? Jonah stopped by the pond and leaned against the railings, panting hard. He'd been running since he left the school, swerving to avoid the arriving parents, up the hill and then in a zigzag across the park, checking the starflower tree, the paddling pool, the playground and the skate ramp, before heading back across the grass and through the trees. *You told Ilaria you were going to school, because you didn't want any of her beetroot juice . . .*

Jonah stared into the pond. Rays of sun were falling through the leaves of the trees and making golden, dancing scribbles on the dark water. There was no sign of the white stick. He straightened, his breath coming easier now, and felt for the four coins in his pocket. 'I've got a plan, Raffy. Don't you want to hear my plan?' He realised he was saying the words out loud, actually talking to himself, or whispering, and in a sudden rage he kicked at the railings: Raff wasn't there, Lucy wasn't there; it was just him, all alone.

He turned and walked towards the gate. Parents and children were passing through it, coming into the park on their way home. He stopped in front of the starflower tree.

When he was little, he'd watched bigger children climb it, amazed, but now he and Raff found it easy. This year, when it was in blossom, they had scrambled up together, to sit among the lemony smelling stars and peer down at Lucy's dreamy, upturned face. He climbed up now, just to the first perching point, where a branch forked from the trunk at a ninety-degree angle. The bark of the branch was smooth, from all the children's bottoms that had sat there, and that section of the trunk was covered in scratches: letters and numbers and signs.

'It's because they're boys. That's why you like them more than me.' Emerald's voice, loud and whiny. 'Because they're boys, and there are two of them, and I'm just a boring girl, who doesn't like cricket.'

'Emmy, don't be stupid. You are my daughter. I would always put you first.' They were coming through the gate. Jonah drew his legs up, out of sight, and watched them through the layers of stiff, dark leaves.

'Well, it doesn't feel like it! It feels like you're sick of me, and you wish you could go and be *their* dad.'

'I don't want to be their dad, Em! Jesus!'

They had passed him, and were heading across the grass towards the pond, but their angry voices drifted back to him.

'They're just trouble!' Emerald stopped, her fists clenched. She was working herself into a state. 'That's what Mum says! She says we've been far too generous with them, and now they need to learn how to stand on their feet!'

They kept going, Emerald storming ahead. Jonah could just hear their voices, but he couldn't make out the words any more. He watched them: Emerald tall and pale, her long legs like scissors; Saviour short and wide, toddling behind her.

Though you've such a tiny body, and your head so large doth grow. The poem started chanting itself in Jonah's head. *Though your hat may blow away, Mr Yonghy-Bonghy-Bò!* Poor Yonghy. That huge, baby head, that wretched face, that little pot belly. Saviour's body wasn't at all tiny, but he was short and there was something Yonghyish about him. What was it? The look of him when he was crying on the bench: a child, trapped in a grown-up's body. Is that what happened to some people? That their bodies became adult, but they didn't ever feel like adults, and they just had to pretend?

They disappeared into the trees, and Jonah's eyes ran over the scratches in the bark. An X, like the X on the card that came with the flowers, and the X on the unnamed text message. He leaned his forehead against the bark. What if *all* grown-ups were just children, pretending? He'd heard people saying that the prime minister was just an idiot. Say if there wasn't *anyone* clever enough to know the right thing to do, to be in charge?

'I fucking hate you!' Emerald's voice again, far away, but she was shouting at her highest volume. They'd come out of the trees and were on the way to the top gate. Jonah watched Emerald punch Saviour a few times, before running off up the hill. *Such a drama queen!* Lucy had said that once about Emerald – or muttered it. On the holiday in France, Emerald had had a fit because she didn't like her new swimming costume. Emerald was spoilt, because she was an only child, and Dora and Saviour treated her like a little princess. He watched Saviour jogging, catching up with her, Emerald punching him again and then falling against him, and his arms going around her. The Martins only really loved themselves. He and Raff and Lucy were just their lame ducks. *Roland was right, Lucy. You shouldn't have made friends with them. And you shouldn't have let them give us things.*

They went through the top gate, and Jonah couldn't see them any more. He let his legs drop down, but stayed sitting on the branch. *'This holiday hasn't exactly been* cheap, *you know!'* That's what Dora had said, the day they'd gone on a trip to a nearby town. They'd looked around a church and then they'd had lunch, sitting outside on the pavement. Dora had said, *'Nice to get away from it all!'* and Lucy had suddenly snapped, *'Why do you keep* saying *that, Dora!'* And Dora had looked shocked, but then she'd had a massive go at Lucy about being such a misery-guts. The holiday must have cost a fortune. It was an amazing house. And then, when they got home, the Martins had given him and Raff the Wii player. *You shouldn't have let them, Lucy. That's why they got sick of us. Because of all the money they spent on us.*

He slithered out of the tree and brushed his hands on his shorts, and then felt in his pockets to check the keys and the four coins were still there. He went through the park gate, heading back to Southway Street, but the long way, so that he didn't have to pass the school. Jingling the coins, he thought about the Martins. Dora had taken them to the Olympics. How much had that cost? And Saviour had taken him, just him, to the Oval to watch England play Sri Lanka. *He wasn't getting sick of me then. He liked having someone to go to the cricket with.* Emerald was right, in a way, about the 'boy' thing.

A strange shout brought him back into the present. He

was on Southway Street, drawing up outside his own front door. There was no one outside the squatters' house any more, but the beer drinkers were still outside the Green Shop. The clouds were breaking up now, into pretty cirrus wisps, and it was getting really hot again. It was the old raggedy woman with the plaits who had shouted; she shouted again, but it seemed to be just a sound, not a word. She was sitting on the pavement with her back against a wheelie bin, and her legs stuck out in front of her. The gold-toothed woman was sitting a few feet away, on a crate, and the red-faced pirate was coming out of the Green Shop with three more beers. The London Kebab Man was watching them, and Leonie was opening her door now, and shouting at the one with plaits to stop shouting – and then Jonah's heart jumped for joy, because there was Raff, looking like a girl, trying to squeeze past Leonie.

'Raffy!' Jonah ran across the road. With his hair pulled back, the bones of Raff's face were too beautiful. They threw themselves at each other, and Jonah hugged his brother hard, smelling hair oil and bubble gum and onions. 'Where have you *been*!'

'I found him in the kebab shop.' Leonie nodded at the London Kebab Man, who nodded back. 'Eating a plate of food as big as himself. Appetites on you boys! He said your ma wasn't in, so I brought him in with me and Pat.'

'Where did you get the money for the kebab?' whispered Jonah.

'It was free,' whispered Raff.

Jonah looked at the London Kebab Man, who nodded again and went back inside his shop.

'I just put it in this knot for now,' Leonie said. 'It won't last, but I can't see him running around looking like a ruffian. Tell your ma I'll do him cornrows, twists, whatever she wants. I don't want her money, but I can't do nothing more without her say so.'

47

As they went into the house, they heard Lucy's phone ringing. Jonah slammed the front door closed and they circled the kitchen and the sitting room, picking things up and putting them down again, until Jonah found the phone on the floor in the hallway. There were ants all over it, and he tried to brush them off.

'Quick!' said Raff.

Jonah blew at the ants, before pressing the green button and putting the phone to his ear.

'Hello?' In the moment's pause before the caller spoke he realised he probably should have let whoever it was leave a message.

'Oh hello, this is Christine Wicks, from . . . Is that you, Jonah?'

'Who is it?' Raff mouthed. Jonah batted an ant off his cheek, trying to think what to say.

'Jonah? Can you put your mum on, please?'

There was an ant on his earlobe now. He held the phone away to flick it off.

'Hello-o-o. Can you hear me?' called tiny Christine, at the end of his arm. Jonah looked at Raff, who was trying to blow a bubble with his gum.

'Yar,' he said shortly. Raff giggled. Jonah held his finger to his lips.

'Hello? Is that . . . am I speaking to Jonah's mum?'

'Yar.' Jonah made the same brief, curt sound, which made Raff giggle even more.

'I'm afraid I can hardly hear you.'

Jonah clamped the phone back to his ear. 'Yar.' This time the sound was longer, but also growlier. Raff sputtered and gurgled.

'Mrs Armitage?'

'Mwembe.' The two syllables came out deep and Zambian. Raff screeched.

'Oh yes, Mrs, ah, Wemby, apologies. It's Christine Wicks here, school manager at Haredale.'

'Yar.' He moved over and tried to clap his hand over Raff's mouth, but without success.

'Mrs Wemby, both your sons were absent today, but we have received no notification from you?'

Jonah stayed silent. He was trying to swallow back his own laughter, and was scared that it might burst out of him if he opened his mouth.

'Mrs Wemby, we need to be notified of all absences by the time the registers are taken.'

'Yar, yar.' The doubling of the syllable brought another shriek from Raff. Jonah quickly backed away from him. There were ants crawling down the back of his neck.

'The next time this happens, please will you phone, Mrs Wemby. And, for today's absences, we will need a note – Jonah for half the day, and Raff for the whole day.'

Shaking with laughter, Raff had fallen to the floor. Jonah looked down at him, sucking in his cheeks to stop himself from exploding.

'I will need a note from you tomorrow morning, Mrs Wemby. Explaining that your boys were unwell. Otherwise they will go down as unauthorised, I'm afraid.'

Raff was stuffing his fist into his mouth, his face was wet with tears.

'Mrs Wemby?' Christine said.

'Yar,' said Jonah, and Raff exploded yet again. Now Jonah had to clap his hand over his own mouth. Christine kept talking.

'I'm sorry if I've got you at a bad time, but it's very important that we get the note tomorrow. It's the last week of term, and we need to have our records up to date . . .'

'Yar,' he said weakly and for the last time, because the laughter rushed out of his nose in a huge snort. He sank to his knees, and the phone fell from his hand and shot across the floor.

'Mrs Wemby? Are you OK, Mrs Wemby?' As Christine's voice squeaked from the other side of the room, both boys lay on their backs, rolling from side to side and gasping for air.

Once she'd rung off and they'd laughed properly for a few minutes, they fell silent, watching the flies circling above them.

'I swallowed my gum,' said Raff. 'By mistake. When I was laughing.'

'It won't kill you.' Jonah remembered that Raff had eaten a massive kebab. 'Did you say thank you? To the London Kebab Man?'

'Yeah, bro.' Raff sat up. 'I fancy an ice cream now. A chocolate Cornetto.'

'You're such a pig.' Jonah sat up too, and pulled the three pounds and fifty pence out of his pocket.

'Is that enough for two Cornettos?' asked Raff.

Jonah shook his head. 'I don't think so. But anyway, I've got a plan.'

'Can't we just buy one Cornetto? I'll share it, this time, I promise . . .'

'No.' Jonah stood up, and held his hand out to Raff. 'Come on. We're going to put it on a horse.'

48

The betting shop was a small, square room with two big roulette machines and a row of TV screens high up on one of the walls. The times they'd been in before, it had been packed with men, staring up at the screens or scribbling with half-size pens on tiny pieces of paper. Jonah remembered the smell of sweat and the noisy jumble of emotions. Today obviously wasn't a big race day. There were two men in the shop, sitting on tall stools, hunched over the high, narrow counter. Behind their heads only one of the screens was on, showing horses being led around by their jockeys, waiting for their race. There were just two balls of crunched-up paper on the usually litter-covered floor, and the only sound was the quiet burbling of voices coming out of the screen. Even the lights on the roulette machines looked like blinking, sleepy eyes. On the other side of the glass, on a chair behind the till, Egg-eye was drinking tea and watching her own tiny little television.

Jonah and Raff stepped further into the shop, not sure whether Egg-eye would turn them out. One of the men was the London Kebab Man, looking like a gnome, perched up high on his stool, with his reading glasses on. The other man was white, with tattoos on his arms, and very dirty hands, and he was wearing one of those bright orange bibs over his T-shirt. His huge, filthy boots rested on the rung of the stool, and there were crumbs of earth on the floor beneath them.

Jonah approached the London Kebab Man, who was chewing one of his fingers like a cat gnaws a bone, while his other hand filled out a betting slip. There was a copy of the *Racing Post* lying on the counter beside him.

'Excuse me,' he said. 'But can I have a look at your paper?'

The London Kebab Man peered at Jonah over his glasses, then glanced back at Egg-eye, who had put her mug down to cough, but was still turned towards her screen. He looked back at Jonah with a gleam in his eyes and a finger to his lips. He folded the paper so that half a page was showing, and passed it to him. Jonah looked. It was details of the 4.20 at Chepstow. The London Kebab Man jabbed at the names of the horses with his little pen. 'Five minutes,' he whispered, pointing at his watch and holding up five fingers. It was as if he thought Jonah couldn't speak English, but Jonah knew it was because he was used to people not understanding him, because of his strange voice and his strong accent. 'Quick, quick, chop, chop!' he whispered, making a little chopping movement with the edge of his hand.

Still coughing, Egg-eye finally turned and looked out at them from behind the glass. She turned her microphone on and the room filled with her cough. The cough had lots of layers to it, from the splutterings of her lips to the rasping deep in her chest. There was also an engine noise coming from somewhere. Jonah turned and saw, through the open doorway, a van pulling up outside their front door.

'They're not allowed to bet, you know,' said Egg-eye, eventually. 'They shouldn't even be in here. I let them in with their dad sometimes. Where's your daddy, dearies?'

'He gone!' cried the London Kebab Man impatiently. 'He gone long time!' He slid off his stool to help Jonah onto the one next to it. Then he drew another one over for Raff and lifted him up too.

Jonah looked back at the van. It was Saviour's van. Leaving the engine running, Saviour was getting out.

'You choose,' said the London Kebab Man. 'You give me money. How much you got?'

Jonah held out his coins.

'Yes, yes, good, good. Now, choose! Chop chop!'

Saviour was knocking at their front door. The squatters were back outside. Would he ask the squatters where they were? Had the squatters noticed them coming into the betting shop? Jonah gazed down at the horses. There were eight of them, and the odds ranged from 3 to 1 to 50 to 1. It was a flat race, which meant outsiders were less likely to win, he remembered.

'We should go for the 3 to 1, really,' he said to Raff. 'Blue Orchid.' He didn't really like the name, it sounded like a perfume and, even though it was a flat race, Roland always hated to go for the favourite. He stared at the jockeys' silks, and then back at the printed names, looking for a clue, feeling the toga gods' eyes on him. He glanced back outside. Saviour was calling over to the squatters. Now Ilaria was crossing over to talk him. She wasn't pointing in their direction, though. She can't have seen them come in. His eyes dropped back to the paper and fixed on a horse called Tooth Fairy. His tongue licked at the hollow in his gum, tasting blood. Tooth Fairy – a message? Not from a god, but from Lucy? *Sorry I can't be a tooth fairy myself, Joney, but if you bet on this Tooth Fairy, I'll make sure you get lots of money.* It was the Tooth Fairy that had odds of 50 to 1, so it *would* be a lot of money if it won. But the silk was boring, dark blue with white sleeves – and he hadn't really *heard* her voice, he'd just imagined what she might say. They only had one chance. Maybe he should study the form properly.

He looked through the door again. Saviour's van was still there, engine running. Where had he and Ilaria got to? Raff was leaning over the paper now, running his finger along each name as he mouthed it. He could read quite well for his age, but lots of the names were too hard.

'Chop chop!' squeaked the London Kebab Man. He was standing at Jonah's side, peering over his shoulder, and he reached round and pointed at Rabbit Run. The finger was brown and crooked, with only a tiny sliver of nail. Rabbit Run was 12 to 1. Of course, Rabbit Run could be a sign too, because of Dylan. The London Kebab Man pointed to his own chest. 'My horse,' he said, nodding.

The man in the orange bib had turned to watch them. 'How much they got?' he asked. 'It's got to be Blue Orchid or Tailor Made. Believe me, lads, don't waste your money on anything else.'

His stomach starting to churn, Jonah turned back to the list. Raff had come to the last horse now. His finger was blocking Jonah's view of the name, but it was a five-year-old grey mare: 20 to 1, so an outsider. Weighing 9-0. Was that stone? He couldn't remember. Her form was 39978, whatever that meant. The silk was orange, with red diamonds on the front. Lucy would like it.

'She's – Not – There,' Raff read out, slowly and carefully. Then he read it again, quicker. 'She's Not There, She's Not There! Jonah, She's Not There!' Raff grabbed his brother's arm, his eyes lit up, and it was like they were Lucy's eyes Jonah was looking into. *Is it the one, Mayo?* He got a whiff of coconut, and he closed his eyes and saw her, clear as crystal, smiling and nodding at him. He opened his eyes, and turned to the London Kebab Man.

'That one, please,' he said. 'She's Not There.'

'Each way?' asked the London Kebab Man.

Jonah took a breath. 'On the nose.' The London Kebab Man nodded and nodded, writing out the slip for them. *Thank you, Mayo! I'm sorry for not believing in you!* He still had the smell, the feeling of her, right there. The Kebab Shop Man had stopped writing and was looking towards the door. Jonah looked too. Leonie was looking in, her high-heeled feet planted wide, arms folded. Behind her, Jonah could see that Saviour's van had now gone.

'I thought I saw you coming in here,' Leonie said. 'You not allowed in here, you know. Where your mama? You tell her what I said about your hair?' The London Kebab Man waved her away, which made her suck her teeth and step inside. 'You tell her? What she say?' She peered at Raff. Raff shrugged.

Then Egg-eye's heavy sigh came through the microphone. 'OK then, dearies,' she said. 'It's now or never.'

The London Kebab Man scuttled to the counter with the slip and their money. Leonie followed, and muscled in next to him. 'You betting for them? How much they betting? Their mama ain't got no money, you know that.'

The London Kebab Man opened his palm and showed her the coins.

'It's just a bit of pocket money,' said Egg-eye. 'Their dad used to let them. Poor boys, let them have their fun.'

Leonie sucked her teeth some more, and turned to look up at the screen. The horses were assembling at the starting line.

'Miss Leonie, what slope you slipping down now?' Pat had followed her and was standing on the threshold. 'Your 4 o'clock's here, you know.'

'He'll have to wait,' said Leonie, hoisting herself onto a stool. 'Just till this race is finished. The boys got three fifty on it.'

'Three hundred and fifty!' Pat clapped her hand over her mouth. 'Where did they get that!'

'Three *pounds* fifty, fool!' said Leonie. 'Just a bit of fun. Which horse is it, boys?'

'There she is,' said Jonah, pointing up at the screen. She's Not There was white, not grey, as he knew she would be. She was a nervous-looking horse, a bit on the thin side, and his heart suddenly sank, because she didn't look like a winner at all. She stamped and snorted, not wanting to go into her stall, and the jockey bobbed around in his red and orange top, his hands everywhere. And if the horse wasn't a winner, then Lucy wasn't there at all, he'd just made her up. '*You just have to* believe!' That's what she'd said to Roland. But it was rubbish, he should have studied the form properly, like Roland would have. And now they were all in their stalls. The starting gates opened. Jonah felt Raff's hand find his and grip it hard.

'How much will we win, Jonah?' he whispered.

'Something like seventy pounds, I think,' Jonah whispered back. 'But only if she wins. She might not win, you do know that, don't you, Raff?'

'Yeh, but you just got to *believe*, fam!' Raff's sparkling eyes were fixed on the screen.

Jonah squeezed his hand. 'You're right,' he breathed. 'She *is* going to win.'

It was a short race, only twelve furlongs, so it wouldn't last long. Jonah watched as the thirty-two-legged mass became a nose-to-tail line, like a paper chain. Blue Orchid was in the lead, a black, shiny muscle-machine, and a chestnut horse called Foot The Bill was second. Fugitive Pieces was right behind, and then came She's Not There, but she wasn't running very smoothly. Tailor Made was behind her. Brave Dave was next, and Rabbit Run was second to last. The Tooth Fairy was at the back, and fading. As they went round a curve in the track, the horses overlapped, blurring into one shape again. As the track straightened, they separated back into their paper chain. But now gaps were opening up between the horses. Only the three at the front were still nose to tail. Jonah scanned along the line. Where had she got to? Oh, Em, Gee, there she was! She still hadn't found her rhythm, and her jockey was dancing around like a puppet, but She's Not There had moved up to second place.

'Run, She's Not There!' shouted Raff, leaning forward on his stool.

'Which stupid-name horse is it?' said Leonie. 'Is it winning? Tell me!'

'The white one,' Jonah croaked. It was like it was Lucy running. Unsteady, but hurtling, on a deadly mission to get that money for her boys. She was starting to overlap with Blue Orchid now, and not on a curve, so it wasn't just a change of angle. Oh no, but now what was she doing? It was like she was about to crash right into him, and her head was thrashing and her teeth were bared . . . Was she trying to bite Blue Orchid? The jockey yanked her back, and she stumbled, but she kept going, and now she was slowly . . . yes, she was gaining again, she was drawing level with him; they were side by side now, neck and neck.

The grown-ups had all moved forward, screwing up their eyes and craning up at the screen. Leonie had put her hands together and was murmuring, and Pat had both her fists up, like a boxer. The TV voice was getting faster and faster – it was impossible to make out what he was saying. Egg-eye even came out from behind her counter and staggered over to stand by Raff.

'Come on, She's Not There!' shouted Pat, shooting a fist up above her head. His hand on Egg-eye's shoulder, Raff stood up on his stool.

'Run, run, run! Run faster!' he shrieked. And she did. She was definitely ahead now, so if she could just hang on, just for a few seconds more . . .

'Go, She Not There!' squawked the London Kebab Man.

'Come ON, She's Not There!' bellowed the man in the orange bib, scrunching up his betting slip and throwing it on the floor. 'Move your fucking scrawny arse!'

Her nose passed the finishing line ahead of Blue Orchid's and Jonah slid off the stool to the floor. 'Hooray!' he croaked, but the grown-ups had fallen silent. She's Not There's lurch into Blue Orchid was being replayed on the screen.

'She won, didn't she?' said Raff.

'Stewards' Enquiry,' explained the man in the orange bib. 'It'll take a few minutes. I'm going for a beer. Want an ice lolly, boys?'

49

The beer drinkers were up on their feet and milling around outside the Green Shop, crazier than ever, with shiny wet skin and glittering eyes. The man with the exploding face was twirling the little plait-haired woman around, and her skirt was flying up so you could see her baggy black pants. The gold-toothed woman was trying to join in by hooking arms with the plait woman, but she kept missing.

'Steady now,' said the man in the orange bib, moving through them. 'You coming, lads?'

'We'll wait outside,' said Jonah. The Green Shop was packed, and anyway he didn't want to see the Green Shop Man.

'Cornettos do you?'

They both nodded, and watched him go inside and elbow his way to the freezer. Then Raff nudged Jonah.

'The Raggedy Man's taken his top off.'

He was standing in front of London Kebabs, as tall and straight as ever, holding a beer can to his bare belly, staring into space like a statue. His tracksuit top was tied around his waist. It was strange to see the skinniness of his body, the tufts of frizzy grey hair on his chest.

Does he know, Mayo? Does he know where you are?

The beer drinkers were singing now – more like bawling – and meandering sideways, engulfing Jonah and Raff. Raff ducked through them and went to wait for his Cornetto at the door of the Green Shop. *'She's not the-e-ere!!!'* they shouted together. Someone must have told them the name of the horse. The gold-toothed woman went into a wild spin, arms out like an aeroplane. She caught the Raggedy Man with her hand, and he flinched and moved off. She stopped, staggering, and tried to link arms with Jonah, mumbling the words of the song at him. There was no point in trying to find her, she was saying, because nobody knew and nobody cared.

'Find who?' he asked, stepping back out of her reach. She looked confused, and took a swig from her can, and the other two kept going with the song. Just a song. Jonah turned and followed the Raggedy Man.

The Raggedy Man came to a stop just past Leonie's shop, and Jonah stood next to him, craning his neck to look up at his face. *He knows.* Below the racket the beer drinkers were making, Jonah could hear his breathing. It was all snuffly. The Raggedy Man had a cold.

'Excuse me.'

The Raggedy Man stayed still, his eyes looking up at the sky.

'She's not the-e-re!' sang the beer drinkers again.

'Did you see our mum? On Monday?'

His voice sounded so childish, and he felt as silly as when he'd talked to Violet. The Raggedy Man just stared at the sky. Jonah looked at his arm. The skin was more like the skin of a tree than a human, and there were stringy bits, bulging like metal cables, showing how hard his grip was on the can. '*He was a boy like you once,*' she had said. Yes, with smooth new skin, like his own. He put his fingers on the arm, very lightly. 'Did you see her come out of the house?' He asked.

All of a sudden the Raggedy Man looked down and Jonah saw right into his eyes. They were a deep, liquid black, and Jonah got a kind of crackle from them, like an electric shock. His face was covered in tiny little bumps and his beard was lots of frizzy tufts, like the ones on his body. In the middle of the tufts were his lips, all cracked and crusty.

'Do you know where she is?' He whispered.

The Raggedy Man said nothing, and Jonah felt like crying because, yes, he might as well be talking to an animal, an animal that didn't know who he was, and didn't care. Behind him the beer drinkers were bellowing about the girl in their song: her voice and her eyes and her hair. Searching deep in the Raggedy Man's eyes, he tried one more time. This time his voice came out in a whisper. 'I heard you talking on the pavement. Did you see her?'

The Raggedy Man's head moved, in a way that could have been a nod. Their eyes still glued, Jonah's lips managed to form the words. 'Where is she?'

The beer can crashed to the ground, and the Raggedy Man's arm rose, long and straight, his finger pointing up into the sky.

Dead, then. Jonah's stomach heaved. The drunk people's singing got even louder, and below him the pavement pitched like the deck of a boat. The Raggedy Man had killed her, and she was up in Heaven. He retched, dropping his hands to his knees as his mouth filled with bitter juice from his belly. He tried to spit, but the liquid stuck to his lip, hanging down in a long drool. Then everything changed colour, his hands, his feet, the pavement, and the thread of drool glinted like liquid diamonds. He looked back up, and the Raggedy Man had turned into God, his finger still pointing, his face completely gold.

Are you dead? Is that what he means? More of the juice was running over his lips, and he spat again, before looking up to where the gold was pouring from. *Are you in Heaven?* The gap in the clouds was getting bigger, showing the blue. *If you are, you have to come back. Me and Raff are your children.* The tears streamed down his cheeks, and he said it out loud: 'We are your children! We are your children!' The sun was flooding him, like her tenderness. 'We are your children!' It was her, in the sun, he could feel her. He wrapped his arms around himself. 'We are your children,' he whispered. The Raggedy Man had lowered his arm. The blue was getting bigger and bigger. He squeezed himself harder – *stay, Mayo, stay* – but the feeling of her was ebbing away. The Raggedy Man was gazing at him with his God face, and as Jonah gazed back, he saw tears well up in his eyes. 'Did you kill her?' he whispered. One of the tears spilled out, and made a streak on his cheek.

'Come on, little Romeo!' It was the plait-headed woman, who had taken hold of Raff's hands, trying to get him to dance with her. Raff was pulling away. Jonah wiped his face and looked again at the Raggedy Man.

'Tell me. Just tell me.'

The Raggedy Man bent his knees and brought his arms up to shoulder height. He swayed and turned from side to side like a surfer. Jonah watched intently, trying to work out what he meant. 'Was she drunk? Did she go out all drunk, in the middle of the night?'

The Raggedy Man made fists with his hands, and put them one on top of each other, just below his belly. Jonah didn't understand until he started circling his hips. 'Sexing,' he whispered.

'What are you *doing*, Raggedy Man?' Raff had escaped from the plait-headed woman and was standing next to Jonah. The Raggedy Man thrust his hips, moving his fist penis backwards and forwards, and Raff burst out laughing. The Raggedy Man thrust his hips again, and then again, and his fist penis got faster and faster. Raff stopped laughing and drew back. 'What is *wrong* with that guy?' he whispered to Jonah.

Jonah kept his eyes on the Raggedy Man, who seemed to be working himself into a frenzy. The beer drinkers had stopped singing and were all watching him too, but from further away. 'I think he knows what happened to Lucy.'

'How does he know? Did he see? What *did* happen?' Raff grabbed his arm, his fingernails digging in.

'I don't know. Shush, Raffy.' The Raggedy Man stopped, worn out. Snot was trickling from both his nostrils, and his tracksuit bottoms had slipped down to where there were more frizzy tufts, clumped together, like his beard. He stood still, staring at nothing for a moment, and then walked off, pulling his tracksuit up over his skinny bottom.

'Tell, me, Jonah! What did he say?'

'Nothing. He said nothing. I just – I thought he was trying to tell me something. With signs. Miming.' They watched him cross the road and walk up Southway Street, towards the park. 'But maybe he's just mad.'

'Here you go, boys.' It was their Cornettos. Raff tore at his wrapper, full of glee.

'Thank you,' said Jonah. Behind them, the beer drinkers had started milling about again.

Then Pat came out of the betting shop. 'Gentlemen!' she announced. 'You have just won yourselves a whole seventy pounds!'

THURSDAY

50

He was in a palace, a broken palace, deep in the jungle, by a river. The Raggedy Man was there and lots of other raggedy people, and a woman was talking to them all through a loudspeaker. He looked out at the river, trying to think about where she might be, but a boat was arriving, full of soldiers with machine guns. Amongst them was the Thin One, looking up at the palace with his strange, dead eyes, and Jonah ducked down, terrified.

But then someone knocked on the door.

Mayo! He tried to move, but it was difficult. His headache was worse than ever and the loudspeaker voice was saying it was raining in Scotland. More knocking and banging – it was her, she was there, not dead, not dead! – the stupid Raggedy Man's signs were just *random*. But there was shouting now, shouting through the letter box, someone shouting his name, a man's voice.

So it wasn't her.

The knocking stopped, and his tongue found the hole in his gum, the spongy flesh, the bone beneath it. His belly churned: if she was dead, she would never know his tooth had come out. He saw the Raggedy Man's finger, pointing up at the sky, and his terrible face, lit with gold. *Remember,* *he was a boy like you once.* Her voice in his head made his belly worse. It was like there was a creature in there, shifting, trying to turn. He tried to roll over, to curl up on his side, but he couldn't, something was stopping him. Then he felt the roll of notes pressing into his leg through his pocket, and remembered that it was OK actually, because even though she was dead, she was still looking after them – as long as he believed. He just had to believe. How much of the money had they spent on their feast? He tried to move his hand, get it in his pocket, but it was stuck, why was his hand stuck? Raff groaned, right in his ear. He opened his eyes.

A gang of flies was hanging out on the ceiling, about fifteen of them, bumping gently against the cracked white surface. There were wasps too, drifted in from the fruit crate in the hall, two of them crawling across the weather map on the television screen. He must have fallen asleep, right at the end of the film, while the bald-headed man was doing all that strange talking. His hand found the remote control and he lowered the volume. Now that the weather woman was quieter, he could just hear the Tibetan bells ringing upstairs. He pushed Raff off him and sat up. Raff groaned again and turned his chocolate-covered face into the sofa.

'Jonah! Raff! It's me! For fuck's sake, open the door!'

Saviour. Jonah swivelled his eyes and looked across the hallway at the raised metal flap, remembering that Saviour had come round twice the night before. The first time it had been still light and they'd been feasting, and playing Slingsmen. They'd seen his van drive up and park outside the sitting-room window, and had paused the game and lain down flat on the floor. He'd knocked and peered through the window, and they'd got the giggles.

'Jonah! Raff!'

He was really bellowing. *But we are just your lame ducks.* Jonah looked around the room. The remains of their feast were strewn across the floor, and now the ants were enjoying it. The second time he'd come had been really late; Raff had been fast asleep and he'd been watching the film all by himself, a wild, scary film about an American soldier hunting for a bad man in the jungle. The bad man, bald and shadowy, kept stroking his huge, smooth head and whispering things. The sound of Saviour's van outside had brought him suddenly back into the messy sitting room, lit only by the flickering brightness from the screen. He had muted the TV, and when the van's engine stopped there had been complete silence. Then the letter box had opened, and Jonah had been able to hear his breathing. It had been like he and Saviour were two soldiers, hunting each other, listening hard, either side of the flimsy door.

'Jonah, Raff, please! I know you're in there!' Now it was daytime, everything was more ordinary. But Saviour wasn't shouting Lucy's name. And why *was* that, actually? The letter box snapped shut, and Jonah felt a little stab at the thought of him going away again. *I used to like you. I used to like you more than Roland. More than anyone.* He let his eyes close, suddenly flooded by a memory: the smell of garlic and bluebells, and that David Bowie song about being a boy. A morning in the summer – maybe last summer – driving back into London in Saviour's filthy old van, him and Saviour in the front, Emerald and Raff asleep in the back. The four of them had got up before dawn to go and pick wild garlic, and they'd picked bluebells too, and Saviour had wrapped the stalks in damp newspaper. Now they were on their way home, and the radio was crackling and the air rushing in through the rattling windows, and the sunshine glinting on the hairs on Saviour's thick brown arms. Jonah had looked down at his own arms, thin and much less hairy, and Saviour had turned up the radio, and there had been the drum, with a voice counting, and then the rough, jangling guitar. '*Heaven loves us, mate,*' he'd said with a wink, and then they'd both sung along with David – *Boys! Boys keep swinging!* – Saviour's big hand slapping the rhythm on the steering wheel . . .

'And they're definitely not at school?' Saviour was still on the doorstep, talking to someone. Jonah turned the volume down even more.

'No. Definitely not.' It was Alison. 'I looked out for Raff when I dropped Mabel off, and then I went to the Juniors with Greta, and Jonah wasn't there either.' Her voice was loud and fretful. 'I've been really worrying about them. I haven't been sleeping at all. God, I'm really glad I ran into you. I do really feel for her, it's terrible, what she's been through, even if you've brought it on yourself, you wouldn't wish it on anyone. But I've been feeling lately that she's just not looking after the kids properly . . .'

'She looks after them fine.' Saviour sounded clearer because he had walked round the corner of the house and was standing on the Wanless Road pavement. There was a pause. Then Alison said: 'So you think sending them over to a neighbour to get their breakfast is fine? Without checking with the neighbour first?'

'When was this?' Saviour was just outside the sitting-room window now, and his familiar shape through the dirty net curtains made something give in Jonah's chest. Not an alien. Not an enemy. Not a bad man of any kind.

'Yesterday! *Really* difficult, my first day at this new job and I was running late, because my mother had phoned.' Now Alison came into view. She was dressed for work, with a bag over her shoulder. She was taller than Saviour, and much thinner, and was wearing dangly earrings. 'They came asking for food, basically. I should have – I don't know *what* I should have done.'

Saviour was trying to see into the sitting room. 'Given them some?' he suggested.

'Oh God,' said Alison. 'You think I'm – you're probably right. I just didn't want to get *involved*, really.'

'Sure.' Saviour cupped his hands around his face and peered through the glass.

'I was running late, Saviour, because my mother had phoned . . . I don't know if you know about my mother.' Alison's voice had gone very high.

'And you didn't have time to give them some cornflakes.' Saviour stepped back. He put his hands on his hips and tilted his head to look up at their bedroom window.

'I just didn't want to get – sucked in,' said Alison. 'You and – and Dora, you obviously know Lucy much better than I do, but I find her – *really* difficult, and I decided a long time ago . . . she doesn't respect boundaries, and I have a *real* problem with . . .'

'Jonah! Raff! Are you in there?'

Saviour had put his hands around his mouth and called

up to their bedroom window. Behind him, on the other side of the road, the Green Shop Man had come out and was watching.

'Anyway. I'm here now. Though I can't be for long, I can't be late today, because I've got to leave early for Sports Day, and then this talent thing they're doing . . .'

Thursday. Jonah looked down at his brother's sleeping face.

'I don't see why they had to bother rescheduling Sports Day. The school just doesn't seem to *realise* that most parents have actual *jobs* . . .'

Saviour grunted. He came up to the glass again, and squatted down, trying to look under the net curtain.

'Why don't you phone her?' said Alison. 'You've got her number, presumably.'

'Yeah.' Saviour looked back at his watch and rubbed his forehead with his fingers.

'Are you OK?'

'Yeah. I need to get back for Dora.'

'Oh God, yes. I heard she – isn't very well again.'

'It's her op today.' Saviour fished his phone out of his pocket. 'I need to get her there for 9.30.'

'I'm so sorry. You must get off. Just give me Lucy's number.' Alison's head dipped as she rummaged in her bag.

'It's OK.' Saviour hunched over his phone and, a moment later, from the kitchen, very faint, came Lucy's ringtone. It was like the phone was a tiny, electronic Lucy, a drop of her bright red essence. The creature in his belly shifted, and he saw her face that moment when Saviour gave her the bluebells: her shining eyes, and her gasp as she buried her nose in them.

'No answer,' said Saviour. The ringing stopped, and he put his own phone back in his pocket.

'OK, that's it. You've got to go, I've got to go. I'm going to phone the police.'

Jonah stiffened. He shook Raff's shoulder, and his brother curled up, making squeaky puppy sounds. Saviour had put his hand on Alison's arm.

'Ali, I'm as worried as you are, but I don't think the police are the answer.'

'I'm sorry, but you just accused me of turning my back on them. You can't now try and stop me from actually doing something about this situation!'

Jonah saw Saviour looking at his watch again. He had started to breathe heavily, as if he'd been running. He moved away from the window, and Jonah heard him coming back to the front door.

'OK, open up, guys!' he bellowed through the letter box. Raff sat up straight, his eyes open wide. 'This is your last chance! Alison's about to dial 999!'

The letter box snapped shut again, and Raff rolled off the sofa and fled upstairs.

51

'Jonah! Thank fuck!' Saviour's brawny arms scooped him up. He was sweaty and bristly, and his breath smelt awful, but Jonah melted into his big, warm body.

'It stinks in here!' Alison had pushed past them. 'Oh God!' She was looking down at the fruit crate.

Saviour put Jonah down and squatted in front of him, his eyes brown and kind. 'What's going on, mate?'

I think Mayo's dead. I think the Raggedy Man might have killed her. Jonah opened his mouth to say the words, but Bad Granny's passionflower face was suddenly there, buzzing like a wasp.

'We're ill,' he said. 'Mayo said we could stay at home.'

The brown eyes narrowed, lasering into him.

'Is there actual petrol in this?' Alison was inspecting the red and yellow can. 'It looks ancient. There are laws about storing petrol.' She pushed past them again. 'Lucy! Is she here?'

Saviour stood up, taking Jonah's hand, and they followed Alison into the kitchen.

'Oh shit.' Saviour let go of Jonah's hand. Alison had cupped her hand over her mouth and nose, too shocked to say anything.

'Jonah, mate.' Saviour sounded like he might cry. Batting

the flies out of his way, he walked over and pushed the lid of the bin open. He closed it again quickly, and Jonah saw him swallowing a retch.

'Lucy!' Alison had left the kitchen and was calling up the stairs.

Saviour looked at Jonah. 'Bit heavy, even for a strong boy like you.' His voice was husky. 'I'm so sorry, Jonah love,' he whispered. 'I've let you down.'

'It's OK,' Jonah stepped forward and wrapped his arms around his waist. Saviour ruffled his hair. Then he pushed Jonah gently away. 'Right!' he said. 'First things first! Let's get this thing out of here!'

He took the top off the bin and Jonah held his nose. He watched him take a dirty mug from the draining board, and use it to push the maggoty rubbish down into the bag.

'Where's Mummy, Jonah?' Alison had come back in. 'And why is her alarm clock ringing?'

'She's out.'

'Yes, but where?'

Jonah watched Saviour's hands tying the ears of black plastic.

'Where's she gone, Jonah?' Alison's earrings jangled as she lowered her pointy nose towards him.

'To the shops.'

'Which shops?' The earrings spiralled on either side of her jaw. 'Which shops? Jonah, can you please answer my question!'

'She's gone to the chemist,' he said. 'To get us some medicine. We've got bad tummies.'

Saviour was carrying the bin bag to the back door. He shot a look at Jonah.

'I'm not surprised, given the state of this place.' The earrings spiralled some more. 'So where's Raff, then?'

'Upstairs. He's probably hiding.' In Lucy's wardrobe maybe, hiding from policemen and the orphanage van man, with his net. Saviour came back in from the yard, wiping his hands on his jeans.

'Why would he be hiding?' Alison walked back out of the kitchen. Saviour and Jonah looked at each other as her feet thudded up the stairs.

'Have you really got a tummy ache?'

Jonah nodded, listening to Alison calling Raff's name. He needed to make a plan, a good one, one that would get them through the whole day, and Saviour's eyes were like torches, shining around his brain, looking for his thoughts.

'I know she's gone,' Saviour whispered. 'You don't have to keep pretending.'

There was a moment of complete silence. Down in Jonah's guts, the creature's eyes were open, but blind, in the darkness.

'She's gone. You and Raffy have been all alone. It's OK. I know.'

The creature moved, and made a sound, but a silent sound. Jonah nodded. Saviour let out a long, soft sigh.

'*There* you are, Raffy!' Alison's voice came through the ceiling. 'What are you doing in there? If you're ill, you should be in bed!'

Jonah was crying, and Saviour had knelt down and hugged him.

'Sshhh,' whispered Saviour. 'It's going to be OK. I've let you guys down, big time, but now I'm going to sort it.'

'I think she's dead.'

He felt Saviour's silent gasp. Then his hand started stroking his head. 'Do you, mate?' His voice so quiet, so gentle.

'The Raggedy Man saw her. With her boyfriend.'

'Her boyfriend?' The hand stopped stroking.

'The one who made her pregnant.' He was crying harder. 'Don't let Bad Granny take me but not Raff. Please, Saviour. Don't let anyone take Raffy away from me.'

'Never!' It was a whispered shout, and it came with a jolt, like electricity. He let Jonah go and crossed his heart, to show it was a promise.

'Why is Jonah crying?' Raff was behind them, standing next to Alison, who had tight hold of his limp arm. His voice was nonchalant, but his eyes were wide.

'I'm not,' Jonah said, quickly wiping the tears from his face.

'Because I'm going to an orphanage?' Raff said, tugging his arm from Alison's hand and turning to kick at a piece of broken piggy bank.

'You're not an *orphan*, Raffy,' said Alison, getting out her phone again. 'No need to over-dramatise things.'

Saviour cleared his throat. 'You get off, Ali,' he said firmly. 'I'll take it from here.'

Alison sighed. 'Well,' she said, 'if you're sure.' She put her bag higher over her shoulder. 'Maybe we could catch up later. Or get Lucy to phone me, when she turns up. I suppose you'll be in the hospital all day. I do hope it . . . all goes OK. Will you make it to the talent show?'

'The talent show!' Raff's face had lit up. He looked just like Lucy. 'Oh, *man*! I need to find my trilby!'

52

'Careful of the piles.'

'What?'

The tiny mounds of fingernails and the pencil shavings were still standing, after all these days, like the Pyramids. Jonah cupped his hands around them, protecting them from Saviour's tidying. He watched the calendar being hung back on its nail. The Camel woman arched backwards, her heart chakra open to the sky; beneath her the days, turned into squares. PED. Whatever it was, it was happening tomorrow. Saviour picked the wine bottle up off the table. 'Don't throw that away!'

'Why not?'

'It might have DNA.'

'DNA?' The bottle thudded on the bottom of the bin. 'Jonah, mate, go and help Raffy find his hat. I need to get you to school.' He was back at the table now, scrabbling through the flower pictures. He seemed to be looking for something. 'This is Dora's.' Saviour picked up the African mask book.

'I know. She lent it to ma—, to Lucy.' He'd said it in a way that sounded as if he thought one of them had stolen it. Jonah had an urge to snatch it from him, but instead he watched him open it and look at Lucy's pencil scribbles.

But her real name is CORDELIA. How uncordial, Cordelia! Giving me things, and then wanting them back.

Saviour closed the book and went back to tidying. He seemed to be in a terrible hurry, and Jonah wondered why he was bothering to tidy now, when he needed to get Dora to hospital. He was getting that feeling again, that strange, scary feeling, that Saviour – and all adults – were just children, pretending.

'Where's your mum's phone?'

'I don't know.' Her tiny red essence. He'd heard it ringing. Where was it? As he tried to remember, he saw the three African uncles, looking at him seriously, their fingers to their lips.

'Jonah, mate, I know you've been using her phone. Tell me where it is.'

On the floor. He'd dropped it, during the conversation with Christine – 'Are you there, Mrs Wemby!' – and it had slid under the table. He didn't want Saviour to find it, although he wasn't sure why. He sat down at the table. 'Why do you want it?'

'Because I want to look at her calls, and her messages.' Saviour had turned away and was hunting along the windowsill. Jonah reached for the phone with his foot, and drew it towards him.

'It'll be here somewhere.' Saviour pulled out his own phone and scrolled for Lucy's number. 'Can you remember the last time you used it?'

Turn it off. Don't let him hear it ring. The three Zambian uncles, frowning, urgent. But why? Jonah reached down, trying to look as if he was scratching his leg. As he straightened, he saw that the orange squash had nearly evaporated, and the dead ants were a thick, squishy mess at the bottom of the jug.

'Saviour.'

'What?' He looked up from his screen.

'Do you remember – when we went on holiday?' His finger searched for the red phone's Off button. 'And Mayo kept rescuing the insects.' He pressed it, hard.

'Insects.' Saviour walked out of the room, his phone held to his ear. Jonah followed him into the sitting room and watched him searching through the things on the mantelpiece. He picked up the Ophelia card, and turned it over.

'Was it good of her, to rescue the insects? I mean, does that – is that a good thing to do?'

Saviour folded the Ophelia card in half and shoved it into the back pocket of his shorts. 'Insects?' He glanced at him. 'Must be out of juice. It's going straight to voicemail.' He ended the call and looked at his watch. 'OK, we need to get going. Jonah, go and help Raff find his hat.'

53

'The ukelele's under here!' Raff was on his hands and knees, peering under Lucy's bed. The Tibetan bells were still going, but the battery must be running down, because they sounded weird. Jonah went over to the clock and tried to turn it off, but the button didn't work. The numbers on the clock's face had gone wrong as well; not numbers any more, just random flashing lines.

'My slingshot!' cried Raff. He aimed the catapult at Jonah. 'Phwoof! Clock's broke, fam.'

'What did you do to it?' Jonah tried to prise the back off the clock, but he couldn't.

'Nothing!' Raff was aiming at the lightshade. 'I just tried to turn it off, and it wouldn't. Phwoof! I need the ball. Where's the ball?'

Jonah looked down at the tea mugs and the lipsticked wine glass, crowded together on the bedside table. He picked up the little card with the X drawn on it, which had come with the flowers. *One long kiss, then?*

'I reckon my hat's in here somewhere.' Raff had dropped the catapult and was on his hands and knees again. Carrying the alarm clock, Jonah came and stood behind him. Long ago, maybe before Raff was born, he and Lucy had played Hide and Seek together. She chose different places to hide, but when it was his turn he always hid under her bed. Even though she knew where he was, she would still look all over the house. *'Joney! Where are you, Joney boy!'* The creature in his belly stirred.

'Bun dat clock, fam! Something *wrong* with that thing.'

Jonah looked down at the lines that used to form numbers. He picked the grey cardigan off the bedpost and wrapped it around the clock to muffle the sound; and then held the woolly parcel to his nose. So many different smells. He imagined all the molecules, clinging to its fibres: washing powder molecules, cooking molecules, sweat molecules coconut oil molecules, molecules of dust.

'What you doing with Mayo's cardigan?'

'It's Saviour's. He lent it to her, the day we took Dylan round.' She'd been all shivery, sitting on the grass, and he'd put it over her shoulders.

'What's Saviour doing?' Raff was looking over his shoulder. From downstairs came the sound of Saviour banging about.

'Tidying up. Kind of.'

'Kind of?'

'He's looking for Mayo's phone.'

'Why?'

Jonah shrugged. Then he said: 'He knows.'

'He knows she's gone?'

Jonah nodded.

'Is he going to phone Bad Granny?'

'I don't think so.' He reached out to ruffle Raff's hair, like a grown-up would. 'What about your hat? Is it there?'

Raff lowered himself back onto his stomach and got right under the bed, shoving things out of his way. The ukulele shot out in a cloud of dust. One of the strings was broken. The Tibetan bells seemed to be getting louder, and faster.

'Here it is!' The whole of Raff's body was under the bed, and his voice was muffled. Jonah went to crouch at the foot of the bed and peered into the dark, dusty space, remembering. '*Oh*, there *you are!*' He would roll himself out and jump into her arms, laughing. Now he lay flat and edged himself under. There had been much more room, back then, not only because he'd been much smaller, but because there'd been less stuff. His nose itching, he peered at the other dust-covered objects. Hair straightening tongs. Roland's weights. Part of a toy train. Right over by the skirting board, though, was that . . .? As Raff wriggled backwards with the trilby, Jonah wormed further forwards. Yes, a book. He couldn't reach it. He scooted himself back out the way he had come and stood up. Raff was whacking his hat against the bed, getting the dust out of it. Jonah walked around him to the head of the bed, dropped down and moved the tub of coconut butter out of the way. There it was; there it had been all the time he'd been looking for it, behind the coconut oil, propped up on its side against the skirting board.

Her diary.

54

'How do I look, fam!' Raff was putting on his hat. It fitted him properly now, and it suited him just as well as it always had. He went over to Lucy's mirror to admire himself, and Jonah sat on the bed with her diary in his lap. It was heavy, with a fancy leather cover. He opened it, and there she was – Mayo-Lucy – on the first page, in bright green ink, all big and small and twirly and loopy and higgledy-piggledy.

So D has bought me this new book, and this pen, with bright green ink in it. A present, for my 40th birthday!!! Would you believe it!

Down the sides and in between the paragraphs, her doodles.

She said it would be good to write things down.

Then some zigzags and spirals.

I've been a little low, these past few months. We make our own luck.

And I've done some bad things, and then I've got what
I deserved . . .

Some shapes that might be fishes or birds. He skimmed
down to a paragraph surrounded by hearts:

Then sometimes I just can't believe how lucky I am.
My lekker, lekker boys. Sometimes I look at them,
and I just melt into joyful nothingness . . .

'Ah wooo! Ah wooo!' Raff was doing his dance moves, pulling
faces and shooting his arms about.

Jonah flicked through the book. There weren't that many
entries: she hadn't written in it that often. Some were in
green and some in blue, and some in black. The longest one
was in brown felt-tip. Jonah kept turning the pages until he
found what she'd written sitting on the corduroy cushion.

Brighter today.

The softness of her against his back, the sun-warmed
concrete, her smell, her dry brown hand flipping the book
closed. He touched his finger on the words, and then read
down the page.

You were in my dream.
You stroked my face, such a tender touch, and when
I woke up I could still feel it. So sad. Then I
remembered. Despite everything, I am a mother, still.
Went tiptoeing in to look at them. Their snuffly breathing.
My treasures.

But then the text pinged, such a small sound, but into my mind like a gunshot, and my thoughts fluttered up like a bunch of crazy old pigeons.

'Bun this flippin' clock!' Raff had unwrapped it from the cardigan and was trying to get the back off it, like Jonah had done. 'Stupid fucking thing!' He threw it on the floor. It bounced and rolled before it settled, but the bells kept on ringing. Jonah looked back at the book. There was one entry after that, the last entry, quite long, in spluttery black biro.

Sunday, 8.30 p.m.
Felt better. Then up and down. J's eyes on me, so anxious. I tried. Took them to the lido, it was so HOT. Their wet, slippery bodies. My treasures. On the way home I saw that the passionflowers had opened. Hundreds of them, all over the Broken House fence.

The Tibetan bells suddenly went crazy, all squeaky and very fast, not like bells at all. Raff got up and started kicking it around the room.

Back at home, I made a jug of orange. Raff kept chattering. I couldn't talk back. The heaviness. I try to heave it, but it's like a sumo wrestler.

Waiting. My default position. You say you'll come soon, and I wait, and then I wait some more.
There are fairy tales about it.

There was a tiny sketch after that, of a tower, with a face looking out of the one high window.

I try to be patient, and remember that you love me, and, like you always tell me, I try to see it from your point of view. And then the panic takes over. I am tied to a railway track, and I can feel the train is coming. I writhe, it is no use. The only thing I can do is beg you.

Don't leave me. Just don't leave me. Please don't leave me.

'There's a devil in it. A spirit.' Raff picked the clock up and threw it against the wall. It left a dent in the paint and fell to the floor, finally silent. Raff gave a whoop, and kicked it again. Jonah turned the page. Some doodles, mainly spirals, and then the writing was much bigger, and the pen had gone deep into the paper.

BUT I HEREBY DECLARE that if you leave me I will tell EVERYONE. You will stagger down the road and everyone will point their finger, saying, 'THATS WHO DID IT!' That's the man who told ALL THOSE LIES. And ordered the death of his own child.

Just saying. Ruin my life, and I will ruin yours.

That creature again, deep in the pit of his belly, shifting about. The writing kept going on the other side of the page, but his eyes got sucked towards the picture covering the page on the right. It was a horrible, sexy drawing. He slapped his hand over it.

'What's that! Let me see!'

'No.' He slammed the book shut.

'Is that Mayo's diary? What does it say?'

'Jonah! Raff! What are you doing up there!' Saviour's voice, calling from down in the hall. 'Have you found the hat?'

'Go and show him how cool you look, Raff. Go on. We'll look at this later.'

Raff shot out of the room, and thudded down the stairs. Jonah went and squatted by the pile of letters on the floor. The hospital letter was near the top. He smoothed it out.

You have opted for the surgical procedure, under local anaesthetic. You will experience mild discomfort, and will need to rest afterwards. Please arrange to be collected from the clinic no earlier than 11 a.m.

He opened the diary again, to the page before the horrible drawing, the page he had just read, and ran his finger under the words until he found what he was looking for.

Ordered the death of his own child.

The tadpole baby. Swimming around in her tummy. Jonah looked back at the letter.

You are likely to experience some bleeding after the procedure.

Her bloodstained pants. The doctor's sucking machine. He dropped the hospital letter and, with a kind of shivery sigh, he turned to the next two pages of her diary.

The drawing on the right-hand page was of a naked man

with a huge penis, which was pointing up at the sky like an arm, and a woman, or a kind of woman, with a wild, evil face, wrapped around him like a boa constrictor. He put his hand over it again and read the words on the left page.

Of course they will hate me too. No, they will hate me more. I will be cast out, and you will be forgiven, poor helpless victim of my monstrous allure.

So then there's the suicide card.

Worthless too, because you know I could never leave my living, growing boys.

But it's the only one left in my hand, and I dream and dream of playing it, because then I'd be with you all the time. Not some pitiful washed-out wraith, whimpering and scratching on a window pane. No — dead, I will coil myself around you like a snake. Dead, you will NEVER get rid of me! Baby, I'll be so HOT, though, I'll be whispering your favourite filthy sweet nothings, I'll be your brazen necrobabe and you'll cry for me to stop, but you'll be so hard.

Jonah lifted his hand away from the drawing and quickly turned the page.

Alive, I lose, any which way you look at it. But dead, I win. Dead, I come into my own.

'Jonah! What are you doing up there!' Saviour's heavy tread was coming up the stairs. He slammed the book shut.

55

They stood outside waiting for Saviour, who had gone back to banging around in the kitchen. The clouds were strato-cumulus again, and the air smelt of dog poo and roses.

'What's he doing now?' asked Raff.

More rummaging and tidying. He'd been around Lucy's room, collecting the mugs from the bedside table, and the glasses. And his grey cardigan. He'd tied the arms of the cardigan around his waist.

'Yuk.' Raff had spotted the dog poo. Holding his nose, he stared down at it.

When Saviour came out, he was carrying the swimming bag. 'Right. I've got your toothbrushes and some clothes. We'll put a wash on later. Anything else you need?'

Jonah peered into the bag. The African mask book was in it. Would Saviour let Dora read Lucy's scribbles?

'Why do we need our toothbrushes and clothes?' asked Raff.

'Because you're coming to stay with us. I'm not having you two staying here on your own.' He slammed the front door shut, like they were never going to go back into that house again.

Jonah hoisted his book bag onto his shoulders. It was heavy, because of the diary.

But dead, I win

'Come on then.' Saviour took Raff's hand and they started walking.

'I think Mayo will come to Sports Day. And the Talent Show,' said Raff. 'Don't you, Saviour?'

Jonah looked up at Saviour's face. It was all scrunched up.

'She forgot to come to Sports Day last year,' said Raff. 'She was really upset she'd missed me winning all the races. So she'll definitely come this year.'

'She won't come, Raff,' said Jonah. 'Tell him, Saviour.'

They all stopped walking. Saviour cleared his throat, but didn't say anything.

'*He* thinks she's dead.' Raff kicked a stone. 'But Jonah, she might not be, you know.' He kicked the stone again. 'Anyway, Daddy might come. They might let him out of prison for it.'

Saviour put a hand on Raff's shoulder. 'Raffy, the main thing is to enjoy today.' His voice was croaky.

'Will *you* come?'

'I'll see how it goes at the hospital. See how Dora's op goes.'

'You have to come to the Talent Show! Em's doing her tap dance.'

'Yep. Hoping to get to that.'

'And our rap. You want to see that too, don't you?'

Saviour nodded.

'But Dora won't be able to, will she? She'll have to stay in hospital.'

'That's right.'

'You could film it! Then they could both see it! They could watch it together, when Mayo gets back!'

Saviour nodded again.

Raff looked up at him. 'Why are you crying?' He frowned. 'Do you think she's dead too?'

Jonah fixed his eyes on Saviour's lips, waiting for the answer.

'I know you'll make her very proud, Raffy,' he whispered. 'Wherever she is.' He reached for Jonah's hand. 'Both of you will. You always do.'

All holding hands now, the swimming bag slung over Saviour's shoulder, they started walking again.

'Saviour?'

'Yes, Raff.'

'You know Furtix?'

'Furtix?'

'That man. The one Daddy hit, because he was sexing Mayo on the table.'

'Felix. Felix Curtis,' said Saviour slowly.

'Yes, him.'

The swimming bag had slithered down Saviour's arm. He let go of Jonah's hand to sling it back onto his shoulder. 'What about him?'

'Do you think she might of gone to *his* house?'

'Felix Curtis,' Saviour whispered, his thumb still hooked under the handle of the bag, his eyes looking far away. Then he shook his head. 'I shouldn't think so, Raffy.' The bag across his back, his big, rough hand took Jonah's.

56

Miss Swann was wearing a stripy vest top, and her strange long shorts – or were they short trousers? She had been writing numbers on the whiteboard as he came in, but when she saw him, she put her pen down and took a step towards him.

'Jonah! There you are! Where have you been! You look . . .' As her eyes travelled over him, he became aware of the filthiness of his slept-in clothes. 'Jonah, have you got a note today?'

He shook his head. Feeling the whole class watching him, he walked to his place and sat down, sliding his book bag under the table. There was a long silence. He looked down into his lap, not wanting to meet anyone's eyes.

'Right.' Miss Swann swept up her whiteboard pen. 'Jonah, we're reviewing fractions. What do you remember about fractions?'

Jonah glanced at Harold, who pulled one of his lightning elastic faces. 'They're like . . .' He felt the heaviness of his school bag against his shins. 'Like half, and quarter.'

'OK.' Miss Swann wrote ½ and ¼ on the board, her pen squeaking. 'Shahana has just asked what the smallest fraction is.' She looked back at him. 'Any ideas, Jonah?'

Lots of people had shot their hands up. He shook his head, looking down at his desk.

'Bethlehem, then.'

'A millionth,' said Bethlehem. Jonah leant forward and slipped his hand down towards his bag, but now Harold had put his hand on his arm and was peering at him.

'Is she back?' he whispered.

Jonah shook his head. He didn't want to talk to Harold.

'You need to tell someone, man,' Harold whispered.

'I did.'

'Who?'

'Emerald's dad.' Jonah looked over at Emerald, and was surprised to see a boy in her place. 'Who's that?'

'It's her. She's had her hair cut off.'

As Jonah gazed at her, Emerald lifted her hands and ran them over her velvety head. Her face looked different, grown-up and brooding, and the bald, whispering man from his dream came back to him.

'What did he say?' Harold's eyes were gleaming. 'He's going to tell the police, right? Have you still got the wine bottle?'

'OK. So which is smaller, a millionth or a billionth?' asked Miss Swann. As hands went up, Jonah leaned forward and unzipped his bag.

'What are you doing?' whispered Harold out of the corner of his mouth.

'Nothing. Shut up.'

Harold's face closed, and he edged away.

'A millionth is smaller. No, a billionth, a billionth!' shouted Bethlehem.

'Absolutely sure?' asked Miss Swann. The book lay heavily in his lap now, and his right hand rested on it.

'A billionth would be smaller. But I think it would be too small,' said Daniella.

'Too small for what?'

'Too small to – see?'

'What about if you had a microscope, though? Tyreese?'

Tyreese said that there was no such thing as 'smallest', because whatever it was, you could always cut it in half, and Jonah sat still for a moment, wondering if things could be infinitely small, like the universe could be infinitely big. Then he opened the book and shuffled his chair back a few centimetres, so that he could look down into it as the voices around him carried on. He'd opened it at a brown felt-tip page. At the top of the page, in big, curly writing, she'd written 'Sunday'.

I'm like a child waiting for Christmas. I'm like . . .

Harold was arguing that you couldn't cut a molecule in half, because there were always six-hundred and seventy-five duodecillion molecules in the world, no more, no less.

What am I going to do if he regrets it? If he just doesn't phone? If that was it, beginning, middle and end?
I will DIE!

There were some spirals and zigzags. Then it said:

You are right, I am a Very Bad Person.

'But what about an atom?' Santi called out.

'Yes! Can an atom be split? What happens if we split an atom?'

Miss Swann's pen squeaked as she wrote on the board. Jonah was interested in atoms, but he only glanced up for a second, and as his eyes dropped back down, her voice faded, she was outside somewhere, they all were, and he was on his own, down among her words.

That Sunday feeling. Boys gone to Olympics with Dora and Em. All on my own.

The Olympics day, the best day of his life. Their seats couldn't have been much better: only a few rows from the track, overlooking the 100-metre finishing line.

And of course I'm hungover, which always emphasises everything.

But what is HE doing? Why is he taking so long?
I took so long getting ready, you wouldn't believe. The boys at the Martins already, so I had the house to myself, and it was like the old days, I smoked a cigarette in the bath!

I wore my red Lycra dress in the end, and my sparkly shoes. I kept dancing, imagining he was watching me, and I drank the bottle of wine I was meant to be taking.
I set off at 10 p.m. It was still warm, and the smell of bins, and people everywhere, because of the summer, and lots of them stared at me.

Because you were drunk. Jonah pictured her, slinking and swaying in her sparkly shoes. Then a blast of Angry

Saturday, the kitchen table, Roland coming in through the French windows.

D threw herself at me, she was so happy to see me, and I went through the motions but I didn't even hear what she was saying. Her hair was too yellow, and her skin was too pink, and her voice was too loud and screechy. I felt sorry for her, but also.

I don't know. She had lipstick on her teeth. I'm just a Very Bad Person.

Jonah turned the page. The brown writing went on and on.

The garden had been watered, it was all cool and leafy, and the smell of wet earth, and the fig tree. We were threading through all the people, and then D was introducing me to some chap, like she does, always matching me up. I kept laughing, but I wasn't concentrating, because I was getting anxious, because I couldn't see him, say if he wasn't THERE?! The chap, I can't remember anything about him, apart from how he stared at my boobs. Went back into the house. It was all bright, and I saw myself in a mirror and I looked like AWFUL, cheap yellow balloon-type, messed-up little slut. I had another glass of wine but I just hated myself, and he wasn't there, and I couldn't ask where he was. STUPID BLAZED BITCH. I saw D coming to find me, so I bolted. I was starting to cry, and then I turned the corner.

His silhouette. Bobbing towards me, my beloved, my

redemption. I was blazed, I couldn't walk in my stupid shoes, but oh lord – he was running! Literally running towards me through the darkness, whispering, Lucy! Baby!

He pushed me against the wall, into this tent of buddleia, and he started kissing me, and his hands were everywhere.

He called me baby. No one ever in my life has called me that.

The brown felt-tip ended. Miss Swann was talking about a war that was cold, and a curtain made of iron. He took a breath and flicked forward to the rude drawing. The man's penis, as big as an arm, an angry arm, shaking its fist; the woman's mad face, and the hairy hole in her bottom, like a cockroach. He turned over to read the very last page.

Alive, I lose. Any way you look at it. But dead, I win. Dead, I come into my own.

(And everyone will say, how could she DO that, what a selfish fucked-up BITCH. Her poor children, they'll say, but thinking, they will be SO much better off without that bitch.)

'Right! Has everyone remembered their PE kit for Sports Day?'

57

The clouds were smaller: altocumulus, maybe. He measured one, by holding up his fist to it, and then his thumb. They walked in twos to the park and, wanting to avoid any more of Harold's questions, he was walking with Roxy Khan, the new girl. He could see Harold's head, bobbing about at the front of the line, looking for him probably. Roxy Khan had black trainers on, but they were falling apart. Her white-socked big toe peeped out of the left one. Seeing her toe, without thinking, he found himself reaching for her hand. You were meant to hold hands with your partner, but you didn't, unless a teacher was actually looking right at you. Roxy snatched her hand away, as if he'd given her an electric shock, but he kept his held out, like you would with a very shy animal. After a couple of seconds she took it. Her hand was hot and damp, but he held it firmly.

A Sports Day without Lucy, or Dora, or Saviour. Or Roland, of course. He pictured Roland in his prison cell, looking at the sky through his tiny window and wondering what they were up to. And Saviour, in the hospital, maybe shaking and crying on a chair in the corridor, like he had on the Kumari bench, while Dora lay on the operating table, having her insides cut out by men in white masks. And Lucy? They were in the park now, passing the star-flower tree. He looked across the meadow to where the trees stood around the pond, imagining her leaning on the railings, talking in her proper English voice to Olive Sage.

'Oh, Miss Sage! I can't be long, I'm afraid. Both my sons will be running their races very shortly, and are very likely to win. Maybe you'd like to join me? My younger son in particular is such a talented athlete!'

They were coming to the field with the short grass, and the track marked out in white chalk. They slowed to a halt, waiting to be pointed to their allotted place. The sky was nearly all blue now, and the infants, already sitting cross-legged, had their sunhats on. Jonah scanned for Raff. There he was, his black trilby like a shark's fin among those bobbing bonnets. Beyond the children, adults were thwacking balls in the three tennis courts.

The signal came, and the crocodile swayed into motion. Jonah settled onto the grass next to Roxy, and looked over the track to the parents. There were a lot fewer of them than usual. Last year's Sports Day had been huge, coming just before the Olympics, and today felt very low-key in comparison. He scanned the adults, wondering if X was among them.

He pushed me against the wall, into this tent of buddleia, and he started kissing me, and his hands were everywhere.

His eyes swept along the line, resting for a moment on a white man in a suit, a bit fat, and very hot-looking. There weren't that many men: it was mainly mums. Alison hadn't arrived yet, and Harold's mum wasn't there. She never came. He wondered if Roxy's mum was there, or her dad – if she had a mum or a dad. She still had hold of his hand, and he was wondering about how to free himself, because it was too weird, holding hands while you were sitting down.

There was a screech as the loudspeaker was turned on and then Mr Mann announced the first race. A group of Reception children got up and followed their teacher, like ducklings. It was the dressing-up race, and a scarf, a hat and a handbag had been placed at intervals down each lane. Jonah watched the tiny children take their places at the starting line, remembering his own very first Sports Day. Lucy, in her red jumpsuit and clogs, little Raff on her hip, had arrived with the Martins. When Raff had caught sight of him, he had slithered down and charged towards him. As they'd hugged, Jonah had glanced around at the teachers, worried they might tell Raff off and send him back to Lucy; but they were all smiling and smiling, because three-year-old Raffy was the cutest thing they'd ever seen.

Roland had arrived later, with Bad Granny. Roland had been in his usual tidy hiking clothes, but Bad Granny had been all dressed up, in a huge floppy hat, a tight lacy dress and very high-heeled shoes. Lucy and Raff and the Martins were all sitting down on the Martins' huge picnic rug, but Bad Granny and Roland had stayed standing on the pavement above the field, because of Bad Granny's shoes. He had waved at them, and they had waved back. He had felt sorry for Roland. It had kept nearly raining, and Roland would put his umbrella up, and then put it down. Afterwards, Lucy and Dora had talked about Bad Granny's outfit. They'd both liked it, but it was ridiculous for a Sports Day and she was a bit old for the dress. Saviour had told them to leave the poor woman alone.

The Reception races were all over, Jonah realised. He hadn't been aware of any of them. Now the Year Ones were lining up for the Egg and Spoon. They weren't real eggs, they were plastic, like ping pong balls, which made it harder, because they were so light. It was the one he had won, when he was that little. He remembered how he'd kept his eyes fixed on that egg, the way Saviour had told him to. When he got his sticker, Lucy and Raff had come running over to hug him. Lucy had refused to be in the Mums' Race. He and Raff had begged and begged, but she'd said she would just wee herself, after the can of lager Saviour had given her. So they'd cheered for Dora, who had won easily. She was so tall, with such long legs, that the distance had only taken her about ten strides.

Saviour had persuaded Roland to be in the Dads' Race. He had gone over and shaken hands with him, and had bravely kissed Bad Granny on each cheek, and then taken Roland's arm. Roland had kept shaking his head, but had given in after a while. On the starting line, they neither of them looked like runners. Roland was too stiff-looking, with his high shoulders, and Saviour too heavy and close to the ground. Jonah knew neither of them would win, but he really hoped Roland didn't come last, because he knew how embarrassed he would be. Roland was always getting embarrassed about things. Lucy had told Dora it was because of Bad Granny: because she couldn't accept him for who he was. *'She once spent a whole day trying to teach him to tie up his shoelaces. A whole day! Imagine!'*

Roland had been in last place, and no wonder, because he leaned so far back behind his high-flying knees, he looked like he was riding one of those circus bicycles. Saviour had been doing nearly as badly, though his style was better, and they were neck-and-neck at the back, until right at the end when Saviour suddenly slowed down. Saviour had let Roland beat him, so he wouldn't come last. Had that been kind of him, or had it been treating him like a lame duck?

The Egg and Spoon was finished, and the clouds had cleared completely, leaving that beautiful emptiness. Jonah shaded his eyes and looked across at Raff. He and Tameron had their heads together and were muttering, probably rehearsing their rap for the millionth time. Saviour had helped Raff so much with that rap, coming up with rhyme after rhyme. Roland was a good person, who had done a bad thing. What about Saviour? And what about Dora? And what about Lucy?

He had managed to slip his hand out of Roxy's, but he realised she was looking at him. He looked back. Her eyes were green, the exact colour of peas. The pupils were small, because of the sunshine, of course. He focused on just the left eye, and saw that there was a yellow circle around the green, and that the white around it had tiny red threads in it. As he looked into the black space in the centre of the green, he thought of Miss Swann's question about whether there was a smallest fraction. There was infinity both ways, out in space and into Roxy's eye. *Where are you, Lucy?* He asked it silently, into Roxy's eye.

Then Roxy nodded over at the track, and there was Raff,

with his hat tipped down over his eyes, sauntering up to
the starting line. The Year 2 sprint was the first proper
race, and all the children had now sat up a bit. Raff would
win, unless Tameron beat him: it would be between the two
of them. Apart from . . . Out of the corner of his eye, Jonah
could see that a car had come into the park and was creeping
along the path towards them. He turned and looked, and
his stomach turned over. It was a bright yellow car, with
little green squares on it, and a light on its roof, which was
flashing on and off, but slowly.

He turned back to look at Raff. He'd been given a spare
PE kit, but he had his ordinary school shoes on. They
hadn't remembered to find his trainers. He got the middle
lane, in between two white boys: Charlie, who was pretty
fast, but better at longer distances, and Milo, who was
Rufus's little brother, and might be good, Jonah wasn't
sure. Tameron got the outside lane. Would Raff mind if
Tameron beat him this year? A handful of Year 2 parents
had come to stand along the track and call out their sons'
names.

Jonah jumped to his feet, ready to yell Raff's name, but
the trouble was that the yellow and green car was getting
nearer all the time. And now, all around him, other people
were noticing, and it felt like everything was braking,
going into slow motion. Mr Mann's body straightened,
and his big nose swung sideways. He looked over his
shoulder and slowly lowered his loudspeaker. Most of the
parents were swivelling round now, and the children's
heads were turning too. Jonah looked at Raff. Raff looked
at Jonah.

The police car stopped up on the path, right where Roland

and Bad Granny had been, the year they came. Two policemen climbed out, all padded and hot-looking, and came walking heavily over the grass. Parents were getting to their feet, and Mr Mann was picking his way through them, on his way to meet the bulky officers. Behind them, Jonah saw that another vehicle had turned into the park, a big yellow van. But he'd told Raff that there was no such thing as an orphanage van. He looked at Raff again. Everyone else was moving forwards, but he had edged backwards, as if he was about to turn and run. Is that what they should do? Jonah glanced at Miss Swann. Like everyone else, she was looking at the policemen. They might make it, if they went now, and ran for their lives. But where should they go? Not back to the house: that would be the first place the police would look.

It was getting really noisy. The parents were all talking to each other and moving towards their children, and the children were standing up, but the teachers were shouting at them to sit back down. There was an engine noise as well – not the car, or the ambulance – but something else, far away, and getting nearer. Mr Mann was talking to the policemen now, and he suddenly turned and looked straight at Jonah. Too late, then. Expecting to be beckoned over, Jonah looked towards Raff, but he couldn't see him because all the parents were blocking his view. As he pushed his way through, he noticed they'd stopped moving and were all looking up at the sky. Raff was already running away, his arms pumping like mad. He would have definitely won the race, it was amazing how fast he was, and it was amazing that his hat was staying on. Jonah started running after him. In the tennis courts, the players had all stopped playing and were looking up too, their hands on their hips. The engine noise was louder now, and very recognisable. Jonah turned and, running backwards, watched the whirling black dot emerge from the blue.

58

He followed Raff along the side of the courts without a hope of catching up, but the long grass behind the courts slowed his brother down. It was that stalky, sticky grass, and it was alive with insects, and there were nettles too, and litter, and lots of tennis balls. Treading the channel Raff had left in his wake, Jonah caught up with him as he reached the trees. They were gnarly old trees, bramble-covered, bent double, their branches reaching down into the litter-strewn weeds. Bent double himself, Raff wormed his way in. Jonah dropped to his knees and peered into the smelly darkness. He could just see his brother, crouched against a tree trunk, with his arms wrapped around his legs. The noise of the helicopter was everywhere now, and Jonah had to shout.

'Raff! Come back out! We need to keep moving, they'll find us if we stay here!'

Raff blew a fly off his nose, and said something Jonah couldn't hear.

Jonah looked back. He was surprised the policemen hadn't followed them yet, and weren't beating their way through the grass with their truncheons, handcuffs dangling from their belts. Only a matter of time, because the helicopter was circling, presumably looking for them; there would be a man staring down, through very powerful binoculars. Jonah lay himself flat, his hands over his ears, looking up through the grass. It came directly above them and he could see its underside, its long, thin feet and its angrily whirring tail. The noise was deafening.

He put his face down, his nose squishing against the dirt, and covered his head with his arms. *Please God.* He tried to summon up the underwatery feeling, to believe in him enough, so that he would be real, but all he could see was the Child Catcher, ringing his bells, his enormous nose sniffing the air. *Please God, don't let them find us. Let us escape.* But where would they escape to? There was something stinky very close to him, probably fox poo, but he didn't dare move an inch. *Please God. If they do catch us, don't let them take Raffy away from me. Please God. Let me go to the orphanage too.* The helicopter seemed to have moved away, because the noise wasn't quite so loud. He turned his head to one side.

'My hat fell off.' Raff had crawled next to him. Jonah reached for his hand and squeezed it. 'I suppose I don't need it anyway. They won't let me have it in the orphanage.'

The helicopter had definitely moved away. Jonah sat up, looking to see where it was going. It seemed to be circling again. He brushed the dirt off his face and his shirt.

'Will they let me stay for the Talent Show?' Raff sat up too. 'Or will they take me away straightaway?'

Jonah put his arm around his shoulder, his eyes fixed on the helicopter. 'I don't think they've seen us. I think maybe . . . if we stay here . . .' The helicopter was moving away again, over the tennis courts and towards the chalk-marked field, which was empty but for the policemen. He looked behind them, into the undergrowth. 'Or we could go further in. Slither in, like snakes, and then stay very still.'

'But if they've got dogs, the dogs will find us,' said Raff. 'They'll find my hat, and give it to the dog to sniff.'

'*Ice cream! Lollipops!*' The Child Catcher's nose, twitching. Jonah got on his stomach again, and edged his way under the tangled branches. Just beyond him, he saw that there was a gap, a little clearing, and he crawled into it. A dusty little space, with a low roof of branches and leaves, but big enough to kneel in, even crouch in. The trees were so close together that they muffled the sound of the helicopter. 'Raffy, come,' he called quietly.

Raff came slithering through, and they sat together, looking around. 'Sick,' Raffy breathed. It was like their own leafy little room, made by a circle of the gnarly, stumpy trees. 'We could live here!' said Raff. 'With all our guards guarding us.' He pointed at one of the trees. 'Look at that one. It's an elephant.'

Jonah looked. In some places the bark had swollen into smooth lumps, and in others it had fallen into folds, like a curtain. He frowned for a moment, but then saw it. It only had one ear, a flag of ivy dropping from a short, thin branch, but it had a smooth, wide brow and a long, wide trunk, with tusks either side. The best thing was its eyes, which were far apart, but exactly level with each other, and small and kind and wise.

'I remembered those two girls,' said Raff, 'those two twins.'

'Scarlett and Indigo?'

Raff nodded. 'I remembered us going to their house, and you jumping with them on the trampoline.'

The barbeque. Raff had been too little to go on the trampoline, but Roland had lifted Jonah onto it. It had been a bit scary, but Scarlett and Indigo had each taken one of his hands and helped him jump.

'They used to play with us in the park on Sunday mornings,' said Jonah. They were the kind of girls who liked playing with littler children – looking after them, like big sisters. 'Their mum went to Pilates, so their dad used to bring them to the playground.'

'Furtix?'

Jonah nodded. The thought of Felix Curtis made him turn and look back through the leaves to the park. He pulled down a couple of branches to make a window.

'Why don't they come any more?'

'To the playground?' Jonah peered out. The helicopter was low now, about to land. A cloud of what looked like smoke, but was actually dust from the ground, was billowing around it. 'You know what, Raffy.'

'What?'

Jonah pushed down on the branches and leaned further forward. The green and yellow van was parked on the path, and people in green uniforms were opening the doors. The children, teachers and parents were in a big huddle further along the path. 'I think it might be the hospital helicopter.' He turned and looked at his brother. 'It's not looking for us at all.'

Raff came to see, his cheek against Jonah's. The people in green uniforms were bringing something out of the van: a trolley of some sort.

'It's an ambulance,' said Jonah. 'It's waiting to take the person in the helicopter to hospital.'

'Mayo!' Raff was on his feet, trying to force his way through the branches. 'It's Mayo, in the helicopter! They've found her! They've rescued her from the bad man's house!' He kicked and punched his way out of the tree room and started crashing through the undergrowth.

'It won't be Mayo, Raff!' Jonah shouted after him.

'It is! They've put the bad man in prison and they're bringing her to hospital!' Raff took off, charging through the grass like a rhinoceros calf.

'Raff!'

Jonah threw himself after him, brambles slashing his shins. When he reached the grass, something tripped him up and he fell. By the time he'd got to his feet Raff had nearly reached the tennis courts. The helicopter had landed, and the propellers were slowing. He waded through the grass winded from his fall. Raff was running back along the tennis courts, now. As the helicopter noise died to nothing, he could hear his shouts. Could it . . . was there any chance . . . *might* it be her? The words from the hospital letter in her bedroom suddenly danced in front of his eyes. *You are likely to experience some bleeding after the procedure.* There were people climbing out of the helicopter, and the side door was being opened, and the ambulance people were wheeling the trolley over. He broke into a jog, but his slashed legs were really hurting, and he suddenly felt incredibly tired. He dropped back to a walk, watching one of the policemen walk towards Raff with his hand held up.

On the tennis courts, the players were gathered at the far end, watching the stretcher being passed out of the helicopter. The body on it seemed to be wrapped up in some kind of plastic and there were tubes coming out of it, and two of the ambulance people were carrying the things the tubes were going into. Whoever it was, that person was seriously, seriously hurt. He stopped, leaning against the wire fence. So would it be better if it *wasn't* her? Maybe a spirit mother who lived mainly up in the sky was better than a mother who was so hurt she needed tubes coming in and out of her? He squinted his eyes to try and see if the injured person was male or female, black or white, but it was impossible to tell.

Now the policeman had picked Raff up, and he was kicking and punching, and still shouting, 'Mayo!' Mr Mann was running over, and Mrs Blakeston, and Miss Swann, though you couldn't call what Miss Swann was doing running . . . *Oh, Raffy.* Jonah found he was pressing his hands together. *Oh, God, please let it be her. Please God. Even if there's a dead baby in her, and it's made her arms and legs go rotten . . . even if she's just a head and body, or just a head. We'll look after her, God, we'll feed her, and get her dressed, and everything. She'll be our roly-poly Mayo and we'll roll her down the hill, and we'll roll after her, and lie next to her, and it will be the three of us, looking up into the sky, and laughing . . .*

The stretcher was lifted into the ambulance, and the doors were closed. The policeman had passed Raffy to Mr Mann and was talking to Miss Swann and Mrs Blakeston, and now, peeling away from the group on the path, there was Alison, walking over to join them. But now Raffy was slithering out of Mr Mann's arms and running towards the ambulance, just as it started moving. It was going slowly, and Raff's legs were still surprisingly fast, and it looked like he might catch it, but Mr Mann was running after him, shouting, 'Raffy! It's not your mum!'

So no roly-poly Mayo to roll down the hill; just some smashed-up stranger, probably from a car accident. Jonah slumped against the wire fencing, wondering whether the person was a mother, and whether she had two boys. How old were they, and did they already know what had happened? Had they been collected from school, were they on their way to the hospital, crying and holding hands? He felt the creature again, waking up in his belly, like a baby seal, moving its head from side to side, trying to see in the blackness. The ambulance was still crawling, because they weren't allowed to go fast in the park. A stocky, familiar figure was coming the other way, and he stepped off the path to let it pass. Raff was still running – how could he keep running that fast! But Saviour was stepping back onto the path, and Raff was running into his open arms.

As Jonah started walking again, the ambulance drove away and the helicopter men were letting the children come and look at the helicopter. The teachers came with them, and the parents, and they all swarmed around the black and yellow machine. Saviour still had Raff in his arms and was talking to Miss Swann.

'It's all over, Mayo,' Jonah whispered. 'They all know you're gone.' He could feel the creature still, a package of dread and sadness, but there was a kind of relief in realising he was no longer in control. He walked slowly towards the helicopter, but then stopped at the edge of the crowd.

Saviour put Raff down, and spoke to Emerald, who was standing beside him. Then he took Raff's hand and led him through the crowd to the open door at the side of the helicopter. The pilot leaned down and was shaking his head, but Saviour was talking and laying his hand on the man's arm. The pilot listened for a while, and then he looked down at Raff and nodded. Saviour lifted Raff up, and the pilot reached for him. Raff was getting to go inside the helicopter. *Thank you, Saviour.* He was a good man. He was their friend. They weren't his lame ducks. He was a good man who *hadn't* done a bad thing, hadn't ruined lives, like Roland had. Ruined lives. What *had* happened to Scarlett and Indigo? If the Curtises were all living in that same house on the Angry Road, why didn't they ever come to the park?

Everything was starting up again. The parents were in groups, chatting; the tennis players were knocking up, and the teachers seemed to be trying to organise the children. Saviour and Emerald were still peering up into the helicopter. Jonah pushed his hands into his shorts pockets. Maybe Felix Curtis's wife had left him, and taken Scarlett and Indigo to live somewhere else. He was remembering her now: Jules, her name was. Small and thin, with a ponytail, and she wore sunglasses, like Felix Curtis did. When she took off her sunglasses, her eyes were all red and puffy . . . but when was that? After Angry Saturday, or before? She had come round to their house, to tell Lucy what she thought of her. In that icy voice. Jonah winced and gripped the roll of money in his pocket. Jules Curtis. Had she taken Scarlett and Indigo, and left Felix Curtis all alone in that house? He saw him jumping on the trampoline, all by himself, in his white shirt and his blue jeans, jumping and jumping, because there was nothing else to do. Had Lucy ever gone to see him? Had she ever cycled round there, on her golden bicycle?

Jonah let go of the roll of money. There was something else in his pocket: a piece of card. As Mr Mann's loudspeaker shrieked, he pulled it out. The flowers card, with the X on it.

'Ladies and gentlemen, boys and girls . . .' boomed Mr Mann. Raff was standing in the door of the helicopter now, and Saviour was reaching up to him. 'We need to be heading back to school.' It was all a bit chaotic. Teachers were trying to round up their classes, but lots of children had attached themselves to their parents and were already walking towards the gate. 'As you know, Haredale's Got Talent will be kicking off at 3.30.' There was a cheer, but quite a small one, because everyone was swarming away. Jonah stared at the X. 'Parents, please let your child's teacher know if your child will be going back to the school with you . . .'

Felix ended in X. Might you use the last letter of your name as your signature? Jonah looked up the hill. You could get to the Angry Road that way, it was somewhere behind the Martins' road and over to the right. Miss Swann was running around, trying to count up the Year 4s, and Saviour, Raff and Emerald were still talking to the helicopter men. Jonah looked up to the top of the park, and then to where the trees started, around the pond. Not that far away, and once he was among the trees he would be invisible.

59

The Angry Road was up near Bellevue Road, about ten minutes' walk from the school. Jonah hadn't been there since Angry Saturday, and it wasn't as wide as he remembered, and the houses weren't as grand; but the trees were still angry, shaking their coppiced fists at him. Very thirsty again, the scratches on his legs throbbing, he walked from tree to tree, looking at each house, feeling each house look back at him. Which one was it? That one. He remembered the stained-glass panel with the red poppies. Those were the railings that Lucy's gold bike had been chained to. And that was the dark blue gate he and Raff had watched Roland go through, as they waited in the car.

Jonah went through the gate and up to the front door. Of course they'd been here that other day, the barbeque day, when Lucy had worn her tight denim shorts. He could only remember the garden, though, with all the people, and jumping on the trampoline with Scarlett and Indigo. Roland had got Raff's toys out of his backpack for him, and had sat playing with him on the grass, sometimes looking up at Jonah and giving him a wave.

The picture of the poppies was made out of lots and lots

of tiny bits of glass. Like jigsaw pieces. He trailed his finger along a black lead line, remembering Lucy's pencil, drawing the skeleton lily. Then he knelt down and looked through the letter box, like Roland had done, like they'd seen him do through the raindrop-covered windscreen. The hall was clean and bare, with those floor tiles – brown, blue and cream – like at the Martins'. He could hear music playing, faint, but beautiful. It seemed to be just one instrument, but he couldn't work out what it was. It sounded almost like a human voice, telling a story, a very sad story. He listened for a while, then let the letter box close gently, stood up and went to the side gate, as Roland had. Through the wooden slats of the gate, beyond the shady passage, he could make out a sunlit slice of garden. He tried the handle. It turned and, as it had for Roland, the gate swung open.

He walked through the deep gloom of the passage and stopped when he got out into the dazzling sun. He could hear the music again – sad, but warm and velvety. What *was* that instrument? The garden was smaller than he remembered, and empty. On the day of the barbeque it had been packed. Then his eyes adjusted to the glare and he saw that the trampoline was still there; and that there was a figure by it, which was either a scarecrow, or a very still man. He shaded his eyes with his hand. It was a man. He was wearing a suit, for some reason. He had one hand in his jacket pocket, and he was staring at the flower bed in front of him. His hair was grey, and his shoulders were hunched so that his neck and head came out of them like a turtle's. He looked too old to be Felix Curtis.

Jonah stepped onto the grass. The movement made the man's head turn, and he looked frightened to see him there.

He took a step back, and looked towards the house, as if
for help. The French windows were open, as they had been
on Angry Saturday. Jonah and the man both gazed at the
shadowy space between the glinting glass, but only the
music came out into the garden.

Jonah looked back at the man, who shuffled on the spot
for a moment, his hand still in his pocket, and then came
walking up the grass. Jonah licked his lips. They were all
crusty still, and he could taste blood in the deep crack. The
man shuffled to a stop, about a metre away. His suit was
covered in hairs and fluff, and he had socks on, but no shoes;
and instead of looking at Jonah, he looked at the space next
to him.

'Are you Felix Curtis?' Jonah managed to whisper.

Still looking at the space, the man took a while clearing
his throat. 'That's right,' he said. His voice sounded like it
had cobwebs in it, as if he hadn't tried speaking in a very
long time. In the long pause, the instrument soared, like a
bird or a comet. Jonah noticed the purple veins on Felix
Curtis's nose.

'I was just wondering if you'd – seen my mum.'

Felix Curtis shuffled himself round, and shaded his eyes
to look down the garden. His lips were moving, as if he was
rehearsing some lines for a play. Finally he said, 'Have you
lost her, then?'

'Yes,' Jonah said. 'She's gone.'

'Oh,' said Felix Curtis. There was a long pause, and then
he sighed. 'Not sure if I can help you, I'm afraid.'

'You haven't seen her, then?'

Felix Curtis shook his head. He lifted his unpocketed hand
and looked at his fingernails. They were yellow and very long.

'Did you send her some flowers?'

Felix Curtis frowned, and his eyes finally met Jonah's, just for a second, but long enough for him to see that they were green, like Roxy Khan's. 'Flowers,' he whispered. 'I don't think . . .' He looked back at his fingernails, thinking.

'Lucy,' said Jonah. 'She's called Lucy. Lucy Mwembe.'

Felix Curtis stepped back, shocked. His lips fumbled and mumbled, and his skin went as grey as his hair.

'Felix? Who's that?'

A woman had come out of the French windows, a small, fat woman, with a ponytail. Wrapping her cardigan around her body, she walked barefoot across the grass and came and stood next to Felix Curtis.

'Who are you?' She peered at him, suspicious, not recognising him, and he realised how much he must have grown since the last time she'd seen him – and how filthy he was, from crawling around in the undergrowth.

'Jonah.' As he said it, he felt warm blood trickle from in his lip.

'Jonah. And what are you doing in our garden, Jonah?' She had noticed the blood, and was watching it travel down his chin.

'I was wondering if . . .'

'Yes?' Softer now. Because of the blood. He wiped it with the back of his hand.

'If I could have a glass of water?'

The woman looked at Felix Curtis, wrapping her cardigan tighter. 'Do you know who this is?'

'It's Lucy's son,' whispered Felix Curtis.

The woman stiffened. She stared down at him, her throat pulsing. 'Jonah! Of course it's Jonah. What are you doing here? Did – did your mother send you?' She was looking down at the scratches on his legs now.

'No. I just – I think I must have got lost. I'm sorry.' Jonah turned to go, but she put her hand on his shoulder. When he looked back up at her, the kindness in her eyes made him want to cry and cry. 'You look like you've been in the wars, Jonah. Come and get a glass of water.'

The three of them walked very slowly across the grass, past the barbeque area and through the French windows. The kitchen was big, with a high glass ceiling, and the beautiful music swirled around it like invisible liquid. The ceiling glass was very dirty, so the light coming through it was throwing spots and clumps and speckles over everything. The room was divided by a long counter, with a sink in it, and some tall stools around the end. The music was coming from two speakers on the shelving unit against the far wall. The speakers were on either end of the highest shelf, and the player was on the shelf below. It was so strange to think that the beautiful sound was being built inside that small silver box, from number patterns, long streams of 0s and 1s. Right in front of them was a long wooden table, piled with papers and books, and there was a bowl, with two shrivelled oranges in it, and some elastic bands.

The table Lucy had been lying on.

There were four elastic bands in the fruit bowl: two small thin ones, one blue and one red, and two thick strong ones, the ones that postmen used around their bundles of letters, the ones you could ping like a catapult. This was where she had been lying, and where Felix Curtis had kept going: creating the force which had sent Roland hurtling towards the saucepan.

The music came to a sudden stop. The woman had turned it off, and now she was going round the counter to the fridge. Felix Curtis shuffled himself onto one of the stools. He put his hands on the counter and stared down at them, his mouth was twisted into a kind of smile. Was he remembering? Remembering how he kept on going? The woman got a jug of water out of the fridge. Seeing her face from the side, with the ponytail sticking out at the back, he suddenly realised that it was Jules who had come to their house, with that same ponytail. She'd been much thinner then. As she reached into a cupboard for a glass, Jonah approached the counter. It was dusty. Everywhere was dusty.

'Here you are,' said Jules. They had been Felix and Jules. Or maybe Jules and Felix. Standing together at the barbeque, his arm around her waist. Taking the glass, Jonah noticed the pots and pans hanging above the olden-days, cream-coloured oven, and wondered if the ratatouille saucepan was there. The water was freezing. He glugged all of it, and Jules took the glass back off him and went to refill it. He hiccupped, and both adults looked at him. Embarrassed, he pointed at the photograph on the wall. 'Scarlett and Indigo.' Their freckled faces were grinning, like they'd just heard a very funny joke.

Jules glanced at the photograph. 'Yes, that's right.'

Felix Curtis was suddenly on his feet again, and moving towards the shelves. His hands had left two marks on the dusty counter.

'Are they at school?' Jonah asked.

'Yes. Boarding school. They'll be home at the weekend.' As she handed him the glass again, that velvet caramel yearning sound flooded the whole of the room. Jules opened her mouth and closed it again, and wrapped her cardigan very tight. They watched Felix shuffle back to his stool and fit his hands very carefully into the marks they'd left. *You kept on going. And then my father hit you with the saucepan. Do you remember?*

Jonah stared at Felix's hands, suddenly seeing him on the park bench, with his cup of coffee, and his black shiny sunglasses, and his crisp white shirt. The instrument was murmuring, and then wailing, and then dropping into a whisper, like it was telling the story of Felix and Lucy and Jules and Roland; and Scarlett and Indigo; and Jonah and Raff. Listening, it came to Jonah that it was the story of why sadness had to exist. *It has to exist, Mayo, doesn't it?* He saw her nodding, saw her eyes watching him, with the wise, patient love of an elephant.

'Jonah.' He looked up. Jules was trying to say something, but the music was too loud. She shook her head and went over to the music player. 'That's better.' She had turned it right down, so you could hardly hear it.

Felix pressed his hands onto the counter, his face twisting. *He kept going.* It was impossible to imagine.

'Jonah.' Jules had laid her hand on his shoulder again.

'Yes.'

'Why are you here?'

Her eyes were blue and very pretty. They had been so red and puffy, the day she'd come into their house and sworn in that icy voice. The instrument was faint, but it was still telling the story, and it was like it was the voice of an elephant. He strained his ears towards the sound.

'Jonah?' Her hand was still resting gently on his shoulder, and he realised he had closed his eyes. He opened them, and drank some more water, and her hand slid off. He put the glass down on the table where Lucy had lain. 'Are you alright?'

He nodded, glancing at Felix, who was getting off his stool again.

'Are you here because of tomorrow?'

'Tomorrow?'

'Yes. Because of – your dad? It is tomorrow, isn't it?'

'My dad?'

'Yes.' As Jules started scrabbling through the piles of paper on the table, Felix turned the volume back up, very high. She wheeled round. 'It's too *loud*, darling! We can't hear each other if it's that loud!'

Felix stood by the music player, his hands in his pockets, grimacing down at his socked feet. Jules sighed, and turned back to the piles of paper. Jonah watched her hands sort through them. *Daddy?* His heart was fluttering, and the steam train came to him, the steam train at the end of *The Railway Children*.

'Here it is!' Jules was holding up a letter. She looked at it for a moment, and then handed it to him. The words, all printed and official, danced around, and as they settled, three of them jumped out at him.

Parole Eligibility Date.

Jules was saying something and shaking her head. She crossed over to the shelves again, putting her hands on Felix and moving him to one side. Parole Eligibility Date. P-E-D. That's what Lucy had written on the calendar.

The music came to another sudden stop. Jules turned around.

'Jonah, I don't understand. Did you even *know* your dad was being released tomorrow?'

The steam, clearing from the station platform. Jonah cleared his throat. 'Not – exactly.'

'But why not? Your mother must know.' Jules took the letter back and folded it, staring at him, her pretty eyes deeply puzzled. 'So why *have* you come?'

Jonah's mind was completely blank. He looked over at Felix, who was still staring at his feet. 'I don't know,' he said. 'I mean, I was thirsty. But anyway . . .' He looked back through the French windows. 'I think I'd better go now.'

'Where?'

'Where?'

'Yes, where? Are you going home?'

'No, I'm going back to school. For the Talent Show. It will be starting soon, and my brother's in it.'

'Your brother – Raphael? I remember.' Jules put the letter in her pocket. 'Well, OK.' Jonah took a step towards the door, and then stopped. 'You know the music.'

Felix looked up.

'The music?' said Jules.

'I was wondering what it was. The instrument.'

'A trumpet. Why? Did you like it?'

Jonah nodded. Felix's eyes rested on him, for the first time.

'A man called Miles Davis was playing it.'

Jonah nodded again. 'Miles Davis,' he said, and looked towards the door.

Jules stepped forward and held her hand out. 'Well, goodbye, Jonah.'

He took her hand and shook it. 'Thank you for the water.'

'You're welcome. I'm glad you liked the music. And I . . .' She paused, and then gave him a very sweet, twinkly smile. 'I do hope Raffy does well in the Talent Show.'

60

The playground had been decorated with balloons and flags, and there was a tombola stall, and a hoopla, and a hook-a-duck. There was a drinks table under the big tree, and Jonah caught sight of Harold, who was taking money while Mrs Blakeston poured glasses of wine. He wormed his way through the swarming people, desperate to find Raff and tell him about Roland. He couldn't see him. He made his way to the hall.

The hall was much quieter than the playground. The loudest thing was the big banner over the stage, proclaiming, 'HAREDALE'S GOT TALENT!' Rows of seats had been put out for the show, and on the stage itself stood a drum kit and a piano. Ms Watkins, still in her Sports Day shorts, was setting up some microphones. A few parents were wandering up and down, looking at the history projects on the walls. There was no sign of Raff.

A woman in a yellow cardigan was looking at Jonah's project. He sidled closer, looking up.

'Did you do this one?' She was quite old, maybe a grand-parent. He nodded, and she said, 'Very well done!'

'Thank you.'

'Who took this?' She pointed at the photo that looked up into the swimming-pool sky.

'My mum.'

'She's a very good photographer.' The old woman looked down at him again, with a smile. Jonah smiled back.

'My father's coming out of prison tomorrow.'

'Really? How nice. I'm very pleased for all of you.' She nodded and moved off, to look at the next project, and he looked up at the photograph. *You're a very good photographer, Ma—* He got a sudden, strong whiff of coconut, and kept perfectly still, his whole body alert. It was as if she had come to stand behind him; as if her arms were about to wrap around him and her chin about to rest on his head. But when he turned, he found himself looking into Emerald's wide grey eyes.

'Hi, Jonah,' she said. She was wearing a silver baseball cap, and a dark blue vest and leggings. Her feet were bare, and she was holding a silver tap shoe in each hand. He looked around the room, inhaling. The coconut smell had gone. 'Yours is definitely the best, you know.'

'What? Oh, thank you.' He glanced back up at his project. Up on the stage, Ms Watkins was tapping the microphones and saying, 'One, two.'

'Where's Lucy?' asked Emerald.

'She's not here,' said Jonah.

'She's coming though. She can't miss Raffy's rap!'

Jonah shrugged.

'*My* mum isn't coming,' said Emerald.

'I know.'

Mr Mann's loudspeaker voice was telling all performers to go backstage, and asking people to start taking their seats. Emerald sat down to put her tap shoes on. She took her hat off and laid it beside her, and Jonah gazed at her shorn, velvety head, wanting to reach out and touch it.

'After the show, you and Raffy are coming for a sleepover!' Emerald jumped up, the metal on her soles tapping the wooden floor. 'Dad needs to go back to the hospital, so Ben from next door is going to babysit. It's going to be really fun! We're going to watch films and get takeaway pizza!'

Jonah smiled back at her. 'Why did you get your hair cut off?' he said.

'To look like Mum. Last time she went completely bald.'

'And then it grew back again.'

'Yes.' Behind her, Ms Watkins bent over to fiddle with the sound system.

'You know my dad?'

Emerald looked at him, frowning. 'Roland.' She said his name doubtfully. She'd probably only met him a couple of times.

Jonah nodded. 'He's coming out of prison tomorrow.'

Emerald screeched and wrapped herself around him. Then she took hold of both his hands and danced him round, her shoes clattering on the floor.

There was a sudden burst of Justin Bieber. Ms Watkins killed it, and called over to them. 'Children, you need to be backstage. Especially you, Emerald, you're first up.'

'Come on, Joney!'

'I'm not going backstage,' he whispered. 'I want to be in the audience. To watch Raffy.'

61

The hall was filling up, and he hesitated, wanting a place near the front, but not wanting to be spotted by a teacher and sent backstage. Then he saw Saviour, already sitting at the end of the second row, waving at him and pointing to the empty seat beside him.

'There you are. Where have you been?'

'Just' . . . Jonah slipped into the seat. 'Is Raff OK?'

Saviour nodded. Jonah looked up at the blue velvet curtains, which had been hung specially for the show. It was about to begin. *Are you coming, Mayo?* He turned and looked at the audience. All the seats were filled now, and there were some people standing at the back. It was very hot, and people had begun fanning themselves with their programmes. Jonah picked up the programme lying on Saviour's lap. Emerald first, tap-dancing to 'Baby' by Justin Bieber, but where were Raff and Tameron? Second to last. The last item being what he was meant to be in: the whole school choir singing 'Starman' by David Bowie. Saviour would love it. He loved all David Bowie songs. He had wanted Emerald to do a tap dance to 'Changes', and he'd explained his idea to her dance teacher. '*She just looked at me like I was a nutter,'*

he'd said, and Lucy had said, with a laughing groan, '*Saviour,
you are a nutter!*' But when had that been? When had Saviour
talked to Lucy about his tap-dancing idea?

Ms Watkins, who had managed to change from her shorts
into a smart shirt and trousers, was walking up the steps
and sticking her head through the blue velvet curtains. And
now she was beckoning Mr Mann, and he was following
her up onto the stage, and the last people standing were
quickly cramming themselves into the remaining seats. The
tap-dancing conversation. He remembered now. Dora hadn't
been there, and neither had Emerald, he didn't think. No,
Saviour had come on his own, with a box of tiny strawberries. It was the time they'd all helped Raff with his rap, out
in the concrete backyard – Saviour lying back on the corduroy
cushion and Lucy pulling the cork out of a bottle of wine.

Ms Watkins stood next to the sound system, and Mr
Mann stood in front of the curtains, waiting for everyone
to quieten down. When they did, he talked for a bit, about
what a good year it had been and how wonderfully talented
all the children were. He mentioned Sports Day, and said
he hoped *this* event wouldn't suffer any interruptions.
Everyone laughed, even though it wasn't *that* funny. Saviour
had his camera ready. It was actually Dora's, a proper film
camera. The lights went down, and the blue velvet curtains
slowly opened. And then there was Emerald, holding a pose
as Justin Bieber went '*Oh-oh-oh-oh-oh-oh aah,*' like an electronic angel.

When the words began, Emerald fell into their rhythm.
Jonah didn't really like Justin Bieber, but watching her face
and her clever feet, he felt the sadness of the song and what
it might be like to want and want to kiss someone, and be

their boyfriend. Some of the children started to join in, and as Justin got to his second verse, you could feel the whole audience getting ready to flood the hall with the chorus. *'Like Baby, Baby, Baby, oh!'*

'He called me Baby.' Why did people who sexed each other call each other 'Baby'? He imagined himself as a teenager, calling a girl 'Baby'. Not Emerald – although he did actually really like her. He looked sideways. Saviour had stopped filming. He was slumped, staring, and his cheeks were wet with tears. Was he crying about Dora? About the doctors rummaging around in her opened-up body, while their nine-year-old daughter danced? Jonah looked over his shoulder again. *Are you coming, Mayo?* He sniffed, trying to get that coconut smell back. Beside him, Saviour wiped his face. Jonah put his hand on his leg. Saviour nodded, and held the camera up again.

After Emerald came a saxophone player from Year 5 called Jake, accompanied by Ms Watkins on the piano. It was quite a long, jazzy piece, which went well with the weather. If Lucy was here, she'd be humming along under her breath. Then came a gymnastics routine from four Year 1 girls, and he imagined Lucy shrieking at their cuteness. But then a big group of recorder players came on, which would make her groan, because the recorders always went on too long. A laughing groan: the same groan she'd made when Saviour had told her about his tap-dancing to 'Changes' idea. The strawberries were wrapped in wet newspaper, and they looked like tiny red jewels, and Lucy had said, *'Fancy a glass of wine?'*

Ms Watkins was turned to the audience now, holding her finger to her lips, because there was lots of talking and the recorders were waiting to start their last piece, which was 'Greensleeves'. Jonah looked at Saviour again. He was looking at the programme, and then at his watch. *'Fancy a glass of wine?'* she'd said, smiling her sparkly smile.

Phew! The recorders finally finished, and trooped off down the steps. Violins next, and they were awful, really screechy; Lucy would be giggling, and putting her fingers in her ears. He glanced behind him a third time. Would she arrive just in time for Raff and Tameron, laughing at the joke she'd played on them, teasing him for being so worried? She was always teasing people.

'You want poor Emerald to dance to some octogenarian?'

'He's in his early sixties! And he was in his thirties when he recorded "Changes"!'

'He's never been a proper pop star, though, not like lovely Justin . . .'

'What are you talking about!' He'd grabbed her wrists, pretending to be furious, and she'd giggled.

Two to go, before Raff and Tameron. The guitarists were good, they always were, and for their last song Lola from Year 6 came onstage to sing with them. She had a great voice, and it was 'Summertime', which Lucy would have loved. Next came the whole of Reception, singing 'Frère Jacques' in a round. Adorable, as Lucy would have said, but Jonah's stomach was churning now, because the moment was about to arrive.

There was a long pause after Reception had toddled down the steps, and everyone in the audience started talking. Saviour picked up Dora's camera, getting it ready to record. Jonah gazed at the empty stage, refusing to allow himself to look back again. Finally Ms Watkins came and sat at the piano, and a boy called Izzy from Year 6 put what looked like a small circle of cardboard in the middle of the stage, before sitting himself behind the drum kit. A group of Year 2 girls came on next, five of them, led by Diahan, all wearing swimming costumes and sunglasses and carrying beach balls. The audience burst out laughing, and they were being really funny, wiggling their bums and blowing kisses. Then they got into a line, and Izzy was tapping a beat, and Ms Watkins was playing some chords. And, as the chatter died down, you could hear that the girls were murmuring something. Jonah leant forward, cupping his hands around his ears, and it was the chorus, the Camber Sands chorus.

Smelly Shelly, Uh-huh, Smelly Shelly

They were stepping from side to side now, and clapping their hands, and it was so weird, and it was also VERY funny. Jonah looked at Saviour, who looked back and winked, and held the camera to his eye.

It was a big build-up. The clapping got louder and louder, as the audience all joined in, and lots of them joined in the chant too. Mrs Blakeston and Christine were walking up and down the aisles, handing out sheets of printed paper, and when Jonah got his he saw that it was the words they were going to hear.

When Raff and Tameron finally came on, there was a roar of laughter. Tameron had sunglasses and Raff had his trilby, and they both had their trousers hanging down so their pants showed. They slouched around for a bit, doing their shoulder shrugging and their hand movements, and then, once

TAMSIN GREY

the audience had calmed down, Raff went over to a microphone.

Woke up early put some bread in da toastah

He and Lucy had heard it so many times before, but this,
finally . . .

Bright sunny day and da world is ma oystah

That's Raffy, Mayo! My brother Raffy! Why wasn't she here?
He leaned forward again, bursting with pride and wrenched
with sadness.

Me and ma homeys takin' off for da beach
Blockin' up da road wid our double-decker coach

Raff looked at the girls and made a sign, and they all put
their hands on imaginary steering wheels as they chanted.
He and Tameron high-fived, and then it was Tameron's
turn at the microphone.

Dat coach had SPEED, man! Fast as a Ferrari!

The girls all started zooming around the stage, honking
their horns.

But dat driver he OLD, man, all beaky and gnarly

Raff staggered to the microphone, bent double, with an
imaginary walking stick.

He said

Tameron stepped back and Raff was on again, being the bad-tempered old coach driver.

> *No eating, no drinkin' and no vomit*
> *Control these evil children*

'And the teacher says,' said Tameron.

'I'm on it!' shouted Diahan, and there was a quick burst of clapping. Jonah turned the word sheet over. On the other side there was a short explanation of the song.

> *Raphael and Tameron's rap was inspired by the Year 2 trip to Camber Sands in June. I think you'll agree it's a colourful and imaginative account, capturing a very special day.*

> *I was lookin' all around for the White Cliffs of Dover*
> *But something caught my eye and I bent right over*

That had been his rhyme! Right back at the beginning, when Raff had first started writing it, just after the trip. He watched Raff bend over and pick up the piece of cardboard, which was meant to be a shell, of course.

> *A shell, a whole one, two sides tightly closed*
> *The creature inside it havin' a doze*

He didn't remember that bit. Of course Tameron had written loads of it. Tameron took the cardboard shell off Raff.

Fitted in my hand like a mobile phone
I held it to my nose and I started to groan

All the girls groaned, and Diahan shouted:

There's a creature in that shell
And it ain't very well!

The audience laughed again. Jonah looked back down at the explanation.

The idea came from the boys themselves, and the song is their own work, with a little help from a few friends!

Saviour had been so good at thinking of rhymes. Jonah looked at him again. He was recording still, his lips mouthing the words.

Gimme Smelly Shelly please don't take it away
Teacher, that's my creature and it's here to stay

'Teacher, that's my creature' – that was one of Lucy's. A really good one.

Tameron would like to thank Tyreese, Talcott, Theodore and DaMarco . . .

His brothers. '*So all the brothers' names begin with T, apart from DaMarco.*' Lucy had pointed that out, in a conversation about the Thompson boys, long ago. '*Does DaMarco mind, do you think?*'

I showed it to my ma and she started to bray
She said that Shelly's smelly, will you throw that thing away

There were some more people that Tameron wanted to thank: Anthony, who was his dad, and someone called Reubina. Jonah looked down to the next line.

Raphael would like to thank Jonah, Lucy . . .

Why had they written Raff's long name? Had he asked them to? He hardly ever got called Raphael. There was a third name, after Lucy's, a French name. There had been a boy with that name in the book that Madame Loiseau had read with them in Year 2.

Uh-huh Smelly Shelly . . ..

They were coming to the scary bit, the bit when Shelly opens up. Jonah looked up at the stage. Tameron and Raff were rapping together now, more quietly, and the rhythm had changed slightly, as they built up to the terrible climax.

Lay down in ma bed with ma Shelly by ma head
But I shoulda listened to what my mama said
Cos ma eyes slammed shut and the moon rose up

'Aah Wooo! Aaah Wooo!' cried the girls.

Saviour had put the camera down. Why? Because he was crying again, crying his eyes out this time. Was he crying because he was sad or happy? Was he remembering lying on the corduroy cushion, coming up with all those rhymes?

Jonah looked back at the programme. 'Jonah, Lucy and Xavier'. He stared at the name, remembering how Madame Loiseau had pronounced it.

> *My eyes opened wide, the light was pouring inside*
> *I looked at Smelly Shelly and I wanted to hide*
> *Cos I heard a creak, the thing was startin' to break*

'Xavier'. But you pronounced the *X* as a *Z*. Zavier. Za-vee-eh.

> *It was oozing from the shell, this big jelly ghost*
> *And I ran round the room with my fingers on my nose*
> *Ooh! Smelly Shelly should have listened to my teach!*
> *Ooh! Smelly Shelly should have left you on the beach!*

It was the crescendo, and they were wailing now, Raff and Tameron, wailing and stamping, and the girls had pushed their sunglasses onto their heads to show their terrified eyes.

> *I ran through ma house and that smelly creature followed*
> *I ran into the street and with my lungs I hollowed*

'Hollowed' should really be 'hollered'; Raff hadn't been sure about it, but Saviour said it would be fine. Jonah tapped Saviour's arm, and he wiped his face and looked down at the name Jonah was pointing at.

> *Save me from the slimy ghost, the big smelly jelly*
> *Save me from the creature who's come*
> *out of Smelly Shelly!*

'Who's that?'

Saviour frowned, not understanding.

'Xavier.' Jonah pronounced it carefully, just like Madame Loiseau had.

Saviour had looked back at the stage, so he tapped his arm again. 'Who's Xavier, Saviour?'

62

It was like suddenly remembering a dream, a dream he couldn't believe he'd forgotten; all those glad-eyed looks, and their hands, always touching. As the rap ended and the clapping began, the memories came tumbling like a flipbook. Her red dress, the smell of mince pies, his soft voice saying, 'Lucy, love'; and in summertime, the bluebells – yes, the way he gave her that bunch of bluebells, the way she took them, her glistening eyes. The clapping was very loud, and he heard Xavier Martin shout, 'Encore!' which was French, like his name. Xavier, on their doorstep, with the box of tiny strawberries, deciding to come in for a glass of wine. The relief of it: the way the house suddenly filled with her happiness. People were getting to their feet now, and he was down, down, down, below the frantic clapping hands. 'That's why Dora stopped coming,' he whispered. 'That's why you stopped being friends with her, Lucy.' But she wasn't there.

He looked up at the stage. Raff and Tameron and the girls were standing in a line, and Raff was sucking his cheeks in to stop himself from grinning. Some people had sat down, but lots were still standing, including Xavier Martin. The clapping was going on and on, and someone at the back wolf-whistled, and Ms Watkins and Izzy were joining the line. As Jonah slid off his chair, the Camber Sands word sheet slipped off his lap and fell silently to the floor.

It was nice and quiet in the playground, and the air was fresh and cool. He went to his classroom to fetch his bag and noticed, in the empty room, a trace of Miss Swann's rosewater. As he walked back across the playground, he heard 'Starman' beginning, those first chords, and the Year 6 girls singing 'Goodbye love' in ghostly voices. His bag was heavy, because of her diary, and he hoisted it onto his shoulder as he went through the school gate. He didn't know what time it was, and the lights were . . . He imagined the rows of children now on the stage, the 'Oh, Oh, Oh' coming from their little round mouths. He couldn't hear the singing any more, but the tune continued in his head and he hummed along to it as he walked home.

The house felt very tidy, and even quieter than the street. Still humming, he went into the sitting room, and looked across the road. Leonie was standing outside her shop, smoking thoughtfully, her other hand cupping her elbow. As he looked at her, he thought about Lucy setting off to see Felix Curtis on Angry Saturday, riding her golden bicycle, in her sparkly shoes. He wondered why she had wanted to sex him so much, why she couldn't just sex Roland, and he stopped humming, trying to understand the bigger part of her, the part that was Lucy, not Mayo; trying to *hear* and *feel* the actual, silent voice in her head.

Leonie went back inside, and he walked into the kitchen and sat down at the clean, bare table. He remembered watching Saviour – *Xavier* – clearing up, throwing the wine bottle away, and how he hadn't wanted him to find the red phone. Then he remembered the first time they ever saw him, in the playground, holding hands with Emerald; his messy clothes, and his friendly smile and his truthful eyes. 'We just liked him straightaway, Mayo, didn't we?' he whispered.

He looked through the window at the concrete backyard. The yellow-flowering weeds had multiplied, and the plants in the plant pots were thriving, too. As he gazed at the delphiniums, he suddenly thought of Dylan – Dylan in his cage, coming out, very slowly, into the Martins' huge-seeming garden. 'Just a few weeks ago, wasn't it?' he murmured. 'It was cold, though.' He wrapped himself in his arms. *You were already pregnant.* Cold and sunny, the grass damp and very green. Lucy silent and shivering, Dora chatting away, Xavier bringing out the tea tray and the grey cardigan.

Dora had kept talking and talking, while he put the cardigan around Lucy's shoulders; talking about the rabbits. Elsie had stayed still, watching Dylan, who had hopped about, sniffing at things. *'Oh, they're made for each other!'* Dora had cried. *'Aren't they adorable? They'll have the sweetest babies!'* And he'd turned his head and seen them, Lucy Mwembe and Xavier Martin, locked into each other's eyes.

He unwrapped his arms, and rested his head on the table, wondering if the tadpole baby had been a boy or a girl. Then he pulled her diary out of his school bag, and her red phone, and laid them side by side. He looked at them both for a while, and then he opened the diary up and found the page he'd skimmed over in the classroom.

I want to tell someone about today. Who, though. No one left. Just a lack. It was raining, and I got soaked through, and the receptionist laughed when she saw me. Don't you have an umbrella! I told her my sons had taken it to school. I was glad to mention my sons, to let her know I have actual, live children. I got to take off my wet clothes anyway, because they wanted me to put on a nylon gown. Dark green with a white trim, and a tie at the side.

He did pick me up, though. I was all groggy, and shivering. I couldn't talk. The busy room, the monitors, the metal instruments, the noise. My tears rolling sideways, into my ears. He drove me home, but he couldn't stop. He said he'd come back later.

That's what he says. And then I wait for him.

He's going to tell her. That's what he said. We just need to get this bit over, he said. But now I don't know if I believe him. I want him to come, and hold me, and say he feels sad too, about our baby. Then I don't want him to come, ever, because I don't want to hear what I think he might say.

Jonah blinked and wiped his eyes, and looked into the yard again, thinking about the sucking machine, and what might happen to a thing that hadn't actually been born. Would it still grow into a person, in Heaven or wherever, or would it stay a tiny tadpole, blind and wordless? *There's a Staarmaan!* He imagined the baby growing into a Star Person, luminous and alone, wishing it could meet its earthly brothers.

There was another clump of writing at the bottom of the page. He wiped his eyes again.

Dora pops up, amongst all my thoughts, a kind of jack-in-the-box octopus.
'Riddled with cancer.'
My darling friend. If it weren't for all this, I would have looked after you, D. I would have sat by your bed and stroked your hair.

Jonah saw a movement out of the corner of his eyes. He closed the book, looked back out of the window and saw the Raggedy Man. He was sitting on top of the wall, staring back. When Jonah stood up, he beckoned, before disappearing behind the wall.

63

Out in the yard, he could smell the dampness of the corduroy cushion. The dip was still there, and his eyes fixed on it, the shape of it, the shape she had left behind. As he stared, the dip seemed to become something alive, seemed to be looking back at him, knowing how afraid he was. *Fear is a kind of magnet . . .* He looked up at the wall, at the space the Raggedy Man had been in. *It can actually make bad things happen . . . It sucks them towards you, like iron filings . . .* He turned away and looked into the kitchen, at where he'd just been sitting, and saw her phone on the table, and her diary, closed, with all her words inside. He looked up again, and felt the Broken House sucking him in.

Using the golden bike, he climbed up, and sat looking down at the big hole that used to be a window. The Raggedy Man must have already gone inside. He looked down at his legs. The scratches from the brambles were actually really bad. *I want my mummy.* That's what little children said, when they hurt themselves. He put his hand on his belly, feeling the creature, and gazed at the hole.

I can't, Mayo. He got a flash of her face, but only a flash. *I'm too tired.* Even if he managed to get down from the wall, his legs would be too weak to carry him into the Broken House. The dread icy in his stomach, he looked over his shoulder at their yard. Then he looked back at the hole, which was like the entrance to a cave, and he saw them again, his three Zambian uncles, peering out at him. Their faces were a bit like Lucy's face, because they were her brothers: the brothers she had looked after when her own mother died. They were waiting for him and, with a rush of courage, he jumped down off the wall, but his landing jolted him and made too big a sound. He froze and looked at the hole, which was just a hole, with no uncles. He tiptoed over and leaned into the coolness, which smelt of dust and birds and foxes. He looked behind him again, up at the wall, and the blue sky above it, and then he put his hands where the windowsill used to be, climbed over and dropped down onto the rubble.

It was dark, and really quite cold, and he could smell another smell, very faint, but it made his heart race, because it was incense. He looked around for the Raggedy Man, who was real, not like the uncles, but it was too dark to see anything much. He stayed still until he could see better, and then he started picking his way over the rubble, remembering coming in the other direction with Raff on Monday. He was glad Raffy wasn't with him. He could see better now, and the room seemed empty, but he had that feeling that he was being watched. *Breathe.* Yes, he hadn't been breathing. He tried to take a proper deep breath, but somehow he couldn't. He looked across at the Wendy house, and wondered if that's where the Raggedy Man was. No, he was too big to fit himself through the little door. He started walking again, the rubble very hard through the soles of his shoes, the cold air picking out the scratches on his legs. *Breathe.* He breathed, and the 'Star Man' chorus started up in his head, very quietly. His eyes had adjusted enough now for him to be able to see the objects mixed up with the rubble. He saw the Monopoly board, and a ping pong ball, and the toy train, and the one-armed doll. He noticed that, as well as only having one arm, part of its head was smashed in. *Like Felix Curtis.* There was the bed again, such a strange bed, all spick and span, with its mattress and sheets and blankets on. Maybe the Raggedy Man was lying beneath it, looking out at him. *Two old chairs and half a candle* . . . The way she read the words to them, the soft loveliness of her voice. He could hear the pigeons now, because he was almost below where the hole in the roof was, with the light falling through; and he could see the carpet; yes, that lumpy old carpet, with the noughts and crosses pattern – he'd stepped over it on Monday.

Jonah stopped, sniffing for the incense, the way he'd sniffed for the coconut. 'Are you here, Mayo?' he whispered. He didn't feel like calling her Lucy. He looked round for the Raggedy Man, slowly and carefully this time, peering into each corner; but either he was hiding under the bed, or he'd gone through to the hall and into the kitchen, or maybe up the stairs. He looked up. He was in just the right place to see the complete rectangle of sky, bird-edged, their tails poking out into the blue. 'It's like a swimming pool,' he whispered. 'We could dive into it. Couldn't we, Mayo?'

His eyes filled with tears then, and the tears rolled down his face, because he wanted her so much. But then he heard a noise from somewhere above, and the dread stopped the crying. 'Mayo?' He stared up. Maybe it was the Raggedy Man, though, watching him through a peephole. He stayed still as a statue, his neck craning, listening for another sound. All he could hear was the pigeons, and after a while he straightened his neck and looked around the room again. There was the bed. And the Wendy house. And that piece of concrete pipe which he'd crawled into, but she'd been too big. And there in the wall, the hole of light, the hole that he'd come through, from the world outside. He shivered. Then he walked over to the carpet.

It was very dirty, but you could still just about see the pattern. There were lines, crossing over each other, making squares, and fitted into the squares were other shapes, circles and crosses and crowns. Some were red and some were black, and actually it was more of chessboard than noughts and crosses. Gazing at the shapes, he put his hands in his pockets and felt the roll of leftover horse money. 'You won us that money,' he whispered, 'Didn't you, clever Mayo?'

He bent down and picked up one of the corners of the carpet. It was sticky, and the underneath side was kind of rubbery, and it was very heavy. He needed both of his hands to lift the corner high enough to throw it back. He staggered, found his feet, and then looked down. He hadn't managed to move very much of the carpet, and it was starting to unflip itself, roll itself back over what he'd uncovered. Just before it did, he saw the foot.

64

He stood very still. In that quick glimpse he'd seen that the foot had red toenails and gold rings. He thought about her feet in her clogs, and in her sparkly high-heel shoes, and her bare feet, padding around the house. Then he thought of the sunlight on Monday morning, *his* feet in the tangled sheet; his dream, the screeching birds, and then seeing on the clock that it was 04.37.

He stayed like that for quite a long time, pictures forming and evaporating in his head. The Lido, on Sunday, her feet dangling in the water; not coming in – he'd wondered why. Much longer ago, when he was really little, sitting in a sandpit, he'd buried her feet. Such strong brown feet, with the gold toe-rings. Her toenails had been purple then, though. The holiday in France, her feet walking along the edge of the swimming pool, rescuing the insects with the net. '*Nice to get away from it all!*' Dora's bright, fake voice, and Lucy's closed face, her hard mouth, her eyes slitted like letter boxes.

'*Nice to get away from it all!*' The pictures had gone, and it was just those words, on a loop in his head. After a while, he decided that he should try and lift the carpet again – but not with his hands, because he didn't want to accidentally touch the foot. He looked around. He could see quite well now, in the gloom, and he found what he was looking for quite quickly. A stick, which was actually more a piece of wood, all splintery, with nails in it. He turned back and levered the stick under the corner of the carpet. It was tricky, because the carpet kept slithering off the wood, but then the rubber caught on one of the nails and, using all the strength in his biceps, he managed to lift it high enough to see the foot again.

Yes, the gold rings and the red nails, but he would have recognised it without them, because a foot is actually as particular as a face. Then his arms gave way and he let go of the stick, and the carpet flapped back down over her foot. *Mayo.* He crouched down, wondering if she might be a tiny bit alive. Alive enough to have lit the incense? They burned incense at funerals. Maybe she'd been getting everything ready.

He glanced around the room. When he looked back at her shape, it seemed very small and flat. *You are very well hidden, Mayo!* He remembered their hide and seek game, such a long time ago. Had Raff even been born? Taking it in turns to count, and him always hiding under the bed, and she looking for him round the house. Everything had gone quiet. He looked around again, wondering about the Raggedy Man. *Where did you go, Raggedy Man? Are you hiding, too?* He turned himself slowly around, pivoting on the spot, looking carefully, until his eyes came back to the carpet. *Have you been playing with the Raggedy Man, Mayo?* He got a flash of her counting, hands covering her eyes, and then, 'Coming!' The creature inside him was awake, staring in the darkness, and then it shifted, and a sound came out of his own mouth that he'd never heard before. *Mayo.* He hadn't wanted to be near the foot, but now, because the longing was unbearable, he wondered whether he might crawl under the carpet and snuggle up to her. Even if she wasn't alive, it would still be her body: it would still be his Mayo.

He tipped onto his hands and knees, and tried to move himself forwards, like a baby, trying to crawl. Then he tipped sideways, so that he was lying in the dirt, curled up in a little ball. He could feel the creature moving, trying to turn in that small space, and it couldn't, because it was expanding – not a worm, not a seal, but something stranger, one of those prehistoric creatures. And it was dangerous. Not evil, how could it be evil, it was just a few days old, it knew nothing, just the blackness, but still dangerous, because if he let it, it could take over not only his body but also his mind. He had to soothe it back to sleep. It couldn't get any bigger, and it mustn't open its mouth, mustn't learn to scream. *Shhh.* He held his belly. It was like he could see it, see its ancient, newborn face, those unformed features, those sightless eyes. *Shhh.* It was part of himself, but if he gave it voice, it would be *his* voice, and the old Jonah would be obliterated.

And then he heard someone jumping down from the garden wall.

He stiffened, but stayed still, curled up on the sharp stones. The person was out of breath, panting, and he pictured the face, pausing, looking at the hole in the wall. Next was the blocking out of the light by the person's shape – he sensed it rather than seeing the difference with

his eyes. A grunt, and then the heaviness of the landing
on the rubble, and the wheezing breath now, with him, in
the Broken House.

65

'Jonah, mate.' His cockney voice was cracked and terrible. He stooped over him, trying to scoop him up, but Jonah curled tighter and pressed himself down against the ground, resisting. Xavier stopped trying, and let out a long, rickety sigh. He sat down next to him, grunting and creaking, and laid his hand on his back. 'Jonah, mate,' he said again.

'*Jonah, mate. Where's the whale?*' He'd winked and they'd high-fived. So long ago: the playground on Monday morning.

'Jonah, I need to get you out of here.'

'Why do you?' His own voice sounded dreamy, small and faraway, but clear and kind of sparkly.

'Because . . .' Xavier turned away, looking around the room. 'This isn't the place for you, Joney boy.'

'Why isn't it the place?' Such a strange voice, coming out of him, the way it was so faint and yet so clear, like he was a ghost child, or it was being transmitted from another planet.

'It . . .' Xavier paused, and Jonah could feel a kind of panic coming from him, and it came to him that Xavier had a creature too. But then he heaved himself back to his feet and, in a firm, grown-up voice, said, 'Come on.' He bent, trying to get a grip on him again, but Jonah rolled away from his hands.

'No.' He'd rolled so that he was lying nearly next to her, his knees and his hands actually on the edge of the carpet. 'I want to stay here.' Out of the corner of his eye he could see the rectangle of sky. 'I want to stay with Mayo.' Now his voice was like Raff's young voice, high, with a quiver in it.

'Mate, please.' This time Xavier did manage to lift him, and staggered with him for a few steps, before Jonah slipped out of his arms.

'No. I'm staying with Mayo.' He crouched, and took hold of the edge of the carpet, but it felt horrible, all sticky and spongy. He dropped it, and wiped his hands on his shirt. 'I'm not leaving her on her own,' he said, and sat back down.

'Jonah, she's not . . .' Xavier sighed a groaning sigh. 'She's not here, mate! You've got to understand! It's not her!'

It's not you! Jonah's heart lifted like a crazy, flapping bird. It was all pretend – a joke! 'Where is she then?' He twisted round to look up at Xavier.

'I didn't mean . . .' Xavier covered his face with his hands, and the flapping bird dropped like a stone. *He means you're not in your body. He means your body is just your worn-out clothes.* A wildness took hold of him, and he found himself on his feet, backing away and screaming her name. From the wildness he could see Xavier, in front of him, shouting too, trying to shut him up, and then crumpling, giving up, clapping his hands over his ears. 'Mayo!' He turned and screamed at her shape, because she *had* to come out, she *had* to be alive – until his screams became sobs and he fell down on his knees.

'That's enough, mate.' This time, when Xavier picked him up, he had his arms pinned to his sides. 'That's enough for now, OK? She won't be on her own for long, the police will come, and – and look after her. They'll take her away.'

'No!' Jonah struggled with all his strength. *I won't let them take you away, Mayo.* Now that he'd found her, he wouldn't lose her again. But Xavier had him so tight, he wore himself out, and, crying, softened into a dead, hopeless weight. Xavier hoisted him up, so that he was half hanging over his shoulder, and started trudging with him back towards the hole in the Broken House wall, but he couldn't see where he was treading and kept losing his footing. By the Wendy house, he staggered and fell backwards, all the way down onto his bum, and Jonah squirmed away, and Xavier stayed on the ground, whimpering. Jonah looked back to the carpet. A smoky, pearly shaft of light was falling from the sky right onto her shape, and he stayed still, staring and trembling. *Are you a ghost, Mayo?* Would he see her diving up, into the swimming pool and through it, all the way up to where the gods in their togas were? *Don't go. You need to stay.* She could be like the bench ghosts, Olive Sage and Hilda Jenkins, and little Kumari; she could stay, and wait for him and Raffy, and then they could go together, hand in hand.

'Jonah.' Xavier had managed to get up. 'Let's keep it together, mate. Just for a little while. OK?'

Jonah looked at the Wendy house. Such a dear little house, with a tiny porch and a railing, and curtains in the windows and the knocker on the front door. The door was ajar, and he dropped to his knees and pushed it open.

'Mate, don't go in there.'

As he crawled through the doorway, his face hit a blanket

of cobwebs. He stopped and wiped them away, and then kept on going, patting his hands over the dusty floor to see what was there. Plastic things. Toys. He felt with his fingers, a little teapot and a cup, and what must be a banana. Something bigger, also plastic, a bit jingly and rattly. He pushed it to one side so that he could get himself all in, and turn around and close the door.

It's nice to get away from it all. Although it was just a box really, a wooden box, lodged in the rubble. Above him, the roof had a tear in it, and through it he could see up to the Broken House rafters. A broken house inside the Broken House. Like a Russian doll. The two windows were just empty squares, but they had their little checked curtains, hanging from hooks. He tucked the curtain of the back window up over itself, feeling insects scurry across the fabric, and over his hand. Now there was more light coming into the Wendy house, and he could see the concrete pipe, and all the way across the room, to the hole in the wall. He lifted the plastic jangly thing onto his lap, and smiled to himself because, yes, it was one of those plastic shop-tills, copied from the ones they used to have in olden-days shops. *Do you remember, Mayo?* There'd been one at the play group she used to take him to. She'd shown him how to press the keys and make the numbers pop up, and then press the button that popped out the drawer.

Xavier was scrabbling at the door. Jonah pushed his feet against it to keep it closed, letting go of the till, and taking hold of both windowsills. As he listened to Xavier's breathing, which was like a saw cutting through wood, he remembered the picture in the *Alice in Wonderland* book: Alice grown too big, from drinking the stuff in the bottle.

'I didn't kill her, Jonah.'

Xavier's head was outside the curtain of the front window. Jonah let go of the windowsills and, drawing his elbows in, he put his fingers on the shop-till's keys. He could feel that there was plastic money in the drawer, and he badly wanted to pop it open.

'Jonah, I need you to listen, because after this the police will come, and I might not get another chance.'

Jonah's fingers ran over the keys. If he pressed one, would there be a little ring? Xavier's breath was quickening up, and he thought again that he must have his own creature.

'I didn't kill your mum, Jonah.' His voice was very shaky. 'But people might think I did. And I want you and Raff to know the truth.'

Jonah frowned, thinking about Xavier not having killed her. He remembered Shahana's auntie, the murdered ghost, with a knife sticking out of her, and pressed firmly on one of the keys. A ring, and a nice click, as the number popped up.

'What was that? What are you doing?' Xavier's hand was on the curtain now. He lifted it, and at the sight of his enormous face, trying to peer in, Jonah nearly got the giggles.

'What did you think of "Starman"?' he said, in his clear, faraway voice, feeling all numb and light.

'What?' Xavier's face disappeared, and he shifted on the stones, which must be digging into his knees. 'I didn't stay for it. I came looking for you.'

'Oh.'

'I ran out to the road,' said Xavier. 'But you weren't there. So I went back and searched around the school.'

There's a Staar-maan! A whole octave's leap, just like 'Somewhere Over the Rainbow'. 'I didn't realise you had a French name,' he said.

'No reason why you should.' It sounded like Xavier was playing with some stones, scooping them up and letting them drop from his fist. 'My real mum was French. She said it differently.'

'Za-vee-eh. Like Madame Loiseau said it.'

'That's right,' said Xavier.

'Why did you change it?'

'I didn't change it. It was my English family. They didn't know how French people pronounced it.'

Jonah listened to the stones falling from Xavier's hand, thinking about the photograph of the curly-haired, sad-eyed little boy hanging in the Martins' hallway.

'Why did your real mum give you to the English family?'

'She didn't.' There was a moment's silence. 'She didn't want me to go. They just came and took me.'

Jonah pressed another key down, and the number popped up. Xavier stayed silent.

'But why did they take you?' asked Jonah. He could hear the stones again, and he pictured them dropping from Xavier's big fist, one by one.

'She used to leave me on my own,' said Xavier, after a while.

'And they thought she shouldn't? They thought that was bad of her?' He pressed another key.

'Yes. Sometimes it was for quite a long time.'

Jonah thought about little Xavier, all on his own in a messy kitchen somewhere. He leant his head against the Wendy-house wall, and remembered Monday morning

again. Saviour and Emerald, hugging in the Juniors' playground, and Saviour looking up, and the high-five. It was
very tiring, thinking about it, but he went back, all the way
to the beginning: the screeching birds, the empty bed, the
bath of water, the open front door; the fox, standing on that
dirty white van; the mango and the wine bottle, and all the
ants, and then the glimpse of red, in the plant pot outside.

'The texts I sent.'

'What?'

He frowned, trying to piece it together. 'When I pretended
to be Mayo – Lucy. You must have thought . . .' He stopped.
What *had* he thought? What had he known? Tiring, like a
chess game, but in reverse.

'I knew it was you and Raff.' Xavier pushed the curtain,
peering through again. A pause, and then the curtain dropped
back into place. 'I knew that she was dead.' Xavier made
another horrible animal sound, and then he whispered: 'And
you and Raff were on your own.'

'Then you must be a bad man.' He said it wonderingly
rather than angrily, but another horrible sound came out
of Xavier's throat. He thought of Roland, who was a good
man who'd done a bad thing, and of Felix Curtis: well, it
was difficult to know. He pressed another key on the till,
and this time the drawer popped out. *There's a Staar-maan!!!*
The children's voices were so lovely, and they were looking
at him, smiling. '*Xavier Martin is a bad man*,' he told them
and, still singing, they nodded, and he remembered those
pearly, alien eyes when he came over with the crate of
plums on Monday evening. '*I did think he might be. Sometimes.
But I wasn't completely sure. I did used to really like him. More
than anyone.*'

He put his fingers in the drawer, feeling the plastic coins. There were five of them, a fifty-pence piece, and four small round ones. He was trying to remember that word, the word that was like 'seaside'; he'd seen it written in her diary, but now he couldn't remember it again. 'So she killed herself,' he said.

'No. That's not what happened.' Xavier's voice was lower, firmer.

'She wrote it in her diary.' Jonah ran his finger around the edges of the fifty pence. 'She thought if she did that, she could be your . . .' What was that word? He closed his eyes, trying to see her handwriting.

'People write all sorts of things in their diaries.' Xavier cleared his throat. 'But Lucy didn't kill herself, Jonah.' His voice was even firmer. 'She would never have done that, whatever she wrote, and no matter how bad she was feeling. And you know why, don't you?'

Then I remembered. I am a mother, still. The creature moved, but it mustn't; there was no room. He pushed the drawer shut and folded himself around the toy, so that its hardness dug into his flesh.

'Jonah?' Xavier was at the window, pushing back the curtain. 'Jonah, it's very important that you know this. Lucy would not have taken her life, because whatever else was going on, she loved you and Raff.'

Went tiptoeing in to look at them. Their snuffly breathing. My treasures. He clamped the toy into him, feeling it bruise his ribs.

'It was an accident, Joney. It was a – a stupid fucking accident.'

'You're not going in there! It's too dangerous, you hear me!'

Leonie's face, stretched with anger – no, with worry, even fear. Afraid of what might happen to him and Raff. *You never get scared, do you, Mayo? You think that fear is a magnet. Daddy said you shouldn't be such a daredevil. And now look what's happened. Mayo, now look what's . . .*

'Joney.' The softness of Xavier's voice made Jonah cry harder. 'I'm so sorry, mate. Please come out.'

66

'How did the carpet get on her?' he asked, after a while.

'The carpet?' It sounded like Xavier had been crying too. 'It was me,' he said.

'Oh.' Jonah frowned. 'Why did you do that?'

'I don't know.' Xavier's voice had gone very high.

'You should have left her looking up at the swimming pool,' he whispered.

'What?'

'She likes the swimming pool.' She wouldn't be able to dive up into it, not with the carpet on her. The creature had started shifting again. He let the plastic shop-till slide away, and put his hands on his belly.

'When people are dead,' Xavier was saying. 'It's just what you do. I didn't want . . .'

He didn't want anyone to find you, Mayo. An icy, glinting chip, like a knife. It was good, the icy chip, it stopped the creature – it blocked it from rising up. *He* didn't want anyone to find you, in case they thought he'd killed you.

'You hid her,' he said. 'You thought everyone would forget about her.' The chip was burning now: a steady, ice-blue flame.

'That's not . . . Oh *Christ!*' Xavier was crying, which was making it hard for him to talk.

'You left her on her own.' *Please don't leave me.* Her pen marks, cut deep into the paper. Xavier was whispering something. Jonah leaned forward, but he couldn't hear. 'You put that smelly carpet on her, and then you left her,' he said.

'I didn't want. . .' whispered Xavier. 'I didn't want animals . . . or insects . . .'

Jonah got a flash of the wriggling bin worms, and the shape of her, under the carpet. His belly heaved and he clapped his hands over his mouth, and the plastic shop-till rolled to the ground.

'I didn't just . . .' Xavier was speaking more clearly. 'Joney, I lay down next to her. I tried to . . . I said her name.'

He said your name, Mayo. His hands were still over his mouth, his fingers were wet with his spit.

'And I stroked her face. I kept stroking her face.'

You stroked my face, such a tender touch. And when I woke up I could still feel it.

'And I – I talked about the baby. You know – the test you found.'

I want him to come and hold me, and say he feels sad too.

'I kept telling her she was my . . . my Lucy. My precious beloved.' His voice dropped to a whisper.

Jonah dropped his hands into his lap. 'Could she . . . hear you?'

There was no answer, but then Jonah realised Xavier was still whispering. He pushed the curtain aside and peered out, and saw that he had turned away from the Wendy house, towards the carpet. The light was still streaming down from the open rectangle, a pale, dusty shaft. *He's talking to you, Mayo. He's calling you 'Baby'. Can you hear him?*

Xavier suddenly looked back, over his shoulder, and their eyes met. 'She died straightaway, Joney.' His voice was calm now, calm and clear. 'It didn't hurt. I looked down, and I could tell from the way she was lying. Her neck had broken.'

'Down?'

'Yes. From up there.' He nodded towards where the light was coming from, and Jonah remembered the Raggedy Man, outside the betting shop, pointing up at the sky. 'That's where we were,' said Xavier. 'And she fell.'

Jonah remembered the birds, so early in the morning, screeching like crazy, as the planet tilted towards the sun. *You fell. Was it the sunrise that made you fall?* He saw her tilted by the turn of the planet, her bare feet slipping, her mouth opening, and her eyes – all surprised.

67

'How long did you stay lying next to her?' Jonah asked. He'd been thinking about Monday morning, and seeing Violet standing on Xavier's white van. He'd looked at Violet, not at the van, which was why he hadn't realised.

'Until I heard the Green Shop blinds.' So he'd been there all that time, while he and Raff were having Weetabix. 'I thought, I must get Em to school. I just – I knew I couldn't protect you and Raff from it. But I wanted Em to be in school. Before the police came.'

'But the police didn't come. Why did you think they'd come? When no one knew?'

'I thought someone would have heard.' *Heard you scream.* 'The Green Shop Man, or you, even. And failing that, I thought you'd tell someone anyway. When you realised she wasn't there.'

'But then you saw us in the playground.'

'Yes. You asked me about the cricket.'

'And you didn't say anything.'

'I just . . . I needed to get Dora to her appointment. That was the next thing. Get Dora to the hospital, then deal with it.' He paused. 'But then there were more next things. There was always a next thing.' He fell silent.

'But you knew we were on our own.'

'Yes.' He made the horrible sound again. Then he said, 'I thought about you all the time.'

'How could you think about us, and not . . .'

There was another long pause. Xavier sounded like he was crying. Then he whispered, 'I came in the night.'

'What night?'

'Monday night. I came in through the back.' Waking up on Tuesday morning, thinking he'd heard her come in, and then the punch of her empty bed. Going downstairs, and seeing that the back door was open. 'I sat on the landing, listening to you and Raffy breathing.'

'You were drunk.' Those eyes, that breath, when he brought round the plums.

'I was. I was totally smashed.'

Smashed, going through the Broken House, past her body; smashed, on the landing, listening to him and Raff. 'Why did you go away?'

'To tell Dora. I wanted to be there when she woke up, and tell her, get that bit over with. And then come back.'

'But you didn't tell her. Or come back.'

'No. She said she'd heard from Lucy. She said you and Raff were coming to tea.' He paused, and when he started again, his voice was wobbling. 'So I went to buy the chicken. It was easier.' A long, shaky sigh. 'But not because . . . Jonah, it wasn't *myself* I was trying to protect. I was going round in circles. Knowing I must tell, but knowing that once I did, I wouldn't have any control over what happened to you. Do you see? I didn't want you to get carted off by

Roland's mother.' His voice was wobbling and quivering, but Jonah was feeling ice-cold, miles away. 'I just wanted to cook you roast chicken.' A whining dog, that was what he sounded like. 'I thought, I'll cook them roast chicken, and then . . . And then I'll figure it out. Maybe get Dora to let you stay.'

'You mended the fence.' He'd remembered the drilling in the night, and the van, driving away.

'Yes. Which night was that?'

'The night it rained. You were trying to hide her.'

'Mate.' He shook his head. 'I didn't want you and Raffy to find her.'

'You didn't want anyone to find her. Because of Dora. You didn't want Dora to know. Or Emerald. You cared about them more than us.'

'I kept waiting for *you* to tell, Joney.' He was making that whining noise again. 'I thought you'd tell someone. Every day. Every hour. I wanted you to. I wanted it taken out of my hands. But you didn't. I even – I even felt angry with you. I just . . .' His crying took over.

'You made her pregnant. And then you made her have an operation, to kill the baby.' He shivered. 'That's why she stayed in bed. You told her you were coming round, on Sunday night.' Her face in her mirror, her eyes, her too-thick lipstick. 'You went to the Green Shop first, and got the mango and the wine, and then you came. Why?'

'I had to tell her. We had to stop seeing each other. Because of Dora being so ill.'

'No, why did you bring the bottle of wine?'

'I don't know. I thought . . . maybe a drink together. That she understood and it would be OK. We would still be friends.'

But you got upset, Mayo. Jonah hugged himself hard, remembering that he'd heard her, but that he'd thought it was a dream. Then he remembered the wine again, and the glasses, by the side of the bed. 'You sexed her, didn't you? You drank the wine, and you sexed her.' His fist tightened, and he bashed it against the Wendy-house wall. 'Why did you *do* that, when you came round to tell her you weren't going to sex her any more?'

The sound of Xavier breaking down gave Jonah a shock, jolting him out of his anger. He listened from inside his little house, feeling himself going numb and light again. He remembered a visit to a church. Where? When? Oh, the French holiday, the day they'd gone into the town. An old, sun-baked town, with a green river and a tiny old lady in black hobbling over the bridge. The church had been very big and cool, with stained-glass windows, and he and Raff and Emerald had run off to explore. They'd played with the wax dripping from some thin white candles, and Emerald had kissed a weird statue baby, and they'd all stared into a glass case at what seemed to be a dressed-up skeleton. And then they'd found the wooden cubbyhole with the curtained window. Raff had thought it was a toilet to begin with, but the seat inside was just a seat. They'd played in it for a while, until Dora had come along and told them not to. '*It's a confession box,*' she had explained. '*The priest sits inside, and if you've been naughty you go and talk to him through the window, telling him the bad things you've done. And then he asks if you're sorry, and if you are, then it's all OK. You're back to being good again.*'

Xavier was talking on the other side of the curtain. 'I loved her,' he was saying. 'You have to realise that. I kept . . . my brain was haywire.'

'So did you change your mind? Were you going to stay and live with us?'

'I couldn't. I wished I could. But how could I? And I thought she realised. You can't leave someone who's . . . who's . . .'

Dora. Adora. Adorable Dora. 'Riddled with cancer'. My darling friend.

'But she went crazy.'

I heard you, but I thought it was in my dream, and I stayed asleep. If only I'd have woken up. I would have come and hugged you.

Xavier was telling him what had happened next, stopping and starting, and stopping again. Jonah held himself tighter, seeing what Xavier was remembering, his eyes squeezed closed. He saw the sleeping houses behind the orange street lights, with their greasy roofs, and the sky like clay. Xavier opening the door and stepping out into the still-cool air, and Lucy coming out after him, crying, in her red sarong and her unravelled hair. Holding her little red phone, which matched her sarong and her toenails. He saw her flipping it open, saying she was going to phone Dora. And Xavier trying to snatch it; and Lucy jumping back, all wild and snarling, and then her bare feet on the pavement, and his Crocs, running after her, and the street lights switching off and the sudden soft greyness of everything. Slipping through the gap in the fence, slipping through easily, but Xavier having to kick and push before he can follow her. Running along the path, the thorns scratching her legs, and into the big, dark kitchen, where she stops and looks down at her phone. But she hears him coming, and she runs into the hall, and the planet tilts, and the light flows down the stairs like a golden carpet.

Then she's running up the stairs, her face lit up with the gold, and the birds all go tumbling upwards. It's so strange being up there, among the crumbly walls, like an olden-days soldier on a castle. She looks up at the birds, feathery, screeching blotches across the candyfloss sky, and then across at their house – yes, and through a jaggedy gap she can see her own bedroom window. And then she hears him, right behind her, on the stairs, and the beam is there . . . *Mayo, don't.*

The beam is wide, but it's so high up, and Xavier is frightened, seeing her walking across it. He says, 'Baby! Please, come back!' But her bare feet keep going, squelching through the bird poo, and she reaches the other side and holds onto the wall. Jonah sees through her eyes now, as she looks over, and sees their little concrete yard, with the plant pots, and the corduroy cushion, and the golden bicycle. Their little life together, Lucy, Jonah and Raff – but she turns away from it and, leaning against the wall, she flips open her phone again.

Xavier is talking about Dora now, saying that she'd taken a sleeping pill and gone 'out for the count', but that it would have worn off by then. Jonah sees them both, like he's watching a split screen: Lucy, up on the beam, the screeching birds and the dazzling sunlight, her face frowning down as she brings up Dora's number; and down in the Martins' house, all silent and curtained, Dora's slack, sleeping face against her pillow in her enormous bed. And then Xavier, in a panic, stepping onto the beam, telling her not to be crazy, not to ruin all their lives. She turns away from him, leaning against the wall, putting her phone to her ear, and she's safe still, her tummy against the brick. The sun is already hot, and the molecules are scattering the blue light waves; Dora's phone is ringing, but probably all the way down in their kitchen. Dora's never going to hear it, but stupid Xavier doesn't know that. He's in a panic, trying to stop her from ruining all their lives. He's across the beam, and he snatches the phone, gripping the wall with his other hand; she turns around again, angry, trying to get it back, and there isn't enough space for them to be jostling and wrestling like that. And then Xavier manages to lift his arm, and he bowls the phone into the air, really hard, to get it away from her. But she reaches after it, she thinks she can somehow . . . reaches with both hands, and then her foot slips and her hands grip the air. Xavier feels the shift, and his hand scrabbles for her, finds her locket, but the chain is just a wisp around her neck. It's so quick, quick as a flash − she's there on the beam, and then she's gone. Jonah doesn't see her falling. Instead he sees the phone, as it arcs, high above, before plummeting, bright red, into the soft earth of the plant pot.

68

'Are there any actual *good* people?' he asked, through the Wendy-house window. They'd been sitting in silence for a while, and he saw Xavier's head jerk up at the sound of his voice. 'I mean, good people who don't do bad things?'

'I don't know. There might be,' Xavier answered. 'But I think nearly everyone has done at least one or two bad things.'

Letting go of the curtain, Jonah leaned back, trying to think of the bad things he'd done. He'd been getting cross with Harold, and Emerald. He'd called Emerald a cunt. He had lots of fights with Raff. He'd got really cross with him for finishing the can of Coke and had let him go off on his own. Had that been his fault? Or had it been a force moving through him, that he could do nothing about? He was feeling light and numb again, his thoughts drifting in the never-ending space of his brain. But then he heard Xavier getting to his feet: his grunts and the shifting rubble. 'Come on, mate.'

Jonah looked at the Wendy-house door. His body was full of pins and needles, but he couldn't bear to move and stir everything up. Instead, he unhooked the checked curtain so that he could see out of the window properly. Xavier, his hands in his pockets, was looking towards the carpet, which was still in the shaft of light. 'Was it you who lit the incense?'

'Incense?' Xavier looked around. 'What incense?'

'Can't you smell it?'

Xavier sniffed the air and shook his head.

'What are you going to do now?' Jonah asked.

'Now?' He sighed. 'Now, I'm going to get you home. You and Raffy, and Em. Back to ours. And then.' He sighed again. 'And then I'm going to phone the police, like I should have done on Monday morning.'

'What about Dora?' Dora in hospital, all bandaged up, like an Egyptian mummy, waiting and waiting for Saviour.

'You don't have to worry about Dora, mate. That's not your job.'

Jonah looked up into the old, crumpled face, which had once been the little-boy face in the photograph. 'I don't want you to,' he said.

'Jonah, mate.' He had gone croaky again. 'Jonah. It's just – what has to happen.'

'They'll take you away. Like they took Roland away. Even though you didn't actually push her. They'll think it was your fault.'

'Well.' Xavier cleared his throat. 'It *was* my fault. It's all my fault. I deserve what's coming to me.' His shoulders rose and then fell.

'I don't want them to take you away,' Jonah said. 'I don't want to – be on my own.'

'It'll be OK, mate. Ben's babysitting. I've already booked him.'

'The police might think you murdered her. They'll put you in prison, for ever and ever, and Dora and Em . . .'

'I've got to tell them, mate.' He spoke softly. 'There's no way out of it.'

In a sudden panic, Jonah kicked open the Wendy-house door. 'But it's too late! Don't you see?' He scrambled out and got to his feet, and stood, facing Xavier. 'They'll think you kept it a secret because you actually killed her, on purpose!'

'Who knows what they'll think. But no more lies. I can't do any more lies.' He held out his hand.

Jonah crossed his arms and shook his head. 'Not tonight.'

'What do you mean?'

'Don't phone the police tonight.' Xavier's eyes scrunched closed and his arm dropped to his side. 'I don't think Dora should find out, straight after her operation.' Jonah paused for a moment. 'And I don't want to tell Raffy. Not tonight. I want him to be happy, and have pizza.' He stepped closer. 'Then you could go and see Dora for a while, and come back and put us to bed.'

There was no answer. Jonah uncrossed his arms and placed them around Xavier's middle. They stayed like that, neither of them moving, and then Jonah put his head against Xavier's belly, and Xavier put his hand on Jonah's hair.

'And then tomorrow Roland will come. You can phone the police after he's got here.'

'Roland?'

'Yes. He's coming out of prison. Didn't you know?'

'Thank fuck.' Xavier was crying again. 'I think I did

know. But I'd forgotten.' He wiped his eyes and nodded his head. 'OK. Tomorrow then.' He looked over his shoulder. They both looked. The shaft of light had gone.

FRIDAY

69

He was back in the Broken House, searching through the rubble, and there was the doll again, lying face down, apart from it wasn't a doll at all – it was the baby. He squatted down and peered: the dent in its head didn't look too bad, but it must be dead, a newborn baby couldn't have survived all these days all alone. Then he realised he could hear a sound, just the trace of a sound, repeating itself. Such a sweet little sound. Its baby suit was filthy, but he could see the yellow elephants on it. He rested his finger in the tiny space between its shoulder blades and felt its heartbeat. Next, it was in the crook of his arm. He looked down into its face, and it looked a lot like its father, Xavier Martin; but then it opened its eyes, and they were just like *his* eyes, the eyes he saw in the mirror, dark and thoughtful.

'Hello, little one,' he whispered. The eyes stared back at him. It had a patient little mouth, and tiny, octagonal nostrils. He felt very tender towards it, but it was a panicky tenderness, because it was too late, it had been neglected for too long. Its eyes closed again, but its nostrils kept sucking on the air. He looked up then, and saw Violet, watching them from a few feet away. 'So it's you that's been feeding the baby!' He felt hopeful, because maybe Violet would do, maybe she could become a mother to them both. He looked into her eyes, searching for warmth in the curdled stillness, and the silence sang in his ears.

It was the singing of the silence that woke him back into his curled-up shape on the futon, in the airy, curtained cool of Emerald's room. He kept his eyes closed, listening – *is it the sound of the Universe, Mayo?* – and then the creature moved, huge and dense. He curled tighter.

He stayed like that for a while, and then he must have dozed off again, because he'd been looking at the dent in the baby doll's head, and the head had been a skull, and he'd been able to see the soul trapped inside. It had been Pearl who had said that dead people's souls escape through the tops of their skulls. *Through that soft bit, Mayo. That babies have.* She had let him touch Raff's, very gently, when he was a newborn baby. But they hardened up as you got older. That's why they need to be cracked. *I should have freed you, Mayo.* He should have rolled the carpet back and cracked her skull open. His eyes pricked with tears. He opened them, and rolled onto his back.

The room looked the same as it ever did, as if none of it had happened, which was strange; like the strangeness of stepping out onto Southway Street with Xavier the day before, and seeing the trees, still in their cages, and hearing the bees in the lavender bushes, and feeling the sun's blast on the back of his neck. It was a big room, big enough for Emerald's flouncy, fairy-tale bed, and the double futon that he and Raff were lying on. They had slept on that futon many times, and he had always loved its firmness, and the airy lightness of the duvet, and the smell of the washing powder the Martins used. Now, he wanted to be in his and Raff's bedroom, with the fallen-down curtain, and Raff's fallen-down poster, and her bedroom right next door. He would be able to get up and go in to her – or at least to her smell, and her bed, and all her things, lying on the floor. *It was better then, Mayo,* he told her, desolated. He couldn't be bothered to try and call her Lucy any more. *I thought it was really bad, but it was better when we didn't know where you were.*

He had his clothes on, he realised, his dusty, filthy clothes, and the horse money was still in his pocket. Ben the babysitter had managed to bundle them upstairs, but hadn't bothered getting them to undress. He rolled back onto his side. Her diary was there, and her phone, lying on the floor beside the futon. He'd brought them both to bed with him, not wanting to leave them downstairs. He reached out and rested his fingers on the diary. Back in their kitchen, after the Broken House, he'd tried to give it to Xavier, and the phone, because they were 'evidence' to be got rid of, like the Ophelia card and the wine bottle. But Xavier wouldn't take them. He'd said that he and Raff were Lucy's sons, and everything of hers was now theirs; and anyway, it was time to come clean.

He'd held the diary to his chest as they'd walked along Southway Street, to protect himself from the unrealness of the sunshine, and the bin sheds, and the lavender bushes. Back at school, they'd pushed through all those noisy, happy people and found Raff with Tameron, surrounded by admirers. Raff, all lit up, had thrown himself at Saviour, with no idea that he was really Xavier. Raff had been so excited that they were going to the Martins and having pizza, he'd run ahead of them, all the way across the park. Jonah had walked next to Xavier, holding the diary to his chest. There had been a cumulonimbus a mile or two ahead of them, and a rainbow, very bright, but the colours only existed because of the cones in the backs of their eyes.

Jonah and Xavier had watched the cricket highlights together, Xavier's arm around his shoulders, while Raff and Emerald ran around like loonies. Then the pizzas had arrived, and Ben, the teenager from next door, and Xavier had got up from the sofa. He'd tried to hug Emerald, but she'd been too busy being chased by Raff. Jonah had kept his eyes fixed on him as he got ready to leave. *You're coming back, though*, he'd said to him silently. *You're not going to tell anyone until tomorrow, are you?* It had been horrible, that feeling of weak, silent panic. He'd wanted to throw himself at him like Raff had, hold him tight around his legs, to stop him going: the only other person in the whole world who knew the truth, who could feel and share its weight. Instead he'd watched Xavier give Ben a beer, and call to Em and Raff to be good; and then pick up his keys.

Once Xavier had gone, Ben had rolled himself one of those fat smokes, and put *The Jungle Book* on, and Raff and Emerald had kept jumping up to sing along and dance. Jonah had sat with his back straight, her diary on his lap, staring hard at the bright screen. He'd wanted to run out into the night and across the park, through their house and over the wall, back into the Broken House, and pick his way across the stones. Better to be with her dead body on those cold stones than alone in this pizza-strewn nothingness.

Now, in Emerald's room, he tried to focus on Roland.

'Ro.' He could see his prison letter handwriting, but for some reason he couldn't get a clear picture of his face. The Ganesha story kept popping up, the father who doesn't recognise his son and chops off his head. *No.* He brought up the steamy platform from *The Railway Children* instead, the steam clearing, Bobbie's voice crying 'Daddy!'

His eyes wandered up to the poster of Justin Bieber above Emerald's fairy-tale bed. Justin's moody face didn't fit in with the rest of the room at all. He didn't want Em to know about Xavier and Lucy. *Or Dora.* They would hate her. Everyone would hate her, even more than for Angry Saturday. Maybe even the gods would hate her, and they wouldn't let her be reborn, and they wouldn't let her into Heaven either. As he stared at Justin, the nothingness of Violet's eyes came back to him from his dream, and then the dead fox, the half-flattened one that Tyreese had wanted to set light to. He saw the row of boys squatting on the hot pavement and the flame of Theodore's lighter, singeing the fur. '*Look at its eye.*' he heard Tameron say. '*You lookin' at me, Mr Foxy?*' He started having an idea, and he closed his eyes to see it in pictures, but it was strange and frightening, and he opened them again.

So quiet, the Martins' house. He listened to the singing of the silence. *Was* it the sound of the universe, always there, under the other sounds, or was it just coming from his own ears? He touched her diary again. *The first thing is to tell Raff, isn't it, Mayo?* The silence rang and rang in his ears. He took a deep breath, trying to think about telling Raff. *It will be OK, because I can tell him about Roland.* He got a flash of him in the Dads' Race, with his pale, ironed trousers, his knees going up too high, and Saviour

– no, Xavier – dropping back to take last place. *It will be OK because* . . . He propped himself up on his elbows to look down at Raff. The eyelashes curving against the rounded cheek, and the fat little mouth, and that nostril. Raffy loved Xavier more than he loved Roland. He didn't really know Roland. *The first thing is to* . . . He lay back, remembering the feeling of panic as Xavier left the house. *The first thing is to stop Xavier from telling.* If he begged him, if he promised him that he wouldn't tell either . . . He sat up and pulled the diary onto his lap. The word like seaside . . . He found the page.

So then there's the suicide card.

Worthless too, because you know I could never leave my living, growing boys.

But it's the only one left in my hand, and I dream and dream of playing it.

Suicide. Which meant to kill yourself. Which Lucy's mother had done – but Lucy hadn't. He stared down at Raff's pretty face, and then looked at the horrible rude drawing, before turning to the next page.

Alive, I lose, any which way you look at it. But dead, I win. Dead, I come into my own.

(And everyone will say, how could she DO that, what a selfish fucked-up BITCH. Her poor children, they'll *say, but thinking, they will be SO much better off without that bitch.)*

He closed the book, and stared at Justin Bieber, having the idea again. The idea was turning into a kind of plan, but he didn't know if the plan was good or bad. *Mayo?*

Maybe if he went downstairs. Maybe if he lay on her sofa.

Stay asleep, Raffy boy. He got out of bed and padded out of the room.

70

Their pizza boxes and drink cans were all over the floor, and Ben's ashtray had tipped over. There were no ants, he noticed, or flies, even though the window had been left open. He went and looked out. Beyond the park, under the colourless sky, London huddled, still asleep. As he stared at the shapes of the buildings, he became aware of a sound, coming from the back of the house; a rhythmic gasping that reminded him of the baby's snuffles. He turned, and as he did, he noticed that Lucy's portrait had been taken down and turned to face the wall. Following the sound, he picked his way through the pizza boxes. In the kitchen the gasps became weird cries. They would be scary if you didn't know what they were, but now he knew. He walked into the conservatory.

The orchids had gone crazy. There must be thousands of those kittenish faces now, mostly speckled, but some spotted and some plain. They were so silently awake, and Xavier so noisily asleep, lying on Dora's sofa with his shoes still on. Why had he chosen Dora's sofa? Did he actually love Dora the most? Who was he dreaming about? Dora in her bandages, or Lucy in her red sarong? He'd loved Dora first, and they'd lived together for so long, they'd got all mixed up with each other. When you mix two paint colours, you can't separate them out again. Everything in this room, in this whole house, including Emerald, was the result of that mixture.

So what was Lucy? What was she, to both of them? They'd drawn her into their lives, but she wasn't part of them, like they were of each other. He suddenly saw Dora's fingers take hold of Lucy's chin, showing Xavier her mouth. *'Do you see? The asymmetry?'*

Just their doll, then, their brown-skinned doll. Something red caught the corner of his eye, and his head whipped round, feeling a spark of her. It was the painted nipple of the mannequin over by the door. Ariadne the Sad. Turning, he looked at the orchids, and the paper cranes and the mirror chimes, and the wood-burning stove, and the empty pink sofa. She wasn't there. Not even a trace of her. He was alone, completely alone, apart from the mannequin and the snoring man. He felt the randomness of the room, and of his presence in it: the randomness of everything. Molecules, some heavier, some lighter, but just molecules, six hundred and seventy-five duodecillion of them, caused by nothing but a big bang.

He walked over to the mannequin. The first time he'd come into this room she had towered above him, up on her pedestal. Now his nose came up to her elbow. He touched her white arm. It was smooth and powdery. He looked at her face, which gazed out at the garden. He turned and looked too, and there in the morning shadows was the scarecrow, slouching languidly in its pinstripe jacket and straw hat. He glanced back at the mannequin: were they looking at each other? But the mannequin's face didn't have eyes, just smooth dips. Hating the emptiness of those dips, he looked back at the orchids. The orchids, too, looked blindly back at him. There was something spiteful about them, the way they were all sticking out their tongues, sticking them out even though they couldn't actually see him. He looked up at the cranes, but they were pieces of paper hung on threads – and then back out at the lifeless scarecrow.

'*Mayo.*' He closed his eyes and said it in his head, trying to stop the emptiness from seeping into him. The word hung in his brain. It was empty; all words were. His thoughts were in words, so they were empty too, and he should have kept his eyes open, because the emptiness was actually coming from inside him. In a panic he thought of his own name – 'Jonah' – but it was emptiest of all. His jaw clenched, he stood spinning in the emptiness.

It took a great effort to open his eyes again, and he knew that when he did, he mustn't look at the statue's dips. He must be careful, really careful, because that emptiness was far, far worse than the creature. He walked across the cool stone floor, and stood looking down at Xavier. He was sprawled on his back, with his fists clenched on his chest, and his snores were rattling cries for mercy. Jonah remembered the hunger of the doll baby's quivering nostrils in his dream. Could Xavier be dying? Could sadness, fear and guilt mixed together actually kill a person? Jonah stepped closer. Xavier was wheezing back down from the top of the snore, a much softer, sadder sound than the inhalation. He looked so old and ugly, with his slack jowly cheeks and his pores all open and glistening, but then you could also see the *boy* in him, the sleeping, dreaming boy, and if you were his mother you would have stroked his forehead.

Xavier shifted as he climbed next to him, rolling onto his side and hugging him to his chest. He stank, worse than ever, but Jonah nestled into him. Xavier's mouth found the top of his head, and he mumbled into it. His snores quietened into much shorter, wheezy breaths. Jonah lay still for a few minutes, his face buried in Xavier's chest. Then he decided what to do. He slipped out of Xavier's arms and went back upstairs.

71

Raff didn't want to wake up at first, but when Jonah whispered to him that he needed to tell him about Mayo he sat up straight, his eyes wide. Jonah put his finger to his lips and pointed to the door. He picked up the diary and put the phone in his pocket, and they crept down the stairs. Raff collected his hat from one of the pigeonholes, and they left the house.

The park was still closed, but the top gate was easy to climb. There was a wind, and the cirrostratus blanket was rolling fast across the sky. Once they were over, Raff started running. His hat blew off, and Jonah caught it and ran after him, calling to him to wait. Raff pounded down the hill, through the trees and out again, stopping when he reached the pond. Jonah stopped too, panting. They were in front of the Kumari bench, and he saw that there was a squirrel on it, sitting on its back legs and holding a morsel of something between its hands. Raff walked around in a circle, looking at the ground. Then he stopped, and they stood facing each other.

'What's that book?' asked Raff. 'Is that Mayo's diary?'

Jonah nodded. Raff's eyes fixed on his. Up in a tree, a crow cawed. Raff raised one eyebrow about a millimetre.

Jonah took a breath. 'She's dead,' he whispered.

Raff nodded. He put his hands in his pockets and looked down at the ground. Then he said, 'Who?'

Jonah didn't understand, but only for a second. 'Mayo,' he said.

Raff frowned at the ground. 'Say her name,' he said.

'Lucy.'

'Her whole name.'

Jonah cleared his throat. 'Lucy Mwembe. Lucy Mwembe is dead.'

'How do you know?' Raff's face was small and tight, straining to understand. 'Did you read it in her diary?'

Jonah shook his head.

Raff looked across at the pond. He pushed his hands deeper into his pockets and his face softened. 'I knew she was, anyway,' he said, with a deep sigh.

The squirrel was still there, looking at them both, as if it was deciding which one to offer its morsel to.

'How did you know?'

Raff shrugged. 'If she'd of been alive, she'd of come to the concert.' He took his hat from Jonah's hand and put it on. His hands in his pockets, he walked up and down.

Jonah looked at the squirrel. He knew he should try and help Raff, say something to make it not so bad, but the creature was moving a lot, so he couldn't say anything at all. When Raff stopped walking and sat down on the Kumari bench, the squirrel skittered away. Jonah tried to see where it had got to. Then he sat next to Raff.

'Will she get a bench, then?' Raff asked.

Jonah shrugged.

'Next to Olive Sage?'

'She didn't want to be down here. She wanted to be up the hill, remember?'

'Oh, yeah.' They both looked at the pond.

'Is your white stick still in there, do you think?' asked Raff.

Jonah nodded. It would have sunk down by now, through the thick brown water to the muddy bed.

'What is it, anyway?'

'It's just a – it's a thing.'

'A thing!' Raff stuck his elbow into his brother's side. 'Tell me what it is, fucking Peck.'

The squirrel hadn't gone far, it was there on a branch to the side of them; still looking at them, but the morsel was in its mouth now.

'It's a stick that can tell if you're pregnant.'

Silence. Then Raff said, 'Is she pregnant, then? As well as dead?'

'I don't think you can be pregnant and dead at the same time.' The squirrel seemed to nod at him. 'Anyway.' He shivered. *You have opted for the surgical procedure.* 'She stopped being pregnant before she died.'

'Anyway,' said Raff. 'Anyway. Anyway!' It was like when he copied him to annoy him, apart from he was starting to cry. The squirrel hopped up a branch, the morsel still bulging from its mouth. Jonah started crying too. The squirrel watched them, both slumped and crying, sitting side by side.

72

'Where is she?' asked Raff.

Jonah wiped his wet face, and wiped his hand on his shirt. 'She's in the Broken House,' he said.

'What!' Raff stared at his brother. 'Why is she in the flippin' Broken House?'

'Because that's where she died. That's where she's been all this time.'

Raff shook his head. 'The Broken House!' Jonah noticed that the squirrel was still there, listening. 'You got some bad snot, bro.'

Jonah nodded. He had given in to the creature, and had been crying hard, rasping and shaking, just like Saviour on Tuesday night.

'That's where you went,' said Raff. 'At the end of the concert. With Saviour.' Jonah nodded again, licking the salty goo from his lips. 'But how did you know she was there?'

Jonah looked back at the pond. 'I just – realised.'

Raff stood up and kicked a stone. He followed it and kicked it again. Dribbling it in front of him, he reached the edge of the pond. Then he turned round.

'Was it Furtix who killed her?'

Jonah shook his head. 'No one killed her.' Then he said. 'I went to see Felix.'

'When?'

'Yesterday. After the helicopter. I didn't go back to school, I went up to the Angry Road instead.'

Raff went back to kicking the stone. 'Were those twins there?'

'No. They go to boarding school now.' Ruined lives. That's what Roland had written in his letter. And then, what had Xavier said, when he was explaining why he'd been so desperate to get the phone from her: *So she wouldn't ruin all our lives.*

'What made her die, then?' Raff turned around, his face small and tight again. 'If no one killed her?'

'She fell. She went to the top of the Broken House, and she fell.'

Raff walked up and down again, staring at the ground as if he was looking for something. He seemed to be humming to himself, making some kind of sound. When he finally stopped and looked at Jonah, his eyes were wet and very clean, like a puppy's. 'Did she fall on purpose?' His teeth were chattering.

I tiptoed in and listened to their snuffly breathing. Jonah hugged the diary and shook his head.

'Jonah.' His chattering teeth were making it hard to speak. 'What, Raffy?'

The wet eyes locked into his as, with great effort, the mouth formed the words. 'Tell me if it was on purpose.'

'It wasn't on purpose, Raffy.' *You know I could never leave my living, growing boys.* 'She didn't want to die.' Jonah put the diary on the bench, and stood up and walked over to

Raff. He put his hands on his shoulders. 'She didn't *want* to miss the concert.'

Raff nodded. Then he placed his hands on either side of Jonah's face and pressed away, stretching the skin tight. Jonah felt his features widen and flatten. Raff's mouth formed the words, but without any sounds. 'Tell me what happened.'

Jonah pulled his hands away. 'OK, Raffy, I'll tell you,' he whispered. He hadn't thought he would, he'd thought it would stay just his and Xavier's secret; but Raff was his brother, and her son. He took his hand and led the way back to the Kumari bench, and they were side by side again, and Raff was shivering. 'It's a secret though, Raff.'

Raff nodded, looking down at his lap. Then he looked up, his eyes raw and naked, nodding and nodding, like he couldn't stop. Jonah picked up the diary and hugged it as he started to speak.

It didn't take long, just a few sentences, to get from the kissing in the buddleia tent the night before they went to the Olympics to the wooden beam and the tiny red phone. He used his own words, mainly, with some words from her diary, and some of Xavier's. He listened to himself tacking them all together, and they sounded silly, like some meaningless tongue-twister.

When he stopped, Raff was silent. Then he said, 'So it was an accident?'

'Yes.'

Raff nodded. 'Silly Mayo!' He tried to grin, which made Jonah start crying again.

'Stop, fam,' said Raff. He patted Jonah's leg for a while, then tried to put his arm around his shoulders. Jonah shook his head, his body heaving.

Raff dropped his arms and sat on his hands. He waited
for a bit, and then he tried putting his hand back on his
brother's thigh. 'Come on, Little Pecker.'

'Don't call me that!' Jonah managed to gasp.

Raff leant in, pushing Jonah's hair away, so that he could
see his face. 'Poor Joney,' he said softly. Jonah turned and
put his face in Raff's chest, which was very small. 'Poor
Joney,' Raff said again, his voice shaking.

Jonah threw his arms around him, and the diary slid off
his lap and fell to the ground. 'Poor Raffy,' he croaked. It
was better to be crying together, it stopped the creature.
Raff's hands were patting and stroking his back, and he
patted and stroked Raff's. They hugged each other for a
long time.

'Why is it a secret, Joney?' asked Raff eventually.

'Because of Dora,' Jonah whispered. 'It would make Dora
very sad. And she's not very well.'

Raff nodded. 'And Em would be sad. I don't want Em to
be sad.' He let go of Jonah and straightened up. 'So Xavier
will keep it a secret too?'

'I think so. As long as . . .' He tried to think about the
plan. 'As long as no one asks him.'

'Do you still like Xavier?'

Jonah mate. Where's the whale? He shrugged.

'I don't think he's actually a bad man,' said Raff. 'I just
think he's done some bad things.'

Jonah stayed silent.

'What are we going to do now?'

'We're going to go to the Broken House. To see Mayo.'

Raff looked scared. 'Does she – look the same?'

'I don't know. She's all covered up. Xavier covered her up.'

'But we're going to uncover her.' Raff swallowed. Jonah nodded. 'And then what?'

'We need to help her soul get out. If it stays trapped inside her, then she'll have to be a ghost.'

'How will her soul get out?'

'It will come out of her head.' Jonah paused. 'It will be – like a funeral. It'll be OK, Raffy. It won't take long.'

'What are you going to do with her diary?' Raff picked it up from the ground. 'Can we keep it?'

Jonah took it from him. 'I don't know. I want to. But it's got the secret in it.'

'And you don't want anyone to know.'

Jonah shook his head.

'I don't want anyone to know either.' Raff was quiet for a moment, thinking. Then he said, 'We could bury it. You know, like treasure.'

Jonah looked at him, nodding. 'Like treasure. And when we're older, we can dig it back up.' He pulled the red phone out of his pocket. 'We could bury this too.' As he looked at it, he remembered the tree elephant.

73

There was the same safe feeling inside their circle of guardsmen trees. It was cooler than the day before, and there were fewer insects. Birds were chirruping above them, and the earth smelt of the rain.

'Where?' whispered Raff.

Jonah pointed across the green gloom. The elephant was still an elephant, as wise and kind as ever. Raff crawled over, and started digging with his fingers, in the dip between two of its roots. Jonah looked around and spotted an orange plastic bag, half hidden in a pile of leaves. He glanced at Raff to check he wasn't looking, before tearing the last page carefully out of the diary. *Alive, I lose, any which way you look at it.* Trying not to look at the rude drawing, he folded it up and put it into his pocket, before putting the diary into the plastic bag. He dropped the phone in too. 'It has to be deep, Raffy. Or a fox might dig it up.'

'Help me, then.'

The earth was only soft for a few inches, and after that the digging was hard work. Jonah used the heel of his shoe, and then Raff found a beer can, which they squashed and bent into a kind of trowel. Squirrels came to watch, and Raff thought he might be able to get them to help, but when he called and beckoned to them, they ran away. They had to take lots of rests, and it took a long time until the hole was wide enough and deep enough. Jonah tied the handles of the orange bag tight, and laid the package in the hole.

'It's like a funeral,' whispered Raff. 'Is this what we're going to do to Mayo?'

'No.' They both stared at the orange package for a while, before pushing the earth on top of it. They patted the earth flat and laid leaves and twigs on it, and then they crawled out. Over on the other side of the tennis courts, a man in shorts and a vest loped along the path. Jonah looked up at the sky, to the pearly glimmer through the cirrostratus. It was still very early.

Southway Street was still asleep under the fast-flowing cloud. They let themselves back into the house, and stood in the hallway for a moment, listening to the silence.

'It's not smelly,' whispered Raff.

'No. Because Xavier emptied the bin, remember?'

'And tidied everything up.' Raff walked through into the kitchen, but then he came back. 'I need a wee.'

Upstairs, the bathroom was just as it had been all week. Maybe there were a couple more dead flies in the bathwater. They took it in turns, and while Raff was weeing, Jonah looked into the bath and imagined her lying in it, her face under the water, like Ophelia's. When they went into her bedroom, he felt a ghostly trace, but it was just the smells and the clothes and all those molecules. Raff lay down on her bed, but Jonah told him to get off again.

'Why?'

'I need the sheets.' He pulled the top one off.

'Why do you need it?' whispered Raff.

'To wrap her in.'

'What, like how you wrapped up the diary?'

'A bit.'

'Are we going to dig a hole?'

'No. We're going to burn her. Like in India. Then her soul will be able to get out.'

Raff stared at him. Then he turned, kicking off his shoes, and put on Lucy's sparkly ones.

'Don't do that.'

'Why?'

'We've got to hurry. We've got to do it before everyone wakes up.' As Jonah bundled up the sheets, he saw the wine glass down by the side of the bed. Xavier's wine glass. He picked it up.

'Jonah?' Raff was still in the sparkly shoes, but his face was scared.

'What, Raff?' Jonah examined the wine glass. It was smeared and dusty, and there was a spot of dried-up wine down in the bowl. He held it up to the light, wondering what DNA looked like.

'What about Bad Granny?'

Jonah bundled the wine glass into the sheet. 'It's OK,' he said. 'I forgot to tell you, but we don't need to worry about Bad Granny any more, because they're going to let Roland out of prison.'

'Out on patrol?' Raff frowned.

'Parole.' As Jonah put the sheet bundle under his arm, he remembered the hospital letter. Another clue. He crouched over the pile of papers by the chest of drawers.

'When?'

'Today, Raffy. We're going to see him today.'

'So will he live with us? In this house?' Raff was still frowning, and he was right, it was difficult to imagine.

'I don't know. But come on.' He scrunched the hospital letter into a ball.

Raff stepped out of the shoes. 'Can these shoes be mine?' he asked. 'Will Daddy let me keep them?'

'Why do you want them? They're girls' shoes.'

'We could sell them, then,' said Raff. 'They're worth a lot of money.'

'They're not, Raff. They're not worth anything. Come on.'

74

They got the petrol can and the stepladder from the hallway and went out into the yard. Jonah set the stepladder against the wall. He stood still for a moment, thinking, and felt in his stuffed. The scrunched-up hospital letter was in with the horse money. Her diary page, carefully folded, was in the other pocket.

'Wait a sec.' He ran back into the kitchen and took the page out. *Alive, I lose* . . . He unfolded it, and smoothed it against the table.

Outside, Raff was already up on the wall. Jonah passed him the sheets, and then, with more difficulty, the petrol can, before climbing up next to him. He jumped down the other side, and turned and lifted his arms. Raff threw him the bundle and then tried to lower the petrol can into his hands, but it was very heavy and he let go before Jonah could take hold of it. It thudded heavily to the ground and tipped onto its side. Out in the light, it looked very rusty. Raff jumped down and picked the can up, and carried it manfully over to the broken window. Jonah followed. They looked into the darkness.

'I can smell incense,' whispered Raff.

'Yes.' The smell was much stronger than the day before. 'Did Mayo light it?'

'You can't light incense when you're dead, Raffy.' Jonah was whispering too.

'So it was Saviour.'

'It wasn't him. I asked him and he said no.'

Raff was silent. Then he whispered, 'Might it be, like, God or someone?'

'I don't think so. Anyway, you don't believe in God.'

'Oh.'

'Pass me the can.'

Still clutching the sheets with one arm, Jonah lifted the can onto the ledge of uneven bricks and hoisted himself next to it. He gazed across the room, to where the light from the sky was falling through the beams – to where the carpet was. As he did, he became aware, from the very corner of his eye, of a tiny orange dot of brightness.

He turned his head. It seemed to be floating in the air, like a firefly, apart from it was completely still. Still, because it was the glowing head of an incense stick. The incense stick was sticking up from the crate next to the bed. And behind it, on the bed, was a very long shape.

And the shape was a person.

Raff heard Jonah's gasp, and leaned in, so that he could follow Jonah's gaze. He gasped too. They leaned into each other, their hearts racing.

'Who is it?' Raff breathed.

'I don't know,' Jonah breathed back. The person was lying on its back, with its hands behind its head.

'Is it a man?'

'Yes.' On the jutting chin, the fuzz of a beard.

'Is he asleep?'

As if he had heard, in a smooth, gliding motion, the man sat up, swivelling his hatted, bearded head to look towards them.

'Oh my days,' Raff whispered. 'So he *does* live here.'

The Raggedy Man. Of course. They watched him swing his long legs round, bringing his feet to the rubble and his hands to his thighs. He seemed to be staring back at them, but it was hard to tell in the gloom.

'So it's him, burning the incense,' whispered Raff. 'Where does he get it from?'

'Maybe the Green Shop Man gives him it.'

'It's weird that he likes incense. I mean, considering what *he* smells like.'

'Yes.' The sadness of the Raggedy Man and his incense. Jonah watched him lean forwards, over his knees, and stay bent over like that, doing something, but he couldn't see what.

'It's his shoes. He's putting them on,' said Raff. 'He's doing his laces.'

'Oh,' said Jonah. He could hear her voice, softly chanting. *On the Coast of Coromandel, where the early pumpkins blow.* He glanced around the gloomy cavern, half expecting to see pumpkins pushing out of the rubble. The Raggedy Man finished tying his laces and stood up, very tall and straight. He turned and tugged the blanket smooth.

'He's making his bed,' whispered Raff, fascinated.

In the middle of the woods, lived the Yonghy-Bonghy-Bò. The Raggedy Man had finished tidying the bed, and had brought his hands to his hips. He was like an actor on a stage, looking across the room to where the light was falling from the sky – to where the carpet was. *Two old chairs, and half a candle, one old jug without a handle.* Jonah's eyes scanned the graffiti on the walls. Words and shapes, and more faces – geometric, like the one in the kitchen that had scared Raff on Monday afternoon. He felt the history of the room, layered under its surface: in the wallpaper under the graffiti, the plaster, the bricks, and in the rubble and the objects buried in the rubble. *These were all his worldly goods: in the middle of the woods.* He became aware of his thoughts as layers, shifting layers: the Yonghy-Bonghy-Bò picture, with the tall thin trees, and the curling feather on Lady Jingly's hat, giving way to the actual room before him, in all its murky complexity.

'What should we do, Joney?'

'I'm not sure.' Jonah stared at the Raggedy Man. 'I think we might have to come back later,' he whispered. But then the Raggedy Man's long oval head swivelled on his long thin neck. His arm lifted – what a graceful arm – and he beckoned.

'He wants us to go in,' said Raff.

Once, among the Bong-trees walking, where the early pumpkins blow, to a little heap of stones came the Yonghy-Bonghy-Bò . . . The Raggedy Man had his hands on his hips, waiting for them. Raff slid off the ledge into the room, and lifted down the petrol can. The heaviness of it made him stagger on the rubble. Jonah got a strong whiff of petrol. He looked down at the ledge, and saw the wet patch the can had left.

'Come on.'

'OK.' Clutching the bundle of sheets, he jumped down next to Raff. They looked at each other, their eyes gleaming in the darkness.

'Where's Mayo?' whispered Raff.

'Over there.' Jonah nodded in the direction of the carpet. The Raggedy Man was watching them, as still as a statue. He led the way across the rubble, feeling the Raggedy Man's eyes following them.

Of course it wasn't that far to where the carpet was – ten or fifteen steps – but it seemed to take a very long time. Hearing Raff stagger again, he glanced over his shoulder. Like a ghost, the Raggedy Man had crossed the room and was there, next to Raff, steadying him.

I am tired of living singly, on this coast so wild and shingly. Lucy's voice was a warm, lisping wisp in his brain. He watched the Raggedy Man take the petrol can from Raff, unscrew the cap and sniff. *If you'll come and be my wife, quite serene would be my life.* But she'd said no, because of Handel Jones, her husband, and the Yonghy had fled. *So sad, Mayo.*

The can hung, dripping, on the end of the Raggedy Man's long arm. The Raggedy Man and Raff were both looking at Jonah. It was time to get going.

When he reached the carpet, he stopped, and the other two stopped either side of him. The patterns on the carpet. More like a chess board than noughts and crosses.

'Where is she?' whispered Raff.

'There. Underneath.'

Raff stared at the carpet. Jonah peeped up at the Raggedy Man. He was hugging the petrol can to his chest, his eyes sad and brooding.

'How do you know, Jonah?' Raff's voice was taut and high, like a whistle. 'Did you look? Did you see her?'

Jonah stayed quiet, the nursery rhyme words rolling on in his head. Beside him, Raff was making little sounds, like a dog's whimper. He lifted the sheets to his face, and smelt the coconut. Then he placed the bundle on the ground, and took out the wine glass. He straightened up and threw it, hard, into the gloom. They heard it smash.

Raff stopped whimpering. 'Why did you do that?' he asked.

'It was a clue. It had Saviour's DNA on it.'

'What's DNA?'

'It's like – bits of him.' Suddenly embarrassed, Jonah glanced at the Raggedy Man, but he didn't seem to have heard. He looked at Raff's face. It had shrunk, his cheeks sucked inwards, as if he'd suddenly become malnourished, his huge eyes fixed on the carpet. Jonah took a breath, trying to focus. They needed some wood, something that would burn easily. He looked around. He'd been thinking about the Wendy house, of maybe pulling it apart, but perhaps the books would do, maybe they could make a pile of them and lay her on it. First they needed to wrap her. Jonah stooped to pick up the sheets and tried to shake them out, but they were too big – his arms couldn't stretch wide enough.

'What are you doing now?'

'We need to spread them. Raffy, can you help me.'

'But what for?'

'So we can. . .' He'd had it so clear in his head, the neat, white cocoon, but it came to him that he wouldn't ever be able to wrap her body up like that, and he didn't see how he'd ever thought he could. He couldn't even bear to lift the carpet. 'It's OK, Raffy.' He dropped the sheets back on the ground. Maybe he could just pour the petrol onto the carpet and set light to it, so she would burn inside. What difference did it make, wrapping her in sheets, if she was going to end up a pile of ash? But then – to burn her without seeing her. Without Raff seeing her. To leave her under that filthy carpet.

'What's the matter, Joney?'

'I can't do it. We can't do it, can we? It's just stupid.'

'Shall we go home then?'

Raff looked over his shoulder, but then the Raggedy Man put the petrol can down, and was taking hold of the edge of the carpet with both hands.

There was a whirl of movement: the Raggedy Man's arms lifting and throwing, the carpet falling back; Jonah jumping back, cupping one hand over his nose, using the other to pull Raff with him. The red of her sarong, her legs, the strange angle of her head, and Raff's scream as he turned and fled.

Jonah took two more unsteady steps back, both hands now clasped over his nose. He heard Raff trip and fall onto the stones, but his eyes stayed on the red. It was very dirty, the sarong, and hitched up high on her thighs. There was the knot, on her breastbone, the ears of the knot lying up towards her throat. She wrapped it twice around her body, then gathered those two corners, pulled it tight and tied that knot; he'd seen her do it, loads of times. 'Mayo!' Behind him, Raff was sobbing the word over and over, the most terrible sound he had ever heard.

He let his eyes move to her face.

It was her, but not quite: a version of her, from a long-ago dream about the future. The skin oddly pale, and the forehead jutting out, like a caveman's, shadowing her eyes. Her mouth was smiling a weird, sideways smile, like she was remembering the fun of being alive.

'Mayo.' He whispered it into his cupped hand. Raff's sobs got even worse, and tears filled Jonah's eyes. '*Mayo,*' he said silently. '*Please come, because Raffy fell over. He's crying, Mayo. Please come, because I don't like your dead face.*' He looked up. Blurred slivers of the sky, clouds racing.

Then the Raggedy Man stepped forward and took the sheets off him. He laid them out in a big white square right next to Lucy's body and, very gently, he slid his long thin hands under her and rolled her onto the white. She was face down now, and Jonah caught a glimpse of her bottom, because, at the back, the sarong had ridden up to her waist. Her bottom had changed – it was flat and very dark, like an all-over bruise – and it made him cry. But the Raggedy Man had hold of the sheets now, and was rolling her up in them, quite tightly, until she was just her shape. Quite a small shape, really. Not as neat as he'd imagined, but a white cotton shape. Then the Raggedy Man straightened up and, wiping his hands on his tracksuit, looked at Raff. Jonah looked too.

'It's OK, Raffy. You can come back now.'

Raff stayed where he was, huddled by the Wendy house, so Jonah walked back and put his arm around the shaking shoulders.

'It's not her, Raffy. Her body isn't actually *her*. She's not in it, any more. It's like – an empty pod. A shell.'

'Where is she, then?'

'She's here. She's . . .' *Mayo, come. Come for Raff. Let him feel you. Please come.*

The Raggedy Man had joined them. He put his hand in his pocket and pulled something out – and offered it, the way he had on Monday morning.

Jonah stared at the glinting object in his palm, and then reached out to take it. 'Thank you,' he whispered. He wondered why the Raggedy Man had removed it from her throat, but then he remembered that Xavier had grabbed it as she fell: he saw the snapped chain, swimming in the air like a golden snake, the heavier locket beating it down to the stones. He snapped it open and looked at the tiny, black and white photo: *her* mother, who'd been dead now, for a long, long time. He closed it again, and gave it to Raff.

'We need to burn her body, Raffy boy. Then she'll – then you'll . . .' He pulled him to his feet. 'We need the books.' He looked down at them. They were mainly ordinary paperbacks, with pictures on the covers. On one of them, a crazy-looking woman, running, with her clothes billowing out behind her. *Wuthering Heights.* He stooped and picked it up. A huge spider scuttled onto his hand and he gasped.

'Jonah?'

'It's OK.' He brushed the spider away and tried to pass Raff the book. 'Come on, Raff, we need to make a pile. For the fire.'

'I don't want to,' whispered Raff, staring at the locket.

'I tell you what, Raffy.' Jonah dug in his own pocket and pulled out the roll of horse money. 'When we've finished, we'll go and buy some sweets. Any sweets you want.'

Raff shook his head, his teeth chattering horribly.

Jonah looked back at the books. 'OK. You stay there. I'll do it. It won't take long. And when I light it, we don't have to stay.' He had thought they'd watch for a while, maybe get to see her soul rising out of her cracked skull. 'We'll run back to the house. We'll go home, OK? Raffy?'

Raff managed to nod. Jonah scooped up an armful of books and so did the Raggedy Man.

Once they'd made a long pile of them, Jonah tried to pick up the petrol can, but he was all wobbly and the Raggedy Man took it off him. He opened the lid and tipped the can, and a thin stream poured down onto the books. *I love the smell of petrol . . .* That's what she'd said, on the bus, holding the can on her lap, on the way to rescue the car.

The Raggedy Man picked up her white shape and placed it carefully on the bed of books. Then he poured on more petrol, and the white cotton got wet and clung to her. When it was empty, the Raggedy Man dropped the petrol can and it clattered on the stones. Then he turned and looked at Jonah again, waiting, alert. It took Jonah a second or two to work out what for.

'Oh no!' he whispered.

'Jonah! What's the matter?' From behind him, Raff's panicked voice.

'I just – I forgot to bring any matches.'

There was a slight change in the Raggedy Man's face – not a smile, or a frown, but a kind of softening. He turned and crossed to the doorway, light of tread. Then he sprang up, out of the room, and disappeared into the hall.

'Where's he gone?' asked Raff.

'To get a light. From the kitchen.' That pot of honey on the table and the little camping stove. And that jar of little sticks that smelt of mince pies. Cloves, that's what they were. Why did the Raggedy Man have a jar of cloves? He must have been making himself a hot toddy. Because of his cold. Had the Raggedy Man's mother ever made him a hot toddy? Did he think of her, when he made himself one?

Jonah pulled out the scrunched-up hospital letter and dropped it among the books, by her petrol-soaked white feet. He stepped back and the Raggedy Man appeared at the doorway, holding a lit candle and a cardboard box. He couldn't jump down with the candle, Jonah realised, not without the flame going out, so he walked over to him and the Raggedy Man passed it down.

Jonah turned back. From here the room looked very long, all the way back to the broken window. Her white shape lay on its nest, bathed in the soft grey light from the sky. Further back, Raff was still huddled by the Wendy house.

As he and the Raggedy Man walked back to her body, a drip of wax ran down the candle and onto Jonah's hand. It was hot, but not too hot. Raff was whimpering again, and he wanted to go to him, but he was holding the candle. The Raggedy Man was rolling and twisting the cardboard into a kind of wand. More wax rolled onto his hand.

'Raffy?'

There was no answer. The Raggedy Man was dipping the wand into the petrol can, so that the cardboard would soak up the last dregs. Then he finally took the candle back and Jonah picked the warm wax off his hand. He wanted to move *around* the Raggedy Man, to go and stand next to Raff, but the Raggedy Man was making a sign for him to move back the other way. He obeyed, and the Raggedy Man kept waving, so he backed away further, which was wrong, because it was away from Raff.

'You move back too, Raffy!' He saw Raff's head turn towards him, like a rabbit's. The flame burst out of the cardboard wand, lighting up the graffiti on the walls.

The faces leered, like an impatient audience, and the Raggedy Man stepped forward and held the wand to the white shape.

'Raffy, get back!'

There was a massive whoosh, and for a second it looked like the Raggedy Man had caught fire too, but he threw himself down and rolled across the rubble, and none of the blaze came with him. He got onto all fours, and then to his feet and, as he looked back at what he'd done, his face turned dark orange. Jonah looked too, at the still shape in the flames, already black, like the black, flaming shapes in the children's paintings. The way the flames clung to the shape, the way they needed it, for their energy, so that they could whip up and up, towards the birds.

'Jonah!'

'Raffy!' Jonah headed towards him. He needed to get him out of there. Poor Raffy. He stopped, because a runaway flame had cut him off, racing nimbly over the rubble. *Gingerbread Man, Gingerbread Man.* Of course, because of the petrol, the drips that had fallen from the can, it was feeding on the drips, because petrol is energy, the liquid energy of things that were alive a million years ago. The flames were small, ankle-high, but when they reached the leftover books there was another whoosh.

'Raffy, quick! We need to go home!' Where was he? Had he already gone, or was that him, over by the Wendy house? It was hard to see, because of the smoke. He called Raff's name again, over the noise of the whooshing and the crackling. He looked back at her body, but it was hidden in thick smoke.

He turned towards the broken window. There were ribbons of flames now, flickering and dancing, but there was still time.

'Jonah!'

'Raffy!' Where was he? The room was full of flickering silk curtains, feeding on the energy of the objects, and the sounds were getting louder.

'Jonah!'

There! He *had* moved – behind the Wendy house now, over towards the wall. He shouldn't have gone that way. Never mind, there was still time. He just needed to . . . It was hot. And the smoke.

'Raffy, it's OK! Raffy, we need to get out the other way!'

'What other way?' He had started coughing.

'To the kitchen! Go towards the kitchen!'

Raff coughed and coughed. He was behind the Wendy house, maybe too close to it still, because the flames were licking at its walls.

'Raffy!'

The fire took hold of the Wendy house and poured upwards, like an upside-down waterfall. It was hot, very hot, and Jonah backed away. He could get around it, though, he could reach Raff, he could get to where the coughing was. He went left first, but turned back, not wanting to pass through those pretty silk curtains. He was coughing too, now, but yes, this way was better, less hot. He couldn't see, though, he couldn't see Raff, he couldn't see anything, and the sound of the fire was so *loud*.

'Raffy!' He licked his hot lips and closed his eyes against the smoke, realising that they were in mortal danger. MORTAL DANGER. He saw the words in zigzagging neon on his closed eyelids. 'Raffy.' He tried to shout, but it came out in a croak and he started coughing again. *Raffy. I'm coming to get you.* He must be very near, maybe an arm's length, but he wasn't sure in which direction.

It's OK Mayo, I'm going to get him. He opened his eyes and surged crazily forwards, his hands groping between the flames. There was a roaring, not the fire, but a roaring in his brain, and there was something on his hand and he had to snatch it back, and the fire seemed to have got onto it. He staggered, shooing the fire off, stuffing his hand under his armpit, and then, crouching down, between his thighs. It was very dark now, like night-time. *Was* it night-time? How long had they been there? *'Keep down.'* Who said that? Something bad had happened to his hand. He curled it against his chest, and curled into a ball. Had it been *her*, telling him to keep down? Had she escaped through her own skull? Was she there with him now? *'Keep down, Joney boy, because heat rises.'* He was crawling now, on his knees and one hand. Heat rises. He must tell Raff. But where *was* Raff? *Such a fierce, strong baby . . .* He was just here, a minute ago. Maybe he went out that other way.

Shush. It was like he was under a mountain, and there were clouds covering the mountain. And the mountain was moving. A moving mountain coming closer, and a face, some kind of face, in the cloud. Was it the mountain's face, or was it just the cloud? Very thick. Nimbostratus. The face of the cloud loomed down, and the arms of it came round. Was it God? A blank face, a long, sad oval, with a tall, sad hat. The long, gnarly arms. Raggedy Man. Hot zip on his tracksuit chest.

He was up. His face was on the Raggedy Man's shoulder, and the Raggedy Man's arms were holding him. But what about Raff? They were at the doorway. It had been so near. And now they were up, in the hallway. He tried to speak, but he couldn't, so he tried to bang on the Raggedy Man's chest. In the kitchen, the smoke was much thinner and he could see trees through the open back door. But what about Raff? They had to go back. He struggled harder, and the Raggedy Man put him down. He started back towards the hallway, but the Raggedy Man grabbed him. 'Raffy.' It was a whisper: no one could have heard it. The Raggedy Man had let him go, he was down on the floor, his hand . . .

Then he could hear water, which was good, clever Raggedy Man, he'd turned on the tap, strange that the tap still worked after all this time. Water was streaming out, down onto the broken sink below, and the Raggedy Man was holding something into the stream, a big piece of cloth, maybe a sheet or a blanket. *Quickly. Because Raff is alone.* Poor Raffy. He could feel that the horse money was in his pocket still, which was good, because he was going to let Raff buy whatever he wanted. He watched the Raggedy Man drape the soaked cloth over his head and shoulders, like a cloak. It was stripy, and very big, covering nearly all of him, which was good. Jonah got to his feet and followed him to the hallway. He saw him pause, on the threshold of the burning room, and look back at him, through the smoke. Then he brought one end of the cloth over his nose and mouth like a desert man, and he jumped down into the burning room.

It's OK, Raffy. The Raggedy Man's coming. Jonah stayed in the hallway, his eyes fixed on the doorway, until there was too much smoke and he couldn't see it any more. *If I stay here. If I stay here, looking . . . If I believe. If I wish. If I pray.* And then he could hear another sound, cutting through the roaring sound, a sound he knew very well – *neee naaaw neee naaaw.* It would be OK. Help was coming. *Raffy, can you hear it! Just hold on!* There was a groan then, a long, deep groan, the groan of a mournful giant, and Jonah couldn't help edging backwards. Another groan, and it was the Broken House groaning, groaning from its bones as they broke, and the ceiling of the hallway started coming down, in showers, and then big lumps. He threw himself back into the kitchen.

He was on the floor again, under the table, which was an OK place to wait. They'd be here soon. They just needed to get through the fallen-down hallway. He felt for the horse money. *Anything you want, Raffy.* He couldn't see the trees any more, but he could just make out the back door, the rectangle of very faint light. There were noises coming from outside, but he decided to stay where he was and wait for Raffy and the Raggedy Man, who were on their way. Then he noticed that the rectangle changed, because there was a shape in it, a human shape, in a great big coat. *Daddy?* He pulled himself out from under the table and tried to stand up. The smoke, though. It was the opposite of the train platform in *The Railway Children*, because instead of getting clearer, the shape was getting fainter. *Daddy, is it you, are you there?* He lurched forward and fell back down. *Daddy?*

SATURDAY

75

It had been a fireman, not Roland, standing in the Broken House door, but the man sitting in the chair next to him *was* Roland, he was nearly sure of it. He could see his pale-trousered thighs and his strange blue hands clasped between them, but he couldn't turn and look at the rest of him – he couldn't move at all. He tried to say his name, but he had something in his mouth, going all the way down his throat, it was horrible.

He seemed to be in a kind of tank. Or was it a submarine? There were lots of machines, and the chair next to him, which was empty now – and another chair by the wall. *Two old chairs, and half a candle . . .* A man in a dark pink uniform kept coming in and looking at him, and going out again. Was he going to see Raff? His name was Bo, it was written on his badge: 'Bo Jensen'. 'I am Bo,' he'd said, smiling, pointing at the badge (with his blue finger), but he was small and neat, with a small, neat head: absolutely nothing like the Yonghy-Bonghy-Bò. 'And you are Jonah. Is this your first time in hospital?' Jonah had tried to answer, but of course he couldn't, because of the tube, and Bo Jensen had put his finger to his lips. His strange blue finger.

He dreamed that *he* was Yonghy, fleeing down the slopes of Myrtle, to the calm and silent sea, where the Turtle was waiting. 'She won't marry me,' he explained. 'So we might as well go.' The Turtle's eye was like Ganesha's eye, very kind and twinkling, and it was easy to climb up onto his broad back. *Through the silent-roaring ocean did the Turtle swiftly go.* He kept looking behind him, though, because he could hear Lady Jingly, crying and crying, on her heap of stones.

He opened his eyes. Roland, definitely Roland, sitting in the other chair now, the one by the wall, so he could see all of him. His hands were still blue, and he was wearing a blue apron. Maybe he'd been making mince pies. He slipped back into the dream, but the turtle had changed into a kind of sea rocking horse, which reminded him: where was the horse money?

Now both of the chairs were empty. Roland must have gone to see Raff. Why didn't they bring Raffy in here? *Two old chairs and half a candle.* No candles. But there was a jug, a plastic hospital jug, over there on the special hospital table. It was actually the second time he'd been in hospital. That's what he'd wanted to say to Bo. The first time, though, was a long time ago, and he could only remember tiny flashes of it. His new Wellington boots, walking up a ramp, a very steep ramp, red boots, and then they were in the long yellow corridor. Granny Sadie had given him the toy to hold, the stripy monkey rattle. He'd been *so* excited, looking through the open doors into the rooms on either side, but Granny Sadie had his hand and they kept going.

Now Roland was back in the chair next to him, and the blue hands were holding a piece of paper. He remembered that piece of paper, he remembered leaving it in the kitchen.

Oh yes, it was that page, the page from her diary. *Alive I lose* . . . The word that was like 'seaside', meaning 'to kill yourself'. He'd forgotten it again, but it didn't matter. It was a bad thing to do, to pretend something, to tell a lie, and he worried about the karma boomerang, whizzing back. But they were probably all just snooker balls, and the gods were leaning on their cues, looking down, watching them roll and bounce.

The blue hands turning the page over now, to look at the rude drawing. And then Bo Jensen was back, and he couldn't see Roland any more, because Bo was in the way, looking at the machines, and looking at him, and writing things on his clipboard. He wanted to tell Bo about the first time he'd been in hospital, how excited they'd been, he and Granny Sadie, walking along the busy yellow corridor. People said he couldn't possibly remember, but he could, he could remember holding the stripy monkey, and his red Wellington boots, and looking and looking . . . where were they?

Bo was gone, and Roland was crying again, weeping and moaning, with the pumpkins, into the jug without a handle. If only he would get up and take the thing out of Jonah's mouth, and pour him some water. *Still she weeps, and daily moans; on that little heap of stones.* His red Wellington boots on the steep ramp, the excitement, and the long yellow corridor. And then, into a big, wide room, with lots of people lying in beds, and through the window, the enormous sky. And there! Finally! Over in the corner! Mayo and Daddy! Daddy, on the chair, smiling, not crying, and Mayo, his lovely Mayo, smiling too, in her big bed. In her arms, a bundle. A bundle of what?

'Hush.' Roland, right there, standing over him, his face

all twisted. 'Daddy's here.' The strange blue hand was stroking his shoulder. If only he would take the tube out. If only he would tell him where Raffy was. *Where is he, Daddy?!* The question rose up in him, urgent, and he tried and tried to make a sound. 'Hush,' said Roland. 'Hush, my darling. Daddy's here.'

Daddy got out of his chair and lifted me up, and out of the window was the park. And in the bed was Mayo, smiling and smiling, kind of pale and underwatery. Then she gave the bundle to Granny Sadie, and Granny Sadie's eyes shined, and everyone was so happy. Can you guess what that bundle was, Raff? I know you think I can't really remember, but I can, I can remember all of it. Then I was on Mayo's lap, and Granny Sadie put the bundle on my lap, and I looked down, and saw your scrunchy, monkey face. I gave you your toy, and you grabbed it, with your tiny fist, and you looked so fierce! I laughed, and so did everyone else, because you were so funny! And Mayo said, 'I'm glad he's a boy, because you two boys are going to have so much fun together.'

Such a strong little fist. Such a fierce little face. Such a strong, fierce little brother.

JULY 2018

76

He'd been a while at Leonie's. Her 6.30 hadn't shown up, and he'd got immersed in his playing, and now his mouth muscles ached and his shadow was long. The ice-cream van was in its usual place in the park, a knot of dishevelled children under its serving window. A little girl in just her pants was getting one of those rocket lollies that Raff had liked. He should hurry, they would all be wondering where he'd got to, but something made him stop and watch her. She had recent, bloody grazes on both her knees. She scuttled off a little way, on her very bandy legs, before ripping the wrapper off and dropping it on the ground. He frowned, but to be fair on her, there was already litter everywhere. Sucking the lolly, she stared back at him, her bulgy eyes latching onto the scarring. He'd presumed she was in just her pants because she'd been in the paddling pool, but then he noticed that the paddling pool hadn't been filled. Three teenagers on skateboards were circling the cracked concrete like sharks.

'My lolly dropped.' The girl was looking up at him, her lips and chin stained purple. The lolly lay in melting chunks on the gravelly ground.

There was something annoying about her expectancy, but he felt in his pocket anyway. 'I'll get you another one.'

One of the teenagers threw him a look, presumably of scorn. The girl took his hand and led him to stand at the back of the queue. It was his bad hand – he was carrying his trumpet with his good one – but she held it with a tight grip. He thought about just giving her the money and walking off, but her grip and the way she was leaning into him made it impossible. He got a cornet for himself, and as he took the first lick of it he wondered again if Xavier would be there. He'd come the year before, with a bag of runner beans from the eco-village, but he hadn't been on good form. He'd shown them photos of his yurt, which he'd built himself. A low, circular hut, made of latticed strips of wood. The inside was very bare: just a camp bed, neatly made, and a candle. Looking at the photos had brought back that poem that Lucy used to read to them . . . *These were all his worldly goods: in the middle of the woods.* What was his name, the man in the woods, with the huge head and the tiny hat? He couldn't remember.

The girl wandered off without saying thank you. Jonah gazed after her. She seemed very little to be on her own. He walked along until he drew level with the hospital, and looked up, trying to identify the window he'd lain under, after they'd brought him up from Intensive Care. He'd been there for weeks, watching the clouds, all alone in his little room off the main children's ward, always thirsty, and that terrible itching under the dressings.

Not alone, Jonah, love. He saw his grandmother shaking her head at him. It was true, there had pretty much always been a visitor – they'd taken it in turns, even through the night. They had read to him, especially at the beginning, when it hurt too much for him to talk. Sadie had chosen the books and had been the best reader by far, with a different voice for each character. Roland had been OK. A bit monotone. Better than Xavier, though, who kept stopping, having drifted off into his own thoughts. In the quiet, he would listen to the faint sounds of the other children on the ward, sometimes thinking he could hear Raff's voice. Inside the room there was Xavier's breathing, the odd bleep from the monitor he was attached to, and the ticking of the big, round clock above the door. He had watched that clock a lot, as a break from the sky and the clouds, enough to know that the second hand slowed ever so slightly on its upward journey, quickening again on its way back down. He had thought of asking Xavier if he was glad about the secret, but he'd felt too tired, and his throat had been too sore.

He wasn't enjoying his ice cream that much, and he'd be having roast chicken soon. As he stuffed what was left of it into an over-filled bin, his phone pinged in his inside pocket, and he reached for it. The message was from Sadie. Sadie, previously known as Bad Granny. Who turned out to be not that bad after all.

Dinner is ready. We are waiting for you. I hope you didn't decide to go to Frank's?!

Poor Sadie. She'd be feeling worried about him, worried he'd got lost, or run into some kind of trouble. 'Big Soz', he wrote, '5 minutes'. And then, because he was feeling guilty, 'XXX'. He pocketed the phone and walked fast up the hill, thinking about how they'd been so scared of her, and as he got to the pond a quacking flurry on the water brought back that scream and that circle of staring eyes. What had happened, maybe, was that they'd got her all mixed up with the peacock. He and Raff had been hysterical, screaming too, mouths wide open. Screaming and running, holding hands, bodies jarring as their feet thudded on the ground. Round the side of the house, then diving under Sadie's car, clinging to each other on the dirty gravel. She had had to drag them out, first him, then Raff, and she'd brushed them down, sobbing; in about the same state as them.

He'd stopped, he realised, and put his trumpet case down, to put his hands over his ears. Funny how a memory can be held, dormant, in various neurons in the cortex, then suddenly fire up, as powerful as ever. He still couldn't remember the name of the sad man in that poem, though. The peacock had died not long afterwards, Sadie had told him: run over, just outside the house. He wriggled his shoulders, shrugging the memory away.

The ducks had all simmered down, and it was quiet and dark under the trees. He lolled against the railings, knowing he should be hurrying, but reluctant to extract himself from the past. They'd been so little, he and Raff. He'd had no idea, at the time, quite how little they were. He thought of the bandy-legged girl, and wondered if he should look for her, ask her if she was OK, if she needed his help. Pat and Leonie weren't the only people who'd felt bad about not noticing his and Raff's predicament, or not acting on their suspicions. Poor Miss Swann had been beside herself, as had Christine, and Mrs Blakeston, and Mr Mann. At the funeral, which they'd had to wait months for, because of the inquest, Alison had gripped him, tearful. '*If only you could have trusted me!'* she had wailed. Sadie had said more or less the same thing, in that chair by his hospital bed. *'Jonah, I am so sorry you didn't feel you could turn to me.'* She had closed the book on her lap, to make her little speech. *'I know I was awful that day, shouting at Raffy.'* The vase had been her mother's, just a stupid bit of glass, but poor Roland, what he'd done – something had snapped in her. Unforgivable that she'd scared them like that, and then the peacock. It had haunted her. A terrible thing on a terrible day.

He looked across at Olive Mary Sage's bench – *She is not far away* – and remembered again, clear as crystal, how he used to feel his mother's presence: her smell and the loving, smiling touch of her eyes. He turned, his back against the railings, and his blurred gaze fell on the words on the bench in front of him.

KUMARI
ETERNAL, RADIANT BEAUTY

Such familiar words. The bench where Xavier had sobbed, and he and Raff had tried to comfort him. The creature was shifting, and he sat himself down on the bench. He was a totally different person now: every cell in his body had been replaced, his hormonal balance had changed, and five years of experience had reshaped his personality. So where was that nine-year-old boy that he'd been? Was he dead too? Or was he dormant in his neurons, dormant but complete, like the sleeping princess in that fairy tale?

'We were so little.'

He'd said it out loud, and there was the tiniest ghost of an echo. He glanced around at the other benches, half-thinking he might catch a glimpse of Olive Sage, or Hilda, or Kumari – or the little dog Snowy. *We were so little.* It was Xavier he wanted to say it to. So complicated, thinking about Xavier. He stared into the pond, imagining the white stick, still intact, down in its muddy bed.

'You *have a secret, Jonah Armitage. You can tell it to me, if you want.*' Kitten's voice. Sadie had sent him to see Kitten, once he was out of hospital and living with her. The name Kitten didn't suit her: she was very tall, with a huge nose and lots of bushy white hair. He'd gone to see her once a week for a few months. He had liked her. She was cleverer than Miss Swann, and also funnier and more relaxed. She had an amazing amount of knowledge. They had talked about religion, and beliefs about what happens to you after you die; and he'd told her about the gods in their togas, looking down, through their pool of water, and about Lucy, looking up and wanting to dive into the sky. They'd had an interesting conversation about free will, and she'd taught him the Latin term *causa sui*, which meant to be the cause of itself; and that quote from a philosopher, a German, what was his name? Something about pulling yourself by your hair out of the swamps of nothingness. She had been very interested in the creature, and in working out what it actually was. In the end she'd decided it was a little Jonah – very little – who had no words to make sense of what was happening. '*Whereas, you, Jonah . . .*' She had leant forward, tucking her bushes of hair behind her ears. '*The Big Jonah, sitting here with me in this room . . .*' It had been a lovely room, with a thick carpet and a big window looking out onto trees. '*The Big Jonah has language, and understanding. Even if he won't tell me everything, he can tell himself, and discover its meaning, and shape the story . . .*'

Kitten had been very enthusiastic about stories. The Bad Granny nickname had come up at some stage, and she'd pounced on it and told him about Baba Yaga, the old hag from ancient fairy tales. He hadn't told her the secret, but he had eventually told her about listening to Sadie talking on the phone, the evening of Angry Saturday, huddled with Raff on the top stair. *'She said she didn't want him, because of his afro hair?'* Kitten had looked astonished, and he'd started wondering if he'd imagined it all. Kitten had told him he must talk to Sadie about it. *'You can't live in the same house as someone without clearing something like that up.'*

He hadn't asked Sadie, but he'd brought it up with Roland, and Roland had got them all to sit down together. Sadie had explained that she'd been talking to a lawyer friend about the possibility of adopting them both, on the grounds that Lucy was an unfit mother. *'Of course I wanted you both. But I . . .'* She had paused, looking over at Roland. *'I had this doubt about Raff. About Roland being his dad. And I was worried that if he wasn't Roland's son, then I wouldn't be allowed to adopt him, and that he would maybe end up in care.'*

The sky was glimmering pink through the trees, and the air was getting cooler. The chicken would be all dried out by now, and Sadie and Dora would be a bit drunk. And Xavier, if he was there. Not Roland, who didn't really like drinking, and who would drive them all home in Sadie's car. Wondering if there would be another argument about politics, he set off again, out of the trees and up the path towards the top gate. The people he passed all looked feverish in the rosy light. *'Do you trust me, Jonah?'* Kitten's eyes, golden black, like treacle. The white stick, sunk deep into the mud. He kept an eye out for the bandy girl, but he didn't see her.

Hopefully someone had got her dressed and put plasters on her poor knees.

The plaque was quite new and shiny still. Jonah traced the words with his finger.

LUCY NSANSA MWEMBE –
BELOVED MOTHER OF JONAH AND RAFF

It was Lucy's father, Tomas, who had told them about her middle name. A Bemba name, he'd explained, meaning 'happiness'. And Raff's middle name – Bupe – meant 'a gift'. Tomas had come to London for the funeral, with Collins, his eldest son. They had brought a gift – a book about the Zambian football team – and also the medal Lucy had won at the All Africa Junior Swimming Championships.

Her bench was under a maple tree, which had been shedding its seed-filled helicopters. *Samaras.* He sat down and picked one up to examine it closely. Four wings, angled downwards to ride the breeze, like a helicopter. That buzzing dot, growing bigger and louder, and Raff's charge through the itchy long grass. He looked down past the tennis courts, all the way to the scrubby trees, and suddenly remembered how they'd buried her diary and her phone. Would they still be there, in that orange bag, under the elephant tree? Had their little hands dug deep enough? He closed his eyes and saw her scribbly writing, with all those doodles in the different-coloured pens. The smell of the earth, his and Raff's hands, scooping it onto the plastic parcel. But that was on the fire morning. It wasn't good to think about the fire. Clenching his bad hand, he thought instead about what Sadie had been saying on the phone that night, and how he

had misunderstood. And then he'd told Lucy what he
thought he'd heard, and it had become part of the Bad
Granny story.

'Mayo,' he whispered. He used to talk to her all the time,
straining to feel her near him. There had been times when
she'd suddenly popped up, as a cat prowling along a wall, a
nodding sunflower, a bright red sports car. 'Mayo,' he whispered again. 'I love you, Mayo.' He'd been trying to call her
Lucy, he remembered, to be more grown up. He wanted to
think of something funny to tell her, because it would be
nice to share a joke, make her laugh, but the sadness and
the strangeness were pressing down on him. Instead he asked
her what she thought about the way things had turned out.
*It's good that Sadie turned out to be nice. And that we live with
her. Don't you think, Mayo?* He watched the tennis players,
trying to feel her answer, to see a sign, but there was another,
more important question, rising up. *Do you mind, Mayo?* He
squeezed his eyes shut. *You don't mind, do you?* The inquest
had finished with 'an open verdict', but everyone thought
she'd committed suicide. You weren't meant to say 'committed'.
Kitten had told him it made it sound like a crime, and it was
better to say 'Died by suicide' or 'Took her own life'. Kitten
had gone on and on about how he shouldn't feel rejected, or
that it was his fault. 'She had an illness like a cloud,' she had
said. 'A very thick, dark cloud. But underneath the cloud,
she loved you both.' He'd pretended so much, it was easy to
forget what had actually happened. And now, it was easy
not to think of it at all. But *did* she mind? Or *would* she
mind? And what about Xavier? Did he go over and over it,
in his yurt, with his beer and his candle? Did he wish he'd
told the truth? Was he angry that he hadn't had to?

The sound of the upper gate opening and closing. A clink of trinkets, a familiar tread. Jaws chewing. The smell of bubble gum.

'Yo, Peck.'

Jonah smiled, his eyes still closed. 'Don't call me that.' The chewing was normally an annoying sound, but he was suddenly feeling incredibly soft and mellow. 'How d'you know I was here?'

'Saw you from the window. Been looking out. Where you been?'

Jonah opened his eyes. The sun was slipping away fast, apart from it was the Earth moving, spinning on its axis. Above it, a rib of cirrus, neon pink.

'I went to the house.'

More chewing, as Raff digested this.

'Could of told me.'

'Sorry. I only thought of it on the train.' Jonah suddenly remembered his flying dream, the cranes tilted up at him. 'Guess who I saw.'

'The Raggedy Man.'

The Raggedy Man. Jonah flinched. Then he cleared his throat. 'Don't be stupid, Raff. He's been dead for five years.'

'Oh yeah.' A pause, then a flat pop as Raff's bubble burst. 'Who, then.'

'You didn't like her.'

'The hippy.'

'What hippy?'

'With the white clothes. Weird accent.'

'Ilaria!' He'd forgotten about Ilaria. He'd asked her what Om meant, and she'd said it was the sound of the universe. 'No, not her. Think!'

'Not that fucking witch, that wouldn't give us no break-fast?'

'Alison? Not Alison.'

'Well, who then?' Raff, impatient now.

'Leonie. Leonie and Pat.'

'Oh, them.' Raff chomped, not interested. Above the neon rib, the first star.

'Is Xavier there?'

'Nah.'

Relieved, Jonah pictured Xavier in his yurt, lighting his candle and opening a can of beer, all alone. *Two old chairs, and half a candle.* The Yonghy-Bonghy-Bò, that's what he was called. Poor old Yonghy. He remembered Xavier at the David Bowie street party in Brixton, crying his eyes out, and Roland trying to hug him. He noticed the star again. Venus, Earth's sister planet. He looked across at Raff, who had joined him on the bench. 'What's happening? Are Sadie and Dora drunk yet?'

'Getting there. But we ain't been there that long.' Raff was playing with his trinkets, holding them in his fist, then letting them run out, down the chain. 'Took ages in the car. Traffic was jarring. Should of all come on the train.'

'Is Dad OK?'

'Not really.' Raff grinned. 'Dora's giving him grief about Helen.'

Helen was Roland's new girlfriend. Jonah laughed, imagining his embarrassment. He looked at his brother's face. So grown up now, the skin tight on the bones. 'What about Em?'

'Chatting to Sadie.'

'What about?'

'I dunno. Clothes or something.' Raff was examining Lucy's swimming medal: 25m Butterfly, Gold, 1986.

'Do you remember when we called Sadie Bad Granny?'

Raff nodded.

'We thought she'd put you in an orphanage.'

'Oh yeah.' Now Raff was playing with Lucy's locket, prising it open and peering at the picture of his other grandmother.

'You know it was all just a mistake, don't you?'

Raff flipped the locket shut, but didn't answer.

'Do you remember the diary?'

Raff nodded. He was preparing another bubble, his tongue pushing into the gum.

'And the phone. Do you remember her Nokia flip phone?'

Raff frowned, starting to blow.

'Maybe we should go and dig them up.'

The bubble failed. 'Could do.'

The chewing was now irritating. Jonah sighed and stood up. He could feel his missing fingers hurting, and he nursed the bad hand with the good one. The sun had gone, leaving a murky orange line on the horizon. Across the city, the starry flickering of electric light. Was it OK to let sleeping dogs lie?

He looked down at his brother, who had returned to fiddling with his trinkets.

'We should get the Raggedy Man a bench, you know.'

'Oh yeah.' He was looking at his own medal, won two weeks ago at the Cross-County Athletics Championships. 'Why?'

'Why d'you fucking think!' Jonah shoved his shoulder. Raff tutted, shaking his head, and Jonah shoved him harder. Raff righted himself, still casual, rearranging his chain, and Jonah grabbed him under the armpits and pulled him off the bench. They both fell to the grass and wrestled for a bit, until Raff managed to free himself.

'Simmer down, bro!' Raff stood up, patting his hair into place, and brushing the grass off his jeans. Jonah rolled onto his side, wanting to cry. The Raggedy Man, staggering out, with his still, stripy bundle, the whole of the back of him on fire.

Raff sauntered up and down for a bit, humming to himself. Letting the tears come, Jonah breathed in the smell of the already-damp grass, and the soil beneath it.

'We'll get the dude a bench, bro.' Raff dropped down beside him and put a hand on his shoulder, but Jonah shrugged him away.

'You don't remember it, do you? You don't remember him screaming.'

Raff was silent. Not even chewing. Through the blades of grass, Jonah could see the red lights on the cranes, and the emerald bracelet that was the London Eye.

'The Wendy house went up,' said Raff. 'And I crawled into that pipe. Then I don't remember nothing.'

Along from the London Eye, silhouetted, wearing a witch's hat, was St Stephen's Tower, Big Ben a giant medal on its throat. What drove people to do things? What had driven the Raggedy Man to save Raff? And what had driven him, Jonah, to try and save Xavier Martin?

'How much is a bench?' asked Raff.

'Quite a lot.'

'I'll get the dough. No sweat.' He was chewing again. 'I'll sell the flip phone. You can get bare peas for them old Nokias now.'

'Fuck off, Raff.' Jonah rolled onto his belly and buried his face in his arms.

'OK, OK! No need to swear, fam!' Raff's hand was back on his shoulder. 'I won't sell the phone.' He chewed, thinking. 'I'll do a sponsored run. I'll do the London Marathon!'

'You can't run a Marathon. They won't let you. You're too young.'

'I bet they will. If I tell them what it's for.' Raff sat back, thinking again. 'What do you want the writing to say?'

'The writing?'

'On the bench.'

Remember, he was a boy like you once. Jonah stared at the tiny tower until he couldn't see it any more. What made people do good things, and what made them do bad things? Did they have a choice, or was it written in their genes; or to do with their childhoods? And anyway, who was to say what was good and what was bad? He used to imagine the gods looking down at them: the ultimate grown-ups, the sense-makers, the ones in charge. But if there were gods, then who had made *them*? Or had they managed, somehow, to pull themselves by the hair out of the swamps of nothingness?

'Anyway,' said Raff. 'We should go. I'm hungry.'

'Me too.' Jonah sat up and rocked forward, about to stand, but then he gasped and sat back again. Across the darkness, great, ghostly scribbles of bright silver had appeared.

'What's that?' Raff's voice quivered.

'Cloud,' breathed Jonah.

'Weirdest cloud I've ever seen.'

'It's a long way away. In the mesosphere. It's made of frozen meteor dust.'

'Frozen?' Raff hugged his knees. 'How can it be frozen, on a day like this?'

'It's cold out there.'

'How cold?'

'About minus 130 degrees Celsius.'

Raff's soft whistle. 'How far away is it then? Like, light years?'

'No! Around fifty miles.'

'Fifty? That's not far. We could go there!'

'If we had a rocket.'

'We need a rocket! I want to go there, man!' Raff sprang to his feet, his arms spreading and lifting as if he might launch himself, dive up into the sky. Across the city, the cranes saluted him. Like slingsmen. Like brothers in arms.

Acknowledgements

I would like to thank the many talented artists and writers in my family, mostly unsung, for providing inspiration and delight. Gratitude to Judith Laurance, Shaun Growney and Flick Allen for nurturing and validating my writing over the years, and to all parents, aunts, uncles, cousins and sisters for their interest and support. I would also like to thank Valerie Goodwin, Tina Cook, and all the members of Tina's group, without whom I would never have got it together to write a novel.

A number of highly-gifted people held my hand throughout the process. Heartfelt thanks to Steve Simmonds, Nicola McQuaid, Catherine Birkett, Angela Coles, Judith Laurance, Shaun Growney and Emily Ingle for their careful attention, ruthless honesty and brilliant suggestions – and for simply keeping me going on a long old haul. Thanks to Rhona Friedman for the use of her flat (and sorry about the teabag); also for the Zombies title, and legal expertise.

Deep thanks also to those who critiqued, applauded or slated early drafts. Flick Allen, Martin Toseland, Alex Uxbridge, Clive Brill, Mike Harris, Sarah Naughton, Alex Goldring, Lisa Jewell, Sarah Bailey, Tony Laurance, Rachel

Bourgeois-About, Miriam Laurance, Cathy Growney, Polly Tuckett, Irene Branach, Sush Amar, Marion Dell, Tom Groves, Suzie Smith, Sophie Lambert and Lennie Goodings were all instrumental in the production of a final, publishable version. I am particularly indebted to the wonderful Lennie Goodings for so kindly devoting her time, talent and expert judgement to my book.

Thanks to St Saviour's School, for being a really great school, and for being the centre of a warm and caring community. I drew heavily on St Saviour's to create Haredale, but would like to make clear that Haredale is a far inferior institution. Thanks to many in the St Saviour's community for their interest and support, and especially Nicola Munyama, for talking to me about Zambia; Ian Proctor, for talking to me about corpses; and Jake Powell-Dunphy, for Smelly Shelly.

Thank you to my agent, Jo Unwin, for her zeal, wit and wisdom. Thanks also to Isabel Adomakoh Young and Milly Reilly at JULA. Thank you to Suzie Dooré for her editorial brilliance, for lunches and cake, and for being laugh-out-loud funny on Twitter. And thanks to Micaela Alcaino for the great jacket design, Jane Robertson for such meticulous copy-edting, Ore Agbaje-Williams and others at Borough Press for all the painstaking work that goes into getting books out into the world.

And now I'll ratchet things up and, tell Steve Simmonds that I do not deserve his steadfast love, faith and patience. I have absolutely no idea how he has tolerated me these past five years.

And lastly – my boys. What can I say? Nothing too gushing, for fear of embarrassing them. Thanks for the laughs, for the London slang, and for being so genuinely impressed with the sheer amount of words. If you ever read this book, guys, I hope it's not too disturbing. I'm here, most days, and my plan is to stick around.